A Ch...

SAY...

# DIAMONDS
### ...this Christmas

Three classic Christmas stories bursting
with glitz and glamour from
Miranda Lee, Sandra Marton
and Susan Stephens

FEATURING A SPECIAL CHRISTMAS
GREETING FROM THE AUTHORS

# SAY IT WITH
# DIAMONDS
## ...this Christmas

MIRANDA LEE
SANDRA MARTON
AND SUSAN STEPHENS

All the characters in this book have no existence outside the imagination of the author, and have no relation whatsoever to anyone bearing the same name or names. They are not even distantly inspired by any individual known or unknown to the author, and all the incidents are pure invention.

All Rights Reserved including the right of reproduction in whole or in part in any form. This edition is published by arrangement with Harlequin Enterprises II B.V./S.à.r.l. The text of this publication or any part thereof may not be reproduced or transmitted in any form or by any means, electronic or mechanical, including photocopying, recording, storage in an information retrieval system, or otherwise, without the written permission of the publisher.

This book is sold subject to the condition that it shall not, by way of trade or otherwise, be lent, resold, hired out or otherwise circulated without the prior consent of the publisher in any form of binding or cover other than that in which it is published and without a similar condition including this condition being imposed on the subsequent purchaser.

® and ™ are trademarks owned and used by the trademark owner and/or its licensee. Trademarks marked with ® are registered with the United Kingdom Patent Office and/or the Office for Harmonisation in the Internal Market and in other countries.

Mills & Boon, an imprint of Harlequin (UK) Limited, Eton House, 18-24 Paradise Road, Richmond, Surrey TW9 1SR

SAY IT WITH DIAMONDS...THIS CHRISTMAS
© Harlequin Enterprises II B.V./S.à.r.l. 2012

*The Guardian's Forbidden Mistress* © Miranda Lee 2008
*The Sicilian's Christmas Bride* © Sandra Marton 2007
*Laying Down the Law* © Susan Stephens 2008

ISBN: 978 0 263 90235 8

012-1112

Harlequin (UK) policy is to use papers that are natural, renewable and recyclable products and made from wood grown in sustainable forests. The logging and manufacturing processes conform to the legal environmental regulations of the country of origin.

Printed and bound in Spain
by Blackprint CPI, Barcelona

# THE GUARDIAN'S
# FORBIDDEN MISTRESS

MIRANDA LEE

**Miranda Lee** was born in Port Macquarie, a popular seaside town on the mid-north coast of New South Wales, Australia. Her father was a country schoolteacher and brilliant sportsman. Her mother was a talented dressmaker.

After leaving her convent school, Miranda briefly studied the cello before moving to Sydney, where she embraced the emerging world of computers. Her career as a programmer ended after she married, had three daughters and bought a small acreage in a semi-rural community.

Miranda attempted greyhound training, as well as horse and goat breeding, but was left dissatisfied. She yearned to find a creative career from which she could earn money. When her sister suggested writing romances, it seemed like a good idea. She could do it at home and it might even be fun!

It took a decade of trial and error before her first romance, *After the Affair*, was accepted and published. At that time, Miranda, her husband and her three daughters had moved back to the central coast, where they could enjoy the sun and the surf lifestyle once again.

Numerous successful stories followed, each embodying Miranda's trademark style: fast-paced and sexy rhythms; passionate, real-life characters; and enduring, memorable story lines. She has one credo when writing romances: Don't bore the reader! Millions of fans worldwide agree she never does.

Dear Reader,

I have always been a traditionalist when it comes to Christmas. As the youngest child in our family, I was often given the job of decorating the Christmas tree on Christmas Eve, which I loved doing. Imagine my horror when one year—I think I was nine—my mother said we weren't having a tree that year because she was sick of the pine needles dropping all over the floor. As darkness fell that Christmas Eve I was in floods of tears, my noisy sobs accompanied by lots of whingeing and whining. As the slightly spoiled baby in the family, I was an accomplished crier and whiner!

In the end, my father couldn't stand it, so he went out into the nearby bush—we lived in the country—and came back with a tree. Well, it wasn't really a tree, just a branch off a nearby eucalyptus. It was positively ugly but I gave Dad a big hug and decorated it all the same. Needless to say next year we had a proper tree and every year after that. I still can't bear Christmas without a tree. Just looking at it gives me pleasure and makes me feel happy. I hope you all have a happy Christmas this year. And don't forget the tree!

Lots of love,

*Miranda Lee*

# CHAPTER ONE

Seven years later...

A frown formed on Sarah's forehead as she watched Derek turn from the crowded bar and slowly make his way back to their table, a full champagne glass in each hand.

In the time it had taken him to be served, she'd begun to worry about having accepted his invitation for a Christmas drink.

Sarah comforted herself with the thought that in the six months Derek had been her personal trainer, he'd never made a pass, or crossed the line in any way, shape or form.

But there was a definite twinkle in his eye as he handed her a glass, then sat down with his.

'This is very nice of you,' she said carefully.

Sarah's heart sank when he beamed back at her.

'I *am* nice,' he said. 'And no, I'm not coming on to you.'

'I didn't think you were,' she lied before taking a relieved sip of the bubbly.

'Yes, you did.'

'Well…'

Derek laughed. 'This is just a little celebratory drink. One you deserve after all your hard work. But do be careful over the Christmas break. I don't want you coming back to me at the end of January in the same shape you were in six months ago.'

Sarah pulled a face at the memory. 'Trust me. I won't ever let that happen again.'

'Never say never.'

Sarah shook her head as she put down her glass. 'I've done a lot of thinking while you've been working my blubbery butt off these past few months, and I've finally come to terms with the reason behind my comfort-eating.'

'So what's his name?' Derek asked.

'Who?'

'The reason behind your comfort-eating.'

Sarah smiled. 'You're a very intuitive man.'

Derek shrugged. 'Only to be expected. Gay men are very *simpatico* to matters of the heart.'

Sarah almost spilled her wine.

'You didn't suspect at all, did you?'

Sarah stared across the table at him. 'Heavens, no!'

'I dislike guys who advertise their sexual preference by being obvious, or overly camp. Other gays sometimes guess, and the odd girl or two.'

'Really?' Even now that she knew the truth, Sarah couldn't detect anything obviously gay in Derek. Neither could any of the women who worked out at the gym, if the talk in the female locker room was anything to go by. Most of the girls thought him a hunk.

Whilst Sarah conceded Derek was attractive—he had nice blue eyes, a great body and a marvellous tan—she'd never been attracted to fair-haired men.

'So now that you know I'm not making a beeline for you,' Derek went on, 'how about answering my earlier question? Or do you want to keep your love life a secret?'

Sarah had to laugh. 'I don't have a love life.'

'What, none at all?'

'Not this last year.' She'd had boyfriends in the past. Both at university and beyond. But things always ended badly, once she took them home to meet Nick.

Next to Nick, her current boyfriend always came across as lacklustre by comparison. Time after time, Sarah would become brutally aware that she wanted Nick more than she ever did other men. Nick also had the knack of making comments that forced her to question whether her boyfriend was interested in her or her future inheritance.

Yet Sarah didn't imagine for one moment that Nick undermined her relationships for any personal reasons. That would mean he cared who she went out with. Which he obviously didn't. Nick had made it brutally obvious since becoming her guardian that he found the job a tiresome one, only to be tolerated because of his affection for and gratitude to her father.

Oh, he went through the motions of looking after her welfare, but right from the beginning he'd used every opportunity to shuffle her off onto other people.

The first Christmas after she'd left school, he'd sent her on an extended overseas holiday with a girlfriend and her family. Then he'd organised for her to live on campus during her years at university, where she'd specialised in early-childhood teaching. When she'd graduated and gained a position at a primary school out in the western suburbs of Sydney, he'd encouraged her to rent a small unit near the school, saying it would take her far too long to drive to Parramatta from Point Piper every day.

Admittedly this was true, and so she had done as he suggested. But Sarah had always believed Nick's motive had been to get her out of the house as much as possible, so that he was free to do whatever he liked whenever he liked. Having her in a bedroom two doors down the hallway from his was no doubt rather restricting.

A well-known man-about-town, Nick ate women for breakfast and spat them out with a speed which was breathtaking. Every time Sarah went home he had a different girlfriend installed on his arm, and in his bed, each one more beautiful and slimmer than the next.

Sarah hated seeing him with them.

Last year Sarah had restricted her home visits to Easter and Christmas, plus the winter school break, during which Nick had been away, skiing. This year she hadn't been home since Easter, and Nick hadn't complained, readily accepting her many and varied excuses. When she finally went home on Christmas Eve tomorrow, it would be nearly nine months since she'd seen Nick in the flesh.

And since he'd seen her.

The thought made her heart flutter wildly in her chest.

What a fool you are, Sarah, she castigated herself. Nothing will change. Nothing will ever change. Don't you know that by now?

Time to face the bitter truth. Time to stop hoping for a miracle.

'His name his Nick Coleman,' she said matter-of-factly. 'He's been my legal guardian since I was sixteen, and I've had a mad crush on him since I was eight.' She refused to call it love. How could she be in love with a man like Nick? He might have made a financial success of his life in the years since they'd first met, but he'd also become cold-blooded and a callous womaniser.

Sometimes Sarah wondered if she'd imagined the kindnesses he'd shown her when she was a child.

'Did you say eight?' Derek asked.

'Yes. He came to work for my father as his chauffeur on my eighth birthday.'

'His chauffeur!'

'It's a long story. But it wasn't Nick who started my eating binge,' she confessed. 'It was his girlfriend.' The one who was there draped all over him last Christmas, a drop-dead gorgeous, super-slender supermodel who'd make any female feel inadequate.

A depressed Sarah had eaten seconds at Christmas lunch, then had gone back for thirds. Food, she'd swiftly found, made her feel temporarily better.

By Easter—her next visit home—she'd gained ten kilos. Nick had simply stared at her. Probably in shock. But his new girlfriend—a stunning-looking but equally skinny actress this time—hadn't remained silent, making a sarcastic crack about the growing obesity problem in Australia, which had resulted in Sarah gaining another five kilos by the end of May.

When she'd seen the class photo of herself, she'd taken stock and sought out Derek's help.

Now here she was, with her hour-glass shape possessing not one skerrick of flab and her self-esteem firmly back in place.

'Amend that to two girlfriends,' Sarah added, then went on to fill in some more details of her relationship with her guardian, plus the circumstances which had led up to her coming to the gym.

'Amazing,' Derek said when she stopped at last.

'What's amazing? That I got so fat?'

'You were never fat, Sarah. Just a few kilos overweight. And lacking in tone. No, I meant about your being an heiress. You don't act like a rich bitch at all.'

'That's because I'm not. Not till I turn twenty-five, anyway. My father made sure in his will that I won't get a dime till I reach what he called a mature age. For years I had my educational and basic living expenses paid for, but once I could earn my own living I had to support myself, or starve. I was a bit put out at first, but I finally saw the sense of his stand. Handouts don't do anyone any good.'

'That depends. So this Nick fellow lives in your family home, rent-free?'

'Well, yes… My father's will said he could.'

'Till you turn twenty-five.'

'Yes.'

'When, exactly, does that happen?'

'What? Oh, next February. The second.'

'At which point you're going to turf that blood-sucking leech out of your home and tell him you don't want to see his sorry behind ever again!'

Sarah blinked, then laughed. 'You've got it all wrong, Derek. Nick doesn't need free rent. He has plenty of money of his own. He could easily buy his own mansion, if he wanted to.' In actual fact, he'd offered to buy hers. But she'd refused.

Sarah knew the house was way too big for a single girl, but it was the only connection she still had to her parents, and she simply could not bear to part with it.

'How come this Nick guy is so flush?' Derek asked. 'You said he was your father's chauffeur.'

'*Was* being the operative word. My dad took him under his wing and showed him how to make money, both on the stock market and in the business world. Nick was very lucky to have a man like my father as his mentor.' Sarah considered telling Derek about Nick's good fortune with *Outback Bride* but decided not to. Perhaps because it made Nick look as though he hadn't become success-ful in his own right. Which he had. 'Have you ever been to Happy Island on a holiday?' she said instead.

'No. But I know about it.'

'Nick borrowed money and bought Happy Island when it was going for a song. He personally supervised the remodelling of its largely derelict resort, built an airport on it, then sold the whole shebang to an international equity company for a fortune.'

'Lucky man.'

'Dad always said luck begins and ends with hard work. He also advised Nick that he'd never become rich working for someone else.' Which was why Nick had set up his own movie production company a couple of years back. He'd already had some success but nothing yet to rival *Outback Bride*.

'Your dad's right there,' Derek said. 'I hated it when I had a boss. That's why I started up my own gym.'

'You own The New You?'

Derek gave her a startled look. 'Don't tell me you didn't know that either.'

'No.'

He smiled, showing flashing white teeth. 'Talk about tunnel vision.'

'Sorry,' Sarah apologised. 'I can be like that. I'm a bit of a loner, if you haven't noticed,' she added with a wry smile. 'I don't make friends easily. Guess it comes from being an only child.'

'I'm an only child too,' he confessed. 'Which makes my being gay especially hard on my parents. No grandkids to look forward to. I only told them a couple of years ago when Mum's pressuring me to get married got a bit much. Dad hasn't talked to me since,' Derek added, the muscles in his neck stiffening.

'That's sad,' Sarah said. 'What about your mum?'

'She rings me. But won't let me come home, not even for Christmas.'

'Oh, dear. Maybe they'll come round in time.'

'Maybe. But I'm not holding my breath. Dad is a very proud and stubborn man. Once he says something, he won't back down on it. But back to you, sweetie. You're simply crazy about this Nick fellow, aren't you?'

Sarah's heart lurched. 'Crazy describes my feelings for Nick very well. When I'm around him, I just can't stop wanting him. But he doesn't want me back. And he never will. It's time I accepted that.'

'But surely not till you've had one last crack at him.'

'What?'

'You haven't been working your butt off because some anorexic model said you were fat, sweetie. It's Nick you're out to impress, and attract.'

Sarah didn't want to openly admit it. But of course Derek was right. She'd do anything to have Nick look at her with desire. Just once.

No, not once. *Again.* Because she was pretty sure she'd spotted desire in his eyes one Christmas, when she'd been sixteen and she'd come down to the pool wearing an itsy-bitsy bikini that she'd bought with Nick in mind.

But maybe she'd imagined it. Maybe she was just

desperate to believe he'd fancied her a little that day, despite his actions to the contrary. Teenage girls were prone to flights of fantasy, as were twenty-four-year-olds, she thought ruefully. Which was why she'd spent all week buying the kind of summer wardrobe that would stir an octogenarian's hormones.

The trouble was Nick wasn't an octogenarian. He was only thirty-six, and he kept his male hormones well and truly catered to. Sarah already knew that the actress girlfriend had gone by the board, replaced by an advertising executive with a penchant for power-dressing.

Sarah might not have been home personally for several months, but she rang home every week to talk to Flora, who always gave her a full update on Nick's comings and goings before passing the call over to Nick. If he was home, that was. Often he was out, being a social animal with a wide range of friends. Or contacts, as he preferred to call them.

'I presume you spend the Christmas holidays back at home?' Derek asked, cutting into her thoughts.

'Yes,' she said with a sigh. 'I usually go home as soon as school breaks up. But I haven't this year. Still, I'll have to make an appearance tomorrow. I always decorate the Christmas tree. If I don't do it, it doesn't get done. Then I help Flora prepare things for the following day. The lunch is partially catered for, but Flora likes to cook some hot food as well. Flora is the housekeeper,' she added when she saw Derek frown at the name. 'She's been with the family for forever.'

'I have to confess I couldn't see your Nick with a girl-friend named Flora.'

'You'd be right there. Nick's girlfriends always have names like Jasmine, or Sapphire, or Chloe.' That was what the latest one was called: Chloe.

'Not only that,' Sarah went on waspishly, 'they never help. They always just swan downstairs at the last minute, with their fingernails perfect and their mi-nuscule appetites on hold. It gets my goat when they sit there, sipping mineral water whilst they eat abso-lutely nothing.'

'Mmm,' Derek said.

Sarah pulled a face at him. 'I suppose you think I'm going to get all upset and make a pig of myself again.'

'It's highly possible, by the sounds of things. But what I was actually thinking was that you need someone by your side at this Christmas lunch. A boyfriend of your own.'

'Huh! I've brought boyfriends to Christmas lunch before,' Sarah informed Derek drily. 'In no time, Nick makes them look like fools, or fortune-hunters.'

'And maybe they were. But possibly they were too young, and totally overawed by the occasion. What you need is someone older, someone with looks and style, someone successful and sophisticated who won't be fazed by anything your playboy guardian says and does. Someone, in short, who's going to make the object of your desire sit up and take notice. Of you.'

'I like the idea, Derek. In theory. But even with my improved looks, I don't think I'm going to be able to snaffle up the type of boyfriend you've just described at this late stage. Christmas is two days away.'

'In that case let me help you out. Because I know just such an individual who doesn't have anywhere to go on Christmas Day and would be happy to come to your aid.'

'You *do*? Who?'

'You're looking at him.'

Sarah blinked, then laughed. 'You have to be kidding. How can *you* be my boyfriend, Derek? You're gay!'

'You didn't know that till I told you,' he reminded her. 'Your Nick won't know it, either, especially if I'm introduced as your boyfriend. People believe what they're told, on the whole.'

Sarah stared at Derek. He was right. Why would Nick—or anyone else at lunch—suspect that Derek was gay? He didn't look it. Or act it.

'So what do you think?' Derek said with a wicked gleam in his eyes. 'Trust me when I say that nothing stimulates a man's interest in a woman as well as another man's undivided attention in her.'

Sarah still hesitated.

'What are you afraid of?' Derek demanded to know. 'Success?'

'Absolutely not!'

'Then what have you got to lose?'

Nothing at all, Sarah realised with a sudden rush of adrenalin. At the very least she would not feel alone, as she often did at Christmas, especially during that dreaded lunch.

This year she would not only be looking her best, but she would also have a very good-looking man by her side.

'All right,' Sarah said, a quiver of unexpected excitement rippling down her spine. 'You're on.'

# CHAPTER TWO

SARAH'S positive attitude towards Christmas lasted till
she pulled her white car into the driveway the following morning and saw Nick's bright red sporty number
parked outside the garages.

'Darn it,' she muttered as she pressed the remote to
open the electronic gates.

She'd presumed Nick would be out playing golf, as
he always did every Saturday, come rain, hail or shine.
Come Christmas Eve as well!

If she'd imagined for one moment that Nick would
be home, she'd have put on one of her sexy new sun-
dresses this morning—probably the black and white
halter-necked one that showed off her slender shoulders
and nicely toned arms. Instead, she was sporting a pair
of faded jeans and a striped yellow tank-top. Suitable
clothes in which to decorate a Christmas tree. But not
to impress a man, especially one who had a penchant
for women who always looked as if they'd just stepped
out of a beauty salon.

Still, with a bit of luck, she might be able to sneak up to her bedroom and make some changes before running into Nick. The house was, after all, huge.

Built in the 1920s by a wealthy mining family, Goldmine had been renovated and revamped many times since then. Its original stone walls were now cement-rendered white, with arched windows and lots of balconies, which gave it a distinctly Mediterranean look.

Because of the sloping site, the house looked double-storeyed from the road, but there was another, lower level at the back where the architecture incorporated a lot of glass to take advantage of the home's harbourside position.

Actually, there weren't many rooms in the house that didn't look out over Sydney Harbour, the view extending across the water to the bridge and the opera house in the distance. On the upper floor, all the bedrooms had individual balconies with water views, the master bedroom opening out onto a walled balcony that was big enough to accommodate an outdoor table-setting.

The enormous back terrace had the best vantage point, however, which was why it was always the place for Christmas lunch. Long trestle-style tables would be brought in, shade provided by huge canvas blinds put up for the day. Only once in Sarah's memory, when the temperature soared to forty degrees, had the lunch been held inside, in the family room, the only room large enough to accommodate the number of guests who swamped Goldmine every Christmas Day from midday onwards.

The tradition had been started by Sarah's father and

mother soon after they'd bought the house nearly thirty years ago, a tradition her father continued after her mother's death, and which Nick seemed happy to honour in the years he'd been living there.

Of course, the cynic in Sarah appreciated that Christmas lunch at Goldmine was more of a business lunch these days than a gathering of family and long-term friends. Most of the guests at the table would be the people Nick did business with, valuable contacts whose priorities were where the next few million were coming from.

Sarah was under no illusion that Nick was any different from the types he mixed with. He liked money as much—possibly more—than they did.

This last thought reminded Sarah of what Derek had implied over drinks last night: that Nick was taking advantage of his position as her guardian to live, rent-free, in her harbourside home. Although she'd defended Nick in this regard, Sarah had to concede that living in Goldmine was a huge social advantage. Not so much because of its size—some of the neighbours' homes were obscenely large—but because of its position. There was no doubt that having such an address had benefited Nick no end in the business stakes. Which was why he wanted to buy the place.

The gates finally open, Sarah drove through and parked next to Nick's car. She frowned over at it, still perplexed that he hadn't gone to golf today.

Thinking about golf, however, reminded her of the

Christmas present she'd bought him. It was a set of minia-ture golf clubs, with the club heads made in silver, the shafts in ebony and the bag crafted in the most beautiful red leather. She'd bought it on eBay and it had cost several hundred dollars, more than she usually spent on him.

The moment she'd seen it, she'd known Nick would like it.

But would he think it odd that she'd bought him something so expensive?

She hoped not.

Sarah grimaced when she realised he might think it even odder that she hadn't bought her new 'boyfriend' anything at all. Which she hadn't. She and Derek had discussed when he was to arrive tomorrow and what to wear, but they hadn't thought of presents.

Sarah sighed, her confidence about this subterfuge beginning to drop.

Not that it mattered all that much. She couldn't seri-ously expect to achieve the miracle of having Nick suddenly look at her and be carried away on a wave of uncontrollable desire. Why should that happen now, after all these years? It wasn't as though she hadn't dolled herself up for him before. She had. With abso-lutely no results at all.

The truth was she obviously wasn't his type. Even with her normally lush curves pared down to the bone, she'd never look or act like the kind of girlfriend Nick inevitably chose and obviously preferred: not only super-slim, but also super-chic and super-sophisticated.

A kindergarten teacher just didn't cut it with Nick, even with a future fortune attached. If anything, that she was her father's heiress was probably a turn-off for him. Nick would not like any reminders that he wasn't entirely a self-made man. Or the fact that she'd known him when he was a nobody.

With every new girlfriend, Nick came with a clean slate.

Sarah had no doubt he hadn't told this latest girl, Chloe, that he'd ever been in jail. Or that his ward's father had been a very generous benefactor. She felt sure Nick always represented her father these days as a long-term friend, thereby explaining his guardianship of her.

Sarah accepted these brutally honest thoughts with a mixture of emotions. There was disappointment, yes. But also a measure of relief. Because it made her realise that to harbour hopes of attracting Nick this Christmas was a case of desperation and delusion. It wasn't going to happen.

Whilst this realisation brought a pang of emotional pain—no one liked to have their longest and fondest dream dashed—the acceptance of reality also began to unravel the tight knots in her stomach. What she was wearing today no longer mattered. She could relax now and act naturally with Nick, which she would not have done with her previous pathetic agenda.

Sarah might have called Derek right then and there and cancelled his coming tomorrow, if she hadn't already told Flora when she rang last night that there'd be an added guest for Christmas lunch; her new boy-friend, Derek. Although Nick had been out at the time, Sarah had no doubt that Flora would have told Nick this news at breakfast this morning. Flora was a dear lady, but inclined to gossip.

No, there was nothing for it but to go through with this charade now.

'You'll probably be glad, come tomorrow,' Sarah told herself as she climbed out of the car and walked round to open the hatchback. Nick's new girlfriend sounded like a right bitch, if Flora's character assessment was to be believed. When Sarah asked what she was like, Flora had said she was up herself, big time.

'Just as good-looking as the last one,' Flora had added, 'but more intelligent. And doesn't she know it! Still, she won't last any longer than the others. Six months is tops for our Nick. After that, it's out with the old and in with the new. If that boy ever settles down, I'll eat my hat.'

Sarah pulled a face as she lifted her two bags out of the boot.

She would, too.

Nick was definitely not a marrying man; never had been and never would be. He wasn't into romance, either. Catering to his sexual needs was the name of his game where women were concerned.

Once Nick got bored with his latest game-partner, she was out.

He'd once admitted to Sarah when she'd been about

twelve—they'd just watched a very sweet romance on TV together—that he could never fall in love the way the characters had in that movie. He'd confessed rather grimly that he didn't have any idea what that kind of love felt like.

Sarah presumed his inability to emotionally connect with women had something to do with his loveless up-bringing, a subject she'd overheard being discussed by her parents not long before her mother died. Apparently, Nick had suffered terribly at the hands of a drunken and abusive father, running away to live on the streets of Sydney when he'd only been thirteen. After that, he'd been reduced to doing some pretty dreadful things just to survive.

Sarah never did find out exactly how dreadful, but she could guess.

Just after turning eighteen, Nick had finally been arrested—for stealing cars—and had been sentenced to two years in jail.

It was during this term that he'd finally been shown some kindness, and given some practical help. By a man who'd spotted his natural intelligence, a man who, for years, had generously given up many hours of his time to help those less fortunate.

Nick was put into a special education programme for inmates that this man had funded, and became one of their most successful graduates, achieving his higher-school certificate in record time.

That man had been her father.

'Sarah!'

Sarah almost jumped out of her skin at her name being called.

But when she saw who it was, she smiled.

'Hi there, Jim. You're looking well.' Flora's husband had to be over sixty by now. But he was one of those wirily built men who aged well and always moved with a spritely step.

'Got a lot of luggage there, missie,' he said, joining her behind her car and staring down at her two very large bags. 'Home for good, are you?'

'Not yet, Jim. Did you get me a good tree?'

'Yep. A beauty. Set it up in the usual spot in the family room. I put the boxes of decorations next to it. And I've hung up the lights out the back.'

'Great. Thanks, Jim.'

Jim nodded. He wasn't one for chit-chat, unlike his wife.

Jim was happiest when he was working with his hands. He loved keeping the extensive grounds at Goldmine spick and span, not such a difficult job after her father had come home from a visit to Tokyo a decade ago and had all the more traditional flower beds and lawns ripped out and replaced with Japanese-style gardens. Now there were lots of rocks and gravel pathways, combined with ponds and water features, all shown to advantage by interesting trees and plants.

Jim hadn't been too thrilled at first with the lack of

grass and flowers, but he'd grown to appreciate the garden's unique beauty and serenity.

Jim picked up Sarah's bags without her asking and started heading along the curved path towards the front porch, putting paid to her earlier plan to sneak in unnoticed through the garages.

To be honest, Sarah still wished she looked better for Nick's first sight of her. It would have been rewarding to see the surprised look on his face.

Sighing, she grabbed her carry-all from the passenger seat, locked the car and hurried after Jim, who by then had dropped her bags by the front door and rung the doorbell.

'I do have keys,' she said, and was fishing through her bag in search of them when the door was wrenched open.

Not by Flora—but by Nick.

If ever Sarah was glad she was wearing sunglasses it was at that moment.

Not because of Nick's reaction to her, but because of her reaction to him.

She'd been so caught up with worrying about her own appearance that she'd forgotten just how devastatingly attractive she found him, especially when he was wearing as little as he was wearing today: just board shorts and a sleeveless white surf top, the colour highlighting his beautifully bronzed skin.

Sarah's thankfully hidden gaze travelled hungrily down his body then up again before fixing on his mouth.

If Nick's black eyes hadn't been so hard, and his other

features strongly masculine, his mouth might have made him into a pretty boy. Both his lips were full and sensual, curving around a mouthful of flashing white teeth, their perfection courtesy of the top-flight dentist her father had taken him to as soon as he'd been let out of prison.

If Sarah had any criticism, it was of his hair, which she believed he kept far too short. Still, the buzz-cut style did give him an intimidating look that probably worked well for him in the business world.

'Well, hello, stranger,' he said, his dark eyes sweeping down to her sneakered feet, then up again.

Not a hint of admiration in *his* expression, however, or even surprise. No reaction at all. Zilch.

His lack of reaction—she'd been expecting some sort of compliment—exasperated Sarah. What did she have to do to make the man notice her, damn it?

'Thanks, Jim,' he said, bending to pick up her bags. 'I'll take these now.'

'Yes, thanks, Jim,' Sarah managed to echo through clenched teeth.

Jim nodded, then moved off, by which time Nick had picked up her luggage and turned to carry it inside.

Sarah wanted to hit him. Instead, she gritted her teeth even harder.

Suddenly, she couldn't wait to turn twenty-five. The sooner she got Nick out of her life, the better. He was like a thorn in her side, niggling away at her. How could she have what she wanted most in life—which was children of her own—if he was always there, spoiling things for her? How could she feel completely happy when she kept comparing every man she dated to him?

Out of sight would be out of mind. Hopefully.

Sarah closed the front door after her, smothering a sigh when she saw Nick heading for the stairs with her cases.

'I can take those up,' she said, desperately needing a few minutes away from the man to regain her composure.

As much as Sarah had subconsciously always known that nothing would ever come of her secret feelings for Nick, finally facing the futility of her fantasies was a soul-shattering experience.

He hadn't even noticed that she'd lost weight!

All that work. For *nothing*!

'It's no trouble,' he threw over his shoulder as he continued on up the stairs with the bags.

Sarah gritted her teeth, and hurried up the stairs after him. 'Why aren't you at golf?'

'I wanted the opportunity to talk to you,' he tossed back at her. 'Privately.'

'About what?'

He didn't answer her, instead charging on ahead with her bags.

'About what, Nick?' she repeated when she caught up, frustrated by his lack of reply.

He ground to a halt on the top landing, dropped her bags then turned to face her.

'Flora, for one thing.'

'What about her? She's not ill, is she?'

'No, but she can't do what she used to do. She gets

very tired. This last year, I've had to hire a home-cleaning service to come in twice a week to do all the heavy cleaning for her.'

'I didn't realise.'

'If you came home occasionally,' Nick pointed out drily, 'you might have noticed.'

It was a fair comment, evoking a large dose of guilt. Sarah recognised she'd been very self-obsessed this past year. But she'd been on a mission. A futile mission, as it turned out.

'I…I've been very busy,' she said by way of an excuse.

'With the new boyfriend, I take it?' came his next comment, this one quite sarcastic.

Sarah bristled. 'I have a right to a social life,' she retorted, taking off her sunglasses so that she could glare at him. '*You* have one.'

'Indeed. But it doesn't take over my whole existence.'

His critical tone was so typical of Nick when it came to her having a boyfriend, his condemning attitude often sparking a reckless rebellion in her that had her running off at the mouth.

Today was no exception.

'Derek and I are very much in love. Something *you* could never identify with. When people are truly in love they want to spend every minute of every day with them.'

'I'm surprised you came home today at all, then,' he countered quite sharply. 'Or will your lover be dropping by later?'

Sarah flushed. 'Derek's working today.'

'Doing what?'

'He owns a gym.'

'Aah. That explains it.'

'Explains what?'

'Your new shape.'

So he *had* noticed! 'You say that like there's something wrong with it.'

'You looked fine the way you were.'

Sarah's mouth dropped open. 'You have to be joking! I was getting fat!'

'Don't be ridiculous.'

Sarah rolled her eyes. Either the man was blind, or he cared about her so little that he'd never really looked at her before.

'Maybe you just didn't notice.'

Nick gave an offhand shrug. 'Maybe I didn't. Still, I suppose it's not up to me to tell you what to do.'

'I'm glad you've finally realised that!'

'Meaning?'

'I couldn't count the number of times you've interfered in my life, and my relationships. Every time I brought a boyfriend home in the past, you went out of your way to make him feel stupid. And me to boot.'

'I was only doing what your father asked me to do, Sarah. Which was to protect you from the money-grubbing creeps in this world.'

'They weren't money-grubbing creeps!'

'Indeed they were.'

'I'll be the judge of that from now on, thank you very much.'

'Not till your twenty-fifth birthday, madam. I have no intention of letting you fall into the hands of some gold-digging gigolo at this late stage. I wouldn't be able to sleep at night if I did that.'

'Huh. I can't see you ever losing any sleep over me.'

'Then you'd be dead wrong, sweetheart,' he grated out.

Their eyes met, with Sarah sucking in sharply at the momentary fury she glimpsed in Nick's face. It came home to her then just how much he'd hated being her guardian all these years. No doubt he would be very relieved when she turned twenty-five next year and his obligation to her father was over.

'I haven't given you that much trouble, have I?' she said, her softer voice reflecting her drop in spirits.

As much as she accepted Nick would never be attracted to her, she'd always thought that, underneath everything, he liked her. Not just because she was her father's daughter, but because of the person she was. When she was younger, he'd often told her what a great kid she was. He'd said she had character, and a good heart. He'd also said she was fun to be with, proving it by spending a lot of his spare time with her.

Of course, that had been a long time ago, before Nick had become a success in his own right. When that started to happen, he'd begun to ignore her. Then, after her father died, the rot had set in completely. It was patently obvious that she was now reduced to nothing more than a responsibility, a responsibility that he obviously found both tedious and exasperating.

'Does he know how rich you're shortly going to be?' he demanded to know.

Sarah's mouth thinned. Here we go again, she thought angrily.

Yet there was no point in lying. Better she answer Nick's questions now than to have him put Derek through the third degree on Christmas Day.

'He knows I'm going to be rich,' she bit out. 'But he doesn't know the full extent of my inheritance.'

'He'll know once he shows up tomorrow. People who live in this street have to be multimillionaires at least. It won't take him long to put two and two together.'

'Derek's not a fortune-hunter, Nick. He's a very decent man.'

'How do you know?'

'I just know.'

'My God, you know nothing!' he flung at her. 'Your father thought he was protecting you with his will. Instead, he set you up for disaster. He should have given most of his money away, donated it to some charity, not left it in the hands of a girl such as you.'

'What do you mean, a girl such as me?'

He opened his mouth to say something but then obviously thought better of it. Instead, he picked up her bags and carried them along the hallway to her room, the stiff set of his shoulders very telling. After dumping her cases just inside the door, he retreated back out into the hallway.

'We'll continue this discussion later,' he said in that deceptively quiet manner he always adopted on the odd occasion when he was in danger of losing his cool.

Over the years Sarah had learned to recognise this tactic of his. Nick hated losing his temper. Hated losing control. He preferred to act like the consummate ice-man, both professionally and personally. She'd rarely heard him yell. He didn't even swear any more, as he once had.

But his body language could speak volumes. So could his eyes.

Though not always. He did have the ability to make them totally unreadable. But not straight away. If you were watching him closely, you could sometimes glimpse what was going on in his head before he drew the blinds down.

'We'll have morning tea in the kitchen,' he pronounced, 'then we'll adjourn to my study and talk.'

'Not about Derek,' Sarah retorted. 'I have no intention of listening to you criticising someone you haven't even met.'

'Fair enough. But I have lots of other things to talk to you about, Sarah. Important issues connected with your inheritance. I want to have everything settled before Christmas.'

'But I don't turn twenty-five till February,' she protested. 'We have the rest of my summer break to settle things!'

'No, we don't. I won't be here.'

'Where will you be?'

'I'm spending most of January on Happy Island.'

Sarah's heart sank. She knew Nick had a holiday house there. But he rarely used it at this time of year.

'Flora never said anything about that when I called.'

'The subject probably didn't come up.'

'There's still the week between Christmas and New Year,' she argued, feeling very put out with Nick's choosing to go away for so long.

'Yes. But I'm having a guest stay during that week. And you have your new boyfriend, who you freely admit you wish to spend every minute of every day with. Better we settle everything whilst we have the chance.'

'But I have to decorate the tree today.'

'I just want a couple of hours, Sarah. Not all day.'

'What about tonight? Can't this wait till tonight?'

'I'm going present-shopping tonight.'

Sarah sighed. Wasn't that just like a man to go present-shopping at the last minute?

'Come on,' he said abruptly. 'Let's go downstairs.'

'I need to go to the bathroom first,' she said quite truthfully.

'Fine,' he replied with another offhand shrug. 'I'll go ahead and tell Flora to put on the kettle.'

Sarah shook her head as she watched Nick go. Derek didn't know what he was talking about. Dolling herself up tomorrow and sucking up to a pretend boyfriend wasn't going to make a blind bit of difference. She was nothing to Nick but an obligation that he obviously wanted over and done with. It was clear to Sarah that he couldn't wait for her twenty-fifth birthday to arrive.

Suddenly, she felt the same way. She was sick and tired of letting her feelings for Nick distress her. Sick and tired of secretly pining for what would never be.

Time to move on, girl. Time to get yourself a life. One that doesn't include Nick!

# CHAPTER THREE

FLORA was in the kitchen, cutting up the caramel slice she'd made that morning, when Nick walked in with a face like thunder.

'Wasn't that Sarah at the door?' she asked.

'Yep. She won't be long. You can put on the kettle.'

Flora turned to pop the caramel slice back in the fridge before switching on the electric kettle. 'It's good to have her home,' she said. 'Isn't it?'

Nick scowled as he slid onto one of the four stools fronting the black marble breakfast bar. 'Speak for yourself, Flora.'

'Come, now, Nick. You've missed her. You know you have.'

'I know no such thing. Ray was out of his mind to make me that girl's guardian. I'll breathe a huge sigh of relief when February comes round, I can tell you.'

'I suppose it has been a big responsibility,' Flora agreed. 'Especially considering how much money she's going to inherit. What do you make of this new boyfriend of hers? Do you think he's on the up and up?'

'Who knows?'

'It's strange that she hadn't mentioned him before last night, don't you think? It makes me wonder what's wrong with him.'

'I've just been thinking the same thing. I guess we'll just have to wait and see.'

'I guess so,' Flora said. 'So how does she look?'

'What do you mean?'

'She told me last night that she'd been exercising and had lost weight. Don't tell me you didn't notice.'

'Yeah, I noticed.'

'And?' Flora asked, exasperated with Nick's reluctance to elaborate. He was just as bad as Jim sometimes. Why was it that men didn't like to talk? It would be nice to have Sarah home, just so she had someone to chat with occasionally.

'I thought she looked fine the way she was.'

'Isn't that just like a man? They never want the women in their life to change. Aah, there she is, the girl herself. Come over here, love, and give old Flora a hug.'

Sarah's heart squeezed tight when Flora enveloped her into a tight embrace. It had been a long time since anyone had hugged her like that.

There'd been no hug from Nick this morning. Not even a peck on the cheek. He never touched her, except accidentally.

Her gaze slid over Flora's shoulder to land on the man

himself. But he wasn't looking her way. He was staring down at the black bench top, looking highly disgruntled.

Probably wishing he were at golf.

'Oh, my,' Flora said when she finally held Sarah out at arm's length. 'You *have* lost quite a few pounds, haven't you? Still, now you can have a big piece of your favourite caramel slice without feeling guilty,' she added before turning away to open the fridge. 'I made it for you first thing this morning.'

'You shouldn't have, Flora,' Sarah chided, but gently.

'Nonsense. What else do I have to do? Did you know that the whole of the Christmas lunch is being catered this year? Nick says it's too much for me. All I'm allowed to do is make a couple of miserable puddings. I ask you!'

She rolled her eyes at Sarah, who was thinking to herself that Flora had aged quite a bit this past year. Her face was very lined and her hair had turned totally grey.

'Not that I'm complaining, Nick,' Flora went on. 'I do know I'm getting older. But I'm not totally useless yet. I could easily have baked a leg of pork and a turkey. And some nice hot veggies for those who don't like salad and seafood. Still, enough of that. What's done is done. Now, sit up there next to Nick, Sarah, and tell us all about your new boyfriend whilst I pour the tea.'

Sarah smothered a groan, but did as she was told, though she didn't sit right next to Nick, leaving one stool between them.

'What would you like to know?' she asked with brilliant nonchalance.

'How old is he, for starters?'

Sarah realised she had no idea.

'Thirty-five,' she guessed. One year younger than Nick.

Nick's head swung her way. 'Handsome?'

'Very. Looks like a movie star.'

Was she crazy, or did Nick's eyes glitter when she said that?

'How long have you been seeing each other?' Flora asked.

Sarah decided to use the truth as much as possible. 'We met shortly after last Easter. I hired him as my personal trainer.'

Nick made a small scoffing sound.

Sarah ignored him.

'Why haven't you mentioned him before?' Flora asked.

Sarah winced. She should have realised she'd get the third degree about Derek, from both Nick and Flora. Again, she decided to stick to the truth as closely as she could.

'We haven't been boyfriend and girlfriend all that time,' she replied. 'That's a more recent development. He asked me out for a drink one night after my workout, one thing led to another and…well, what can I say? I'm very happy.'

Sarah smiled, despite the lurch within her chest.

'And very healthy, too,' Flora said with a return smile. 'Don't you think so, Nick?'

'I think she looks like she could do with some of your caramel slice.'

Sarah found a laugh from somewhere. 'That's funny coming from you. All your girlfriends have figures like rakes.'

'Not *all* of them. You haven't met Chloe, have you?'

'I haven't had the pleasure yet.'

'You will. Tomorrow.'

'How nice.'

'You'll like her.'

'Oh, I doubt it. I never like any of your girlfriends, Nick. The same way you never like any of my boy-friends. I've already warned Derek.'

'Should I warn Chloe?'

Sarah shrugged. 'Why bother? It won't change anything.'

'Will you two stop bickering?' Flora intervened. 'It's Christmas, the season of peace and love.'

Sarah almost pointed out that Nick didn't believe in love, but she held her tongue. Sniping at Nick was not in keeping with her resolution to move on. But he'd really got under her skin with his remarks about her being skinny.

When Flora presented a plate full of caramel slice right in front of her, she couldn't really refuse. But she did take the smallest piece and proceeded to eat it very slowly between long sips of tea. Nick chose the biggest portion, devoured it within seconds, then had the gall to take a second salivating slice. The lucky devil had one of those metabolisms that allowed him to eat whatever he liked without getting fat. Of course, he did work out with weights every other day, and swam a lot.

Although thirty-six now, he didn't carry an extra ounce of fat on his long, lean body. Really, other than some muscling up around his chest and arms, Nick hadn't changed much since the day they'd met.

Physically, that was. He'd changed a good deal in other ways, matching his personality to suit whatever company he was in, sometimes warm and charming, at other times adopting a confident air of cool sophistica- tion and *savoir-faire*, both personas a long way from the introverted and rather angry young man he'd been when he'd first come to live at Goldmine.

Though he was never angry with me, Sarah recalled. Never. He had always been sweet, kind and generous with his time. He'd made a lonely little girl's life much less lonely.

Oh, how she'd loved him for that!

Sarah much preferred the Nick of old to the one sitting beside her today.

In the beginning, when he'd launched himself into the business world, she'd admired his ambition. But success had made Nick greedy for the good life, feeding on hedonistic pleasures that were as fleeting as they were shallow. Other than the holiday house on Happy Island, he owned a penthouse on the Gold Coast and a chalet in the southern snowfields. When he wasn't working at making more money, he flitted from one to the other, always accompanied by his latest lady-love.

Whoops, no. Amend that to latest playmate. Love was never part of Nick's lifestyle.

Her father had always said how proud of Nick he was. He'd lauded Nick's work ethics, his intellect and his entrepreneurial vision.

Sarah could see that, professionally, there was much to be proud of. But surely her father would have been disappointed, if he'd been alive today, at the way Nick conducted his personal life. There was something reprehensible about a man whose girlfriends never lasted longer than six months, and who boasted that he would never marry.

No, that was unfair. Nick had never boasted about his inability to fall in love. He'd merely stated it as a fact.

Sarah had to concede that at least Nick was honest in his relationships. She felt positive he never spun any of his girlfriends a line of bull. They'd always known that their role in his life was strictly sexual and definitely temporary.

'Glad to see you're still capable of enjoying your food.'

Nick's droll remark jolted Sarah out of her reverie, her stomach contracting in horror once she realised she'd consumed a second piece of caramel slice without being aware of it.

She kept her cool, however, determined not to let Nick needle her further.

'Who could resist Flora's caramel slice?' she tossed at him airily. 'Next Christmas we'll get back to having a smaller Christmas lunch, Flora, and you can cook whatever you like.'

'You won't keep your father's tradition going?' Nick asked in a challenging voice.

'Is that what you think you've been doing, Nick?' she countered. 'When Dad was alive, Christmas lunch was a gathering of true friends, not a collection of business acquaintances.'

'Is that so? I think perhaps you're mistaken about that. Most of your father's so-called friends were business contacts.'

Nick was right, of course. But people had still liked her father for himself, not just for what they could get out of him. At least, she liked to think so.

But maybe she was wrong. Maybe she'd seen him through rose-coloured glasses. Maybe, underneath his *bonhomie*, he'd been as hard and cynical as Nick.

No, that wasn't true. He'd been a kind and generous man.

Not a brilliant dad, though. During her years at boarding-school he'd often made excuses for not being able to come to school functions, all of those excuses related to work. Then, when she came home for school holidays, she'd largely been left to her own devices.

If she was strictly honest, things hadn't been much better when her mother was still alive. A dedicated career woman, Jess Steinway had been totally unprepared for the sacrifices motherhood entailed upon the arrival of an unexpected baby at forty. Sarah had been raised by a succession of impersonal nannies till she went to kindergarten, after which Flora had taken over as carer before and after school. But Flora, warm and chatty though she was, had mostly been too busy with the house to do much more than feed Sarah and make sure she did her homework.

No one had spent quality time with her, or played with her, till Nick had come along.

She turned her head to look at him, a wave of sadness washing through her. Oh, how she wished he was still their chauffeur, and she the little girl who could love him without reservation.

Tears pricked at her eyes, right at that moment when Nick's head turned her way. She quickly blinked them away, but not before she glimpsed regret in his.

'Sorry,' he muttered. 'I didn't mean any disrespect for your father. He was a good man and a very generous one. Christmas was his favourite time of year. Did you know that every Christmas he gave huge donations to the various charities round Sydney for the homeless? Because of him, they always had a proper Christmas dinner. And no one, especially the children, went without a present.'

Sarah frowned. 'I didn't know that.' She knew about his good work with young prisoners. And he'd given lots of money to cancer research and cancer support groups. There were a few hospital wings named after him, too. But he'd never mentioned his Christmas donations. 'I hope his estate is continuing with that tradition, Nick. Do you know if it is?'

'It wasn't written into his will, so I do it in his name every year.'

'*You?*'

'Don't sound so surprised. I am capable of generous gestures, you know. I'm not totally selfish.'

'I…I never said you were.'

'But you think it. And, generally speaking, you'd be right.'

'Don't be so modest, Nick,' Flora piped up. 'You should see the huge plasma television Nick bought Jim and me a few weeks ago, for no reason at all except that he thought we'd like it. It has surround sound and its own built-in DVD. You can tape any number of shows and watch them later, when you have time. Jim's in seventh heaven, watching cricket and tennis at all hours of the day and night.'

'Why do you think I bought it?' Nick quipped. 'Had to do something to stop my right-hand man from spending every summer's day glued to that TV, when he should be outside working. My motivation was purely selfish, I assure you. And don't be expecting anything too expensive for Christmas, because I'm flat broke now.'

'Oh, go on with you,' Flora said laughingly.

'Don't laugh. I've made two dud movies already this year. And I'm damned worried about the one coming out in the New Year. We've had a couple of test audiences view it and they said the ending was way too sad. The director reluctantly agreed to reshoot it with a happy ending, but I've decided to go with his original vision. If this one flops, I might have to come to Sarah here for a loan.'

Sarah was shocked by this news. She knew better

than anyone that Nick's ego would not survive becoming poor again. 'I can give you as much as you need, come February. And it won't be a loan, either.'

'Lord, what am I going to do with this girl, Flora? I hope you haven't made any similar offers to this boy-friend of yours. Don't ever give a man money, Sarah,' he told her sternly. 'It brings out the worst in them.'

Sarah shook her head at him. 'How many times do I have to tell you? Derek doesn't want my money.'

'He will, when he sees how much you've got.'

'Not every man is a fortune-hunter, Nick. Now, if you don't mind, I do not wish to discuss Derek any further. I know there's no convincing you that no man could possibly love me for myself and not my money, so I'd prefer not to try.'

'Hear hear,' Flora agreed. 'I agree with Sarah. Another piece of caramel slice, love?'

The ringing of Nick's cellphone was a welcome inter-ruption, not only to his incessant questioning about Derek, but also to her escalating exasperation. Tomorrow was not going to be a pride-saving exercise. It was going to be hell!

'Hi there,' she heard Nick say in that voice he reserved for girlfriends. 'Yeah, that'd be great, Chloe. OK. I'll pick you up tonight at seven. Bye.'

He clicked off his phone and slipped off the stool. 'Sorry, folks. Change of plan. Chloe's had a last-minute invitation to a Christmas Eve party at some bigwig's place, so I'll have to dash out and do my present-shopping now. We'll have to put off that talk till I get back, Sarah.'

'Fine,' she said, pretending not to care. But she did. She cared a lot. Not about the talk so much but about his going out this afternoon, then going out with Chloe tonight. Pathetic, really. The way she would accept the crumbs of his company.

'Don't forget I want a new car,' Sarah called after him as he walked away. 'A yellow one.'

Nick stopped walking, then glanced over his shoulder at her. 'Yellow,' he repeated drily. 'Any particular make?'

She named a top-of-the-range model. 'Of course. What else?'

When he smiled his amusement at her, Sarah's heart lightened a little. It was still there, that special bond between them. Because they *knew* each other.

Chloe didn't know Nick. Not the real him. She only knew the man who had graced the cover of Australia's leading financial newspaper last year.

'I'll see what I can do,' he said. 'Bye, girls.'

'Bye,' Sarah trilled back, smiling on the outside whilst inside she was already sinking back into the pit, that moment of pleasurable intimacy wiped away in the face of where Nick would be going tonight.

Do not succumb to jealousy, she lectured herself, or depression. Do not let him do this to you!

'You don't still have a thing for Nick, do you, love?'

Flora's softly delivered question was almost Sarah's undoing.

Gulping down the sudden lump in her throat, she

straightened her spine and adopted what she hoped was a believable expression. 'No, of course not.'

'That's good. Because it would be a mistake. There's no future for any woman with a man like Nick.'

Sarah laughed a dry little laugh. 'Don't you think I know that, Flora?'

'This Derek chap, is it serious between you two?'

Sarah hesitated to answer for a second too long.

'I didn't think so,' Flora said. 'You would have told me about him sooner, if that were the case.'

'Don't tell Nick,' she blurted out.

Flora's eyes narrowed. 'Is this Derek a real boyfriend or not?'

Sarah bit her bottom lip. She knew it would be wiser to lie, but she couldn't, not to Flora's face.

'He…he's just a friend.'

Flora gave her a long, searching look. 'What game are you playing at, girlie?'

Sarah sighed. 'Nothing bad, Flora. I just wanted to bring someone to the Christmas lunch and Derek volunteered. I'm sick and tired of Nick's girlfriends looking down their noses at me.'

'So it's a matter of female pride, is it?'

'Yes; yes, that's exactly what it is.'

'You do realise Nick is going to give this poor Derek the third degree?'

'Yes, he's prepared for that.'

Flora pulled a face. 'I hope so. Because Nick takes his job as your guardian very seriously, love.'

'Derek can hold his own.'

'None of your other boyfriends could.'

'Derek's not a real boyfriend.'

'But he's pretending to be one.'

'Yes.'

Flora sighed. 'Good luck to him, then. That's all I can say.'

# CHAPTER FOUR

SARAH decorated the Christmas tree on automatic pilot, her mind still on Flora's last words.

Flora was right, of course. Derek was going to be in for a rough time tomorrow.

But I did warn him, she reminded herself. And he still wanted to do it. In fact, he seemed to find the prospect of pretending to be my boyfriend an exciting challenge.

Sarah was beginning to find the thought terrifying. Nightmarish possibilities kept popping into her mind. What if Nick somehow discovered that Derek was gay? Or that their so-called relationship was just a sham? How could she explain such a crazy deception? Surely saving her pride wasn't worth the risk of feeling more of a fool in front of him.

And in front of Chloe.

Chloe…

Already she didn't like the woman and she hadn't even met her.

Nick had implied earlier that Chloe wasn't as skinny as his usual girlfriend. Was she blonde as well?

She would have to ask Flora later for a more detailed description.

Finally, all of the ornaments and lights were hung, except for the star that went on top of the tree. A glance at her watch showed that it was ten past six, way past time for a toasted sandwich and some coffee. She'd bypassed lunch after having eaten two pieces of that dreaded caramel slice, believing that they would easily sustain her for the whole afternoon.

Serious hunger pangs told her she'd been wrong. But the Christmas star came first.

Sarah climbed up the stepladder once more, this time having to go up on tiptoe to reach the right spot.

'That's a great-looking tree.'

Sarah jumped at the unexpected sound of Nick's voice, the star dropping from her hands as the back feet of the ladder lifted off the floor and she began to over-balance forwards. How Nick managed to save her she'd never know, but one second she was about to crash head-first into the tree, the next the ladder was abruptly righted and she fell backwards into Nick's arms.

'Oh, lord!' she gasped, her arms flailing wide whilst his wound tightly around her back, pulling her hard against his chest.

'You're all right,' he told her.

Her arms finally found a home around his neck, her heart thudding loudly behind her ribs.

'You…you frightened the life out of me,' she blurted out.

'Sorry. Didn't mean to.'

Sarah opened her mouth to say something more, *anything* to defuse the excitement that had instantly been sparked by finding herself in Nick's embrace. Such physical closeness, however, was not conducive to sensible brain activity, her mind going totally blank when his dark eyes dropped down to her softly parted lips.

For several, highly charged seconds Nick just stared at them.

Time seemed to slow around her, the air stilling whilst her pounding heart suspended its beat, her eyes closing as her head tipped invitingly sideways.

He was going to kiss her. She was sure of it!

To suddenly find herself being lowered onto her feet came as a shock.

'Oh,' she cried out, her eyes flying open to discover Nick frowning down at her with nothing but concern in his face.

'Steady now,' he said.

Sarah could have cried. Clearly, she was so *desperate* in her infatuation with this man that she'd conjured up passion where there was none. Not on his part, anyway.

'I'm fine, thank you,' she said curtly, pride demanding she cool her overheated blood and still that foolish, treacherous heart of hers.

'For a second there, I thought you were going to faint.'

'Faint? Why on earth would I faint?'

'Some girls do, after a shock.'

'I'm fine,' she reiterated.

'In that case, how about thanking me for saving you from a nasty fall?'

'Which you caused in the first place,' she pointed out stroppily. 'What are you doing home, anyway? I thought you were going to a party at seven. It's not far off that now.'

'Chloe forgot to tell me that it was black-tie. So I came home to change.'

Sarah had seen Nick in a dinner suit. Of course, he looked devastatingly handsome. Jealousy jabbed at her as she thought of Chloe on his arm tonight, then possibly in his bed…

Sarah's stomach somersaulted at the thought.

'I'm surprised you're not going out tonight yourself,' Nick said.

'What? Oh, yes, well…Derek wanted to take me somewhere, but I…I told him I'd be too busy with the tree and present-wrapping.' She was babbling and stammering! Why, oh, why did she have to think about Nick with Chloe?

'You should do what I do,' Nick said. 'Only buy presents at shops that do free gift-wrapping.'

And in shops where some smitten female sales assistant did all the choosing for him as well, Sarah thought ruefully.

'I'd better get going,' Nick went on. 'See you at present-opening in the morning. And before you ask, no, Chloe will not be in attendance. So you won't have to sulk.'

'I never sulk,' Sarah snapped.

'Oh, yes, you do, madam. But I agree with you on one score: some of my girlfriends have not been all that nice to you. Still, that's because most of them are jealous.'

'Of *me*?' Sarah could not have been more surprised.

Nick's smile was wry. 'How would you like to discover that your Derek was living with an attractive young female ward? Now I really must go,' he pronounced abruptly, and spun away.

'We still haven't had that private talk,' she called after him.

He stopped and glanced over his shoulder at her, his body language impatient. 'I realise that. It'll just have to wait till after Christmas Day.'

'But won't Chloe be here then?'

Nick had said this morning that he had a guest between Christmas and New Year. Who other than his current girlfriend?

'Chloe and I don't need to spend every minute of every day together,' he said rather pointedly. 'See you in the morning, Sarah.'

Sarah watched him stride across the family room, then leap up the two steps that led to the foyer. She heard him run up the stairs, depression descending at the sound of his hurrying to take out his girlfriend.

'I'm glad Derek is coming tomorrow,' she muttered under her breath.

'Talking to yourself is never a good idea, love.'

Sarah turned, then smiled at Flora. 'I have some of my best conversations with myself.'

'Better than that tea towel you used to talk to when you were a child, I suppose.'

Sarah stared at Flora. 'You knew about that?'

'Nothing much gets by me, love. So was the tea towel your other self? Or a special friend?'

'A special friend,' she confessed.

'Boy or girl?'

'Um...boy. Sort of.'

'He wasn't called Nick, was he?'

Sarah flushed.

'Like I said, love,' Flora continued as she went over and turned the switch that lit up the tree, 'nothing much gets by me. My, now, that is one lovely tree.'

'Jim chose a really good one this year.'

'He did indeed. Was that Nick I heard a minute ago?'

'Yes. He came home to change. The party's black-tie.'

'I'm not surprised. Chloe's a social climber, if ever there was one.'

Sarah shook her head. 'She sounds awful. What on earth does Nick see in her?'

'What does Nick see in any of his girlfriends? I suppose he doesn't much care about their characters as long as they're beautiful and do whatever he wants them to do in bed. He doesn't keep any of them, after all.'

'Flora! I've never heard you talk like this about Nick before.'

Flora shrugged. 'I'm getting old, I guess. When you get old you say things you wouldn't dare say before. Don't get me wrong. I'm very fond of Nick. But where women are concerned, he's bad news. He's never made a pass at you, has he, Sarah?'

'What? Me? No, never!'

'Just as well, with you having that crush on him.'

'I'm over that now.'

'You might think you are, but he'd still be able to turn your head, if he tried.'

Flora had never said a truer word. 'Why would he bother, when he has the likes of Chloe in his bed?'

Flora wrinkled her nose. 'I suspect Madame Chloe is fast reaching her use-by date. I'd watch myself, if I were you, when you swan downstairs tomorrow wearing one of those sexy new dresses of yours.'

Sarah's mouth dropped open. 'How do you know about them?'

'Couldn't sit around doing nothing all afternoon, so I unpacked for you. Which one are you wearing tomorrow? The red and white one, I'll bet.'

'Flora, you're an old sticky-beak!'

Flora remained quite nonplussed at this accusation. 'How do you think I get to know everything? I also put all those lovely Christmas cards you got from your pupils on your dressing table. Didn't leave room for much else, I'm afraid, so I set out all your new make-up and perfume and skin-care stuff on the vanity unit in your bathroom.'

Sarah didn't know whether to be appreciative, or annoyed. 'So, did everything get your seal of approval?'

'Let's just say I think you'll give Chloe a run for her money in the beauty stakes.'

'I sure hope so.'

'And who knows? Maybe your Derek will take one look at you and decide to take your friendship to a different level.

'Somehow I don't think that's likely to happen.'

'You never know, love. You just never know.'

# CHAPTER FIVE

SARAH woke to a less than gentle shake of her shoulder and an unshaven Nick leaning over her. Surprise and shock sent her eyes instantly wide and her heart racing.

'What is it?' she exclaimed. 'What's wrong?'

When he straightened she saw he was already dressed, in jeans and a T-shirt. 'Nothing's *wrong*,' he said.

Then what on earth was he doing in her bedroom at some ungodly hour in the morning?

'Flora sent me to wake you,' he went on, his voice carrying a measure of exasperation.

'What for?' Confusion in her own voice.

'For breakfast and present-giving.'

Sarah blinked. '*This* early?'

'The men with the tables and blinds are due to arrive at nine and it's already eight.'

'Eight!' Sarah sat bolt upright, pushing her hair back from her face as she glanced first at her sun-drenched balcony, then at her bedside clock, which confirmed that it was indeed, just after eight. Yet she had set her alarm for six, wanting to be looking her very best for present-opening with her hair done, make-up perfect and dressed to impress in her sexy new jeans and a very pretty green top.

'I must have slept through the alarm,' she said with a groan.

Or perhaps she'd fallen asleep without actually setting it. She'd stayed up quite late, doing everything she could the night before in preparation for Christmas Day.

'Just get up and come downstairs,' Nick said impatiently before whirling and striding from the room.

'I...I'll be down shortly,' she called after him.

'You'd better be,' he called back.

It wasn't till Nick left that Sarah realised she hadn't wished him a happy Christmas. Still, he hadn't thought to wish her the season's greetings, either. He'd sounded tired and grumpy. Probably hadn't had enough sleep. She hadn't heard him come in last night, so it had to have been very late. Probably went to Chloe's place after the party and...

'Don't think about last night,' she lectured herself aloud. 'Just get up and get on with things.'

Scooping in a deep breath, Sarah threw back the bed-clothes and dashed into the bathroom, where she washed and cleaned her teeth in two minutes flat.

Then she stared at herself in the mirror.

D-Day, she thought with a wild fluttering in the stomach.

In a way it was a good thing that she didn't have time to dress. It would make her transformation later on all the more eye-catching and dramatic.

At the same time, she didn't want to look a total dag.

No time to do much with her hair except brush it, then twist it up into a loose knot on top of her head. Definitely no time for make-up.

Thankfully, her nightie was new and pretty, a lavender satin petticoat that had a matching robe. She slipped the robe on, looped the sash belt and hurried back into her bedroom, only then realising she had nothing suitable for her feet.

She never wore slippers. Sandals didn't seem right and neither did her flip-flops.

Oh, well, it wouldn't be the first time she went downstairs for Christmas breakfast barefooted and in her night things, though usually the latter were a bit longer. This nightie only reached mid-thigh, the robe to her knees. She would have to watch herself when she sat down. At least her legs were nice and smooth, all the way up. Sarah had taken herself off to a beautician late last week and had a full wax. Painful, but worth every penny not to have to worry about shaving for ages.

It felt a bit odd when she wasn't wearing panties, however. Like now, for instance.

Sarah might have slipped some panties on, but there really wasn't time for any more delay. It was already seven minutes past eight. And it wasn't as though anyone would know.

Sarah sucked in one last, long, calming breath, exhaled slowly, then set forth for the staircase.

Breakfast on Christmas morning was always very light; croissants and coffee served in front of the tree during present-opening. The family room in Goldmine was huge, with three distinct sitting areas. The Christmas tree was always placed down the far end, where there were two brown leather sofas facing each other, and a sturdy wooden coffee-table between them.

Everything was set out in readiness by the time Sarah made it downstairs, delicious aromas hitting her nostrils as she padded down the steps into the family room.

Her entry was quiet, due to her bare feet, giving her a second or two to survey the situation and work out in advance where she would sit.

Flora and Jim occupied opposite ends of the sofa facing the terrace, with Nick sitting in the middle of the sofa opposite, sipping coffee. She didn't want to sit next to him, not after what had happened yesterday. She certainly didn't want to sit next to him without her panties on. Physical proximity to Nick made her body—and her mind—go absolutely haywire.

Whilst Sarah was still resolved to go through with her plan to doll herself up for Christmas lunch—and to pretend Derek was her new boyfriend—she no longer held any hope whatsoever that Nick's eyes would be opened to her attractions as a female. She'd come to the dampening conclusion that after her father died Nick had mentally placed her in a box marked 'legal responsibility', thereby killing off any possibility of a personal relationship between them.

Suddenly his head turned her way, his dark eyes travelling swiftly from her tousled hair down to her scarlet toenails before moving back up again.

Was she mistaken, or did his eyes stop to linger on her breasts?

Whatever, her body responded instantly, a tingling feeling spreading over her skin whilst her heartbeat quickened and her nipples peaked alarmingly against the satin.

Sarah swallowed. Surely she was imagining it, as she'd imagined yesterday that he'd been going to kiss her. Yes, of course she was. The man was just looking, the way any man would when a pretty young female presented herself in front of him in her night things. He'd always *looked* at her, just not the way she wanted him to.

'Merry Christmas, everyone!' she trilled, determined not to let the deluding nature of her feelings for Nick spoil present-opening.

Flora and Jim glanced round at once, their kind faces breaking into warm smiles.

'And merry Christmas to you too, love,' Flora returned happily. 'Come on, come over here and sit next to me,' she said, patting the spot next to her.

'Sorry to keep you waiting.' Sarah angled herself past Flora's plump knees to take her place in the middle of the sofa directly opposite Nick. 'I must have slept through my alarm,' she added, once she was safely leaning back with her knees modestly pressed together and her robe arranged to cover as much of her bare thighs as possible.

'That's perfectly all right, love,' Flora said. 'You're here now. Coffee?' she offered, already leaning forward to pick up the coffee-pot.

'Yes, please.' Ignoring Nick—whose eyes had remained on her as she sat down—Sarah picked up a bread plate and helped herself to a croissant. 'Have you all eaten yet?'

'Jim and I have,' Flora said. 'Nick hasn't. He said he wasn't hungry. But I think he's got a hangover.'

'I do *not* have a hangover,' Nick protested. 'I feel fine. I'm just saving my appetite for lunch. But I will have a top-up of coffee, Flora,' he said, putting his mug on the coffee-table and pushing it towards her. 'With cream and sugar. That should keep me going for the next couple of hours.'

'Did you enjoy yourself at the party last night?' Sarah asked before she could snatch the words back. Truly, she was stupid sometimes.

Nick picked up his refilled coffee mug and took an appreciative sip before answering. 'It was a typical party of that type. To be honest, I think I'm partied out at the moment. That's one of the reasons I'm going to Happy Island. So that I can relax and do absolutely nothing for a while.'

'You could do absolutely nothing here,' Sarah pointed out, still hating the thought of his going away.

His dark eyes connected with hers over the rim of the mug. 'I can't, actually.'

'Why not?'

'People will bother me here,' he stated matter-of-factly.

*And get in the way of your spending private time with your girlfriend.*

Sarah could picture them skinny-dipping in his swimming pool on Happy Island, making leisurely love in the water and everywhere else in the no doubt luxurious holiday house.

It was a depressing train of thought.

'I think we should get on with present-giving,' Flora suggested. 'Jim, why don't you play Santa this year? Is that OK with you, Sarah?'

'Sure.' She was more than happy to sit there and devour her croissant, telling herself all the while that she would stop at just one. Because if she didn't, she'd be on her way back to Blubbersville.

But she needed the comfort the croissant gave her, needed to combat the dismay which was crushing her at that moment.

It was all so hopeless, Sarah thought wretchedly as she finished the first croissant in no time flat, then picked up another. Nick was never going to be hers. Not in bed, or anywhere else.

*But then, you knew that, didn't you? You were a fool to listen to Derek, even for a moment.*

Flora's gentle hand on her arm stopped her from stuffing the second croissant into her mouth.

'Perhaps that can wait till after we've opened the presents,' she suggested. 'Pick one of Nick's presents first, Jim, so that Sarah can drink her coffee.'

'Thank you, Flora,' Sarah whispered under her breath as she put down the croissant and picked up her coffee instead.

Jim rose and began moving the pile of presents around, Sarah's stomach contracting when he selected a smallish rectangular gift, wrapped in sparkling gold paper that had Christmas trees all over it.

'That's from me,' she said with false brightness when Jim handed it over to Nick.

Instead of Sarah feeling joyful anticipation at Nick's opening her present, her main emotion now was anxiety over his reaction. Sarah knew he would like it. She just hoped he wouldn't read anything into it. She would hate him to guess how she secretly felt about him. Hate the humiliation that would go with any such discovery.

Nick put down his coffee and ripped off the wrapping paper, frowning when confronted with the plain white cardboard box.

'Not cologne this year?' he said as he struggled to open the tight top, his short nails not helping with the task.

'No,' she replied. 'Do you want me to open it for you?'

'No. I'll get it. Eventually. There. Done.' Nick frowned some more as he upended the box and slid the bubble-wrapped gift into the palm of his hand. 'I have no idea what this could be,' he said with genuine puzzlement in his voice as he unwrapped it.

Sarah found herself holding her breath, rewarded when she saw pure, unadulterated delight fill his face.

'I…I hope you like it,' Sarah said, her cheeks colouring when his eyes lifted to stare over at her. Oh, goodness, she hoped he wasn't jumping to any embarrassing conclusions.

'What is it?' Flora piped up before Nick could answer her. 'Show me.'

Nick placed the miniature golf bag on the coffee-table for everyone to see before shaking his head at her.

'Words fail me, Sarah,' he said. But with amazement, not speculation.

'Look at this, Jim,' Flora said. 'It's a tiny little golf bag, full of the most beautiful little golf clubs.'

Jim leant over to take a closer look. 'It looks expensive.'

'Yes,' Nick agreed. 'It does. You shouldn't have spent so much money on me, Sarah.'

'Oh, it wasn't too dear for a soon-to-be heiress,' she replied airily. 'I thought you deserved something special for having put up with me all these years. The clubs are made from real silver, you know. English silver. They have hallmarks on them.'

'Where on earth did you get it?' Nick asked.

'I bought it on eBay. They have things you just don't see in the shops.'

'It's an exquisite and thoughtful present,' he said as he picked it up again. 'I'll treasure it always.'

Sarah's heart swelled with pleasure. If nothing else, she'd pleased him with her gift today, his genuinely warm reaction lifting her spirits and making her realise that he did care about her. She'd seen the affection in his eyes just now.

If she could not spark his sexual interest, then she would settle for his affection. It was better than nothing. For a while there, over the last few years, she'd begun thinking he didn't even like her any more.

But it was clear that he did. Maybe, once she grew up and got over this mad sexual obsession that had been tormenting her for far too long, they could even become friends again.

'Now it's your turn,' Nick said. 'Jim, give me that box with the red bow on it, please. Yes, that's the one.'

Nick smiled as he handed Sarah the store-wrapped package. 'Sorry it's not quite what you asked for.'

'What are you talking out? Oh, you mean the car. Well, I was only joking, you know. I can't imagine what you've bought me,' she said a bit breathlessly as she removed the bow then lifted the lid off the box.

Inside was a yellow car. A model of the one she'd mentioned to Nick. Not a miniature, but quite a large one. And not cheap, either.

Sarah laughed as she drew it out. 'Look what the wicked devil bought.'

Flora clucked her tongue at Nick. Jim liked it, though, calling it a beauty.

'If you open the driver's door,' Nick said, 'you might find something of more use to a soon-to-be heiress.'

Sarah did as she was told, and discovered a small, rectangular-shaped box made in dark red velvet. She knew, before she opened it, that it contained jewellery, but what?

Nerves claimed her stomach when she started to lift the lid. Nick never bought her jewellery. So why had he this time?

The sight of what was inside took her breath away.

'Oh, my God!' she gasped before gazing with wide eyes up at Nick. 'Tell me they're not real diamonds. Tell me they're zircons, or cut glass.'

'Of course they're real diamonds,' Flora said, leaning over to gaze at Sarah's present.

'They do look expensive,' Jim said, not for the first time that morning.

'Don't you like them?' Nick said drily. 'If you want to return them, I'm sure I still have the receipt somewhere.'

'Over my dead body!' Sarah retorted, snapping the box shut and hugging it to her chest.

Nick smiled. 'I do realise that you have all your mother's jewellery, but what suits one woman doesn't necessarily suit another. I thought these were more you.'

Sarah opened the box again, then picked one of the earrings out of the box for closer viewing. It had a large diamond at the lobe, and two dangling drops of smaller diamonds that shimmered and sparkled with the slightest movement.

'You think I'm a girl who favours flashy jewellery?'

'Diamonds aren't flashy, they're classy. And they never go out of fashion. You can wear them with any outfit.'

'Then I'll wear them today,' she decided immedi-

ately. 'To the Christmas lunch.' And I'll make sure
Chloe knows who gave them to me, she vowed with uncharacteristic bitchiness.

'Yes, do that,' he agreed, an odd glitter in his eyes.

Sarah wished she knew what was going on in his
head. But he was a closed book when he wanted to be.

'I'd like my present from Nick now,' Flora piped up.

'Oooh, did I get diamonds, too?' she added when Jim
handed her a beautifully wrapped gift that was almost
as small as Sarah's.

'Sorry,' Nick returned. 'I thought you'd prefer sapphires, to go with your pretty blue eyes.'

'Oh, go on with you,' Flora said laughingly.

But he *had* bought her sapphires, in the form of an
utterly stunning, sapphire-encrusted watch. Jim got a
watch, too, a very expensive gold one. Both were
thrilled to pieces.

Sarah had never known Nick spend so much money
on Christmas presents. He couldn't possibly be having
serious financial worries, she thought with some relief,
if he was throwing money around like this.

Flora and Jim seemed to like the gifts Sarah had
chosen for them, Flora gushing over her favourite
perfume and a cookbook, a new one that featured
healthy meals. Jim was notoriously difficult to buy
presents for, but a bottle of really rare port, plus a special
glass engraved with his name, found favour.

In return, Flora and Jim gave Sarah a truly beautiful
photo frame and a lovely feminine diary for the follow-

ing year. It had pictures of flowers on every page, along with a special thought for the day. Nick became the proud owner of a new leather wallet, along with a very stylish gold silk tie.

'For the rare occasions when you're forced to wear one,' Flora informed him.

Which was, indeed, rare. Nick looked drop-dead gorgeous in a tux, or any suit for that matter. But he hated wearing them. He much preferred casual clothes. When circumstance demanded, he did wear a business suit, but he mostly teamed it with an open-necked shirt, or a crew-necked designer top. Only when protocol insisted on a tie did he wear one.

Around the house, he lived in shorts and jeans. Like now. Of course, he would change for Christmas lunch into a smart pair of trousers and an open-necked shirt, its length of sleeve depending on the weather. Today the forecast was for twenty-eight degrees, a very pleasant temperature for this time of year.

Sarah was glad it wasn't going to be cool, or rainy, as she would have frozen in her outfit.

'OK, folks,' Nick said, and abruptly stood up. 'Time to clean up the mess we've made here and shake a leg. Jim, I'll need your help getting everything ready outside. But Flora, you're not to rush around working yourself into a lather like you usually do. The caterers are due here at ten. All they require is a clean kitchen. They're providing everything, right down to the crockery, cutlery and glasses. Though not the wine. I bought that last week and stored it in the cellar. Jim, we'll need to bring that up as well. I'll put my presents away first, then meet you on the back terrace in five minutes. The guests are due to arrive from midday on, so, Sarah, leave plenty of time to dress and be back downstairs by five to twelve, ready to help me greet people at the door as they arrive.'

'How many are coming this year?' she asked.

'Twenty, if they all show up. Twenty-four, including us. OK?'

'Fine.'

They all rose to do as they were told, Sarah's heart beating faster when she thought of what lay ahead. Ok, so maybe it had been foolhardy of her to go along with Derek's plan without thinking it fully through, but now that the moment was at hand, it was still better than facing Christmas lunch alone. If nothing else, Derek wouldn't let her eat everything in sight.

But would he be able to withstand Nick's scrutiny?

Flora had told her yesterday that Nick took his job as her guardian very seriously indeed. Which in the past had obviously included vetting her boyfriends and making sure they weren't fortune-hunters.

Bringing Derek home so close to her inheriting her father's estate—not to mention telling Nick that they were very much in love—would only make him extra-protective. And paranoid.

She'd feel more confident if Derek weren't gay. And if she'd met this Chloe before. The unknown made her nervous. And she didn't want to be nervous. She wanted to swan downstairs just before midday, the epitome of cool composure and worldly sophistication. She wanted Nick to take one look at her and think to himself that she was the most beautiful and desirable woman that he had ever seen!

## CHAPTER SIX

BY ELEVEN, Nick had done everything that needed to be done downstairs. The tables and shady blinds had been set up, and the wine brought up from the cellar and delivered to the family-room bar. The caterers had arrived right on ten, the staff consisting of three females and two males, a highly efficient group of people whose job it was to take the stress out of Christmas Day dinners.

Nick smiled ruefully to himself as he went upstairs. He had no doubt that they did a very good job with the food, the serving and the clearing up afterwards. But nothing—and no one—was going to take the stress out of *this* Christmas dinner. Not for him, anyway.

He'd thought he'd finally got a handle on the unwanted desires Sarah had been evoking in him since she turned sixteen. But no, he'd just been deluding himself. Her staying away from home for most of this year had lulled him into a false sense of security. That, and meeting Chloe, whose sexy body and entertaining company had banished his secret lust for Sarah into the dungeon of his mind; that dark, dank place in which Nick imprisoned memories and emotions that were best forgotten. Or, at least, ignored.

He'd honestly thought he was prepared for Sarah's presence at Christmas. Thought he'd taken every precaution to keep the door to that mental dungeon firmly locked.

It had been Flora's news over breakfast yesterday that Sarah was bringing a boyfriend to the Christmas Day lunch which had shattered his illusion of iron self-control, stirring up a hornet's nest of jealousy within him. Next thing Nick knew, he was staying home from golf, just so that he could be here when she arrived. He'd made the excuse that he needed to talk to her about her inheritance, when in fact what he'd wanted most was to question her about the new man in her life.

Finding out that she was madly in love with this Derek didn't do his jealousy any good. OK, so on the surface he'd managed to control himself around Sarah. He gave himself full marks for not kissing her when he'd had the chance yesterday afternoon.

But he'd given in to temptation over those diamond earrings, hadn't he? Spent a small fortune on them, with the full intention of letting dear Derek know who'd bought them for her.

The truth was Nick had behaved badly every time Sarah brought home a boyfriend. He'd always pretended to himself that he was only doing what Ray had asked him to do, justifying his actions with the excuse that he was protecting her from fortune-hunters.

But that was actually far from the truth. None of those poor boys in the past had been gold-diggers. How could they be, when Sarah had never told anyone she was an heiress? They'd just been young men who'd had the good fortune—or was it misfortune?—to be where Nick had always wanted to be.

With Sarah.

The savage satisfaction he'd experienced every time he broke up one of her relationships showed just what kind of man he was: rotten to the core and wickedly selfish.

What would he do this time? he wondered grimly as he mounted the top landing and gazed down the hallway towards Sarah's bedroom.

Nothing, he hoped. The same way he'd done nothing yesterday when she'd been in his arms. He'd wanted to kiss her. Hell, he *ached* to kiss her.

But what would that have achieved, except make her look at him not with adoration as she'd once done, but with disgust? Sarah had finally fallen in love; possibly she was on the verge of having what she'd always wanted: marriage and children.

If this Derek was a decent fellow, then it would be cruel and callous to try to put doubts in Sarah's head about him.

Yet he wanted to…

Still, wanting to do something and actually doing it were two entirely different things. He'd wanted to seduce Sarah for years, but he hadn't, had he?

Nick shook his head agitatedly as he forged on across the carpeted landing into the master bedroom. It wasn't till he shut the door behind him that his mind shifted from his immediate problem with Sarah to another problem he would have to face in the near future.

Come February, he had to leave this house.

It would be a terrible wrench, Nick knew. He'd grown very attached to the place, and the people in it. He could not imagine coming home to any other house, or any other bedroom.

Strange, really. Eight years ago, after Ray died and Nick moved into the house, he hadn't much liked this bedroom.

Ray had gone Japanese-mad after his trip to Tokyo; the gardens hadn't been the only thing around Goldmine to be changed: the master-bedroom suite had been totally gutted, its walls painted white, the plush gold carpet ripped out and polished floorboards laid. The heavy mahogany bedroom suite had been given to charity, to be replaced by black lacquered Japanese-style furniture. The king-sized bed was now large and low, the duvet and pillows covered in scarlet silk with sprays of flowers at their corners.

Other than two matching black lacquered bedside tables, there'd been no furniture in the room, the walk-in wardrobe being spacious enough to accommodate all Ray's clothes.

The bathroom had been changed with an all-white suite during this refurbishment, enlarged as well to accommodate a huge spa bath that you could practically swim in.

Nick liked the bathroom, but had found the bedroom rather stark, and not evocative of the atmosphere he wanted his bachelor boudoir to evoke. So he'd bought three fluffy white rugs to surround the bed, and some white cane chairs for the corners. A huge plasma television now hung on the wall opposite the bed with access to every satellite television channel available. Black silk sheets were his final purchases, along with some new shades for the chrome-based bedside lamps: red, of course.

The effect at night was erotic and sensual.

When in his bedroom, Nick didn't pretend to be anything but what he was: a very sensual man.

Which made his actions last night after the party almost incomprehensible.

Why, when he'd taken Chloe home, hadn't he gone inside and made mad, passionate love to her? She'd been all over him like a rash at the door. Normally, he loved it when she was sexually aggressive, loved it that he didn't have to be gentle with her. At any other time, he would have pushed her inside and had her up against the wall.

Instead her rapacious mouth had repelled him for some reason, and he found himself telling her he had a headache. A *headache*, for pity's sake!

Chloe had been surprised, but reasonably understanding, sending him off with a kiss on the cheek and the advice to have a good night's sleep.

'You won't get off so easily tomorrow night,' she'd added as he walked back to his car.

Nick hadn't gone straight home. He'd driven round and round, trying to work out why he wasn't in Chloe's bed right at that moment, sating his desires to a degree where he wouldn't be capable of feeling any lust for anyone!

Then, when he'd finally come home, he'd fallen into a fitful sleep, his dreams filled with disturbingly erotic images involving the bane of his life. In one dream, Sarah had come down to the Christmas lunch wearing that minute bikini that had tormented him all those years ago. In another, she had been decorating that damned Christmas tree in the nude. In yet another, she'd been in his arms and he was kissing her the way he'd wanted to kiss her yesterday.

He'd woken from that dream incredibly aroused.

When Flora had sent him into Sarah's bedroom to wake her this morning, he'd stared down at her sleeping form for longer than was decent, the dungeon door in his mind well and truly open. Then, when she'd waltzed down to present-giving in that sexy little nightie, he'd been consumed with a desire so strong it had taken every ounce of his will-power to keep himself in check.

Her giving him that exquisite and very expensive miniature golf set had tormented him further, giving rise to the provocative possibility that, despite her new boyfriend, she still secretly fancied *him*. But her rather offhand words that her present was a parting gift of gratitude had propelled Nick back to cold, hard reality.

Sarah was well and truly over her schoolgirl crush on him. He'd lost his chance with her, if he'd ever had one.

It was this last thought that was bothering him the most.

'You should be glad she's over you,' he muttered as

he marched towards the bathroom, stripping off his T-shirt as he went. 'Now all you have to do is concentrate on getting through today without behaving badly.'

Nick wrenched off his jeans, before walking over to snap on the water in the shower.

'No sarcastic remarks,' he lectured himself as he stepped under the ice-cold spray. 'No telling Derek you bought his girlfriend thirty-thousand-dollar earrings. And definitely no looking, no matter *what* she wears!'

# CHAPTER SEVEN

'LET'S go, Sarah.'

Nick's loud command—called through her bedroom door—was accompanied by an impatient knocking.

Sarah's bedside clock showed it was three minutes to twelve, two minutes after Nick had asked her to be downstairs.

'Coming,' Sarah called back after one last nervous glance in her dressing-table mirror.

She did look good: the red and white sundress clung to her shapely but slender body, and her choice of hairstyle— she'd put it up—showed off her new diamond earrings.

It wasn't Sarah's sexy appearance that had the butterflies gathering in her stomach. It was this silly charade with Derek. Nick was going to spot something strange about their relationship, she felt sure of it!

But it was too late now. Derek was on his way, having texted her a while back to say the taxi he'd ordered had just arrived and he should be at her place by twelve.

Sarah pulled her scarlet-glossed mouth back into

what she hoped passed for a happy smile and hurried across the room, movement setting her earrings swinging. When she wrenched open the door, Nick glanced up from where he was leaning with his back against the gallery railing. He still looked tired, she thought, but very handsome in fawn chinos and a brown and cream striped short-sleeved shirt.

'I'm ready,' she said breezily.

Nick's dark eyes swept over her from head to toe, his top lip curling slightly, as it did sometimes. 'Yes, but ready for what?'

His sarcasm rankled, as always.

Sarah planted her hands on her hips, just above where her skirt flared out saucily. 'It wouldn't hurt you to say something nice to me for a change.'

His eyebrows lifted, as though she'd surprised him with her stance. 'That's a matter of opinion. But if you insist…' His eyes travelled over her again, this time much more slowly.

A huge lump formed in her throat when his gaze lingered on her breasts before lifting to her mouth, then up to her eyes. If she'd been hoping to see desire in his detailed survey, however, she was doomed to disappointment.

'You look utterly gorgeous today, Sarah,' he said at last, but in a rather dry fashion. 'Derek is a very lucky man.'

Sarah was tempted to stamp her foot in frustration when the doorbell rang, saving her from her uncharacteristic temper tantrum.

'That'll probably be Derek now,' she tossed off instead, and bolted for the stairs, eager to answer the door without Nick being too close a witness to their greeting.

It wasn't Derek at the door, but an attractive, thirty-something brunette wearing a wrap-around electric-blue dress and a smile that would have cut glass.

Sarah knew immediately who it was.

'Sarah, I presume,' the woman said archly after a swift once-over that made her ice-blue eyes even icier. 'I'm Chloe, Nick's girlfriend.'

Of course you are, Sarah thought tartly. Nick's girlfriends might look different from one another—this one had a very short, chic hairdo, plus a much curvier body than the others. But underneath their varied physical features always lay a hard-nosed piece with no genuine warmth or niceness.

Sarah despised Chloe on sight.

'Hi there,' she managed politely before spinning round to see where Nick was. No way was she going to be caught having to make small talk with the bitch *du jour*.

Nick was still coming down the stairs, his expression none too happy.

'Chloe's here,' she called out to him.

For a split-second, Sarah could have sworn he had no idea who she was talking about. But then the penny dropped and he hurried to the door, his disgruntled face breaking into a smile.

'Happy Christmas, darling,' Chloe gushed as she threw herself into Nick's arms.

Sarah turned away so that she didn't have to watch

them kiss, her stomach contracting when she heard Chloe whisper something about giving him his main Christmas present later that night.

It was extremely fortunate that Derek chose that moment to arrive, Sarah's nervous anticipation over their charade was obliterated in the face of her need to have someone by her side *on* her side.

'Derek, darling!' she gushed in much the same way Chloe had. 'Merry Christmas. Oh, it's so good to see you.' She let out a mental sigh of relief when she took in the way he was dressed. She'd been a bit worried he might wear a pink Paisley shirt, or something equally suspect. But no, he looked very attractive and sportily masculine in knee-length cargo shorts and a chest-hugging sky-blue top that complimented his fair colouring and showed off his great body.

'And you too, babe,' Derek returned, startling Sarah with his choice of endearment, not to mention his leaning over the rather large present he was holding to kiss her full on the mouth, taking his time.

'You look incredible,' he said on straightening. 'Doesn't she look incredible, everyone?'

Neither Nick nor Chloe said a word.

Sarah flushed with embarrassment, but Derek was undeterred.

'I hope this fits, babe,' he said, then pressed the present into her hands. 'I saw it in a shop window and I thought straight away that it was you to a T.'

Sarah didn't know whether to be pleased, or afraid

of the contents. Derek had a wicked streak in him that was proving to be as entertaining as it was worrying.

'I…I'll open it a bit later,' she hedged. 'I have to help Nick greet our guests. Which reminds me. Nick, this is Derek,' she said by way of a formal introduction. 'Derek, this is Nick, my guardian.'

'No kidding,' Derek said as he shook Nick's hand. 'I got the impression you'd be older.'

Sarah tried not to laugh. But it was rather funny, seeing the expression on Nick's face.

'And I'm Chloe,' Chloe said with a sickeningly sweet smile. 'Nick's girlfriend.'

It never ceased to amaze Sarah how females like Chloe possessed split personalities—a super-sweet one for dealing with the male sex, a super-sour one, for their own.

'Why don't you go open your Christmas pressie in private?' Chloe suggested to Sarah with pretend saccharin-sweetness. 'I can help Nick answer the door, can't I, darling? I mean, all of the guests—other than Derek, of course—are Nick's friends.'

'What a good idea!' Sarah said, jumping at the chance to remove herself from Chloe's irritating presence. Of all Nick's girlfriends, she disliked this one the most, the conniving, two-faced cow!

'No, not down there,' Derek whispered when she grabbed his elbow and began steering him across the foyer towards the sunken family room. 'Take me upstairs. To your bedroom.'

'My *bedroom*!' she squawked, grinding to a halt.

'Ssh. Yes, your bedroom,' he went on softly. 'Don't ask why, just do it. And don't look back at either of those two. Just giggle, and then skip up those stairs with me.'

'I *never* giggle.' She hated females who giggled.

'You're going to today. That is, if you don't want to wonder for the rest of your life what it would be like to spend a night in Mr Dreamy's bed.'

Sarah finally saw what he was up to. 'This won't work, Derek, trust me.'

'No, you trust me. I know what I'm doing here, Sarah. I'm a master at the art of sexual jealousy. All gays are.'

'Ssh. Don't say that out loud.'

'Then do as you're told.'

Sarah refused to giggle. But she did laugh, then let Derek usher her with somewhat indecent speed up the stairs.

'Which room is yours?' he asked once they reached the landing.

'The third one on the right.'

'Nice room,' he said on closing the door behind them.

'Nick thinks it's too girlie. He also thinks I'm too thin now. He still doesn't fancy me, Derek. You're wasting your time trying to make him jealous.'

Derek smiled. 'That's not the impression I got when I kissed you.'

'What do you mean?'

'I kept my eyes open a fraction and watched your guardian's reaction over your shoulder.'

'And?'

'He hated it. And he hated me. I could feel his hatred hitting me in waves. Then, when he shook my hand he tried to crush my fingers.'

Sarah shook her head as she walked over and placed Derek's present on her pink quilt. 'I don't believe you,' she said as she sat down next to it.

'Why not?'

'Because I…Because he…Just because!' she snapped.

'You know what, Sarah? I think you're afraid.'

'Afraid of what?'

'Of success. You've lived with this fantasy for far too long. It's time to either let it go, or try to make it real. Which is it to be?'

Sarah thought of lying alone in this bed tonight whilst Nick cavorted with Chloe in his bed. She squeezed her eyes tightly shut for several seconds whilst she made up her mind. Then she opened them and looked into Derek's patiently waiting face.

'So what's the plan of action?'

Derek grinned. 'Stay right where we are, for starters. What time is lunch served?'

'Actually it's not served as such. It's a buffet. Nick usually tries to get everyone heading for the food at one o'clock.'

Derek glanced at his watch. 'In that case we'll make a reappearance downstairs at around five to one.'

Sarah frowned. 'We're going to stay up here till then?'

'Yep.'

'You do realise what Nick is going to think we're doing.'

'Yep.'

'He'll think I'm a slut!'

'If I'm right about him, he'll have trouble thinking at all. Now open your present. And make sure, when you come downstairs, you tell him what I gave you.'

# CHAPTER EIGHT

NICK tried to hide his growing agitation, but where the hell was Sarah and what in God's name was she doing? It didn't take *that* long to open one miserable present. Damn it all, it was getting on for one o'clock.

The obvious answer just killed him: she was up in her bedroom, doing unspeakable things with that lounge lizard she was madly in love with and who had obviously pulled the wool over her eyes.

If ever Nick had seen a fortune-hunter it was darling Derek, with his fake smile, his fake blonde hair and his equally fake suntan!

Unfortunately his muscles didn't look fake, a fact that irritated the death out of Nick. He'd never thought Sarah was the sort of girl whose head could be turned by such superficial attractions. But clearly she was. She even seemed to like being called babe.

Didn't she know darling Derek probably called every one of his girlfriends babe? Saved him having to remember their names, since it was obvious he didn't have enough brains to make his head ache.

'Nick, Jeremy's talking to you,' Chloe said somewhat waspishly.

'What? Oh, sorry.' Nick dragged his mind away from his mental vitriol to focus back on the man talking to him.

Jeremy was his production company's location manager. Quite brilliant at his job, and gayer than gay.

'What were you saying, Jerry?'

Jeremy gave him a sunny smile over the rim of his martini. 'Just that I'm super-grateful to you for inviting *moi* for lunch today. Christmas is the one time of year when gays are severely reminded that lots of people are still homophobic. We try telling ourselves that Sydney is a very sophisticated city these days, but it's not as sophisticated as it pretends to be.'

'Really?' Nick said, his eyes returning to the foyer through which Sarah would have to come. If she ever came back downstairs, that was.

'You'd think the world had more important things to worry about than what people do in their private lives, wouldn't you?' Jeremy rattled on. 'I mean…what business is it of others who or what you have sex with, as long as you're not hurting anyone?'

But what if you were? came Nick's savage thought. What if having sex with someone—right at this moment—was tearing someone else's insides out?

'Well said, Jeremy,' his partner complimented.

Nick's eyes swung to Kelvin, who was a tall, skinny fellow of indeterminate age.

Nick was about to open his mouth and make some possibly rude remark—he suspected he was on the verge of behaving very badly indeed—when the movement he'd been waiting for caught the corner of his eye.

Nick's guts crunched down hard as he watched the object of his agitation waltz across the foyer with a smug-looking Derek hot on her heels.

That Sarah's hair was down—and tousled—did not escape Nick. Neither did her flushed cheeks.

'If you'll excuse me,' he said abruptly, 'there's someone I must speak to. Chloe, could you show our guests out to the terrace? The lunch is a buffet, but there are place cards on the table.'

Nick ignored the flash of annoyance that zoomed across Chloe's face, just before he spun away and marched across the family room to confront Sarah. What he thought he was going to say he had no idea. But he needed to say something; anything to give vent to the storm of emotion building to a head within him.

'Sarah,' he bit out when he was close enough to the lovebirds.

Her eyes jerked round towards him.

'I need to talk to you. *Now.* In private.'

'But we were just going out to the terrace for lunch,' she returned, oh, so sweetly.

He gritted his teeth as his furious gaze fastened on her mouth, where her red lipstick was an even glossier red than it had been before. Courtesy, no doubt, of having had to be retouched.

But the *coup de grâce* to his already teetering control was noticing that she'd removed his diamond earrings.

'I'm sure you won't mind not eating for a further five minutes,' he snapped, his stomach turning over at the thought of why she wasn't still wearing his Christmas gift.

Her shrug seemed carefree, but he detected a smidgeon of worry in her eyes.

'I won't be long, darling,' she said to her lover with a softly apologetic stroke on his arm. 'The buffet's all set up on the terrace out there. You go ahead and I'll join you shortly.'

'Sure thing, babe. I'll choose for you. And get you some of that white wine you like.'

'Would you? That would be wonderful.'

The schmaltzy exchange almost made Nick sick to his stomach. The moment Derek departed he grabbed Sarah by the elbow and steered her back out to the foyer, then along the front hallway towards his study.

When she tried to wrench her arm free, his hand tightened its hold.

'Is this caveman stuff really necessary?' she protested.

Nick said nothing, just pushed her into his study, then banged the door shut behind them. When he glowered over her, she did look a little shamefaced.

'OK, you're mad at me for not coming downstairs earlier and helping you with your guests,' she said. 'That's it, isn't it?'

'Not only was your behaviour rude, Sarah, it was embarrassing.'

'Embarrassing! I don't see how. I mean, it's not as though I know any of the guests this year. Flora told me beforehand that all of them are from your production company.'

'That's no excuse for ignoring them,' he lashed out. 'They have heard me speak of you. They *expected* to meet you, but you were nowhere to be seen. On Christmas Day, of all days! It would have been polite of you to be in the family room, offering drinks and making conversation. Instead, you were upstairs in your bedroom, having sex with that obsequious boyfriend of yours. I would have thought you had more pride, and a better sense of decorum.'

Her cheeks went bright red. 'Derek is not obsequious. And I was *not* having sex with him.'

Nick's laugh was both cold and contemptuous. 'Your appearance rather contradicts that.'

Her mouth fell open, then snapped shut. 'What Derek and I do in the privacy of my room is none of your business. Just as it's none of my business what you'll be doing with Chloe tonight in your bedroom. We're both adults now, Nick. I've been an adult for quite some time, in case you haven't noticed. In six weeks' time, I'll be twenty-five and you'll no longer have any say in my life whatsoever. I will be able to do whatever I like in this house because you won't be in it!'

'And no one will be more pleased than me,' he threw

back at her, his frustration making him reckless. 'Do you think I've enjoyed being your bloody guardian? Do you think it's been fun, trying to keep you safe from all the sleazebags? Do you have any idea how hard it's been for me, keeping my own hands off you?'

There! He'd said it. It was out in the open now. His dark secret, his guilty obsession.

Nick hated the shock in her face. But it was a relief, in a way.

'You never guessed?' he said, his soul suddenly weary.

She shook her head. 'You…you never said anything.'

Nick's smile was wry. 'I owed it to Ray to do what he asked me to do.'

'He asked you to keep away from me?'

'He asked me to protect you from the scoundrels of this world.'

If anything, this statement shocked her more than his admitting his desire.

'But you're not a scoundrel!'

'Trust me, Sarah. I'm a scoundrel of the first order. Always was. Always will be. Believe me, if you were any other man's daughter I would have seduced you when I had the chance. Because I did have a chance with you, didn't I? When you were sixteen.'

'You mean when I kissed you that time? You actually wanted me back then?'

'That's putting it mildly. Don't imagine for a single moment that I was worried about your age. Such things have never mattered to me. I just couldn't bear the thought that the one man in the world whom I liked and respected might look at me with disgust. Ray's words of praise and acceptance meant more to me than my intense but inconvenient desire for you.'

'I…I see…'

Nick doubted it. How could someone as basically sweet and naïve as Sarah understand the dark and damaged undercurrents of his character?

'Go on. Go back to your Derek,' he commanded.

'He…he's not my Derek.'

'What? What do you mean by that?'

'Derek's not my lover. He's just a friend. He's also gay.'

*'Gay!'* Nick repeated, his mind whirling as he tried to make sense of Sarah's confession.

'You've just been brutally honest with me, so I'm going to be brutally honest with you. I brought Derek to today's lunch so that I wouldn't be alone. And hopefully, to make you jealous.'

Nick stared at her.

Sarah looked as if she was about to cry. 'I've had a crush on you for as long as I can remember,' she blurted out.

Nick grimaced. He hated that word, crush. It sound so schoolgirlish. Of course, Sarah was still very young, compared to him. He'd been old from the time he was thirteen.

'You still have a chance with me, Nick,' she went on, her green eyes glistening. 'If you want it…'

If he wanted it. Dear God, if she only knew.

But what he wanted bore no resemblance to what she wanted.

'I'm no good for you, Sarah,' he bit out, surprising himself that he could find the will-power to resist what she was foolishly offering him.

'Why not?' she demanded to know.

'You know why not. I hid nothing from you when you were a youngster. I told you more than once: I can't fall in love.'

'I'm not asking you to.'

He glowered at her. 'Don't you dare lower yourself in that fashion. Don't you dare! I know you, Sarah. You want love and marriage and children. You do not want some decadent affair with a man of little conscience and even less moral fibre.'

'So you're knocking me back again. Is that the bottom line?'

'I already have a girlfriend,' he said coldly. 'I don't need you.'

The hurt in her eyes showed Nick that he'd done the right thing. Sarah's crush would have deepened into love if he slept with her. It had happened to him before, which was why he always stuck to partners like Chloe these days.

But that didn't mean he felt good about rejecting Sarah. His body was already regretting it.

'You'll find Mr Right one day,' he said stiffly.

'Oh, don't be so bloody pompous,' she snapped at him. 'If I wanted Mr Right, do you think I'd have just propositioned *you*? But that's all right, there are plenty of other good-looking studs around. Once I inherit all Daddy's lovely money, I don't think I'll be wanting for lovers, do you? Now I'm going to go eat my Christmas lunch. You can please yourself with what you do!'

# CHAPTER NINE

'DOES that face mean good news or bad news?' Derek asked after Sarah had dragged the chair out next to him, and plonked herself down.

'Don't talk to me just yet. I'm so mad I could spit.'

'Oooh. I wish I'd been a fly on the wall. Here, have some wine. It's a very good Chardonnay from the Hunter Valley.'

'I don't give a damn what it is as long as it's alcohol.'

Sarah lifted the glass to her lips and swallowed deep and hard.

'I hope you like seafood,' Derek said, indicating the plateful he'd collected for her.

'At this point in time, I like anything which is edible. And drinkable!'

Sarah could still hardly believe what had just happened. Her fantasy man had confessed that he fancied her. Had claimed he'd fancied her way back when she'd been fifteen!

She'd been within a hair's breadth of having her most

longed-for dream come true and what had he done? Rejected her, in favour of the brown-haired witch sitting two chairs down from her.

'Sarah!' the witch suddenly snapped. 'Where on earth is Nick? I got his meal for him and now he's not here to eat it.'

Sarah gained some pleasure from seeing that Chloe was not pleased with her lover's absence. Not pleased at all!

'I have absolutely no idea where he is,' came her seemingly nonchalant reply, which was followed up by another large gulp of wine.

'But weren't you just talking to him?'

'Yes,' she replied airily.

The witch's eyes narrowed. 'So what were you two talking about? Or weren't you talking at all?'

Sarah blinked, her wine glass stilling in mid-air. 'What?'

'You don't fool me,' Chloe spat. 'I know what's going on here with you and Nick. I knew it the moment I clapped eyes on you.'

'Knew what, Chloe?'

Both Sarah and Chloe jumped at Nick's reappearance, Sarah quite stunned by the ice in his voice. And his eyes.

Chloe's own eyes stayed hard. 'Don't take me for a fool, Nick. I know jealousy when I see it. And I know you. No way could you have lived all these years with a girl of Sarah's—shall we say?—attractions—without sampling them for yourself. '

Sarah's mouth gaped open whilst Nick's hands tightened over the back of his chair, his knuckles going white. 'Are you accusing me of sleeping with my ward?'

'For want of a better word—yes.'

Sarah suddenly became aware that a silence had fallen over the long, trestle-style table. In the distance she could hear the sound of a speedboat on the harbour. Up close, all she could hear was her own heart beating loudly in her chest.

'If that's what you think,' Nick said, 'then I suggest you leave.'

Chloe looked rattled for a moment, but only for a moment. Her face became a sour mask as she scraped her chair back and stood up. 'I couldn't agree more. I'm not a girl who tolerates being cheated on.'

'I never cheated on you,' Nick stated curtly.

'If that's so, then it's only because Sarah decided she temporarily preferred Derek to you. I am well aware she hasn't been home lately. But be warned, Derek,' she flung in Derek's direction, 'she belonged to Nick first. Isn't that right, Sarah?'

Sarah could have lied. But she wanted this creature gone from Nick's life.

'Yes, that's right,' she said, and there was a immediate buzz around the table. Chloe's face showed a savage satisfaction, whilst Nick's expression carried alarm.

'But not the way you're implying,' Sarah went on, determined not to let this witch-woman ruin Nick's reputation in the eyes of his business colleagues. 'Nick has always had my love, and he always will. He has not, however, ever acted in any way with me but as my protector, and my friend. So yes, I agree with Nick. If you believe he's behaved in such a dishonourable fashion, then you should leave. There is no place in my home for anyone who doesn't hold Nick in the same high regard in which my father did, and in which I do. So please,' she said, and stood up also, 'let me show you to the door.'

'No,' Nick said, and pressed a gentle but firm hand on her shoulder. 'Let me.'

Sarah threw him a grateful glance before sinking back down into her chair, only then realising her knees were very wobbly indeed.

'Good luck,' Chloe grated out with one last vicious look at Sarah. 'You're going to need it.'

As Nick shepherded Chloe from the terrace, Derek began a slow clap, joined by several of the guests.

'Very impressive, sweetie,' Derek said softly. 'But also rather telling.'

Sarah's head jerked around towards him. 'In what way?'

'Blind Freddie can see you're in love with the man.'

Sarah sighed. 'Was I that obvious?'

'Afraid so.'

'Oh, dear.'

'No matter. Now, tell me what happened a little while back that made you so mad. Was Nick as jealous as Chloe said he was?'

'Yes.'

'I *knew* it! He fancies you, doesn't he?'

Sarah shook her head. 'I couldn't believe it when he told me he did. And not just lately. Since I was sixteen.'

'Wow. Did you tell him you fancied him right back?'

'Yes.'

Derek looked confused. 'Then I don't get it. What's the problem? Not me, I hope. You did tell him I wasn't your real boyfriend, didn't you?'

'Oh, yes. I was totally honest with him. I even told him you were gay.'

'*And?*'

'He still rejected me. Said he was no good for me.'

'*What?*'

'He told me my father asked him to protect me from the scoundrels of this world, of which he rates himself the gold-medal winner.'

'For crying out loud, can't the man see that his not sleeping with you all these years makes him one of the good guys?'

'Obviously not.'

'This calls for even sneakier action. Now, tonight I suggest you—'

'Stop, Derek,' she broke in. 'Just stop.'

'You're giving up,' he said, disappointment in his voice.

'No, I'm moving on. And so is Nick. He's already told me he can't wait to leave here.'

'That's because he can't trust himself around you. You've got him on the ropes, sweetie, and he's running for cover.'

'Then let him run. It's over, Derek.'

'How can it be over when it hasn't even begun?'

'Could we just leave this conversation and eat?'

Derek shrugged, then fell to devouring some prawns.

Sarah was doing her best to force some food down her throat when Nick returned to the table. Her hand tightened around her fork whilst he removed Chloe's chair, along with her plate, before pulling out his own chair and reseating himself.

'Sorry about that, Sarah,' he muttered as he shook out his serviette. 'Thank you for standing up for me.'

'That's all right. Chloe shouldn't have said what she did.'

'No, she shouldn't have. But I can understand why she did. Jealousy can make you do...stupid things.'

'Yes, I know. I'm truly sorry for this whole charade today, Nick.'

'I wasn't talking about you, Sarah. I was talking about myself.'

Her head turned and their eyes connected.

'You *were* jealous, weren't you?' she whispered.

'We're not going to go there again, Sarah,' he warned her abruptly. 'Do I make myself clear?'

If his harsh voice wasn't sufficiently convincing, his cold eyes were.

'Crystal clear,' she said.

'Good. Now let's forget about everything that has happened today so far and enjoy our Christmas lunch.'

Sarah sat there in stunned silence when Nick tucked into his food with apparent relish. She was even more amazed when he started up a very lively conversation with the man on his immediate right.

Was he just pretending, or hadn't he been genuinely upset by the events of the day? Chloe had been his girl-friend for the last six months and she'd just been dismissed in an instant.

Hadn't he cared about her at all?

Obviously not.

Maybe Nick was right. Maybe he was a scoundrel.

Sarah slid her eyes to her right, where she surreptitiously watched him eat half a dozen oysters; watched him lift each oyster shell to his lips, tip his head back, then slide the tasty morsel down his throat, after which .he would lick his lips with relish.

Sarah finally found herself echoing this action with her own tongue, moving it over her suddenly parched lips, her heartbeat quickening when his head turned her way.

He stared at her wet lips for a long moment, before his mouth pulled back into a twisted smile. 'You just can't stop, can you?'

'Stop what?' she choked out.

'The tempting. No, don't bother to deny it. Or defend yourself. Everything you've done today has been leading to this moment. Very well. You've won. Though I doubt you'll see it as a win by tomorrow morning.'

'What do you mean?'

Again, that cold, cryptic smile. 'I did warn you. If you insist on playing with the devil, then you have to be prepared to take the consequences.'

# CHAPTER TEN

THE rest of the afternoon was endless, an eternity of wondering and worrying exactly what Nick meant by his provocative yet threatening words.

Several times Sarah tried to draw him into further clarification but he would have none of it, always turning the conversation away from the subject, or turning away from her altogether. After the lunch was over he deserted her to play the role of host, mingling with all his guests and making sure they had a good time. Coffee was served around the pool, with a few of the guests changing afterwards for a swim. Unfortunately Nick joined them, the sight of him in his brief black costume not doing Sarah's agitated state of mind any good.

It was around this time that Derek received a call on his cellphone from his mother, saying that his father had had a change of heart and wanted him to come home for Christmas after all. A delighted Derek called a taxi straight away and rushed off, leaving Sarah pleased for him, but even more lonely and agitated herself. In desperation, she left the party and escaped to the privacy of her bedroom.

But there was no peace for her there. She could still hear the gaiety downstairs through the French doors, the sounds tormenting her. What kind of man was Nick to say what he'd said to her and then ignore her? Finally, she could not bear her solitude any longer and made her way out onto the balcony, where she had a perfect view of the pool below…and Nick.

He saw her watching him, she knew. But he still ignored her, choosing instead to put his head down and swim, up and down, up and down. He must have swum for a good fifteen minutes straight before he stopped abruptly at one end and hauled himself out of the pool. Grabbing a towel, he draped it around his dripping shoulders before throwing her a savage glance, then striding up the terrace steps and disappearing under the roof created by the canvas blinds.

Every female nerve-ending in Sarah's body went on high alert. He was coming upstairs. To change? Or for something else?

She gripped the wrought-iron railing of the balcony, hot blood rushing around her veins at the possibility that it was *her* he was coming for; that he was about to put his teasing words into action. It didn't seem possible that he would do such a thing with the house still full of guests. But he'd said he was a scoundrel, hadn't he?

Sarah did not hear him enter her bedroom. But she

felt his presence in every pore of her body. She whirled
to find him standing in the doorway that led out onto the
balcony. The towel was no longer draped around his
shoulders. His legs were set solidly apart, his hands
balled into fists by his sides.

Sarah had seen him dressed in nothing but his
swimming costume many times, but never in her
bedroom, and never with that look on his face.

She shivered under the impact of the dark passion
emanating from his coal-black eyes.

'Come here,' he commanded, his voice low and harsh.

Shock—and a sudden wave of fear—held her motionless.

He stunned her further by stripping down to total
nudity, leaving her to confront the physical evidence of
his desire.

Now, *that* she'd never seen before, and a dark excitement sent her head spinning and her pulse racing.

'Come here,' he repeated in gravelly tones.

She moved across the balcony like some robot, her
mouth dry, her heart thudding loudly behind her ribs.
When she was close enough he reached up to cup her
heated face, his eyes holding hers captive whilst his
mouth lowered to her still parched lips.

But he didn't kiss her. He just slowly licked her lips
with his tongue. She found it incredibly erotic, her eyes
shutting as her lips fell further apart on a soft moan.

Another moan punched from Sarah's throat when
his tongue suddenly slid into her mouth. Surprise swiftly

gave way to a wild craving to draw him in deeper and yet deeper. The need to pleasure him was great; the need to possess him even greater.

Her eyes flung wide when he wrenched his tongue away, her cry the cry of dismay. But then his hands fell to her shoulders and he was pushing her down onto her knees in front of him.

Any shock was momentary. If this was what he wanted, then she wanted it too.

He tasted clean and salty from the swimming pool. But it wasn't the taste of him that mattered to Sarah. All the years of wanting him to want her made her both reckless and wild. Her secret passion was finally unleashed.

Afterwards, she had no detailed recollection of how long it was before he came. A minute perhaps. Maybe two.

All she could recall was her satisfaction in his release, thrilling to the raw groans that filled the room, exulting in his uncontrolled surrender.

She glanced up at him, still unbearably aroused by what she'd just done. Her body was on fire, her conscience in danger of being totally routed. She did not care if he was a scoundrel. Did not care if he was only using her. She'd never been so excited in all her life.

'You do realise there's no going back now,' he grated out as he lifted her to her feet.

She just stared at him, unable to formulate any reply at that moment.

He stared back with hard, glittering eyes. 'I should have known you'd do this to me today.'

'Do what?' she choked out.

'Make me cross the line. You think you know what you're doing but you don't.'

'I'm not a child, Nick.'

He laughed. 'You are, compared to me. But that's all right. That's your attraction. I like it that you're relatively innocent. It excites me. It'll almost be worth it to open your eyes, to make you see what kind of men there are in this world. And how easily it is for them to seduce girls like you. Hopefully, by the time I've finished with you, you'll have enough experience to protect yourself in future.'

'I'm not that innocent,' she threw back at him.

'No? Why do you say that? Because you think you know how to go down on a man?'

Sarah's face flamed.

'I'm not saying that I didn't enjoy it,' Nick went on, reaching out to stroke a perversely loving hand down her cheek. 'But I'll enjoy teaching you how to do it properly a lot more.'

His hand drifted across to her mouth, where he inserted a finger between her lips.

'Most men prefer not to be gobbled up like fast food,' he advised, sliding that knowing finger back and forth along the middle of her tongue. 'Once you master the art, you can love a man more times than you would think possible. Have you ever been made love to all night long, Sarah?'

A shudder rippled down Sarah's spine at the images he was evoking.

'I think not,' he purred, his dark gaze narrowing on her wide eyes.

His finger retreated, leaving her feeling weirdly bereft and empty.

'But tonight you will, my love,' he promised. 'Tonight, I will take you to places you've never been before. If that's what you want, of course. Do you want it, Sarah? This is your last chance to tell me to go to hell.'

She stared into his heavily lidded eyes, afraid now of the power he had over her.

But her fear was not as strong as her desire.

'So be it,' he snapped when she said nothing. 'Just remember that you must live with the consequences of your decision.'

'What consequences?'

'That one day, I will have had my fill of you and you will go the way of all the others,' he said so coldly it was scary.

'Are you trying to frighten me off?'

His laugh was hard, and lacking in humour. 'Good God, no. I want nothing more than to have that gorgeous body of yours at my daily disposal till at least the end of the summer holidays. But I have a policy of brutal honesty with all my girlfriends. Chloe knew the score. Now you do too.'

'Can I tell Flora that I'm your new girlfriend?'

His face darkened at this suggestion. 'Absolutely not!'

'I thought that might be the case. You want to keep me your dirty little secret, don't you?'

'I do have my pride. Don't you?' he threw at her challengingly.

Her chin lifted. 'Yes.'

'Then it will be *our* dirty little secret. If you're not happy with that, then we can still call it quits. Right now. After all, one swallow doesn't make a summer.'

Sarah sucked in sharply at this most outrageous *double entendre*. 'You really are a wicked devil, aren't you?'

'I did warn you about my character. So what's your final decision? I can leave you and this house asap. Or...' He walked over to the bed, where Derek's present was lying spread out on the pink quilt. It was a black satin and lace teddy, which left little to the imagination, bought with the idea of making Nick jealous.

He picked it up, his eyebrows arching as he turned it this way and that. 'Or you can agree to come to my bedroom tonight, wearing nothing but this and my diamond earrings.'

Sarah tried to feel disgusted with him, and herself. But it was no use. There was no room in her quivering body at that moment for anything but a wild rush of dizzying excitement. She could not wait to do what he asked, could not wait to present herself to him the way he asked.

What did that make her?

A masochist, or just a girl in love, a girl who'd lived for far too long with her romantic fantasies.

Yet he wasn't offering her romance, just a few weeks of the kind of lovemaking she hadn't experienced before. He was right about that. All her lovers so far had been youngish men of little *savoir-faire*.

But the way Nick was talking made her wonder if there were ways nice girls didn't know about.

The thought only excited her further.

'What time tonight?' she asked, and looked him straight in the eye.

No way was she going to let him think he'd seduced her into this. She would come to him willingly, with courage, not fear.

His smile was wry. 'I've always known you had spirit, Sarah. That's another of your many attractions. Shall we say nine? Flora and Jim will have retired to their quarters by then.'

'Nine,' she repeated in pained tones. That was over four hours away!

'Yes, I know. But it will be all the better for the waiting. Now I must go and dress,' he said, bending to snatch up his swimming costume and towel from where they lay on the cream carpet. 'Meanwhile I suggest you go downstairs. People might begin to wonder where we are, and jump to the conclusion that there's some truth in Chloe's accusations. Just don't forget to replenish your lipstick before you go.'

Sarah stared after him as he left. Then she whirled and hurried into the bathroom.

# CHAPTER ELEVEN

'I KNEW Chloe had just about reached her use-by date,' Flora remarked as she packed the dishwasher for the last time that evening. 'But I still can't believe Nick broke up with her on Christmas Day.'

Sarah glanced up from where she was sitting, having a cup of coffee. The clock on the wall showed twenty-two minutes past eight.

'He's a right devil with women,' Flora rattled on, 'but I've never thought of him as cruel.'

Strangely enough, Sarah agreed with Flora.

'He really had no option after Chloe accused him of carrying on with me in front of everyone,' she defended.

Flora pulled a face. 'I suppose not. I just wish I'd been there. Trust something exciting to happen the first year Jim and I decide to eat Christmas dinner back in our rooms. So tell me, what led up to it?'

Sarah shrugged. 'I have no idea. One minute everything seemed fine, the next she just came out with it. We were both shocked, I can tell you.'

'I'll bet it was because of the way you look today. She was probably blind with jealousy.'

'That's what Nick said.'

'He'd have been furious with her for saying something like that in front of his work colleagues. But I heard you set her to rights.'

'Really? Who told you that?' She'd done her best not to provide Flora with too many details, in case she slipped up with her story.

'One of the waiters. He said it was the most interesting Christmas lunch they'd ever catered for.'

'It was darned embarrassing. I'm glad it's over. Next year, things are going to be very different.'

Sarah wished she hadn't said that. Because she didn't want to think about next year. She didn't want to think about anything but tonight.

But once the thought was put in her head, it was impossible to banish it. If Nick had been telling the truth earlier, then by next Christmas she would be long gone from his life, and from his bed.

'You won't change your mind?' Flora asked.

'About what?'

'About letting me cook a hot meal next year. Call me old-fashioned, but Christmas just doesn't feel like Christmas without a turkey and a plum pudding. I know Nick won't mind. He really likes turkey.'

'Nick probably won't be here,' Sarah said a bit stiffly.

'What? Why not?'

'He's moving out in February.'

'So what? You'll invite him here for Christmas, surely. You and he are like family.'

'He might not want to come.'

'Rubbish! He loves having Christmas here. Even when he was building that resort on Happy Island, he always came back for Christmas. And it's not as though he'll go off and get married and make a home of his own.'

'True,' Sarah agreed ruefully, her eyes dropping to her coffee. 'That's never going to happen.'

So don't start secretly hoping that it will. He's not going to fall in love with you, no matter how much you love him. You're just another sexual partner, a temporary object of desire, a source of physical pleasure.

And when that pleasure begins to wane, when boredom sets in, you'll be replaced. That's the way it's always been with Nick and that's the way it will continue.

It might have been a seriously depressing train of thought if she'd been in a sensible, looking-after-her-future-happiness mood. But Sarah was anything but sensible at that moment. Excitement was fizzing through her veins, her insides wound so tight she was having trouble swallowing her coffee. How she managed to appear so composed in front of Flora, she had no idea. Obviously, she had the makings of an Oscar-winning actress!

'Where is Nick, by the way?' Flora asked.

'He went upstairs a little while ago,' Sarah replied as cool as you please. 'He said he was tired.'

'You finished with that?' Flora reached out for her coffee-mug.

Sarah handed it to her. 'I think I'll go up to bed, too,' she said, this time with a slight catch in her voice. 'It's been a long day.'

'There's a good movie on at eight-thirty,' Flora said. 'Got that film-star fellow in it that I like. Sexy devil. Now, he can put his slippers under my bed any time he likes.'

'Mmm,' Sarah murmured as she slid from the stool. Not as sexy as the devil she was about to spend the night with. 'Goodnight, Flora. Don't worry about breakfast. I'm going to sleep in. You should too. You look tired.'

'I am a bit. What about Nick?'

'I'll tell him to get himself something in the morning. I doubt he's asleep yet.'

'Before you go, Sarah, I just want to say how lovely you looked today. I wouldn't mind betting that by next Christmas you'll have a real boyfriend sitting at the Christmas table. Or even a fiancé. Which reminds me, did anything further develop with Derek today?'

'Er—no. He's not interested in me in that way.'

'What a pity. Still, there are plenty of other fish in the sea. Off you go, then.'

'Goodnight, Flora. Enjoy the movie.'

'Oh, I will.'

Sarah's pretend composure began to disintegrate the moment she left the kitchen.

'What on earth do you think you're doing?' she muttered to herself as she walked up the stairs on suddenly shaky legs. 'He's going to break your heart. You know that, don't you?'

Sarah stopped in front of his bedroom door. She even lifted her hand to knock. What she was going to say to him, she had no idea, though *go to hell* came to mind.

But then she heard the sound of Nick's shower running.

He was getting ready for her.

She could picture him standing naked under the jets of warm water, washing himself clean with long, soapy strokes of a sponge. In her mind's eye, he was already wanting her.

It was the thought of his wanting her that was the most corrupting. She'd wanted him to want her like this for years.

Impossible to turn her back on his desire.

Impossible to ignore her own.

Sarah's hand fell back to her side and she stumbled on to her bedroom.

Nick stood under the lukewarm spray, his hands braced against the shower-stall tiles, his eyes down.

Half an hour to go and already he was in agony.

Gritting his teeth, he turned the water to cold. Ten minutes later, he had his flesh under control again. But not his mind.

You should not be doing this, Nick, came the reproachful thought. She's in love with you. Or she thinks she is.

'You're a total bastard,' he growled to himself.

His mouth twisted into a sneer as he emerged from

the shower stall and snatched up a towel. 'So what's new, Nick?'

Still, he *had* given her every chance to escape. She'd been right when she'd accused him of trying to frighten her off. He'd honestly thought when he pushed her to her knees the way he had that she would jump up and run a mile. But she hadn't...

Of course, his desire for Sarah had been building in his head for years. It was no wonder he'd found it difficult to control himself this afternoon.

Still, it was a worry, his lack of control. From the moment she'd taken him into her mouth, he'd just lost it. Totally.

As he stared at his reflection in the bathroom mirror, Nick vowed that tonight would be different. Tonight he would be the coolly confident lover he usually was, patiently taking her on an erotic journey that initially might feel romantic to a girl as young and naïve as she was.

By morning, however, she would see him for what he really was: a cold-blooded and ruthless bastard who used women for nothing but his own pleasure and satisfaction. She would see that any finer feelings would be wasted on him, at the same time becoming a lot wiser to the wicked ways of the world, and of men.

It was a perverse way to protect her, but then, he'd always been perverse when it came to Sarah. Hadn't he lusted after her when she'd been little more than a girl? A lust which had been as obsessive as it was unwanted.

This moment had been inevitable, Nick conceded as

he finished drying himself. The only surprise was that he'd held back as long as he had.

Nine o'clock saw Sarah once again at Nick's door, her hands curling into white-knuckled balls as she struggled to find the courage to knock.

The black teddy fitted her perfectly, the skin-tight mid-section outlining her newly defined waist, the built-in lace bra cut low. More transparent lace inserts covered her hips, making the already high-cut sides seem even higher. But it was the back of the teddy that shocked her, mostly because there wasn't much of it. A couple of inches of material above her waist and next to nothing below, where it narrowed into a satin thong.

The door suddenly being wrenched open brought a gasp to her lips. Nick stood there, a dark red towel slung low around his hips, the expression on his face not a particularly happy one.

But his eyes changed as they swept over her, that white-hot desire she'd always wanted to see making her stomach flip right over.

'I knew you'd look beautiful in that. I didn't realise just how beautiful. And how damned sexy.'

He looked pretty damned sexy himself, she thought breathlessly.

His sudden frown worried her, as did his ragged sigh. 'You've made my life really difficult, Sarah.'

'No more than you've made mine,' she countered. Quite bravely, considering she was quaking inside.

He shook his head as he took her right hand in his and pulled her into the bedroom, kicking the door shut behind them.

'I presume you haven't changed your mind,' he said drily as he drew her across the room towards the bed.

'If I had, I wouldn't be wearing this, would I?' she threw at him with more feigned boldness whilst her gaze flicked nervously around.

She noted the bed, its red quilt thrown back, the black satin sheets glowing under the soft light of the red lampshades.

His suddenly scooping her up into his arms shattered her brave façade.

'You're trembling,' he said.

'Am I?'

'Very definitely.' He sighed for the second time, his eyes shutting for a moment. 'What am I going to do with you?'

'Make love to me, I hope. All night long, you promised.'

His eyes flicked open to glower down at her.

'No, Sarah. That's not what's going to happen here.'

Her heart plummeted to the floor.

'What I'm going to do is have sex with you. Don't mistake it for lovemaking. I never make love. I have sex with women. Of course,' he added with a sardonic smile as he lowered her gently into the middle of the bed, 'it will be great sex.'

Relief—and a rush of excitement—flooded through Sarah as her head and shoulders came to rest against the pile of satin-covered pillows. At this moment, he could call it whatever he liked. Nothing he could say would deter her from seeing this through.

But for Sarah, it would be lovemaking. For her, this was going to be the night of her life!

The satin sheets felt cool against her heated skin. Nick's eyes were cool as well, that white-hot desire she'd spotted earlier now not in evidence.

'Relax,' he advised as he straightened.

'I...I guess I am a bit nervous,' she admitted when he joined her on the bed.

'Yes, I can see that.'

Propping himself up on his side, he ran a teasing fingertip around the edge of the low-cut neckline, making her skin break out into goose-pimples. When he traced the neckline a second time, almost touching one of her nipples, she sucked in, then held her breath.

'Do you have extra-sensitive breasts?'

His question rattled her. Actually his talking rattled her. None of her previous lovers had talked. They'd simply got on with it.

Sarah finally let go of her long-held breath. 'I...I don't know,' she said, her head spinning.

'Let's see, shall we?'

Sarah held her breath again as he levered the satin straps off her shoulders and peeled them slowly downwards till the lace cups gave up their prizes.

'Mmm. Delicious,' he said, and bent to lick her right nipple.

Sarah clenched her teeth hard in her jaw, lest she cry out. But oh, the dizzying pleasure of it.

When he drew her nipple into his mouth, she could not prevent a moan escaping.

When he nibbled at it with his teeth, she squirmed and whimpered.

His head lifted, his eyes glittering now.

'As much as this teddy looks fantastic on you, right at this moment I prefer you without it.'

Sarah gulped but said nothing as he peeled it down her body and off her feet before tossing it carelessly aside. His eyes were like laser beams, honing in on that private part of her body.

'I love looking at you,' he rasped, caressing her smooth pubic bone before sliding his fingers through the already damp folds of her sex.

'Oh,' Sarah choked out, stunned by the sensations that came crashing through her.

'You are so beautiful,' he crooned as he continued to explore her down there, touching her everywhere. Inside, outside, then inside again. More deeply this time, finding erotic zones she didn't know she had. She pressed herself urgently against his hand, her head twisting from side to side, her wide eyes pleading with his as her body raced towards a climax.

'It's OK,' he said, his voice rough, his eyelids heavy. 'I want to watch you come.'

Sexy words, sexy eyes. Pushing her over the edge in a free-fall of pleasure that was wonderfully wanton, till she came to earth with a thud and realised this was *not* what she'd waited a lifetime to experience: Nick watching her come.

But no sooner did these rather dismaying thoughts flash through her mind than he was kissing her, not wildly but gently, his mouth sipping softly at hers.

'Don't be upset,' he murmured between kisses. 'You needed that. You were wound too tight. Next time…I'll be inside you…and it'll be much better.'

She blinked up at him when his head rose.

The corner of his mouth lifted in a quirky smile. 'You don't believe me?'

'Oh, no,' she said truthfully, 'I believe you.'

'Then what is it?'

'I…I'm sorry, but I thought…before we go any further, what…what about protection? I mean…Oh, you know what I mean,' she said, annoyed with herself for stuttering and stammering. 'You've been around.'

His expression carried an element of reproach. 'Sarah, you don't honestly think I would risk making you pregnant, do you?'

'Well, actually, you can't,' she admitted. 'Make me pregnant, I mean. I'm on the Pill.'

'I see. But you still want me to use condoms?'

'I'm not a total fool, Nick.' Even if he thought she was for being here with him.

'You've no need to worry. I've got that taken care of. Relax. No way are you getting out of here, sweetheart. Not till your old Uncle Nick lets you.'

'Don't call yourself that!' she snapped as she struggled to suppress an involuntary moan. Dear heaven, but he was good at that. 'There's nothing wrong with our being together,' she threw at him in desperation.

'That depends on your definition of wrong,' he countered, his devastatingly knowing fingers not missing a beat as he touched her breasts again. 'But no matter. It's like I said this afternoon,' he went on, that knowing hand sliding slowly down over her stomach and back between her legs. 'I'd reached the point of no return.'

'I...I think I'm just about reaching it again, too,' she choked out.

'So soon?'

She squirmed against his hand, her still sensitised flesh unable to bear too much more.

'You have to stop that,' she cried.

He stopped, leaving her panting whilst he rolled away and yanked open the top drawer of his bedside table. He selected a condom and drew it on. When he returned to her body, he did not rush. Neither did he attempt any kind of weird or wonderful position, for which she was grateful. Sarah wanted to look into his face when he was inside her; wanted to hold him and love him as she'd always wanted to.

She tried not to cry out when he finally entered her. But she couldn't quite manage to contain herself, a raw sound escaping her throat. Do not fall apart, for pity's sake, she lectured herself. But there was a great lump in her throat and tears were threatening.

Nick's concern was instantaneous. 'Are you all right?' he asked, smoothing her hair back from her face and staring deep into her by then glistening eyes. 'I'm not hurting you, am I?'

What an ironic thing to say!

'No, no, I'm fine,' she insisted, though her voice sounded artificially high. 'Would you mind kissing me, please? I like to be kissed a lot.' Anything to stop him staring down at her in that thoughtful fashion.

'My pleasure,' he said, and lowered his mouth to hers.

It was a kiss that might have been the kiss of true love, if she hadn't known differently.

How hungry it was, how passionate...how heartbreaking.

When his body began to move in tandem with his tongue, her fragile emotions were forgotten as the physical experience took over. With each surge of his flesh she could feel the coil of desire tighten within her. It was exciting, yet frustrating at the same time. She wanted to come. But as the seconds turned into minutes there was no release for her, only an all-consuming heat that flooded her body and quickened her heartbeat to a point where her mouth was forced to burst away from his.

'Help me, Nick,' she sobbed as she dragged in some life-saving breaths.

'Look at me,' he commanded, cupping her face and stilling his flesh inside her.

She stared up at him, her eyes wide and wild, her mouth panting heavily.

'Wrap your legs higher around my back,' he advised. 'Then move *with* me. Lift your hips as I push forward, then lower them when I withdraw. There's no hurry, Sarah. Just look into my eyes and trust me.'

*Just look into my eyes...*

She never wanted to look anywhere else.

*Trust me...*

Oh, God. How she wanted to do that too.

This is all a big mistake, Nick thought as she blindly followed his instructions. How long had it been since he'd been so damned nice and considerate in bed?

Who was this Nick who was suddenly caring so much?

He didn't approve of him. Couldn't trust him. He might start thinking he'd changed.

Which was impossible. He was what he was and he'd never change. This was just a momentary aberration. He'd get over it.

The trouble was he didn't think he'd get over it in one night.

He began moving faster, and so did she, her eyes growing wider and more desperate-looking.

Her first spasm was so strong Nick almost came then and there, but he held on, watching with wonder as her face became suffused with a seductive mixture of surprise and sheer joy. He'd never seen a woman look like that before. Never felt a woman who felt the way she did, either.

Finally he surrendered his control, astonished at the

intensity of his own climax, and the strange lurch to his heart when she pulled him down on top of her.

'Oh, Nick,' she cried, and nuzzled into his neck. 'Oh, my darling…'

Nick didn't say a word. He couldn't.

He'd never felt so confused. All he was sure of was that he'd never felt what he'd felt just now when she'd called him her darling. The endearment had wrenched at his very soul, that soul which he'd always imagined was too dark for such sentiment.

As he lay there with her cuddled up to him, Nick gradually became sure of something else: he didn't want to frighten Sarah off any more.

Which rather changed his plans for the rest of the night.

Nick didn't delude himself that this more romantic side he'd unexpectedly discovered within himself would last. But, for now, he found it quite irresistible. He could not wait to make love to Sarah again, could not wait to see the delight in her eyes.

But first, there was something he had to do. Carefully he disentangled himself from her arms and headed for the bathroom, where he washed himself fresh and clean then returned to the bed. He was about to stir her with some kisses when the phone next to his bed began to ring.

# CHAPTER TWELVE

SARAH woke to the sound of a phone ringing. For a split-second she had no idea where she was. But the feel of Nick's naked body pressed up against hers swiftly cleared the haze in her head, everything coming back in a rapid series of flashbacks.

Her, coming to his bedroom wearing that outrageous teddy.

Him, carrying her to the bed.

Her, lying back against these satin pillows.

Him, making love to her.

But then came another memory: she'd called him darling afterwards.

When the phone continued to ring, Nick sighed then rolled over to reach for it.

*No, don't*, was her instinctive reaction.

But his hand had already swept the receiver up to his ear.

'Yes?' he said rather abruptly.

Sarah clutched the sheet up over her breasts as she

sat up, pushing her hair back off her face at the same time. Who on earth could it be?

Not Chloe, she hoped, trying to worm her way back into Nick's life with a million apologies.

'For how long?' Nick asked in concerned tones. 'How bad are they?'

She had no idea whom he was talking to or what it was about. But it didn't sound like Chloe.

'No, I think you're right, Jim. Don't listen to her. She has to go to hospital. *Now*.'

Sarah sucked in sharply. Something was wrong with Flora!

'I don't think we should wait for an ambulance,' Nick told Jim quite firmly. 'Get her into the back of the Rolls and I'll drive you straight to St Vincent's. I'll just throw some clothes on.'

Slamming down the phone, he tossed back the sheet and jumped up.

'Flora's having chest pains,' he threw over his shoulder as he strode across the floor towards his walk-in wardrobe. 'I'm taking her to the hospital.'

'Can I come too?' Sarah asked, her heart racing with alarm.

'No, it'll take you too long to dress,' he said as he returned to the bedroom, jeans already on, a blue striped shirt in his hands.

'But I—'

'Let's not argue about this, Sarah.' He shoved his

arms into the shirt's sleeves and drew it up over his shoulders. 'I'll call you from the hospital.'

'You haven't got any shoes on,' she pointed out when he headed for the door, shirt flapping open. 'You can't go to a hospital without shoes!'

He grumblingly went back for some trainers, then flew out of the door. Sarah heard him running down the stairs. Then she heard nothing.

A shiver ran down her spine, nausea swirling in her stomach at the possibility that Flora could be having a heart attack. She might even die!

The thought brought back all those horrible feelings she'd had when her father had been struck down by a coronary. Aside from the emotional trauma of losing her last parent, she'd been besieged with regret that she hadn't even been able to say goodbye to him, or tell him that she loved him.

Flora might not be a parent but Sarah loved her dearly. It pained her that Nick hadn't let her go with him, even though he was probably right—she would have taken longer to dress than him. He'd taken all of thirty seconds!

*But that doesn't stop you from dressing now and following him to the hospital in your own car, does it?*

Sarah was out of the bed in a flash, dashing for her room.

She didn't dress as fast as Nick, but she managed to make herself respectable in under ten minutes. Getting out of the house, however, took her another few minutes, because she had to lock up. Then she had difficulty finding the hospital, not having been there since her mother fell ill all those years ago. At last she located the right street, along with a parking spot not far from the emergency section.

She'd just made it to the ER waiting room when her mobile rang.

It had to be Nick, she reasoned as she retrieved it from her handbag.

'Nick?' she answered straight away.

'Where in hell are you?' he grumbled down the line. 'I tried the home number and you didn't answer.'

'I couldn't just sit there, Nick. So I got dressed and drove myself to the hospital. I've just arrived at the emergency waiting room. How's Flora?'

'Not too bad. They whipped her in and gave her some medication to thin her blood straight away. Then they hooked her up to some kind of heart-monitoring machine that does ECGs and other things. The doctor thinks it might just be angina.'

'But that's still not good, is it? I mean, angina can lead to a heart attack.'

'It can. But at least we've got her where she can have some further tests, and proper treatment. You know Flora. She doesn't like going to doctors, or hospitals. I'm going to make sure she stays in for a couple of days till we get a full picture of her condition. I've rung a colleague whose uncle is a top cardiac specialist here. We're going to transfer her to a private room after the doctor in ER is finished with her, and he'll come in in the morning and take over.'

Sarah felt the tension begin to drain out of her. 'That's wonderful, Nick. How's Jim doing?'

'To be honest, I've never seen him so distressed,' Nick whispered. 'He's sitting by Flora's bed as white as a sheet himself. I'm going to try to persuade him to come with me for a cup of tea and a piece of cake. I think he's in shock. Look, just sit down where you are and I'll be with you shortly. Then we can all go together. There has to be a cafeteria somewhere in here.'

'Couldn't I see Flora myself before we do that? I need to see her, Nick.' To tell her old friend that she loved her. Also that she was coming home to live. Permanently. She would put in for a transfer to a nearer school. No, she'd resign and find work in one of the many local preschools. They were always crying out for experienced infant teachers.

'She's not going to die, Sarah,' Nick said gently.

'You don't know that. What if she took a bad turn while I was sitting near by, having a cup of tea? I'd never forgive myself.'

'Fine. Stay where you are and I'll come and get you. I'll just tell Jim where I'm going.'

Sarah sat down in an empty chair against the wall, only then absorbing her surroundings. The place was very busy, with people rushing to and fro, and lots of people just sitting and waiting to be treated, several of them dishevelled young men with cuts and bruises over their faces. There were half a dozen mothers with crying children, and wailing babies. They all looked poor and wretched. Some of them even smelt.

She dropped her eyes away, upset by this brutal confrontation with the cold, cruel world. Not that she hadn't come across neglected children before. Just not on Christmas Day.

'Sarah? You OK?'

Sarah jumped up from the plastic chair. 'Oh, Nick, I'm so glad you're here.' She grabbed his arm and steered him away to one side.

'Did any of those louts bother you?' he asked.

'No, no, nothing like that. I just…Oh, Nick, the world's a horrible place, isn't it?'

'It can be,' he agreed soberly.

'We are so lucky to be healthy. And rich.'

His smile was wry. 'You're right there, sweetheart. Healthy and wealthy are the daily double. Come on, I'll take you to Flora.'

The sight of Flora's dull eyes and pale face alarmed Sarah. But she tried not to show it. 'What a scare you gave us,' she said lightly as she bent and kissed Flora on the cheek.

'It's just indigestion,' Flora protested. 'But no one believes me.'

The attending nurse surreptitiously rolled her eyes at Sarah, indicating that it certainly wasn't indigestion.

Sarah pulled up a chair by Flora's bed and picked up her hand. It felt oddly cold, which was another worry.

'Best we make sure, now that you're here,' she said.

Flora pressed her lips together. 'That's what Nick and Jim say but, truly, I'd much rather go home to my own bed. All I need is a rest.'

'Now, Flora, love,' an ashen-faced Jim began before his voice trailed weakly away. He'd never worn the trousers in the family and it looked as if he wasn't about to now.

'You'll do as you're told, madam,' Nick intervened firmly. 'Now I'm taking Jim for a cuppa. Sarah's going to sit with you for a while.'

Sarah flashed him an admiring smile. Truly, Nick's command of this situation had been wonderful from the word go. He hadn't panicked, he'd acted decisively and quickly—and possibly saved Flora's life in the process.

'See you soon,' he said to her, then turned and shepherded Jim away.

Sarah's gaze followed him for a while before returning to Flora.

'Have you something to confess, missie?' Flora said softly, but in a very knowing fashion.

Sarah had no intention of letting herself be railroaded into any admissions about Nick. She would not hear the end of it if she told Flora that she and Nick were having an affair.

'I just wanted to say I love you dearly, Flora, and I've been a selfish cow, staying away from home as much I have. Things are going to change from now on, I assure you. I'm going to get a job near by so that I can be there, in person, to make sure you take it much easier, as well as look after your diet. I've become a very good cook of low-fat meals this past year, and you, madam, need to lose a few pounds. If you must work, then you can help Jim in the garden. And you're going to start walking. *Every* morning.'

'Goodness, you're sounding just like Nick.'

'Who has your best interests at heart as well. So I don't want to hear any more nonsense about your coming home just yet. Nick has organised a specialist to come in tomorrow to do some tests and you're going to have them.'

'Heavens to Betsy, is this my sweet little Sarah talking?'

'No, it's your grown-up Sarah.'

'I can see that. And so does Nick. He couldn't take his eyes off you today, Sarah. Or tonight, for that matter.'

Sarah eyed Flora sternly. 'Don't start matchmaking, Flora. You and I both know Nick is not a marrying man.'

'If anyone could make him change his mind about that, it's you, love.'

Sarah bit her tongue, lest she give the game away. But there was a part of her that agreed with Flora.

Nick hadn't just 'had sex' with her tonight. He'd made love to her, with tenderness and caring.

Who knew? Maybe there was a chance of a real relationship between them, no matter what Nick said.

'You're in love with him, aren't you?' Flora said.

Sarah could not bring herself to lie any longer. 'Yes,' she admitted.

'Then go after him, girl.'

'That's what I am doing.'

'And?'

Sarah felt a betraying smile tug at her lips. 'Let's just say it's a work in progress.'

'Ooooh, I like the sound of that.'

'Well, I don't,' the nurse interrupted firmly. 'Your blood pressure is on the rise again. Sorry,' she said to Sarah. 'I think it would be better if my patient rests quietly for a while. Perhaps you could join her other visitors in the coffee lounge for the next half-hour at least. It's thatta way.'

Sarah went reluctantly, with the solemn promise to return. She followed the direction of the nurse's finger, but still had to ask for more directions before she found the cafeteria.

Jim and Nick glanced up with questioning eyes at her arrival, Jim looking particularly anxious. She didn't have the heart to tell him that she'd raised his wife's blood pressure, saying instead that the nurse wanted Flora to rest quietly and they weren't to go back to her bedside for half an hour at least.

'If you want anything, you have to order at the counter,' Nick informed her.

Sarah shook her head. 'I don't want anything.'

'Don't be silly. I'll get you some coffee and cake. You have to be hungry. I know I was.'

Jim said nothing during the time it took Nick to return with the coffee and piece of carrot cake. He just kept staring blankly into space.

'You haven't eaten your cake, Jim,' Nick said as he sat back down.

Jim turned his head towards Nick, his eyes remaining vacant. 'What did you say?'

'Your cake,' Nick said, nodding towards the untouched plate.

He shook his head. 'I can't eat it.'

'She's not going to die, Jim.'

'But what if she does?' he said plaintively. 'I can't live without her. She's all I have.'

'I know, Jim.' Sarah reached over to press a gentle hand on his arm. 'But you won't have to live without her. Not yet, anyway. We've caught this in time. We'll look after her together and make her better.'

His eyes filled with tears, shocking Sarah. She'd only ever seen a man cry once before in her life—her father, at her mother's funeral. Jim's crying propelled her back there, to her mother's graveside and the awful sound of her father's broken sobs as they lowered her coffin into the ground.

'I'm just so worried,' Jim choked out.

'We all are, Jim,' Nick said gently.

'I never thought I'd get married, you know,' Jim went on, his voice cracking some more. 'At forty, I was a crusty old bachelor. Not ugly exactly, but not the kind of chap women went for. Flora used to shop in the same supermarket as I did. Not sure why she took a liking to me but she did. Before I knew it, we were hitched.'

A huge lump filled Sarah's throat as she watched the tears run down Jim's sun-weathered cheeks.

'Best thing I ever did,' he finished up, pulling a hankie from his pocket.

An emotion-charged silence descended on their table. They all fell to drinking and eating, no one saying a word. Sarah noted that the people at the other tables weren't saying much either.

Cafeterias in hospitals, she decided, were not places of joy, especially late at night.

When her eyes returned to their table, she found Nick staring at her.

What are you thinking? she longed to ask.

But she said nothing, her eyes dropping back to her coffee.

Nick could not believe the crazy thoughts going through his head at that moment. Jim's touching little story about his romance with Flora must have totally unhinged him. Because, suddenly, he was thinking that that was what *he* should do: get married…to Sarah.

An incredibly bad idea. Even worse than giving in to his lust and sleeping with her. An affair with a scoundrel could have the beneficial side-effect of educating and protecting her, in a perverse kind of way. But marriage to the same scoundrel had nothing going for Sarah at all. Because such a union would not give her the one thing she wanted most in life: children.

This last thought steeled Nick's strangely wobbly heart,

reaffirming his resolve to keep their affair strictly sexual. That way, when it was over, Sarah wouldn't be too hurt.

Meanwhile, it would be kinder of him if their affair didn't last too long. Best it be over by the time she turned twenty-five. Which gave him what time with her?

Six short weeks. Not long to burn out a lust that had been growing for years, and which he now had little control over. Despite all that had happened tonight, he could not wait to get her home, to bed. Which underlined just what type of man he was; not fit to marry a lovely girl like Sarah, that was for sure.

'I think we should go back to the ward now. See what they've discovered.'

Nick's abrupt suggestion jerked Sarah back to the moment at hand.

'The nurse didn't seem keen on Flora having too many visitors,' she told him. 'I think it would be best if I went home to bed. I'll come back and visit Flora tomorrow morning, bring her some things she might need.'

'That sounds like a good idea,' Nick agreed.

'I'm not going home,' Jim said somewhat stubbornly. 'I'm going to stay with my wife. They said I could.'

'Of course,' Nick soothed. 'I'll stay till I find out the doctor's verdict, then I'll go home too. I'll come back with Sarah in the morning.'

Nick stood up first, coming round to hold the back of Sarah's chair as she rose.

'*My* bed,' he whispered. 'Not yours.'

Shock held her rigid. How could he possibly be thinking about sex at this moment? It was the last thing on her mind.

But by the time she unlocked the front door and made her way upstairs, the thought of being with Nick again was slowly corrupting her. She kept telling herself that she was as wicked as he was; that she should be consumed with worry for Flora, not desire for him.

Nick's brief phone call from the hospital informing her that it had just been angina, and not a heart attack, did soothe her conscience somewhat, though her emotions were still very mixed as she showered and perfumed her body, then slipped, naked, back between those black satin sheets.

She'd heard about people having wildly tasteless sex at wakes, just to prove that they were still alive. Maybe this was something like that.

But she suspected not.

Sarah wanted to believe that it was love behind her behaviour. But she was beginning to wonder if it was more a matter of lust. She'd never experienced the kind of sexual pleasure that she'd had earlier that evening. And she wanted more.

By the time she heard the Rolls throttle down in the driveway, Sarah was beside herself with excitement. When Nick strode into the room already stripping off as he went, desire had rendered her totally mindless.

This time he did not speak and neither did she. Their coupling was fast and furious, a raw, animalistic mating that sent them both hurtling over the edge in seconds. Afterwards, they clung to each other, their skin pearled in sweat, their bodies stuck together.

'I didn't use a condom,' he muttered into her hair.

'I know,' she rasped.

'I'm sorry.'

'Don't be,' she shocked herself by saying. 'I liked it.'

Oh, what an understatement. She'd gloried in his hard, unprotected flesh surging into hers, wallowed in his flooding her womb.

His head lifted, dark eyes gleaming. 'But you're not safe. You've just opened the dungeon door, Sarah, big time.'

Her sex-glazed eyes searched his. 'What dungeon is that?'

'The one I've kept my X-rated fantasies about you imprisoned in all these years.'

Sarah's eyes widened at the rather menacing metaphor.

'Don't ever imagine I'm in love with you,' he snarled. 'Love doesn't live in a dungeon. Now, go to sleep. I've had enough for one night and I'm bloody exhausted.'

# CHAPTER THIRTEEN

'SOMETHING to drink, Sarah?'

Sarah's head turned. She'd been staring through the plane window at the panoramic vista below. They'd not long taken off from Mascot Airport and hadn't yet reached any clouds.

'Yes, please,' she said to both Nick and the hovering stewardess. 'What can I have?'

'How about a glass of champagne?' Nick suggested.

'At seven-fifteen in the morning?'

'Why not?'

'Nick, you *are* terrible,' she chided, but jokingly. 'OK, champagne it is.'

'And you, sir?' the flight attendant asked.

'I'll have what she's having.'

Sarah's laugh enchanted him, as did she. There was no artifice in her, no pretend sophistication. She was a pleasant change from the kind of woman he usually dated.

Once she was handed her glass of champagne, Sarah

turned back to gaze intently through the window, her nose close to the rim.

Truly, she was like a child on her first flight.

Nick stared at her as he waited for his drink. She looked about sixteen this morning, wearing little make-up, no jewellery and a simple black and white sun-dress. Her hairstyle was young too, the sides scooped up into school-girlish combs, the rest falling loosely down her back.

The flight attendant was probably thinking he was a shameless cradle-snatcher. Nick detected a knowing glint in the woman's eyes as she handed him his glass of champagne.

Not that he cared what she thought, or anyone else for that matter. Nick had become so besotted by Sarah that he was already considering extending the length of their affair.

Of course, a month of non-stop sex with her at his holiday house on Happy Island might return him to a wiser course of action. He really hadn't had enough time to burn out his lust for Sarah since the first night they'd spent together.

Apart from anything, they'd been very busy, visiting Flora at the hospital and seeing to her health needs.

Fortunately, the specialist had located the source of the angina, a minor blockage in one artery that had been successfully cleared without the need for open-heart surgery. When the doctor had suggested a holiday for his quickly recovering patient, Nick had offered Jim and Flora his penthouse on the Gold Coast, which was fully serviced, with meals readily available, either in the restaurant downstairs or delivered to their apartment door. They'd jumped at the chance of an all-expenses-paid jaunt and Nick had seen them off at the airport three days ago, New Year's Eve.

Which had left him alone in the house with Sarah.

As Nick settled back to sip his champagne, his mind drifted back to the thirty-first of December…

He'd chilled some white wine, ordered in a five-star meal from a local restaurant, then set everything up on the balcony to the master bedroom, the perfect setting for a romantic, candlelit dinner. The perfect setting for New Year's Eve as well, with the uninterrupted view of Sydney Harbour—the water, the city and the bridge—which was always the showpiece of the fireworks.

Not that they got to see the fireworks, either at nine or at midnight, each occasion finding them otherwise occupied inside. After nearly a week of abstinence, he was insatiable, both for Sarah's beautiful body and her rapturous responses, Nick wallowing with wicked self-ishness in the transparency of her feelings for him.

Nick could not get enough of her that night. Or the next day. Oddly enough, he didn't want to try out lots of different positions. He was content to just be in bed with her.

That evening, however, she suddenly called a halt, claiming she was exhausted. That night she slept alone, in her pink-quilted, little-girl bed.

Nick didn't argue. He could see she was determined. But he wasn't happy, resolving during that long, restless night that the following morning he would persuade her to go away with him to Happy Island, where she wouldn't be able to escape him.

Fortunately, he hadn't cancelled the airline tickets he'd booked for himself and Chloe.

Sarah's reaction to his invitation over breakfast seriously surprised Nick.

'Surely you can't expect me to go away with you on the same holiday you planned with Chloe!' she threw at him.

Nick quickly saw that his sensitivity meter was registering very low, Sarah making it clear what she thought of his suggestion.

He had to work hard all day to make Sarah see he wasn't treating her as a substitute for Chloe. Some tender lovemaking seemed to soften her stubborn attitude a little. But he finally struck the right note when he said that he'd never taken Chloe—or any of his other girlfriends—to Happy Island before. She would be the first female to share his holiday house with him.

It was both the truth, and a lie. He had taken Chloe there for one short weekend back in September. But, as it had turned out, she'd fallen ill with food poisoning on the flight there. She'd been unwell the whole time, unable to do anything but stay in bed and read. Nick decided in his male mind that that didn't count.

After agreeing to go with him, Sarah had surprised him once again when she'd insisted on spending last night alone in her bedroom. She'd said she needed a good night's sleep, since they had to get up so very, very early.

Nick had been wide awake well before his alarm went off, his desire more intense than ever.

But it wouldn't be long now. Soon he would have her all to himself again in a place where she had nowhere to run to. Or to hide.

'Oh, I can't see anything any more,' Sarah said wistfully as she slumped back into her seat, her champagne glass still untouched. 'The clouds are in the way.'

Nick smiled. 'Anybody would think you hadn't flown before.'

'It's been years since I have,' she said, then finally took a sip of champagne.

'Really?'

'I haven't had much money left for holidays, what with paying for my rent and my car and general living expenses.'

Nick frowned. 'You could have asked me for some money for a holiday,' he said. 'I never did agree with Ray for leaving you that short of funds.'

'It was probably good for my character. At least I'm not spoiled.'

Nick's frown deepened. No, he thought. She certainly wasn't. But would spending time with him change her character? He wanted to educate her, not corrupt her. He would hate for her to turn out like Chloe, who thought of no one's pleasure but her own.

'Now, what's that frown all about?' she asked him.

'You're not worrying about Flora and Jim, are you? I spoke to them last night and they're as happy as can be up there on the Gold Coast. It was a brilliant idea of yours to lend them your penthouse. Very generous, too.'

Nick decided not to let her go back into hero-worship mode. Bad enough that she probably thought she was in love with him.

'Come, now, Sarah, you know very well it wasn't generosity that inspired my offer. It was a strictly selfish proposition. I wanted them right out of the way.'

'You're not the only one,' she said, then blushed.

It got to him, that blush, sparking a desire so intense that his flesh ached.

'I wish I could kiss you right now,' he said.

'Why can't you?' she returned, her cheeks still pink.

'Because I wouldn't want to stop there,' he ground out. 'Next thing you knew, we'd be joining the mile-high club.'

Her nose wrinkled with distaste. 'No way could you get me to do that. I've always thought sex on a plane to be the height of tackiness.'

'Hear! Hear!' Nick said, and raised his glass to her. No way, he realised with considerable relief, would she ever become like Chloe.

It would be damned difficult to go back to girls like Chloe after being with Sarah...

As Sarah sipped her champagne, she wondered if Nick really approved of her view. Maybe he thought her prudish, since he'd always claimed to be a roué.

But surprisingly, other than that first incident, when he'd pushed her down to her knees, her sexual encounters with him had not been the least bit decadent. Passionate, yes. But not dark.

On New Year's Eve he'd been very romantic, something he'd claimed he would never be.

Sarah held the opinion that people were as good, or as bad, as you let them be. Certainly, that applied to children. She'd discovered during her teaching years so far that if she had high expectations of her pupils they usually lived up to them.

Especially the so-called bad boys.

Nick was a bad boy. But he wasn't bad through and through, no matter what he thought of himself, and no matter what he'd done in the past. Her father had seen his worth. Her dad had also expected a lot of Nick. And Nick had lived up to those expectations.

Admittedly, he'd lost his way a bit since Ray's death. Sarah could not deny that he had earned his playboy reputation. Women had been relegated to sex toys in his life for so long that it probably was foolish of her to think he would ever embrace a better way of life. With her.

*Very* foolish.

But love was foolish, wasn't it?

Why else was she sitting here, in a seat that had been booked for Chloe? The bottom line was that if Chloe hadn't made that *faux pas* on Christmas Day, she'd be the one sitting here today.

This pessimistic train of thought irritated Sarah to death. Hadn't she decided last night to be positive, and not negative; to view Nick's invitation to share a whole month with him as a step towards a real relationship? Hadn't she vowed to use this time not just to explore the sexual chemistry between them, but also to revive that special bond which had sprung up all those years ago when they'd both been so very lonely?

She hoped that, besides the sex, they would have deep and meaningful conversations during which Nick would tell her everything about himself, and vice versa.

'You're not drinking your champagne,' Nick pointed out.

Sarah turned a rueful smile his way. 'It *is* a little early. I think coffee would have been a better choice.'

'It's a woman's privilege to change her mind,' he said amiably, and pressed the button for service.

Sarah watched with pride as he gave the stewardess back the champagne and asked for coffee instead. She loved his decisiveness, his 'can-do' attitude. Nick was a natural leader, something her father had once commented on.

Sarah believed he would make a great husband and father. But would Nick ever believe it?

'I have a confession to make,' he said after the coffee arrived.

Sarah's stomach contracted. 'Nothing that will upset me, I hope.'

'No reason why it should.'

'Out with it, then.'

'I read all your Christmas cards. The ones on your dressing table.'

Her stomach relaxed. 'Oh? When?'

'Yesterday. When you were having a shower.'

'And?'

'I don't think I've ever seen such glowing words. It's a privilege to be in the company of the "bestest" teacher in the whole wide world.'

Sarah laughed. 'A slight exaggeration. But I am pretty good.'

'And yet you've resigned?'

'Only from my current school. I'll find another position closer to home. Possibly at a preschool. I'm very fond of small children. They have such open minds.'

'I don't have any patience with small children.'

'Lots of men don't. But they change, once they have their own.'

His glance was sharp. 'I won't. Because I don't intend having any of my own.'

Sarah kept her expression calm. 'Why's that?'

'Fathering is a learned skill, passed on from generation to generation. The only example I ever had of fathering is not something I'd like to pass on.'

'Not every child of abusive parents becomes an abuser themselves, Nick,' she said carefully.

'Perhaps not. But why take the chance? The world has enough children. They won't miss mine.'

'You might change your mind if you were presented with one.'

He whipped his head round to glare at her. 'You have brought your pills with you, haven't you? You're not going to try that old pregnancy trap. Because it won't work, Sarah. Not with me.'

The coldness in his eyes sent a chill running down her spine.

But she refused to give up on him. For now, anyway.

'I have no intention of trying to trap you with a baby, Nick. And yes, I have brought my pills. You can feed me one every day, if you'd like.'

'I just might do that.'

'Have you always been this paranoid about pregnancy?'

'Let's just say you're the first female I've ever had sex with without a condom.'

'It's nice to know that I'm unique.'

He smiled wryly as he shook his head at her. 'You are that, all right. Now, drink your coffee before it goes cold and I have to call the stewardess again.'

She drank her coffee quickly, anxious to get back to their conversation. It would be a couple more hours before they landed on Happy Island, with Nick imprisoned by her side all that time. Sarah didn't think she'd ever have a better opportunity to find out all the things she'd ever wanted to know about him. She suspected that once they hit Happy Island, there might not be too much talking done.

'Tell me about your life, Nick,' she said when she finally put the coffee down. 'Before you came to work for Dad. I'm curious.'

'I never talk about that part of my life, Sarah.'

'But that's silly. It's not as though I don't already know quite a bit. I know you had a horrible father and that you ran away from home to live on the streets when you were only thirteen. And I know that you were put in jail for car-stealing when you were eighteen.'

'Then you know enough, don't you?'

'Those are just the bare facts. I want you to fill in the details.'

Nick sighed. 'You do pick your moments.'

'I think I have the right to know some more about the man I'm sleeping with, don't you? You used to give my boyfriends the third degree.'

'But I'm not your boyfriend. I'm your secret lover. Secret lovers are often men of mystery.'

'Sorry, but you're not my secret lover any longer. I told Flora last night that we were together.'

'You *what*?'

Sarah shrugged. 'I said I was sorry.'

'Like hell you are. You're a conniving, manipulative little minx.'

Sarah could see that he wasn't as angry as he was trying to sound. And she had no intention of backing off.

'So are you going to tell me your life story, or not?'

'Do you think you're up for it, little girl?'

'Don't insult my intelligence, Nick. I might not have

been around like you, but I watch the news at night, and I can read. I know about the big, bad world. Nothing you say will shock me.'

What a naïve statement, Sarah was to discover over the next quarter of an hour as she listened to Nick's dreadful life story.

His mother had run off when he'd been too young to remember her, his lone-parent father a violent and drunken good-for-nothing who taught his son to shoplift when he was only five and beat him every other day. Sarah was appalled as Nick described being not only punched and slapped, but also beaten with belts and burned with cigarettes.

Naturally, Nick's schooling had been limited—he was kept away a lot—but he was smart enough to learn to read and write. Love, of course, had been an unknown emotion. He'd counted himself lucky to be fed. Survival had been the name of the game.

When he'd gone into puberty at thirteen, he'd suddenly shot up in height and was able to look his father straight in the eye. For the first time when his father hit him, Nick had hit back.

He hadn't actually run away from home as she'd thought. He'd been literally thrown out into the street with only the clothes he was wearing.

He'd stayed in a refuge for a while, but was unfortunate enough to find one that was run by someone who wasn't interested in helping, just in pocketing his salary. Not the best introduction to the welfare system for an already emotionally scarred child. After running away from there, Nick had made his way to King's Cross in Sydney, where he squatted in derelict buildings and made money the only way he knew: by stealing. Not shoplifting. Mostly he broke into parked cars and stole the contents.

He'd resisted joining a gang, not wanting to rely on anyone but himself. He had made a few friends, but they were all low-life, pimps and prostitutes and drug-dealers. Inevitably, he'd been drawn into drug use himself. Anything to make his existence more bearable.

Addiction of any kind, however, took money. So he had started breaking and entering, plus stealing the cars themselves, rather than just the contents.

'One night,' he said, 'I made a mistake and got caught. I went to jail, met your father and the rest is history, as they say.'

Sarah was close to tears. 'Oh, Nick…'

'I did warn you.'

'You survived, though.'

'Let me tell you about that kind of survival,' he bit out. 'It makes you think of no one but yourself. You become hard, and cold, and capable of just about anything. When I first met your father when I was in jail, I didn't give a damn about him, only what he could do for me. I saw a means of escape and I grabbed it with both hands. When I finally got out of jail and came to work as Ray's chauffeur, I thought he was a sucker. I had no feelings for him whatsoever.'

'But you did, in the end,' she said. 'You *loved* him.'

'I respected him. That's not the same as love.'

'I see…'

'No, you don't. You don't see at all. You can't, till you've lived in my shoes. I've told you once, now I'll tell you again: men like me can't love anyone.'

'I don't believe that,' she muttered. She couldn't. For if she did, her future was unbearable. 'You weren't that bad when you came to live with us. You were kind to me for starters.'

'Was I? Or was I just trying to get in good with the boss?'

Sarah frowned. She'd never thought of his actions in that light before.

'Damn it all, don't look at me like that. OK, so I did like you. You were a nice kid.'

'You still like me,' she said with a smile of relief.

'Yeah. I still like you.'

As admissions went, it wasn't much, but it made Sarah feel better. Things suddenly looked a bit brighter. But she felt a change of subject was called for.

'Have you heard anything about your movie yet?'

She'd never seen Nick look so confused. *'What?'*

'Didn't you say that movie you'd put so much money into was coming out in the New Year? Well, it's the third of January. That's past the New Year.'

The penny dropped for Nick. His lurid background was too much for Sarah. Hopefully, she wouldn't bring it up again. Talking about movies he could cope with. His past was best kept locked in the dungeon.

'It came out yesterday to mixed reviews,' he told her. 'It'll take a few more days before the public's verdict has come in.'

'What's it called?'

'*Back to the Outback*. It's a sequel to *Outback Bride*. It has the same writer-director.'

'That should do well, surely. Everyone who saw and loved *Outback Bride* will come to see it.'

'That's what we're hoping.'

'Is it any good? Sequels often aren't as good as the original.'

'I think it is.'

'But the critics didn't.'

'A couple of them did. The others hated the tragic ending.'

'Who dies? Not Shane, I hope.'

'No, Brenda.'

'*Brenda!* That's even worse. You can't kill off the heroine in a romance. There has to be a happy ending, Nick.'

'Rubbish. Lots of romances have unhappy endings.'

'Only the ones written by men,' she said disgustedly. 'How does she die?'

'She's shot saving her child from the baddies,' he said defensively, as if that made it all right.

'No excuses. She simply cannot die. Why couldn't she have been shot, but still live? Truly, you should have talked to me about this earlier, Nick. I would have advised you.'

'She *needed* to die. She was no good for Shane. Their romance was flawed and their marriage was a disaster waiting to happen. She hated life in the country and was threatening to go back to the city and take the child when the baddies from her earlier life show up. The sequel isn't really a romance, Sarah, it's a drama.'

'You can call it what you like. It sounds awful.'

'Thank you for the vote of confidence.'

The captain announcing that they were expecting some turbulence and everyone was to belt up terminated what was becoming a heated exchange.

'Typical,' Nick muttered as he snapped his seat belt shut.

'What do you mean?' Sarah asked, grabbing at the armrests when the plane shuddered.

'January is cyclone season in this neck of the woods.'

'I wish you'd told me that earlier. We could have just as easily stayed home, especially once Flora and Jim went away.'

'I wanted to show you Happy Island.'

'The island itself, or your fancy holiday house?'

Nick smiled. 'A man's allowed to show off to his girlfriend, isn't he?'

Sarah's heart flipped over. 'You...you called me your girlfriend.'

Nick shrugged. 'I reserve the right to rescind the title if you get stroppy with me.'

'I only get stroppy during cyclones. I also get hysterical.'

Nick laughed. 'Now she tells me. Don't worry. My place is cyclone-proof. Actually, Happy Island hasn't been directly hit by a cyclone in decades. Mostly, it just gets lots of wind and rain. Unfortunately, we might have to stay indoors for days on end,' he added with a wicked twinkle in his eyes.

Sarah grinned. 'Just as well I brought all my old board games with me, then, isn't it?'

Nick groaned. 'Oh, no, not the Monopoly! You always whipped my butt at that.'

'Monopoly and Snakes and Ladders, and Chinese Checkers. I found them in the bottom of my wardrobe when I was packing.'

When Nick looked pained, she gave him a playful dig in the ribs.

'Come on. We used to have great fun playing those games.'

'I had some different kinds of games in mind now that you've grown up.'

Sarah shook her head at him. 'If you think this holiday is going to be just a sex-fest, Nick, then think again. I picked up a brochure about Happy Island from a local travel agent and there's heaps I want to do.'

'Really. Such as?'

'Aside from a tour around the island to all the scenic spots, I'd like to take a boat trip to the barrier reef and a helicopter ride over the Whitsundays. Then there's windsurfing and souvenir-shopping. Oh, and mini-golf. You can have your revenge on me with that. I also saw pictures of a lovely white beach with the most beautiful turquoise waters where I'd like to go for a swim.'

'Uh-uh,' he said with a shake of his head. 'You won't be doing that.'

'Why not?'

'Because of the irukanji.'

'The what?'

'They're a jellyfish. Toxic as all hell. They can put you in hospital for days. Two people have died from their sting since 2001. Summer is their peak season.'

'Oh, great. No swimming.'

'Actually, you *can* go in the sea, if you wear a full body suit. But they don't look too glamorous. Still, not to worry. There are more swimming pools on Happy Island than you can poke a stick at. Mine is fabulous, and solar-heated as well.'

'I didn't doubt it.'

His smile carried amusement. 'You have a tongue on you at times, don't you?'

'I never said I was perfect.'

'Just nearly,' he murmured, and leant over to kiss her on the cheek.

Her head turned fully to face him. 'I thought you said you weren't going to kiss me.'

'You call that a kiss? I'll show you a kiss when I get you to my place.'

A quiver ran through her body at the desire gleaming

bright in his eyes. This was what she'd always wanted, to have him look at her like this. But would it be enough, just being the recipient of Nick's passion? The truth was she wanted more now. She wanted that happily-ever-after ending. She wanted Nick's love, the very thing he claimed he could never give anyone.

'You can relax your hands now,' he said. 'We're through the turbulence.'

Not so, she thought with a tormented twist to her heart. The turbulence has only just begun.

# CHAPTER FOURTEEN

THE beauty of Happy Island just blew Sarah away. The pilot circled it once before landing, giving all the window-seat passengers a splendid view.

Talk about a tropical paradise!

She'd heard people wax lyrical about the colour of the sand and the water in this region, but the beaches and bays were just magic to the eye, framed by lots of palm trees and environmentally friendly buildings that blended beautifully with the green vegetation.

Nick was right about the number of pools, though. They did stand out from the air, because there were so many, in all sorts of shapes and sizes.

Any worry she was still harbouring about the eventual outcome of their relationship was put aside as excitement took hold. It would be wonderful to have a romantic holiday here, with the man she loved. Wonderful to have him all to herself for a whole month.

If nothing else, she would have this marvellous memory.

'No point in rushing off the plane,' Nick said when everyone else jumped up from their seats. 'We'll only have to wait in the heat for our luggage. There's no carousel in the terminal here, just a collection area down near where all the resort shuttles are parked.'

'Will we be taking a shuttle?'

'No. I own a golf buggy, which I keep at the airport.'

'Oh, yes, I read about those in the brochure. It said there weren't many cars on the island, and everyone got around in golf buggies.'

'That's right.'

'Can I drive it?'

'Sure.'

'Oh, wow. That'll be fun.'

Sarah and Nick finally exited the plane next to last, with Sarah surprised to find it not quite as hot outside as she'd been expecting. 'Am I wrong, or is it not all that hot out here?'

'No, you're quite right. But the weather forecast says there'll be a change later in the week. It's going to gradually get hotter, with higher temperatures and humidity. They're predicting a storm on Saturday afternoon, with strong gusts of wind and tons of rain.'

'How do you know all that?'

'Looked on the internet last night for the forecast up this way.'

'You didn't bring your laptop with you, I hope.'

'No need. I have a full computer set-up here.'

'What *don't* you have here?' Sarah heard herself saying half an hour later.

She was standing in the main living room of Nick's holiday house, looking through a wall made totally of glass at the most magnificent pool she had ever seen. It was called a horizon pool, so named because the far side of the pool seemed to have no edge, the water meeting the sky the way the horizon did out at sea.

'It cost me a pretty penny,' Nick agreed.

'You mean the pool, or the rest of this place?'

Actually, the house wasn't all that huge. Only three bedrooms. But everything was beautifully and stylishly decorated in cool greens and blues that complemented its tropical setting. There was also every mod con available, including a kitchen to die for and a king-sized plasma television.

'The foundations cost the most,' he told her.

Sarah could understand why. The house was built on the side of a cliff, its half-hexagonal shape creating one-hundred-and-eighty-degree views. All the rooms had huge glass windows or walls that looked out to sea and the other islands beyond. The glass was specially toughened to withstand even the worst storms, Nick told her, and tinted to soften any glare.

'It took two years to build,' Nick said. 'It was only completed last June.'

'Really?' Sarah said. So that was why Nick hadn't brought any of his girlfriends here before. He hadn't had the opportunity. Still, it was nice to think she was the first girl to stand here with him. And the first to share this particular master bedroom. She could hardly make the same claim about the bedroom back home.

'It's spectacular, Nick,' she said, throwing a warm smile up at him. 'So's this view.'

Nick slid an arm around her waist and pulled her close. 'Wait till you see it at sunrise.'

When he turned her towards him, Sarah knew he was going to kiss her. And this time, there would be no stopping him. Not that she wanted to. Her heart was already pounding by the time his lips met hers.

'I don't think I'm going to let you unpack,' Nick said to her some considerable time later. 'I like you like this.'

They'd eventually made it to the master bedroom, though Sarah's clothes were still on the living-room floor. Nick's as well.

Sarah sighed with pleasure as Nick gently caressed her stomach.

'I like you like this as well,' she returned dreamily.

The lovemaking between them was getting better and better, and gradually more adventurous. Sarah had thought she preferred the missionary position with Nick, where their eyes could meet and she could hold him close in the traditional way. But she found this spoon position very much to her liking, thrilling to the hot feel of Nick's body cocooned around hers. She loved that it left his hands free to play with her breasts and the rest of her body whilst he was inside her. The sensations had sent her head spinning.

He hadn't withdrawn afterwards, and she could feel

him slowly coming back to life. He groaned when her bottom moved voluptuously against him.

His hands lifted to her breasts, where he pinched her nipples.

'Oh,' she gasped, startled by the odd mixture of pain and pleasure.

'You liked that,' he muttered thickly in her ear.

'Yes…no…I don't know.'

'*I* liked it,' he said, and did it again.

She moaned, then squirmed. Yes, she definitely did like it.

'Do it again,' she urged breathlessly.

He obliged and her head whirled with the dizziest pleasure. Now he was fully erect again, and began thrusting harder than the first time. Heat enveloped her, her forehead breaking into a sweat.

'Yes,' she bit out, everything inside her twisting into exquisitely expectant spirals. 'Yes. Yes,' she cried out as her body broke into little pieces, splintering apart with a violent release.

With a raw groan Nick rolled her over onto her stomach, cupping her breasts and lifting her up onto her hands and knees. Sarah thought she was done, but she was wrong. When he reached down and rubbed her clitoris, another orgasm ripped through her. This time he came too, hot and strong. At last she fell, face-down, onto the bed, his body collapsing on top of hers.

For a couple of minutes they just lay, glued together by sweat, their breathing ragged.

'See?' he said at last, his voice low and thick. 'A woman can come lots of times in a row. I could keep you coming all day, if you want me to.'

Sarah went weak with the thought of his doing such a thing.

'I…I think what I need right at this moment,' she said shakily, 'is a shower.'

'Mmm. What a good idea. I'll join you.'

# CHAPTER FIFTEEN

NICK lay stretched out next to Sarah's sleeping form, his hands linked behind his head, his body temporarily sated but his mind not even remotely at peace.

It wasn't working, his plan to burn out his lust for Sarah. It seemed the more he had her, the more he wanted her.

Thirty-six hours had passed since their arrival, with their hardly leaving the master suite, except for food and the occasional dip in the pool.

Nick's flesh began to stir once more as he recalled their erotic encounter by the pool last night, not to mention the wildly passionate one in the kitchen this morning.

Sarah had confessed afterwards she'd never had sex whilst sitting on a granite bench-top before. Or sitting anywhere, for that matter.

It seemed her sex life so far had been limited and unimaginative, a fact that Nick found surprising, yet primally satisfying. He was beginning to understand why some men married virgins. There had to be something intensely pleasing about being a female's first lover.

At the same time, Sarah's lack of sexual experience troubled him. Young, naïve girls like her fell in love so very easily.

Though she'd never said she loved him, he'd seen adoration in her lovely but very readable eyes. Seen it, and wallowed in it.

Was that the reason behind his growing addiction for her? Not the sex so much but the way Sarah made him feel whilst he was making love to her?

How would it be to always have her in his bed? he began to wonder. To put his ring on her finger? To legally bind her to him?

Crazy thoughts, Nick. Crazy.

Shaking his head, he rolled over and propped himself up on one elbow to stare down at her, his eyes roving hotly over her lusciously naked body. Before he knew it he was touching her again, waking her, *wanting* her. He groaned when she opened her arms to him on a sigh of sweet surrender.

*Say no, damn you,* his mind screamed as he plunged into her.

But she didn't.

Sarah crept from the bed, lest she wake Nick. Night had fallen and he was sleeping soundly at long last.

Pulling on her lavender satin robe—her only item of clothing as yet unpacked—she made her way quietly out to the kitchen, where she began to search the large freezer for something substantial to eat. During the past two days they'd only eaten enough to survive—mostly toast and coffee—and Sarah was suddenly feeling ravenous.

Half an hour and two microwaveable meals later, Sarah carried a second mug of coffee into the living room and curled herself up in a corner of the blue sofa. She sighed as she sipped, only then allowing herself to think about what they'd been doing since they'd arrived on Happy Island.

So much for her saying this holiday was not going to be just a sex-fest!

Truly, she should put her foot down and demand that they leave the house occasionally. It wasn't right to just loll around, having sex all the time.

Sarah pulled a face. Maybe it wasn't right, but it felt good. *She* felt good. Better than she'd ever felt.

But enough was enough, she decided. Come tomorrow, she would insist on their getting dressed and going out somewhere.

Hopefully Nick would not make a fuss, or start seducing her again. Her head whirled at how good he was at doing that. And how successful. She just couldn't seem to say no to him.

But she would, come tomorrow morning.

Easier said than done, Sarah thought ruefully. He only had to roll over and start touching her, and she was a goner.

Maybe she should spend the rest of the night out here on this sofa; it was big enough to sleep on.

Whatever, she didn't need sleep for a while. After her eating binge, she was wide awake. Watching television was not an option, however. The noise might wake Nick. Maybe she would read for a while. There were a few paperbacks on the shelves that flanked the large built-in entertainment unit.

Sarah put down her coffee and made her way across the tiled floor. There was only one title that appealed, called *Dressed to Kill*, the back blurb promising a page-turning thriller with twists and turns and a spine-tingling climax.

Sarah's spine certainly tingled when she opened it and saw the handwritten name on top of the first page.

Chloe Cameron.

Her mouth went dry as she stared down at that hated name, her head filling with a hundred horrible thoughts, the main one being that Nick had lied to her. Chloe *had* been to Happy Island with him—how else would this book be here? Nick was not a reader.

Various repulsive images popped into Sarah's mind. Of Nick having sex with Chloe by the pool and on the kitchen counter. Of his doing all the things with Chloe that he'd done with her.

The hurt was overwhelming. So was the humiliation. What a fool she'd been to be so easily tricked! A besotted fool!

But no more.

Gripping the book tightly in both hands, Sarah marched back into the bedroom, snapping on the overhead light, then slamming the door with deliberate loudness.

* * *

Nick woke with a start, blinking madly as he sat up. Sarah's glowering at him from the side of the bed brought confusion, then a jolt of alarm.

'What is it? What's wrong?'

She threw something at him. A book. It struck his bare chest before he could catch it, tumbling down into his lap.

'You said you'd never brought her here,' Sarah bit out. 'You lied, you bastard.'

The penny dropped for Nick, as did his stomach.

'It's not what you're thinking,' he defended.

Her laugh had a hard, hollow sound to it. 'And why's that, Nick?'

'I didn't have sex with her.'

She laughed again. 'You expect me to believe that? Mr I-have-to-have-it-ten-times-a-day!'

'Chloe was sick, with food poisoning. She spent the whole weekend in bed in the guest room.'

Sarah crossed her arms, her expression scornful. 'If that's the truth, why didn't you tell me?

'I'll tell you why,' she went on before he could say a single word. 'Because that might not have got you what you wanted, which was stupid me, filling in for Chloe on this holiday. Better to let the silly little fool think she's unique and special. Make her believe your inviting her to come with you here is a one-off. Whatever way you look at it, Nick, you lied to me for your own selfish ends.'

Nick was not at his best when backed into a corner. He always came out fighting.

'And you haven't done the same?' he counterattacked. 'I seem to recall your telling me in my study on Christmas Day that all you wanted from me was sex. Obviously that wasn't the truth, was it? You want what you've always wanted: marriage. That's why you've been so damned accommodating all the time. And why you're so upset right now!'

Her face flushed with a shaming heat, her hurt eyes making him feel totally wretched.

'If that's what you really think, Nick,' she choked out, 'then I can't stay here with you. I just can't.'

In all his life, Nick had never felt so dreadful. Even when he'd been in jail. But it was for the best, wasn't it? He was no good for her. Better they call it quits now before she got even more hurt.

'If that's what you want,' he snapped.

'What I want…' She shook her head, her shoulders slumping as a soul-weary sigh escaped her lips. 'I'm never going to get what I want. Not with you. I can see that now.' She straightened, putting her shoulders back and lifting her chin up. 'I'm sorry for throwing that book at you, Nick. Generally speaking, you have been honest with me. Quite brutally at times. I just didn't want to hear what you were saying.'

Now Nick felt even worse, his heart like a great lump of iron in his chest. The temptation to jump up and take her in his arms was almost overwhelming. He wanted to tell her that *he* was the sorry one, that she *was* unique and special and that he *did* want to marry her.

But he resisted the temptation. Somehow.

'I…I'll move my things into one of the spare bedrooms for tonight,' she went on, her eyes glistening. 'Then first thing tomorrow I'll see if I can get on a flight back to Sydney.'

'Fine,' he said, and threw back the sheet. 'Now, if you'll excuse me, I need to go to the bathroom.'

# CHAPTER SIXTEEN

SARAH couldn't sleep. Not only was she still very upset,
but she was also hot. The weather forecast had been
right: the temperature had risen sharply over the last few
hours, so the air-conditioning was struggling in the
higher humidity.

In the end, Sarah got up, put on the pink bikini she'd
bought before Christmas, grabbed a towel and headed for
the pool. Who cared if it was the middle of the night and
pitch-black outside? The pool had underwater lighting.

The strength of the wind surprised her. She had to
anchor her towel underneath a banana lounger to stop it
from blowing away. The same banana lounger, she
realised, that she and Nick had had sex on the day before.
Wild, wanton sex, with herself a very willing partner.

Shuddering at the memory, Sarah dived into the
water, and began stroking vigorously up and down,
hoping to make herself so exhausted that when she
returned to bed she would immediately fall asleep.

Fat chance, she thought wretchedly, but continued

to punish herself with lap after lap. Finally, the lactic acid in her joints forced her to stop. Slowly, she swam over towards the lounger that was down near the far edge of the pool.

Sarah shivered as she hauled herself out of the water. The wind was much stronger than before. That storm couldn't be far off now. Hopefully, it wouldn't last too long. She didn't want there to be any reason for the airport to be closed tomorrow. She needed to get off this island and away from Nick as soon as possible.

Sarah was bending to retrieve her towel when a wildly swirling gust of wind lifted a nearby table and umbrella off the tiled surrounds and hurled them against her back. She screamed as she was catapulted with tremendous force into the air and right over the horizon edge of the pool. She screamed again when she hit the water-catching ledge below with a bruising blow to her shoulder, another scream bursting from her mouth when momentum carried her right off the edge and into the void.

Nick was lying on top of the sheets, wide awake, when he heard Sarah's terrified screams. He was off the bed in a flash, fear quickening his heartbeat—and his legs— as he raced in the direction of her cries.

The pool area.

The security light was already on, indicating that Sarah must have come outside here recently. But he couldn't see her anywhere.

And then he saw them: the table and umbrella floating in the far end of the pool.

'Oh, my God!' he exclaimed, his first thought being that she was under them in the water, knocked unconscious and already drowning.

When Nick dived in and found no sign of her, an even worse possibility came to mind. Swimming to the far edge, he peered over it to the ledge below, hoping against hope that he'd see her sitting there, waiting for him to pull her up into his arms.

The most appalling dread consumed him when the dimly lit ledge proved empty as well. The thought that she had fallen down to the rocky waters below was so horrendous that he could hardly conceive of it. For no one could survive a fall like that.

'Nooooo!' he screamed into the wind.

She could not be dead. Not his Sarah. Not his wonderful, beautiful, sweet Sarah.

'Nick! Nick, are you there?'

Nick almost cried with relief. 'Yes, I'm here,' he called back, scrambling over the edge and dropping down to the ledge below. 'Where are you? I can't see you!'

His eyes were gradually becoming accustomed to the lack of direct light, but the wind was making them water like mad.

'Down here.'

'Down where?'

He leant right over as far as he dared, finally spotting her clinging to the cliff a few metres down under the ledge. No, not to the cliff but to a bush that was growing out of a crevice in the rock face—a rather straggly-looking bush.

Hopefully, the roots were tenacious.

'Have you got a foothold?' he called out to her.

'A bit of a one. But I think this bush is coming loose. Oh, God, yes, it is. Do something, Nick.'

Nick knew she was too far down for him to reach. He needed something long that she could get hold of. But what?

Panic turned his head to mush for a moment.

'Think, man,' he muttered to himself.

The umbrella in the pool. It was quite large and its supporting pole was long.

'Hold on, Sarah, I have an idea.'

Adrenaline had him leaping back up and into the pool with the agility of a monkey. He grabbed the umbrella, yanked it down, then jumped back with it to the ledge below.

'Here,' he said, and stretched it out towards her. 'Grab this.'

She did so.

'Hold on tight,' he ordered.

Her weight surprised him at first. But he felt strong, stronger than he'd ever felt. And then she was there, in his arms, weeping and shaking with shock.

Nick held her close, his lips buried in her wet hair, his eyes tightly shut.

'It's all right,' he said thickly. 'I have you now. You're safe.'

'Oh, Nick,' Sarah cried. 'I…I thought I was going to die.'

Nick held her even tighter. He'd thought she *had* died. And it was the most defining moment in his life. He knew now what Jim had felt at that hospital. Because as much as Jim loved Flora, *he* loved Sarah. Oh, yes, he loved her. There was no longer any doubt in his mind.

But did that make any difference? Wouldn't she still be better off if he let her go?

He just didn't know any more.

'I…I can't stop sh-shaking,' she said, her teeth chattering.

'You're in shock,' he told her. 'What you need is a warm bath, and a hot cup of tea with lots of sugar in it. But first, I have to get you up out of here. Very, very carefully.'

Sarah couldn't stop thinking about the moment she'd fallen off that ledge. Couldn't stop reliving the fear, and the split-second realisation that her life was about to be over.

It made one reassess things, facing death like that. Made one see what was important, and what wasn't. Made one more prepared to take a risk or two.

'Here's the tea,' Nick said as he came into the bathroom.

Sarah was lying back in a very deep, deliciously warm bath, her pink bikini still on. Nick, however, was still naked.

'Do you think you could put something on?' she said to him when he handed her the tea. Sarah knew she would find it difficult to talk to a naked Nick.

And she did want to talk to him. Sensibly and truthfully.

Nick pulled a towel off a nearby rail and tied it around his hips.

'This do?' he asked her.

'Yes, thank you. No, please don't leave. I…I have something I want to say to you.'

Nick crossed his arms and leant against the far wall whilst Sarah lifted the mug to her lips and swallowed, grimacing at the excessive sweetness. Finally, she put the mug down and locked eyes with him.

'I've decided I don't want to go home tomorrow.'

His eyes flickered momentarily. 'And why's that, Sarah?'

'I love you, Nick. I've always loved you. You were quite right about why I came here with you. I had this romantic dream that if we spent quality time together, you would discover that you loved me back. And then there was the ultimate fantasy of your asking me to marry you.'

Now he did move, his arms uncrossing as he levered himself away from the wall, his high forehead drawing into a frown. 'Sarah, I—'

'No, no, let me finish, please, Nick.'

'Very well.'

'You may have been right about my reasons for coming here with you. But you were wrong when you accused me of using sex to try to get what I wanted. Not once have I said yes to you sexually with that agenda in mind. I *love* it when you make love to me. I've never experienced anything like it before in my life. I can't describe how I feel when you're inside me. I don't want to walk away from that pleasure, Nick. So if you still want me, I'd like to stay. I…I promise I won't put on any more insanely jealous turns. I just want to be with you, Nick,' she finished, a huge lump having formed in her throat during her brave little speech. 'Please…I…'

When her eyes filled with tears, Nick couldn't stand it any longer. How could his sending her away be the best thing for her? Or him? Seeing her like this was killing him.

'Don't cry,' he choked out as he fell to his knees by the bath. 'Please don't cry.'

'I'm sorry,' she sobbed. 'It's just…I…I love you so much.'

His hands reached out to cup her lovely face. 'And I love you, my darling.'

She gasped, her eyes widening.

'I knew it tonight when I thought I'd lost you. I love you, Sarah. And I *do* want to marry you.'

Her eyes carried shock, and scepticism. 'You…you don't mean that. You can't. You always said…'

'I know what I always said. I thought I wasn't good enough for you.'

'Oh, Nick. That's just so not true.'

'Yes, it is,' he insisted. 'But if you will trust me with

your life I vow that I will do my best never to hurt you, or let you or your father down. I will be faithful only to you. I will love you and protect you. And I will love and protect our children.'

Her already shocked eyes rounded further. 'You're prepared to have children?'

'I'll have your children, my darling, because I know that any shortcomings I have as a father will be more than made up for by your brilliance as a mother.'

'You...you shouldn't say such sweet things to me,' she cried.

'Why not? I mean them.'

Her tear-filled eyes searched his. 'You do mean them, don't you?'

'I surely do.'

'I...I don't know what to say.'

'Yes to marrying me would be a good start.'

'Oh, yes,' she said, and he kissed her. When his mouth lifted she was smiling.

'I'm glad to see I was right,' she said.

'About what?' Nick asked.

'The heroine in a romance never dies.'

## EPILOGUE

'Don't you think people might think it's odd,' Flora said, 'having a sixty-one-year-old bridesmaid?'

'Who cares what people think?' Sarah countered. 'Besides, you look absolutely beautiful.' She did, too. A few weeks of healthy eating and exercising had done wonders. So did her new blonde hair. Flora looked ten years younger.

'Not as beautiful as the bride,' Flora returned with a warm smile. 'I'm so happy for you and Nick, love. If ever a couple were made for each other it's you two. Ray would have been very pleased. Pleased about the baby, too.'

'I think so,' Sarah said, beaming with happiness.

She'd forgotten to take the Pill the morning after that traumatic night on Happy Island, and had fallen pregnant. At first she'd been a bit nervous about Nick's reaction, but he'd been absolutely thrilled.

It seemed mother nature knew what she was doing.

Now here she was, almost four months pregnant, about to marry the father of her baby and the only man she'd ever loved. She was not, however, a super-rich heiress. The day before her twenty-fifth birthday, she'd discussed her feelings over her inheritance with Nick and decided to do what he'd once said her father should have done in the first place: give all the money to charity.

So she had, dividing up the many millions in the estate between various charities that supported the poor and the needy.

Of course, she wasn't exactly broke. She still owned Goldmine, which was worth a conservative twenty million. Not that she would ever sell it. And then there were the royalties from *Outback Bride*, which would continue to flow in, the movie having been re-released after the worldwide success of its sequel. Nick had been so right about that tear-jerker ending.

Generally speaking, however, Nick would be the main provider for their family, an excellent source of motivation for him to keep working hard and feeling good about himself. Sarah vowed to never forget that underneath her husband's façade of confidence lay a damaged child who constantly needed the healing power of love. *Her* love.

A loud knock on her bedroom door was accompanied by a familiar voice. 'Time for the bride to make an appearance downstairs. We don't want the groom thinking things, do we?'

Sarah was smiling as she opened the door.

'Wow!' Derek said, looking her up and down. 'It's at moments like these I wish I weren't gay. And I'm not just talking about the bride.'

'Oh, go on with you,' Flora said, but with a big grin on her face.

Derek had become a frequent visitor to Goldmine, with Nick even warming to him. Derek had been delighted—and touched—when Sarah had asked him to give her away.

'OK, girls,' he said, linking arms with Sarah, 'it's showtime!'

'Goddamn!' Jim exclaimed beside Nick when an elegantly dressed blonde lady walked sedately down the steps into the rather crowded family room. 'Is that my Flora?'

'Indeed it is,' Nick informed his best man. But his own admiring eyes moved quickly to the radiant bride following Flora, his heart filling with emotion as he watched Sarah walk towards him with the most glorious smile on her face. It was a smile of total love and trust, that love and trust which had soothed his soul and brought it out from the dungeon into the light.

Nick still found it hard to believe sometimes that he was happy about becoming a husband and father. Still, anything was possible with Sarah by his side.

'You look amazing,' he said softly to her as he took her hand and they turned to face the celebrant.

'You do, too,' she whispered back.

'Ray would have been so proud of you.'

Her hand squeezed his tightly. 'You, too, my darling heart. You, too.'

# THE SICILIAN'S CHRISTMAS BRIDE

## SANDRA MARTON

**Sandra Marton** wrote her first novel while she was still in elementary school. Her doting parents told her she'd be a writer someday and Sandra believed them. In high school and college, she wrote dark poetry nobody but her boyfriend understood, though, looking back, she suspects he was just being kind. As a wife and mother, she wrote murky short stories in what little spare time she could manage, but not even her boyfriend-turned-husband could pretend to understand those. Sandra tried her hand at other things, among them teaching and serving on the board of education in her home town, but the dream of becoming a writer was always in her heart.

At last Sandra realised she wanted to write books about what all women hope to find: love with that one special man; love that's rich with fire and passion; love that lasts forever. She wrote a novel, her very first, and sold it to the Mills & Boon® Modern™ line. Since then, she's written more than sixty books, all of them featuring sexy, gorgeous, larger-than-life heroes. A four-time RITA® Award finalist, she's also received five *Romantic Times BOOKclub* awards for Best Mills & Boon® Modern™of the Year and has been honoured with a Career Achievement Award for Series Romance. Sandra lives with her very own sexy, gorgeous, larger-than-life hero in a sun-filled house on a quiet country lane in the northeastern United States.

Sandra loves to hear from her readers. You can write to her or visit her at www.sandramarton. com.

Dear Reader,

I think we all have special memories, don't you?
One of my favourites has to do with Christmas.
When I was five or six, we spent Christmas in
a beautiful old house in upstate New York. I, a
child of Manhattan, had always worried how Santa
would find me in our big apartment building. And
we had no chimney. How would he get into our
living room? Somehow, it always worked out but,
still, I was never quite sure that it would. That
Christmas, so far from home, I had a new concern.
Would Santa know we weren't in the city?

As my mother tucked me into bed Christmas Eve,
she assured me that he would. She read me *The
Night Before Christmas*, a tradition I would also
keep years later, when I became a mum. After, I
lay awake, wide-eyed, watching the snow fall
outside the window, wondering about Santa and
his reindeer. I was determined not to fall asleep...

Hours later, in the quiet of that dark country night,
I heard something. Bells. Sleigh bells? Sounds on
the roof. A tapping, like little hooves?

My heart began to beat faster.

The fireplace was just outside my partly-closed
bedroom door. I screwed my eyes shut, pulled the
covers over my head, held my breath...

When I awoke Christmas morning, there were gaily
wrapped presents on the hearth.

Santa had found us.

Years later, I asked my parents about that night.
Had my father made those noises? Had my mum?
They didn't know what I was talking about.

Only Santa and I understood!

Love to you all, and a very Happy Christmas,

*Sandra*

# CHAPTER ONE

THE HOTEL BALLROOM was a Christmas fairyland.

Evergreen garlands hung with silver and gold ornaments were draped across the ceiling; elegant white
faux Christmas trees sparkled with tiny gold lights.
Someone said there'd even be a visit from Santa at
midnight, tossing expensive baubles to the well-dressed
and incredibly moneyed crowd.

Nothing could ever compare with New York's first
charity ball of the holiday season.

Dante Russo had seen it all before. The truth was, it
bored the hell out of him. The crowds, the noise, the in-
your-face signs of power and wealth...

But then, for some reason everything bored him lately.

Even—perhaps especially—the high-octane excitement of his current mistress as she clung to his arm.

"Oh, DanteDarling," she kept saying, "oh, oh, oh,
isn't this fabulous?"

That was how she'd taken to addressing him, as if
his name and the supposed-endearment were one
word instead of two. And *fabulous* seemed to be her
favorite adjective tonight. So far, she'd used it to

describe the decorations, the band, their table and the guests.

A month ago, he'd found Charlotte's affectations amusing. Now, he found them almost as irritating as her breathless, little-girl voice.

Dante glanced at his watch. Another hour and he'd make his excuses about an early-morning meeting and leave. She'd protest: it would mean missing Santa's visit. But he'd assure her Santa would bring her something special tomorrow.

A little blue box from Tiffany, delivered to her apartment building not by Saint Nick but by FedEx.

He would see to it the box held something fabulous, Dante thought wryly. Something that would serve not only as a gift to make up for ending the night early but as a goodbye present.

His interest in Charlotte was at an end. He'd sensed it for days. Now, he knew it. He only hoped the breakup would be clean. He always made it clear he wasn't interested in forever, but some women refused to get the message, and—

"DanteDarling?"

He blinked. "Yes, Charlotte?"

"You're not listening!"

"I'm sorry. I, ah, I have a meeting in the morning and—"

"Dennis and Eve were telling everyone about their place in Colorado."

"Yes. Of course. Aspen, isn't it?"

"That's right," Eve said, and sighed wearily. "It's still gorgeous—"

"Fabulous," Charlotte said eagerly.

"But it's not what it used to be. So many people have discovered the town…"

Dante did his best to listen but his attention wandered again. What was the matter with him tonight? He didn't feel like himself at all. Bored or not, he knew better than to let his emotions gain control.

Giving free rein to your feelings was a mistake. It revealed too much, and revealing yourself to others was for fools.

That conviction, bred deep in his Sicilian bones by a childhood of poverty and neglect, had served him well. It had lifted him from the gutters of Palermo to the spires of Manhattan.

At thirty-two, Dante ruled an international empire, owned homes on two continents, owned a Mercedes and a private jet, and had his choice of spectacularly beautiful women.

His money had little to do with that.

He was, as more than one woman had whispered, beautiful. He was tall and leanly muscled, with the hard body of an athlete, the face of Michelangelo's David and the reputation of being as exciting in the bedroom as he was formidable in the boardroom.

In other words, Dante had everything a man could possibly want, including the knowledge that his life could very well have turned out differently. Being aware of that was part of who he was. It helped keep him alert.

Focused.

Everyone said that of him. That he was focused. Tightly so, not just on his business affairs or whatever woman held his interest at the moment but on whatever was happening around him.

Not tonight.

Tonight, he couldn't keep his attention on anything.

He'd already lost interest in the conversation of the others at the table. He took his cue from Charlotte, nodded, smiled, even laughed when it seemed appropriate.

It bothered him that he should be so distracted.

Except, that was the wrong word. What he felt was— What? Restless. As if something was about to happen. Something he wasn't prepared for, which was impossible.

He was always prepared.

Always, he thought... Except for that one time. That one time—

"DanteDarling, you aren't paying attention at all!"

Charlotte was leaning toward him, head tilted at just the right angle to make an offering of her décolletage. She was smiling, but the glint in her eye told him she wasn't happy.

"He's always like this," she said gaily, "when he's planning some devastating business coup." She gave a delicate shudder. "Whatever is it, DanteDarling? Something bloody and awful—and oh, so exciting?"

Everyone laughed politely. So did Dante, but he knew, in that instant, his decision to end things with Charlotte was the right one.

These past couple of weeks, while he'd grown bored she'd grown more demanding. Why hadn't he phoned? Where had he been when she called him? She'd begun using that foolish name for him and now she'd taken to dropping little remarks that made it seem as if she and he were intimate in all the ways he had made clear he never would be.

With any woman. Any woman, even—

"…would love to spend Christmas in Aspen, wouldn't we, DanteDarling?"

Dante forced a smile. "Sorry. I didn't get that."

"Dennis and Eve want us to fly to Aspen," Charlotte purred. "And I accepted."

Dante's eyes met hers. "Did you," he said softly.

"Of course! You know we're going to spend Christmas together. Why on earth would we want to be apart on such a special day?"

"Why, indeed," he said, after a long pause. Then he smiled and rose to his feet. "Would you like to dance, Charlotte?"

Something of what he was thinking must have shown in his face.

"Well—well, not just now. I mean, we should stay here and discuss the party. When to fly out, how long we'll stay—"

Dante took her hand, drew her from her chair and led her from the table. The band was playing a waltz as they stepped onto the dance floor.

"You're angry," she said, her voice affecting that little-girl whisper.

"I'm not angry."

"You are. But it's your own fault. Six weeks, Dante. Six weeks! It's time we took the next step."

"Toward what?" he said, his tone expressionless.

"You know what I mean. A woman expects—"

"You knew what *not* to expect, Charlotte." His mouth thinned; his voice turned cold. "And yet, here you are, making plans without consulting me. Talking as if our arrangement is something it is not." He danced her across the floor and into a corner. "You're right about one thing. It's time we, as you put it, took the next step."

"Are you breaking up with me?" When he didn't answer, two bright spots of color rose in her cheeks. "You bastard!"

"An accurate perception, but it changes nothing. You're a beautiful woman. A charming woman. And a bright one. You knew from the beginning how this would end."

His tone had softened. After all, he had only himself to blame. He should have read the signs, should have realized Charlotte had been making assumptions about the future despite his initial care in making sure she understood they had none. Women seemed to make the same mistake all the time.

Most women, he thought, and a muscle jumped in his cheek.

"I've enjoyed the time we've spent together," he said, forcing his attention back where it belonged.

Charlotte jerked free of his hand. "Don't patronize me!"

"No," he replied, his voice cooling, "certainly not. If you prefer to make a scene, rest assured that I can accommodate you."

Her eyes narrowed. He knew she was weighing her options. An embarrassing public display or a polite goodbye that would make it easy for her to concoct a story to soothe her pride.

"Your choice, *bella*," he said, more softly. "Do we part friends or enemies?"

She hesitated. Then a smile curved her lips. "You can't blame me for trying." Still smiling, she smoothed her palms over the lapels of his dinner jacket. It was a proprietorial gesture and he let her do it; he knew it was for those who might be taking in the entire performance. "But you're cruel, DanteDarling. Otherwise, you wouldn't humiliate me in front of my friends."

"Is that what concerns you?" Dante shrugged. "It's not a problem. We'll go back to our table and finish the evening pleasantly. All right?"

"Yes. That's fine. But Dante?" The tip of her tongue flickered across her lips. "Hear me out, would you?"

"What now?" he said, trying to mask his impatience.

"I know you don't believe in love and forever after, darling. Well, neither do I." She paused. "Still, we could have an interesting life together."

He stared at her in surprise. Was she suggesting marriage? He almost laughed. Still, he supposed he understood. He didn't know Charlotte's exact age but she had to be in her late twenties, old enough to want to find a husband who could support her fondness for expensive living.

As for him, men his age had families. Children to carry forward their names. He had to admit he thought about that from time to time, especially since he'd plucked the name "Russo" from a newspaper article.

Having a child to bear the name was surely a way to legitimatize it.

Charlotte could be the perfect wife. She would demand nothing but his superficial attention and tolerate his occasional affair; she would never interfere in his life. Never fill his head to the exclusion of everything else.

And, just that suddenly, Dante knew what was wrong with him tonight.

A woman had once filled his head to the exclusion of everything else. And, damn her, she was still doing it.

The realization shot through him. He felt his muscles tighten, as if all the adrenaline his body could produce was overwhelming his system.

"Oh, for heaven's sake," Charlotte said, "don't look at me that way! I was only joking."

He knew she hadn't been joking but he decided to go along with it because it gave him something to concentrate on as he walked her back to their table.

Eva greeted them with a coy smile. "Well," she said, "what have you decided? Will we see you in Aspen?"

For a second, he didn't know what she was talking about. His thoughts were sucking him into a place of dark, cold shadows and unwanted memories.

Memories of a woman he thought he'd forgotten.

Then he remembered the gist of the conversation and his promise to Charlotte.

"Sorry," he said politely, "but I'm afraid we can't make it."

Charlotte shot him a grateful look as she took her seat. He squeezed her shoulder.

"I'll be back in a few minutes."

"Going for a cigar?" Dennis said. "Russo? Wait. I'll join you."

But Dante was already making his way through the ballroom, deliberately losing himself in the crowd as he headed for one of the doors. He pushed it open, found himself in a narrow service hallway. A surprised waitress bumped into him, murmured an apology and tried to tell him he'd taken a wrong turn.

He almost told her she was right, except he'd taken that wrong turn three years ago.

He went through another door, then down a short corridor and ended up outside on a docking bay. Once he was sure he was alone, Dante threw back his head and dragged the cold night air deep into his lungs.

*Dio,* he had to be crazy.

All this time, and she was still there. Taylor Sommers, whom he had not seen in three years, was inside him tonight, probably had been for a very long time. How come he hadn't known it?

*You didn't want to know it,* a sly voice in his head told him.

A muscle knotted in his jaw.

No, he thought coldly, no. What was inside him was rage. It was one thing not to let your emotions rule you and another to suppress them, which was what he had done since she'd left him.

He'd kept his anger inside, as if doing so would rid him of it. Now, without warning, it had surfaced along with all the memories he'd carefully buried.

Not of Taylor. Not of what it had been like to be with her. Her whispers in bed.

*Yes. Dante, yes. When you do that, when you do that...*

He groaned at the memory. The need to be inside her had been like a drug. It had brought him close to believing in the ancient superstitions of his people that said a man could be possessed.

He was long past that, had been past it by the time she left him.

It was the rest, what had happened at the end, that

was still with him. Knowing that she believed she'd left him, when it wasn't true.

He had left her.

He'd never had the chance to say, "You made the first move, *cara,* but that's all it was. You ran away before I had a chance to end our affair."

She didn't know that and it drove him crazy. Pathetic, maybe, that it should matter…but it did. Obviously it did, or he wouldn't be standing out here in the cold, glaring at a stack of empty produce cartons and finally admitting that he'd been walking around in a state of smoldering fury since a night like this, precisely like this, late November, cold, snow already in the forecast, when Taylor had left a message on his answering machine.

"Dante," she'd said, "I'm afraid I'll have to cancel our date for tonight. I think I'm coming down with the flu. I'm going to take some aspirin and go to bed. Sorry to inconvenience you."

Sorry to inconvenience you.

For some reason, the oh-so-polite phrase had irritated him. Was *inconvenience* a word for a woman to use to her lover? And what was all that about canceling their date? She was his mistress. They didn't have "dates."

Jaw knotted, he'd reached for the phone to call and tell her that.

But he'd controlled his temper. Actually, there was nothing wrong in what she'd said. *Date* implied that they saw each other when it suited them. When it suited him.

So, why had it pissed him off? Her removed tone. Her impersonal words. And then another possibility had elbowed its way into his brain.

*Maybe,* he'd thought, *maybe I should call and see if she needs something. A doctor. Some cold tablets.*

*Or maybe I should see if she just needs me.*

The thought had stunned him. Need? It wasn't a word in his vocabulary. Nor in Taylor's. It was one of the things he admired about her.

So he'd put the phone aside and gone to the party. Not just any party. *This* party. The same charity, the same hotel, the same guests. He'd eaten what might have been the same overdone filet, sipped the same warm champagne, talked some business with the men at his table and danced with the women.

The women had all asked the same question.

"Where's Taylor?"

"She's not feeling well," he'd kept saying, even as it struck him that he was spending an inordinate amount of time explaining the absence of a woman who was not in any way a permanent part of his life. They'd only been together a couple of months.

Six months, he'd suddenly realized. Taylor had been his mistress for six months. How had that happened?

While he'd considered that, one of the women had touched his arm.

"Dante?"

"Yes?"

"If Taylor's ill, she needs to drink lots of liquids."

He'd blinked. Why tell him what his mistress needed to do?

"Water's good, but orange juice is better. Or ginger tea."

"That wonderful chicken soup at the Carnegie Deli,"

another woman said. "And does she have an inhalator? There's that all-night drugstore a few block away…"

Amazing, he'd thought. Everyone assumed that he and Taylor were living together.

They weren't.

"I prefer that you keep your apartment," he'd told her bluntly, at the start of their relationship.

"That's good," she'd said with a little smile, "because I intended to."

Had she told people something else? Had she deliberately made the relationship seem more than it was?

He'd thought back a few weeks to his birthday. He had no idea how she'd known it was his birthday; he'd never mentioned it. Why would he? And yet, when he'd arrived at her apartment to take her to dinner, she'd told him she wanted to stay in.

"I'm going to cook tonight," she'd said with a little smile. "For your birthday."

He made a habit of avoiding these things, a home-made dinner, a quiet evening, but he couldn't see a way to turn her down without seeming rude so he'd accepted her invitation.

To his amazement, he'd enjoyed the evening.

"Pasta Carbonara," she'd said, as she served the meal. "I remember you ordering it at Luigi's and saying how much you liked it." Her cheeks had pinkened. "I just hope my version is half as good."

It was better than good; it was perfect. So was everything else.

The candles. The bottle of his favorite Cabernet. The flowers.

And Taylor.

Taylor, watching him across the table, her green eyes soft with pleasure. Taylor, blushing again when he said the food was delicious. Taylor, bringing out a cake complete with candles. And a familiar blue box. He'd given boxes like that to more women than he could count, but being on the receiving end had been a first.

"I hope you like them," she'd said as he opened the box on a pair of gold cuff links, exactly the kind he'd have chosen for himself.

"Very much," he'd replied, and wondered what she'd say if he told her this was the first birthday cake, the first birthday gift anyone had ever given him in all his life.

He'd blown out the candles. Taken a bite of the cake. Put on the cuff links and felt something he couldn't define…

"Dante?" Taylor had said, her smooth brow furrowing, "what's the matter? If you don't like the cuff links—"

He'd silenced her in midsentence by gathering her in his arms, taking her mouth with his, carrying her to her bed and making love to her.

Sex with her was always incredible. That night…that night, it surpassed anything he'd ever known with her, with any woman. She was tender; she was passionate. She was wild and sweet and, as he threw back his head and emptied himself into her, she cried out his name and wept.

When it was over, she lay beneath him, trembling. Then she'd brought his mouth to hers for a long kiss.

"Don't leave me tonight," she'd whispered. "Dante. Please stay."

He'd never spent the entire night with her. With any woman. But he'd been tempted. Tempted to keep his arms around her warm body. To close her eyes with soft kisses. To fall asleep with her head on his shoulder and wake with her curled against him.

He hadn't, of course.

Spending the night in a woman's bed had shades of meaning beyond what he needed or expected from a relationship.

Two weeks after that, he'd attended this charity ball without her, listened to people urge him to feed his mistress chicken soup...

And everything had clicked into place.

The birthday supper. The fantastic night of sex. The plea that he not leave her afterward.

Taylor was playing him the way a fisherman who's hooked a big one plays a fish. His beautiful, clever mistress was doing her best to settle into his life. She knew it, his acquaintances knew it. The only person who'd been blind to the scheme was him.

"Excuse me," he'd suddenly said to everyone at the table, "but it's getting late."

"Don't forget the chicken soup," a woman called after him.

Dante had instructed his driver to take him to Taylor's apartment. It was time to set things straight. To make sure she still understood their agreement, that the rules hadn't changed simply because their affair had gone on so long.

In fact, perhaps it was time to end the relationship. Not tonight. Not abruptly. He'd simply see her less often. In a few weeks, he'd take her to L'Etoile for dinner, give her a bracelet or a pair of earrings to remember him by and tell her their time together had been fun but—

But Taylor didn't answer the door when he rang—which reminded him that she'd never given him a key. He hadn't given her one to his place, either, but that was different. He never gave his mistresses keys, but they were always eager to give theirs to him.

And it occurred to him again, as it often did, that Taylor wasn't really his mistress. She insisted on paying her own rent, even though most women gladly let him do it.

"I'm not most women," she'd said when he'd tried to insist, and he'd told himself that was good, that he admired her independence.

That night, however, he saw it for what it was. Just another way to heighten his interest, he'd thought coldly, as he rang the bell again.

Still no answer.

His thoughts turned even colder. Was she out with another man?

No. She was sick. He believed that; she'd sounded terrible on the phone when she'd called him earlier, her voice hoarse and raw.

Dante's heart had skittered. Was she lying unconscious behind the locked door? He took the stairs to the super's basement apartment at a gallop when the damned elevator refused to come, awakened the man and bought his cooperation with a fistful of bills.

Together, they'd gone up to Taylor's apartment. Unlocked the door...

And found the place empty.

His mistress was gone.

Her things were gone, too. All that remained was a trace of her scent in the air and a note, a *note,* goddamn her, on the coffee table.

"Thank you for everything," she had written, "it's been fun." Only that, as if their affair had been a game.

And Dante had swallowed the insult. What else could he have done? Hired a detective to find her? That would only have made his humiliation worse.

Three years. Three years, and now, without warning, it had all caught up to him. The embarrassment. The anger...

"Dante?"

He turned around. Charlotte had somehow managed to find him. She stood on the loading dock, wrapped in a velvet cloak he'd bought her, her face pink with anger.

"Here you are," she said sharply.

"Charlotte. My apologies. I, ah, I came out for a breath of air—"

"You said you wouldn't embarrass me."

"Yes. I know. And I won't. I told you, I only stepped outside—"

"You've been gone almost an hour! How dare you make me look foolish to my friends?" Her voice rose. "Who do you think you are?"

Dante's eyes narrowed. He moved toward her, and something dangerous must have shown in his face because she took a quick step back.

"I know exactly who I am," he said softly. "I am Dante Russo, and whoever deals with me should never forget it."

"Dante. I only meant—"

He took her arm, quick-marched her down a set of concrete steps and away from the dock. An alley led to the street where he hailed a cab, handed the driver a hundred-dollar bill and told him Charlotte's address.

He'd left his topcoat inside the hotel but he didn't give a damn. Coats were easy to replace. Pride wasn't.

"Dante," she stammered, "really, I'm sorry—"

So was he, but not for what had just happened. He was sorry he had lived a lie for the past three years.

Taylor Sommers had made a fool of him. Nobody, *nobody* got away with that.

He took his cell phone from his pocket and called his driver. When his Mercedes pulled to the curb, Dante got in the back and pressed another number on the phone. It was late, but his personal attorney answered on the first ring.

He didn't waste time on preliminaries. "I need a private investigator," he said. "No, not first thing Monday. Tomorrow. Have him call me at home."

Three years had gone by. So what? Someone had once said that revenge was a dish best served cold.

A tight smile curved Dante's hard mouth.

He couldn't have agreed more.

IT WAS A LONG WEEKEND.

Charlotte left endless messages on his voice mail. They ranged from weepy to demanding, and he erased them all.

Saturday morning, he heard from the detective his attorney had contacted. The man asked for everything Dante knew about Taylor.

"Her name," he said, "is Taylor Sommers. She lived in the Stanhope, on Gramercy Park. She's an interior decorator."

There was a silence.

"And?" the man said.

"And what? Isn't that enough?"

"Well, I could use the names of her parents. Her friends. Date of birth. Where she grew up. What schools she attended."

"I've told you everything I know," Dante said coldly.

He hung up the phone, then walked through his bedroom and onto the wraparound terrace that surrounded his Central Park West penthouse. It was cold; the wind had a way of whipping around the building at this height. And it had snowed overnight, not heavily, just enough to turn the park a pristine white.

Dante frowned.

The detective had seemed surprised he knew so little about Taylor, but why would he have known more? She pleased his eye; she was passionate and intelligent.

What more would a man want from a woman?

There had been moments, though. Like the time he'd brought her here for a late supper. It had snowed that night, too. He'd excused himself, gone to make a brief but necessary phone call. When he came back, he'd found the terrace door open and Taylor standing out here, just as he was now.

She'd been wearing a silk dress, a little slip of a thing. He'd taken off his jacket, stepped outside and put it around her shoulders.

"What are you doing, *cara?* It's much too cold for you out here."

"I know," she'd answered, snuggling into his jacket and into the curve of his arm, "but it's so beautiful, Dante." She'd turned her face up to his and smiled. "I love nights like this, don't you?"

Cold nights reminded him of the frigid winters in

Palermo, the way he'd padded his shoes with newspaper in a useless attempt to keep warm.

For some reason he still couldn't comprehend, he'd almost told her that.

Of course, he had not done anything so foolish. Instead, he'd kissed her.

"If you can get over your penchant for cold and snow," he'd said, with a little smile, "we can fly to the Caribbean some weekend and you can help me house-hunt. I've been thinking about buying a place in the islands."

Her smile had been soft. "I'd like that," she'd said. "I'd like it very, very much."

Instantly, he'd realized what a mistake he'd made. He'd asked her to take a step into his life and he'd never meant to do that.

He'd never mentioned the Caribbean again. Not that it mattered, because two weeks later, she'd walked out on him.

Walked out, he thought now, his jaw tightening. Left him to come up with excuses explaining her absence at all those endless Christmas charitable events he was expected to attend.

But he'd solved that problem simply enough.

He'd found replacements for her. He'd gone through that season with an endless array of beautiful women on his arm.

On his arm, but not in his bed. It had been a long time until he'd had sex after Taylor, and even then, it hadn't been the same.

The truth was, it still wasn't. Something was lacking.

Not for his lovers. He knew damned well how to make a woman cry out with pleasure but he felt—what was the word? Removed. That was it. His body went through all the motions, but when it was over, he felt unsatisfied.

Taylor was to blame for that.

What in hell had possessed him, to let her walk away? To let her think she'd ended their affair when she hadn't? A man's ego could take just so much.

By Monday, his anger was at the boiling point. When the private investigator turned up at his office, he greeted him with barely concealed impatience.

"Well? Surely you've located Ms. Sommers. How difficult can it be to find a woman in this city?"

The man scratched his ear, took a notepad from his pocket and thumbed it open.

"See, that was the problem, Mr. Russo. The lady isn't in this city. She's in…" He frowned. "Shelby, Vermont."

Dante stared at him. "Vermont?"

"Yeah. Little town, maybe fifty miles from Burlington."

Taylor, in a New England village? Dante almost laughed trying to picture his sophisticated former lover in such a setting.

"The lady has an interior decorating business." The P.I. turned the page. "And she's done okay. In fact, she just applied for an expansion loan at—"

The P.I. rattled on but Dante was only half listening. He knew where to find Taylor. Everything else was superfluous.

How surprised she'd be, he thought with grim satisfaction, to see him again. To hear him tell her that she hadn't needed to leave him, that he'd been leaving her—

"…just for the two of them. I have the details, if you—"

Dante's head came up. "Just for the two of what?" he said carefully.

"Of them," the P.I. said, raising an eyebrow. "You know, what I was saying about the house she inherited. A couple of realtors suggested she might want something newer and larger but she said no, she wanted a small house in a quiet setting, just big enough for two. For her and, uh… I got the name right here, if you just give me a—"

"A house for two people?" Dante said, in a tone opponents had learned to fear.

"That's right. Her and—here it is. Sam Gardner."

"Taylor." Dante cleared his throat. "And Sam Gardner. They live together?"

"Well, sure."

"And Gardner was with her when she moved in?"

The P.I. chuckled. "Yessir. I mean—"

"I know exactly what you mean," Dante said without inflection. "Thank you. You've been most helpful."

"Yeah, but, Mr. Russo—"

"Most helpful," Dante repeated.

The detective got the message.

Alone, Dante told himself he'd accomplish nothing unless he stayed calm, but a knot of red-hot rage was already blooming in his gut. Taylor hadn't left him because she'd grown bored. She'd left him for another man. She'd been seeing someone, making love with someone, while she'd been with him.

He went to the window and clasped the edge of the sill, hands tightening on the marble the way they wanted to tighten on her throat. Confronting her wouldn't be enough. Beating the crap out of her lover wouldn't be enough, either, although it would damned well help.

He wanted more. Wanted the kind of revenge that her infidelity merited. How dare she make a fool of him? How dare she?

There had to be a way. A plan.

Suddenly, he recalled the P.I.'s words. *She's done well. In fact, she's just applied for an expansion loan at the local bank.*

Dante smiled. There was. And he could hardly wait to put it into motion.

# CHAPTER TWO

TAYLOR SOMMERS POURED a cup of coffee, put it on the sink, opened the refrigerator to get the cream and realized she'd already put it on the table, right alongside the cup she'd already filled with coffee only minutes before.

She took a steadying breath.

"Keep it up," she said, her voice loud in the silence, "and Walter Dennison's going to tell you he was only joking when he said he'd change those loan payments."

Dennison was a nice man; he'd been a friend of her grandmother's. He'd shown compassion and small-town courtesy when Tally fell behind on repaying the home equity loan his bank had granted her.

But he wasn't a fool and only a fool would go on doing that for a woman who behaved as if she were coming apart.

Was that why he wanted to see her today? Had he changed his mind? If he had, if he wanted her to pay the amount the loan called for each month...

Tally closed her eyes.

She'd be finished. The town had already shut down

the interior decorating business she'd been running from home. Without the loan, she'd lose the shop she'd rented on the village green even before it opened because, to put it simply, she was broke.

Flat broke.

Okay, if you wanted absolute accuracy, she had two hundred dollars in her bank account, but it was a drop in the bucket compared to what she needed.

She'd long ago used up her savings. Moving to Vermont, paying for repairs to make livable the old house she'd inherited from her grandmother, just day-to-day expenses for Sam and her had taken a huge chunk of her savings.

Start-up costs for INTERIORS BY TAYLOR had swallowed the rest. Beginning a decorating business, even from home, was expensive. You had to have at least a small showroom—in her case, what had once been an enclosed porch on the back of the house—so that potential clients could get a feel for your work. Paint, fabric, wicker furniture to make the porch inviting had cost a bundle.

Then there were the fabric samples, decorative items like vases and lamps, handmade candles and fireplace accessories… Expensive, all of them. Some catalogs alone could be incredibly pricey. Advertising costs were astronomical but if you didn't reach the right people, all your other efforts were pointless.

Little by little, INTERIORS BY TAYLOR had begun to draw clients from the upscale ski communities within miles of tiny Shelby. Taylor's accounts had still been in the red, but things had definitely been looking up.

And then the town clerk phoned. He was apologetic, but that didn't make his message any less harsh.

INTERIORS BY TAYLOR was operating illegally. The town had an ordinance against home-based businesses.

That Shelby, Vermont, population 8500 on a good day, had ordinances at all had been a surprise. But it did, and this one was inviolate. You couldn't operate a business from your house even if you'd been raised under its roof after your mother took off for parts unknown.

Tally's pleading had gained her a two-month reprieve.

She'd found a soon-to-be-vacant shop on the village green. Each night, long after Sam was asleep, she'd worked and reworked the costs she'd face. The monthly rent. The three-months up-front deposit. The fees for the carpenter, painter and electrician needed to turn the place from the TV-repair shop it had been into an elegant setting for her designs.

And then there were all the things she'd have to buy to create the right atmosphere. Add in the cost of increased advertising and Tally had arrived at a number that was staggering.

She needed $175,000.00.

The next morning, she'd kissed Sam goodbye, put on a white silk blouse and a black suit she hadn't worn since New York. She'd pulled her blond hair into a knot at the base of her neck and gone to see Walter Dennison, who owned Shelby's one and only bank.

Dennison read through the proposal she'd written, looked up and frowned.

"You're asking for a lot of money."

"I know."

"Asking for it in a home equity loan."

"Yes, sir."

"You understand what would happen if you were unable to pay the loan off, Ms. Sommers? That the bank would have the right to foreclose on your house?"

Taylor had nodded. "Yes, sir," she'd said again. "I do."

Dennison had looked at her for a long moment. Then he'd smiled. "You've got your grandmother's gumption, Tally," he'd said, and held out his hand.

The loan was hers.

She'd made the first payment…but not the second. Or the third. The contractors demanded their money according to the schedules she'd agreed to. Things couldn't get worse, she'd thought…

And the furnace in the house went belly-up.

Pride in tatters, Taylor had gone to Dennison again. If he could see his way clear to lower the monthly payments…

He'd sighed and run his fingers through his thinning hair. In the end he'd done it.

Which brought her back to today's phone call. It had come while she and Sam were having breakfast.

"I need to see you, Ms. Sommers," Dennison had said. "Today."

She'd almost stopped breathing. "Is it about my loan?"

There'd been a little pause. Then Dennison had said yes, it was, and she was to come to his office at four.

"Four," he'd repeated, "promptly, please."

The admonition had surprised her. So had the change from Tally to Ms. Sommers. She'd told herself it wasn't a bad sign. A man who wanted to discuss a six-figure loan was entitled to be a little formal, even if he'd known you since you were a baby.

"Of course," she'd said, all cool New York sophistication. Then she'd hung up the phone and tried to smile at Sam, whose eyes were filled with questions.

"Nothing to worry about, babe," Tally had said airily.

Sam had grinned a Sam-grin, at least until she said she might not be home until suppertime.

"You can visit the Millers," she'd said reassuringly. "You know how much you like them."

She'd smoothed things over by promising they'd have the entire weekend together, doing what Sam liked most: snuggling with her on the sofa, watching videos and eating popcorn.

Dante Russo had probably never watched a video or eaten popcorn in his life...

And what was that man doing in her head again?

Who gave a damn what Dante Russo did or didn't do? He was history. Besides, he'd never meant anything more to her than what she'd meant to him. New York was filled with relationships like theirs. Two consenting adults going out together, being seen together...

Having sex together.

Tally's eyes closed. Memories rushed in. Scents. Tastes. Sensations. Dante's hands, deliciously rough on her skin. His mouth, demanding surrender as he kissed her. His face above her, his silver eyes dark as storm clouds, his sensual lips drawn back with passion...

She swung toward the sink, dumped her coffee and rinsed out the cup.

What stupid thoughts to have today of all days, when she had to be at her best. Still, she understood why she would think of Dante.

Her mouth curved in a bitter smile.

This was an anniversary of sorts. She'd left Dante

Russo a few weeks before Christmas, three years ago. All it took was the scent of pine and the sound of carols to bring the memories rushing back.

She wouldn't let that happen. Dante had no place in the new life she'd built for herself. For herself and Sam.

He was nothing to her anymore.

Or to Sam.

Sam didn't know Dante existed. And Dante certainly didn't know about Sam. He never would, either. She would see to that.

Tally knew her former lover well.

Dante hadn't wanted her and surely wouldn't have understood why she wanted Sam… But that didn't mean he'd simply let her have Sam, if he knew.

Her former lover could be charming but underneath he was cold, determined and ruthless. She refused to think about how he might react if he knew everything.

Tally sighed and turned on the kitchen lights. Night had fallen; it came early to these northern latitudes. The coming storm the weatherman had predicted rattled the old windows.

She'd fled New York on a night like this. Cold, dark, with snow in the forecast.

What a wreck she'd been that night! Pretending to be sick, then packing her clothes and scribbling that final note. All she'd been able to think about was getting away before Dante showed up.

She wasn't stupid. She'd known he hadn't wanted her anymore. He'd been removed and distant for a while and sometimes she'd caught him watching her with a look on his face that made her want to weep.

He was bored with her. And getting ready to end

their affair, but she wouldn't let that happen. She'd end
it first. It would be quicker, less humiliating...

And safer, because by then she had a secret she'd
never have been foolish enough to share with him.

So she'd made plans to leave him. And she'd done it
so he wouldn't be able to find her, even if he looked for
her. Not that she thought he would. Why would a man
go after a woman when she'd saved him the trouble of
getting rid of her?

Even if he had, maybe out of all that macho Sicilian
arrogance made all the more potent by his power, his
wealth, his gorgeous face and body—even if he had,
he'd never have found her. He'd never dream she'd flee
to a tiny village in New England. He knew nothing
about her. In their six months together, he'd never asked
her questions about herself.

Not real ones.

*Would you prefer Chez Nicole or L'Etoile for dinner?*
he'd ask. *Shall I get tickets for the ballet or the symphony?*

Things a man would ask any woman. Never anything
more important.

Well, yes. He'd asked her other things. Whispered
them, in that husky voice that was a turn-on all by itself.

*Do you like it when I touch you this way?* And if what
he was doing seemed too much, if it made her tremble
in his arms, he'd kiss her deeply and say, *Don't stop me,
bellissima. Let me. Yes. Let me do this. Yes. Like that.
Just like that...*

She was trembling even now, just remembering
those moments.

"You're a fool," Tally said, her voice sharp in the
silence of the kitchen.

Sex with Dante had been incredible, but sex was all it was, even though lying beneath him, feeling the power of his penetration, his possession, sometimes made her want to weep with joy. But it didn't make up for the fact that he'd never once spent the entire night in her bed or asked her to come to his.

*Stay with me,* she'd wanted to say, oh, so many times. But she hadn't. Only the once, when the words had slipped out before she could stop them...

Only the once, when she'd forgotten that all her lover wanted was her body, not her heart.

Tally turned her back to the window.

So what?

Why would she have wanted a man to tie her down, give her a baby and then turn his ever-wandering eyes elsewhere as her father had done, as a man like Dante Russo would surely do?

It was the meeting with Walter Dennison that had her feeling so strange, that was all. Once she put that behind her, she'd be fine.

And it was time to get moving. *Be here at four, Ms. Sommers, and please be prompt.*

She smiled as put on her coat and grabbed her car keys. All those years in New York had made her forget how pedantic a true Yankee could be.

AS USUAL, the weatherman had it wrong. Snow was already falling as if someone were shaking a featherbed over the town.

The snow dusting the woods and fields with a blanket of white as Tally drove past would have made a beautiful Christmas card. In the real world, it made for a dangerous drive. The narrow road that led into the heart of town already wore a thin coating of black ice, and the new snow hid stretches of asphalt as slick as glass.

Her old station wagon needed better snow tires. The rear end slewed sickeningly as she turned onto Main Street and her stomach skidded with it, but there were no other vehicles on the road and she came through the turn without harm to anything but her nerves.

Only two cars were parked in the bank's lot, the aged maroon Lincoln she recognized as Dennison's and a big, shiny black SUV that looked as if it could climb Everest in a blizzard and come through laughing.

Dennison would have sent his employees home early because of the storm. The SUV probably belonged to some tourist on his way to ski country who'd stopped to use the ATM.

Tally parked and got out of the station wagon. The double doors to the bank opened as she reached them, revealing Walter Dennison wearing a black topcoat over his usual gray suit.

"You're late, Ms. Sommers."

He whispered the words. And shot a quick look over his shoulder. Tally felt a stab of panic. The black car. The paleness of Dennison's face. His whisper.

Was the bank being held up?

"I'm sorry," she said, trying to peer past him, "but the roads—"

"I understand." He hesitated. "Ms. Sommers. Tally. There's something you need to know."

*Oh, God.* It was true. She'd walked into a holdup in progress—

"I sold the bank."

She stared at him blankly. "What?"

"I said, I sold the bank."

He might as well have been speaking another language. Sold the bank? How could he have done that? The Dennison family had started the Shelby Bank in the early 1800s.

"I don't understand, Mr. Dennison. Why would you—"

"It's nothing for the town to worry about. The new owner will keep everything just as it is." Dennison cleared his throat. "Almost everything."

His eyes shifted from hers, and Tally's stomach dropped. There could only be one reason he'd wanted to see her.

"What about the new payment arrangements on my loan?"

She saw Dennison's adam's apple move up, then down. He opened his mouth as if he were going to speak. Instead, he shouldered past her, turned up his collar and went out into the storm. Tally stared after him as his lean figure was lost in a swirling maelstrom of white.

"Mr. Dennison! Wait!" Her voice rose. "Will this affect my loan? You said the new owner will keep everything just as it is—"

"Not quite everything," a familiar voice said.

And even as her heart pounded, as she swung toward the open bank doors and told herself it couldn't be true, she knew what she would see.

That voice could belong to only one man.

DANTE SMILED when Taylor turned toward him.

Her face was white with shock.

Excellent. He'd wanted her stunned by the sight of

him. Things were going precisely as he'd intended, despite how quickly he'd had to work. He'd put his plan in motion in less than a week, first convincing the old man to sell and then getting the authorities to approve the sale, but he was Dante Russo.

People always deferred to him.

This morning, he'd phoned Dennison and told him he'd be there at three. Told him, as well, to notify Taylor to be at the bank at four.

Promptly at four.

And, of course, not to mention anything about the bank's new ownership.

Dante's lips curved in a tight smile. He'd figured Taylor would be on edge to start with. A woman who'd put up her home as equity for a loan of $175,000.00 she couldn't pay would not be at ease. Add in Dennison's refusal to explain the reason for the meeting and the warning to be prompt, her nerves would be stretched to the breaking point.

His smile faded. The only thing that would have made this more interesting was if Samuel Gardner was with her, but from the investigator's comments, he'd gathered that his former mistress's new lover didn't stand up to life's tougher moments.

"Why didn't Sam Gardner sign for the loan?" he'd asked Dennison.

The old man had looked at him as if he were insane.

"Buying a bank on a seeming whim, suggesting something anyone in town would know is impossible... You have a strange sense of humor, Mr. Russo," he'd said with a thin-lipped Yankee smile.

Dante stood away from the door.

Dennison was wrong. There was nothing the least bit humorous about this situation. It was payback, pure and simple.

And it was time Taylor knew it.

"Aren't you going to come inside and face me, *cara?*" he said, his tone deliberately soft and coaxing. "Perhaps not. Facing me is not your forte, is it?"

He saw her stiffen. She probably wanted to run, but she didn't. Instead, she raised her chin, squared her shoulders and stepped inside the bank. He had to admire her courage, the way she was girding herself for confrontation.

She had no way of knowing that nothing she could do would be enough. The news he was going to give her was bad, and it delighted him to do it.

"Hello, Dante."

Her voice trembled. Her face had taken on some color, though it was still pale. Three years. Three years since he'd seen her…

And she was still beautiful.

More beautiful than his memory of her, if that were possible. Was it time that had made her mouth seem even softer, her eyes wider and darker?

Still, time had not been completely kind. It had affected her in other ways.

Purple shadows lay beneath her eyes. Her hair was pulled back in an unbecoming knot and he had the indefensible urge to close the distance between them, take out the pins and let all those lustrous cinnamon strands tumble free.

He let his gaze move over her slowly, from her face all the way to her feet and back again. A frown creased his forehead. He'd never seen her in anything but elegantly tailored clothing. Designer suits and gowns, spiked heels that could give a man dangerous fantasies, her face perfectly made up, her hair impeccably cut and styled.

Things were different now. The lapels of her coat were frayed. Her boots were the no-nonsense kind meant for rough weather. Her hair was in that ridiculous knot and her face was bare of everything but lipstick—lipstick and the shadows of exhaustion under her eyes.

He spoke without thinking. "What's happened to you?" he said sharply. "Have you been ill?"

"How nice of you to ask."

She was still pale but her gaze was steady and her words were brittle with sarcasm. He moved quickly; before she could step back he was a breath away, his hand wrapped around her arm.

"I asked you a question. Answer it."

A flush rose in her cheeks. "I'm not ill. I'm simply living in the real world. It's a place where people work hard for what they have. Where you can't just snap your fingers and expect everyone to leap to do your bidding, but then, what would you know of such things?"

What, indeed? It was none of her business, of anyone's business, that he'd started his life scrounging for money, that he'd worked his hands raw in construction jobs when he came to the States, or that he could still remember what it was like to go to sleep hungry.

He'd never snapped his fingers and never would, but he'd be damned if he'd explain that to anyone.

"And your lover? He permits this?"

She looked at him as if he'd lost his mind. "My what?"

"Another question you don't want to answer. That's all right. I have plenty of time."

Tally wrenched free of his grasp. "I'm the one with questions, Dante. What are you doing here?"

"We haven't seen each other in a long time, *cara*." A slow smile that turned her blood to ice eased across his lips. "Surely, we have other things to talk about first."

"We have nothing to talk about."

"But we do. You know that."

She didn't know anything. That was the problem. What did he know? Did he know about Sam? She didn't think so. Surely, he'd have tossed that at her already, if he did.

Then, what did he want? He wasn't here for a visit. He hadn't bought the Shelby bank on a whim...

The loan. Her loan. Oh God, oh God...

"Ah," he said slyly, "your face is an open book. Have you thought of some things we might wish to discuss?"

She couldn't let him see her fear. There had to be some way she could gain the upper hand.

"What I know," Tally said, "is that we never talked in the past. We went to dinner, to parties..." She took a steadying breath. "And we went to bed."

His mouth twisted. Had she struck a nerve?

"I'm glad you remember that."

"Is that why you came here, Dante? To remind me that we used to have sex together? Or to ask why I left you?" Somehow, she managed a chilly smile. "Really, I thought you'd understand. My note—"

"Your note was a bad joke."

Tally shrugged her shoulders. "It was honest. Or did it never occur to you that a woman is no different from a man? I mean, yes, we can pretend in ways a man can't, but sooner or later, things grow, well, old."

Dante's face contorted with anger. "You're a liar!"

"Come on, admit it. We'd been together for months. It was fun for a long time but then—"

She gasped as he caught hold of her and encircled her throat with his hand.

"I remember how you were in bed," he said, his voice a low growl. "Are you telling me it was all a performance?"

He tugged her closer, until her body brushed his and she had to tilt back her head to look into his eyes. It was deliberate, damn him, a way of emphasizing his strength, his size, his domination.

God, how she hated him! Three years, three endless years, and he was still furious because she'd walked out on him, but she'd done what she had to do to survive. To protect her secret from his unpredictable Sicilian ego.

"You were fire in my arms." His eyes, the color of smoke, locked on hers. She tried to look away but his hand was like a collar around her throat. When he urged her chin up, she had no choice but to meet his gaze. "You cried out as I came inside you. Your womb contracted around me. Would you have me believe you faked that, too?"

"Is it impossible for you to be a gentleman?" Tally said, hating herself for the way her voice shook.

His smile was slow and sexy and so dangerous it made her heartbeat quicken.

"But I was a gentleman with you. Was that a mistake? Perhaps you didn't want a gentleman in your bed." She gasped as he forced her head back. "Is that why you ran away in the middle of the night?"

"I left you, period. Don't make it sound so dramatic."

"Left me for what, exactly? The glory of an existence in the middle of nowhere? A bank account with nothing in it?" His tone turned silken. "I think not, *cara*. I think you left me for a new lover who isn't a gentleman at all."

"I don't know what you're talking about!"

He thrust his fingers into her hair. The pins that held it confined clattered sharply against the marble floor as the strands of gold-burnished cinnamon came loose and fell over her shoulders.

"Is that it? Was I too gentle with you?" He wound her hair around his fist and lowered his head until his face was an inch from hers. "Had you hoped I would do things to you, demand things of you, that people only whisper about?"

"Dante. This is— It's crazy. I don't— I didn't…" She swallowed dryly. "Let me go."

She'd meant the words to be a command. Instead, they were a whisper. He smiled with amusement, and she felt an electric jolt in her blood.

"I said, let go… Or did you come here thinking you could bully me back into your arms?"

His eyes grew dark; she saw his mouth twist. The seconds ticked away and then, when her heart seemed ready to leap from her breast, he thrust her from him, stepped back and folded his arms.

"Never that," he said coolly. "And you're right. Things were over between us. I knew it. In fact, that was the reason I went to see you that night. I wanted to tell you we were finished." He gave a quick smile. "As you say, *cara,* things get old."

She'd known the truth but hearing it made it worse.

Still, she showed no reaction. He wanted her to squirm, and she'd be damned if she would.

"Is that what this is about? That the great Dante Russo wants to be sure I understand I made the first move only because your timing was off?"

Dante chuckled. "Bright as always, Taylor—though you surely don't believe I bought this bank and made this trip only so I could tell you it was pure luck you ended our affair before I did."

Tally moistened her lips with the tip of her tongue. She was dying inside, but she'd be damned if she'd let him know it.

"No. I'm not that naive. You bought the bank because—" Desperately, she ran through the terms of the loan in her mind. Could he do that? Could he cancel what Dennison had already approved? "Because you think you can cancel my loan."

"Think?" he said, very softly. "You underestimate me. I can do whatever I wish, but canceling a loan that already exists would take more time and effort than it's worth." He smiled. "So I'm going to do the next best thing. I'm reinstating the original repayment terms."

Her gaze flew to his. "Reinstating them?" she said stupidly. "I don't understand."

"It's simple, *cara*," he said, almost gently. "As of now, you will pay the amount you are supposed to pay each month."

Tally thought of the four-figure number the loan called for. She was paying a quarter of that amount now, and barely managing it.

"That's—it's out of the question. I can't possibly—"

"Additionally, you will pay the amount that's in arrears." He took a slip of paper from his pocket and held it out toward her. His lips curved. "Plus interest, of course."

Tally looked at the number on the paper and laughed. It was either that or weep.

"I don't have that kind of money!"

"Ah." Dante sighed. "I thought not. In that case, you leave me no choice but to start foreclosure proceedings against your home."

She felt the blood drain from her face. "Foreclosure proceedings?"

"This was a home equity loan. You put up your house as collateral." Another quick, icy smile. "If you don't understand what that means, perhaps your lover can explain it to you."

"Are you crazy?" Tally's voice rose. "You can't do this! You can't take my house. You can't!" Her hands came up like a fighter's, fists at the ready as if she would beat him into understanding the horror of his plan. "Damn you, there are rules!"

"You've forgotten what you know about me," Dante said coldly. "I make my own rules."

He proved it by gathering her into his arms and kissing her.

# CHAPTER THREE

HE WAS KISSING HER, Dante told himself, because she'd lied to him a few minutes ago.

Why else would he want her in his arms, except to make her confess to the lie?

Taylor had never faked her responses in bed, and he'd be damned if he'd let her pretend she had.

He was over her, but she knew just the right buttons to push. Well, so did he. He'd kiss her until she melted against him the way she used to and then he'd step back and say, *You see, Taylor? That's the price liars pay.*

Which was why he was kissing her.

Or trying to.

The problem was that he had cornered a wildcat. She fought back, twisted her head to the side to avoid his mouth and pummeled his shoulders with her fists.

When none of that worked, she sank her teeth in his ear lobe so hard he hissed with pain.

"Damn you, woman!"

"Let go of me, you—you—"

Her fist flew by his jaw. Grimly, Dante snared both her hands in one of his and pinned them to his chest. Her knee came up but he felt it happening and yanked her hard against him to immobilize her. She was helpless now, pinned between him and the wall beside the double doors.

"Take your hands off me, Russo! If you don't, so help me—"

"So help you, what? What will you do? How will you stop me from proving what a little liar you are?"

"I don't know what you're talking about. I am not a—"

He bent his head and captured her mouth with his. She nipped his lip, her teeth sharp as a cat's. He tasted blood but if she thought that would stop him, she didn't know him very well.

He would win this battle.

He had the right to know why she'd lied about what she'd felt when he made love to her. And to know why she'd left him.

He wanted answers and, damn it, he was going to get them.

He caught her face in his hands. Kissed her again, angling his mouth over hers, penetrating her with his tongue. He remembered how she'd loved it when he kissed her this way. Deep. Wet. Hot. He'd loved kisses like this, too...

He still did.

*Dio,* the feel of her in his arms. Her breasts, soft against his chest. Her hips, cradling his erection.

He wanted her, and it had nothing to do with anger.

It was the feel of her. The taste. The scent of her skin. He remembered all of it, everything making love to her had done to them both, and his kiss gentled, his touch turned from demand to caress, and a little sigh whispered from her lips to his.

She was trembling, but not with fear.

It was with desire. For this. For him.

Something began to unlock inside him. Something so primitive he couldn't put a name to it. He only knew that the woman in his arms still belonged to him.

He swept his hands into her hair. All that lush, cinnamon-hued silk tumbled over his fingers.

"Tell me you want me," he said, his voice rough and thick.

She shook her head in denial. "No," she whispered.

But her eyes were pools of darkness as she looked up at him, as her hands spread over his chest.

"I don't," she said, "I don't…"

He took her mouth again and suddenly she gave the wild little cry he had heard her make a thousand times in the past. It excited him as much now as it had then, and when she rose on her toes and wound her arms around his neck, whispered "Dante," as if he were the only man in the world who could ever make her feel this way, he went crazy with desire.

It had been so long. Oh, so long since he'd possessed her. He was on fire…and so was she.

Saying her name, blind to everything but passion, Dante fumbled with the buttons of her coat. When they didn't come undone quickly enough, he cursed and tore the coat open.

He had to cup her breasts or he would die. Had to thrust his knee between her thighs and hear her cry out again as she moved against him. Had to shove up her skirt, slip his hand between her thighs and, yes oh yes, feel her heat, yes, feel the wetness of her desire, yes, yes…

Her head fell back like a flower on a wind-bent stalk.

She whispered his name over and over, knotted her fingers in his hair as she lifted herself to him.

Blindly, he lifted her off her feet. Spread her thighs. Reached for his zipper. Now. Right now. He would be inside her. Lost in her silken folds...

"Mr. Dennison? I didn't finish cleanin' but considerin' the storm's turnin' into a blizzard, an'... Whoa!"

The thin, shocked voice had all the power of an explosion.

Dante whirled around, automatically shielding Taylor with his body. A grizzled old man in overalls and work boots stood next to the tellers' cages, his eyes wide and his jaw somewhere down around his ankles.

"Who," Dante said coldly, "are you?"

Tally pulled the lapels of her coat together and peered past Dante's shoulder, heart thumping in her ears.

"It's Esau Staunton. The janitor," she whispered in a shaky voice.

The old man was also Shelby's biggest gossip. By tomorrow, the whole town would know what had happened here this afternoon. She gave a soft moan of despair, and Dante put his arm around her and drew her forward so that she was pressed against his side. She stiffened and would have moved away but he spread his hand over her hip, the pressure of it insistent.

Was he trying to brand her? Or was he telling her this wasn't finished? Either way, she had to let him do it. Her legs had turned to jelly.

"Is that your name?" Dante said pleasantly. "Staunton?"

The old man swallowed audibly. "That's me." His

eyes danced to Taylor, then back to Dante. "Where's Mr. Dennison?"

"Mr. Dennison no longer owns this bank. I do. And you're right, Mr. Staunton. You should leave now, before the storm gets worse."

"You sure?" Again, the rheumy gaze fell on Taylor. "My boy's just pulled up at the curb in that red pickup, but, ah, if you or the lady wants—"

"Go home, Mr. Staunton," Dante said, his tone still pleasant but now backed with steel.

"Oh. Sure. Sure, I'll do that. Mr., ah, Mr.—"

"Russo. And there's one last thing." Dante spoke softly, in that same polite but unyielding voice. "I'm sure you understand that Ms. Sommers wouldn't want anyone to know about her fainting spell."

"Her fainting—"

"Surely, I can trust you to be discreet. People who work for me always are. And you do want to work for me, Esau, don't you?"

Another audible swallow. "Yessir. I do."

"Excellent. In that case, have a pleasant weekend."

The old man nodded and opened the double doors. The wind filled the room with its icy breath as he scrambled into the red pickup, which disappeared into the swirling snow.

"The old man was right," Dante said. "The storm's turned into a blizzard."

Tally stared at him. How could he talk about the weather after what he'd just done? Forcing his kisses on her. His caresses. If the janitor hadn't turned up, who knew what would have happened?

As for his admonitions to the old man—did he really

think they meant anything here? By tomorrow, this sordid little story would be everywhere.

Not that it mattered.

Without a house, without an income, she and Sam wouldn't be living in Shelby much longer.

"Nothing to say, *cara*?"

She wrenched free of his encircling arm. "You've done what you came to do, Dante. More, thanks to…to that performance just now."

His eyebrows rose. "Is that what you call it?"

Amusement tinged the words. Oh, how she wanted to slap that smug, masculine smile from his face.

"You are—you are despicable. Do you understand? You are the most despicable, contemptible—"

The world blurred. She raised her hand and swung it, but his fingers curled around her wrist.

"Such a temper, *bellissima*. And all because I caught you in a lie." His smile vanished. "You wanted me three years ago and you want me now."

"If you ever come near me again—"

"Don't make threats, Taylor. Not unless you're prepared to back them up."

She wanted to scream. To weep. To lunge at him again—but none of that would change anything. Because of him, her life had almost come apart before. Now, it lay in tatters at her feet.

The only thing left was a dignified retreat.

"You're right," she said, forcing herself to sound calm. "No threats. Just a promise. I don't ever want to see you again. If you come after me, I'll go to court and charge you with harassment. Is that clear?"

He laughed. And, before he could stop her a second time, Tally slapped his face.

Fury darkened his eyes. He reached for her, a harsh Sicilian oath spilling from his lips, but she slipped by him, yanked the doors open and ran.

She heard him shout her name but she didn't look back. The parking lot was a sea of white; the wind tore at her with icy talons as she fought her way to her station wagon, pulled the door open, got behind the wheel and slammed down the lock.

Just in time. A second later, Dante grabbed the door handle, then banged his fist against the window.

"Taylor! Open this door."

Her hands were shaking. It took two tries before she could jab the key into the ignition. The engine coughed, coughed again—and died.

A sob burst from her throat. "Come on," she said, turning the key, "come on, damn it. Start!"

"Taylor!" Another blow against the window. "What in hell do you think you're doing?"

Getting away. That was what she was doing. Dante had destroyed everything she'd built over the last years. He'd taken her home with a stroke of the pen, her pride with a kiss she hadn't wanted, her reputation with an X-rated scene she didn't want to think about.

And all he'd proved was what they'd both already known, that he was powerful and brutal, that he had no heart. That he could still make her respond to him, make her forget what he was and drown in his kisses....

"Taylor!"

She turned the key again. Not even a cough this time. *Calm down,* she told herself. Take it easy. The engine needed work, she knew that, but it had gotten her here, hadn't it?

The car wouldn't start because of the cold, that was all. Or maybe she'd flooded it. You could fit what she knew about cars inside a thimble and have room for the rest of the sewing kit, but wasn't there something about not giving a cold engine too much—

The station wagon rocked under the force of Dante's fist.

"Damn you, woman, are you out of your mind? Get out of that car! You can't drive in a blizzard."

She couldn't stay here, either. Not with him. And there was Sam to worry about. Was Sam safe at the Millers'? Yes. Of course. Sheryl and Dan were Sam's friends as well as hers. Still, she'd worry until she reached home.

If there was one thing life had taught her, it was that anything was possible.

One last try. Turn the key. Touch the gas pedal lightly...

Nothing. Nothing! Tally screamed in frustration and pounded the heels of her hands against the steering wheel.

"Listen to me," Dante said, calmly now, as if he were trying to talk sense to a child.

How could she not listen? They were inches apart, separated only by glass.

"Come back inside until the storm is over. I won't touch you. I swear it."

She almost laughed. What could he possibly know of a New England winter? The storm might last for days. Days, alone with him? With a man who'd just promised not to touch her in a way that made it clear he was sure she was helpless against him?

"Taylor. Be reasonable. We'll phone for help. This town has snowplows, doesn't it?"

Of course it did. But would the phones work? The first thing that always failed in bad weather were the telephone lines.

"Damn you, woman," Dante roared. "Can't you be without your lover for a few hours? Would you risk your neck, just to get back to him?"

So much for logic and reason.

Dante cursed, yanked at the door and it flew open. Tally grabbed for the handle but he was already leaning into the car, gathering her into his arms and striding to the bank through the blinding snow, head bent against the shrieking wind.

When they reached the entrance, he put her down.

"Just stand still," he said grimly. "Once we're inside, I'll call the police. For all I give a damn, you can lock yourself in the vault until they arrive."

He reached for the brass handle and pulled.

Nothing happened.

He grunted, wrapped both hands around the handle and pulled harder. But the doors were locked.

He spat out a word in Sicilian. Tally didn't need a translator to know what it meant. Here was one situation he couldn't control. Neither could she. The doors were probably on a timer. They wouldn't open until Monday.

People died in storms like this, and she knew it.

So, evidently, did Dante.

He picked her up again. She didn't fight him this time. The footing was slippery; he stumbled, recovered his balance and she automatically wrapped her arms around his neck. Snow crunched underfoot as he made his way toward the black SUV she knew must be his. Halfway there, he dug his keys from his pocket, pointed the remote at the vehicle and unlocked it.

He put her in the passenger seat, hurried to the driver's side and got in. For a long moment, they sat without looking at each other. Then he took a cell phone from his pocket and flipped it open.

"It won't work," Tally said wearily, leaning back in her seat.

Dante turned toward her. Her face was pale. He sensed that her anger had given way to resignation. It was an emotion neither of them could afford in a situation like this.

"Well, then," he said briskly, "we'll just have to come up with another plan."

He turned the ignition key so that he could read the instrument panel. The gas gauge, in particular, though he knew what he'd find. He'd been in such a damned rush to get to the bank before Taylor arrived…

One look confirmed what he'd suspected.

"We don't have much gas. Just enough to run the engine for maybe twenty, thirty minutes. After that—" *After that, they'd freeze.* "So," he said, again in that brisk tone, "here's what we're going to do. I'll go for help. You stay here and turn on the engine every ten minutes. Let the car warm up, then shut if off. Do that as long as you can and I'll do my best to find help quickly."

"Don't be a fool! You won't get a hundred yards."

"Why, *cara,*" he said, the words laced with sarcasm, "I didn't think you cared."

She didn't. But she did care about Sam. A moment ago, she'd almost let despair overtake her. Now she knew she couldn't let that happen. She had to live. To live for Sam.

There was only one choice. It was a risk in endless ways, but staying here was worse.

She took a deep breath. "Are you a good driver?"

"Of course."

Such macho intensity! Any other time, she'd have laughed.

"And is there enough gas in the tank to go fifteen miles?"

He nodded. "Just about."

"Then start the car. I'll get us to my house. My neighbor has a truck and snowplow. He can lead you to a place near the highway—tow you, if necessary— where there's a gas station and a motel. You'll be fine there until the storm's over."

"And you? Will you be fine, as well?"

Tally looked at Dante. His eyes were cool, making it clear his was a polite question and nothing more.

"I'm not your concern," she said. "I never was."

A muscle knotted in his jaw. Then he nodded, turned the engine on and headed out of the parking lot and into the teeth of the storm.

THE WORLD HAD TURNED into an undulating sea of white. Shifts in the wind's direction revealed only an occasional landmark, but that was enough.

The heavy vehicle, Dante's skill at the wheel and Tally's knowledge of the roads combined to get them safely to her driveway.

They battled their way to the door. Tally dug out her keys; Dante automatically reached for them as he used to when he saw her home in New York, and they waged a silent, brief struggle until he held up his hands in surrender and let her unlock the door herself.

She paused in the doorway.

The danger of the drive here had deprived her of rational thought. Now she was making up for it with frantic desperation. Were any of Sam's things in the kitchen? She didn't think so. Besides, it was too late to worry about it now.

If there were, she'd come up with some kind of explanation. In the last hour, she'd learned to be an accomplished liar.

She stepped into the room, fingers mentally crossed, with Dante close behind her, and reached for the light switch. The room remained dark. The power was out, as she'd figured it would be. The phone, too. All she heard when she picked up the handset was silence.

"It would seem you're stuck with a guest," Dante said coolly.

Tally didn't answer. She felt her way to the cupboard and took out the candles and matches she kept handy for just such occasions. When the candles were lit, she put one on the sink and another on the round wooden table near the window.

A shudder raced through her. The kitchen was the smallest room in the house but an hour or two without the furnace going had turned it into a walk-in refrigerator.

"Are you cold?"

"I'm fine."

Dante frowned, shrugged off his leather jacket and

draped it around her shoulders. "You'll never be a good liar, *cara*."

"I don't need—"

"You damned well do! Keep the jacket until the room warms up." He jerked his chin at the old stone fireplace that took up most of one long wall. "Is that real?"

"Of course it's real," Tally said brusquely, trying not inhale the scents of night and leather and man that enveloped her. "This is New England, not Manhattan. Nobody here has time for pretence."

A smile twisted across his mouth. "What an interesting observation," he said softly, "all things considered."

She felt her face heat. "I didn't mean—"

"No. I'm sure you didn't." He held out his hand. "Give me those matches and I'll make a fire."

"That's not necessary."

"Nothing is necessary," he said curtly. "Not if it involves me, is that correct?"

He'd come so close to the truth that she was afraid to meet his eyes, but that had been their initial agreement, hadn't it? Their relationship had been based on accommodation, not necessity. No strings. No commitment. No leaning on him for anything…

"Look, I know you want me gone," he said impatiently, "and believe me, I'll be happy to comply, but until then I'll be damned if I'm going to freeze just so you can prove a point. Give me the matches."

He was right, even if she hated to admit it. She tossed him the matches and watched as he knelt before her grandmother's old brick hearth and built a fire. Just seeing the orange flames made her feel better and she moved closer to them, hands outstretched so she could catch some of their warmth.

"Better?"

Tally nodded. All she could do now was wait for the storm's power to abate. At least she wasn't worried about Sam anymore. She'd seen the Millers' lights glowing when they drove past their house. She'd forgotten that Dan and Sheryl had a generator. Their place would be snug. Sam would have a hot meal, a warm bed…

"So. You inherited this from your grandmother?"

Her gaze shot to Dante. Arms folded, face unreadable, he was looking around the kitchen as if it were an alien planet. It probably was, to a man accustomed to luxury.

"Yes," she replied coldly. "And now I'm about to lose it to you."

"And where is your lover? Out of town? Or in another room, afraid to face me?"

"I told you, I don't have a lover. And if I did, why would he fear you? My life is my own, Dante. You have no part in it."

"You made that clear the night you ran away."

"For God's sake, are we going to talk about that again?" Tally marched to the stove, filled a kettle with water, took it to the hearth and knelt down, searching for the best place to put it. "I left you. I was absolutely free to do that. I know it's hard to face, but I didn't need your permission."

"Common courtesy demanded more than that note."

"I don't think so."

"Damn it," he growled, clasping her shoulders and

drawing her up beside him, "I'm tired of you dancing away from my questions. I want to know the reason you left."

"I told you. Our affair was over." She looked straight into his eyes. "And we both knew it."

She was right…wasn't she? Hadn't he come to the same conclusion? That it was time to end things? Not that it mattered. He *hadn't* ended the relationship. She had.

Wasn't that the reason he was here? Except, she was doing it again. Taking the upper hand, and he didn't like it.

"I never gave you the right to speak for me," he said sharply.

"No. You didn't. So I'll speak for myself." She took a deep breath and turned away. "I wanted a change."

Dante's mouth thinned. "You mean, you became involved with another man."

"That's ridiculous! I didn't—"

She cried out as he caught her and swung her toward him. "More lies," he growled.

"For the last time, there is no other man!"

"There is. I know his name." His hands dug into her flesh. "Now I want to know if you respond to him as you did to me a little while ago."

"Respond?" She gave a harsh laugh. "Is that what you call it? You—you forced yourself on me!"

It was a foolish thing to say. His nostrils flared like a stallion's at the scent of a mare in heat.

"You don't learn, do you?" he said softly. "You keep making statements and I end up having to prove that they're lies."

Tally looked up into the face of the man who had once been the center of her universe. How could she have forgotten how beautiful he was? And how cruel?

"We're both adults, *cara*. Why not admit we want each other?"

"Didn't you just say you knew I was eager to see you gone? That you'd be happy to go?" Damn it, why did she sound breathless? "Didn't you say that?"

He didn't answer. Instead, he cupped her face and lifted it to his. "Kiss me once," he whispered. "Just once. Then, if you don't want to make love, I promise, I won't touch you again."

"I don't have to kiss you to know the—"

His mouth took hers captive. Tally made a little sound of protest. Then his arms went around her and she let him gather her into his embrace, let his lips part hers and she knew nothing had changed, not when it came to this. To wanting his touch. His mouth. His body, hardening against hers...

The door flew open; the gust of wind that followed slammed it, hard, against the wall as a small woman cradling a grocery bag in one arm all but sailed into the kitchen.

"Sorry not to knock," Sheryl Miller said breathlessly, "but I don't have a free hand. I brought you leftovers from dinner and a loaf of oatmeal bread I baked this morning. Dan's going to get his mom and I said I'd go with—" Her mouth formed a perfect circle as she peered around the bag. "Oh! Oh, I'm sorry, Tally. I didn't know you had company."

Neither Tally or Dante answered. Both of them were staring at the toddler, round as a snowman in a raspberry-pink snowsuit, who clung to Sheryl's free hand.

"Hi, Mama," Samantha Gardner Sommers said happily, and flew to her mother's arms.

# CHAPTER FOUR

FOR A MOMENT, no one moved but the child.

Then, as if someone had pushed a button, the room came to life again. The woman in the doorway, her face a polite mask, put the bag she'd been holding on the counter. Taylor scooped the toddler into her arms, and Dante...

Dante forced himself to breathe.

*Mama?* Was that really what the child had said? Taylor was staring at him over the little girl's head. Her face had gone white. So, he suspected, had his.

"Who is this?" he said hoarsely.

The woman glanced at Taylor. Then she took a step forward. "I'm Sheryl Miller. Tally's neighbor."

His head swung toward the woman. He thought of saying he didn't mean her, that he didn't give a damn who she was, but that would have been stupid. He needed time to get hold of himself and she had given him exactly that.

Oh yes, he needed time because what he was thinking was surely impossible.

"And you are?" Sheryl said, breaking the strained silence.

"Dante Russo." Dante forced a polite smile. "Taylor and I—"

"We knew each other in New York," Tally said quickly. A little color had returned to her face but it only made her look feverish. "He was in the area and—and he thought he'd drop by."

A horn beeped outside. The Miller woman ignored it. "Funny," she said, "but Tally never mentioned you."

He wanted to tell the woman to get out. To leave him alone so he could ask Taylor who this child was, why she'd called her Mama, but he knew better than to push things. The tension in the room was thick. Taylor's neighbor was already looking at him as if he might be a serial killer.

"No," he said politely, smiling through his teeth, "I'm sure she didn't."

The woman ignored him. "Tally? Is everything okay?"

Tally swallowed a wave of hysterical laughter. Nothing was okay. Nothing would ever be okay again unless she could come up with a story to change the way Dante was looking at her and Sam.

"You want me to tell Dan to come in?"

"No! Oh, no, Sheryl. I mean—" What *did* she mean? "It's as I said. Dante is an old—an old—"

"Friend," Dante said, his tone level. "I thought I'd stop by and see how Taylor was adjusting to small-town life."

The Miller woman looked doubtful but Tally said yes, that was it, and smiled, and finally the woman smiled, too.

"Why wouldn't she adjust? Didn't she ever tell you she's a small-town girl at heart? That she comes from Shelby?"

"No. But then, I'm starting to realize there are lots

of things she didn't tell me." Dante looked at Taylor. "Isn't that right, *cara?*"

Taylor didn't answer. That was good because it meant she knew that whatever she said now would only fuel the fury building inside him.

The horn beeped again. "Dan wants to get going," Sheryl said. She peeled off a glove and offered Dante a brisk handshake. "Nice to have met you." She leaned forward, as if to share a confidence. "Tally can use the company. I keep telling her she needs to get out more but what with Sam, well, you know how it is."

"No," Dante said, forcing another smile, "I'm afraid I don't."

Sheryl grinned. "Men never do. Anyway, it's good to see someone from her old life drop by."

"That's definitely what I am. Someone from Taylor's old life."

This time, the horn beeped three times.

"Okay, okay," Sheryl muttered, "I'm coming. Tally? I was going to say, if you want to come with us, I'm sure Dan's mother wouldn't mind."

For a wild moment, Tally imagined running out into the storm with Sam, getting into the truck, telling Dan to drive and drive and drive until she'd put a million miles between Dante and her—

"Tally?"

What was that old saying? You could run, but you couldn't hide.

"Thanks," she said brightly, "but we'll be fine."

The Miller woman looked unconvinced. Dante put his arm around Tally. When she stiffened, he dug his fingers into her flesh in mute warning.

"Taylor's right. We'll be fine." He drew his lips back from his teeth and hoped the result would still approximate a smile. "The snow, a fire, candlelight…it's quite romantic, especially for old friends. Isn't that right, *cara?*"

The child, thumb tucked in her mouth, looked at him. *Liar,* her round green eyes seemed to say. But the woman's big smile assured him she'd bought the story.

"In that case, I'm off. It was nice meeting you, Mr. Russo."

Dante held his smile until the door closed. *Now,* he told himself, and dropped his arm from Taylor's shoulders.

"Whose child is this?"

No preliminaries, she thought dizzily. No safe answers, either.

"Taylor. I asked you a question. Is the child yours?"

Sam chose that moment to give a huge yawn. Tally grabbed at the diversion.

"Somebody's sleepy," she said, ignoring Dante and the pounding of her heart.

"Am not," Sam said, yawning again.

Despite herself, Tally smiled. "Are, too," she said gently. She buried her face in her daughter's sweet-smelling neck as she carried her to the small sofa near the fireplace and sat her down. She tugged off the baby's boots, zipped her out of her snowsuit but left on the warm sweater and tights beneath it.

"How about taking a nap, sweetie? Right here, by the fire. Would you like that?"

"Wan' Teddy."

"Teddy! Of course. I'll get him. You just put your head down and I'll get Teddy and your yellow blankey, okay?"

"'Kay," Sam said, eyelids already drooping.

Tally rose to her feet and forced herself to look at Dante. "Don't," she began to say, but caught herself in time. Don't what? Go near my child? That wasn't the problem. The questions that blazed in his silver eyes was the problem.

So was answering them.

By the time she returned, Samantha was fast asleep. Tally covered her, tucked the teddy bear beside her, smoothed back the baby's hair...

"Stop playing for time."

She swung around. Dante, standing only inches away, might have been carved from granite. Her heart was beating in her throat but the biggest mistake she could make now would be to show her panic.

"Please keep your voice down. I don't want you to wake Sam."

"Sam?" His mouth twisted. "The child's name. Not your lover's. Why did you let me think otherwise?"

She busied herself picking up the boots and snowsuit from the floor.

"I had no idea what you thought. Besides, why would I care? This is my life. I don't owe you explan—"

She gasped as his hand closed, hard, on her wrist. "No games," he said in a soft, dangerous voice. "I warn you, I'm not in the mood."

"And I'm not in the mood for being bullied. Take your hand off me."

Their eyes met and held. Slowly, he released her. Tally took a last look at her sleeping daughter, then walked briskly into the kitchen with Dante on her heels.

"I'm still waiting for an answer. Is the child yours?"

The million-dollar question. It wasn't as if she hadn't envisioned this scene before and all the possible ways to handle it. Dante would demand to know whose baby this was and she'd come up with a creative reply.

She'd say she was raising the child of a sister or a dear friend. Or she'd tell him that she'd adopted Sam. Any of those explanations had seemed plausible, but now, with his cold eyes boring into hers, Tally knew she'd been kidding herself.

A man with Dante's resources would prove she was lying in the blink of an eye.

"It's a simple question, Taylor. Is the child yours?"

In the end, there was only one possible response. She gave it on a forced exhalation of breath.

"Yes. She's mine."

She steadied herself for what would come next. Anger that she hadn't told him he'd made her pregnant? A demand to claim that which was his? Or perhaps, by some miracle, a thawing of his ice-clad heart at the realization he had a daughter.

Later, she'd weep bitter tears at the memory of those possibilities and how reasonable they'd seemed.

"So, that's the reason you left me. Because you were pregnant."

She nodded and searched his face for some hint of what he was thinking.

"Answer the question! Was your pregnancy the reason you ran away?"

"I didn't run away."

His mouth thinned. "No. Of course you didn't."

"I'm sure you think I should have told you, but—"

"You were quite right, keeping the information to yourself," he said coldly. "However you imagined I'd react, the reality would have been worse."

Tears blurred her eyes. "Yes," she said. "I know that now."

Dante caught her by the shoulders, his hands as hard as his eyes.

"I made myself clear from the start."

She couldn't help it. The tears she'd tried to control trembled on her lashes, then fell. She pulled free of his hands, went to the sink and made a pretense of straightening things that didn't need straightening.

"I know. That's why I didn't—"

"You were my mistress."

That dried her tears in a hurry. "I was never that."

"Don't mince words, damn it!" He came up behind her and swung her toward him. "You belonged to me."

"This jacket belongs to you," she said, shrugging it from her shoulders so it dropped to the floor. "And that vehicle in the driveway." Tally thumped her fist against her chest. "*I* am not property. I never belonged to you."

"No." His smile was as thin as a rapier. "As it turns out, you didn't." His grasp on her tightened. "I knew things had changed between us. I just didn't know the reason."

"I left you. Final answer."

"I thought it was that our relationship was growing old."

Amazing, that such cruel words could wound after all this time, but she'd sooner have died than let him know it.

"You're right. It was. It had. That's why—"

"Now I find out it wasn't that at all." He caught her face, lifted it to him so that their eyes met. "It was this," he said, jerking his chin toward the next room, where the baby lay sleeping. "You had a secret and you were so intent on keeping it from me that you kept yourself from me, too."

"Maybe you're not as thick-headed as you seem," Tally countered, trying for sarcasm and failing, if the twist of his lips was any indication.

"I could kill you," he said softly.

As if to prove it, one cool hand circled her throat. His touch was light, but she felt its warning pressure.

"Let go of me, Dante."

"There's not a court in the land that would convict me."

"This is America. Not Sicily." Tally put her hand over his. "Damn you, do you think I planned to get pregnant?"

He stared at her for a long minute. Then he dropped his hand to his side.

"No," he said. "I suppose not."

He strode away from her, his back rigid, and paced her kitchen like a caged lion.

Her heart thudded.

What was going on in his head? Would he turn his back and walk away? Or would his pride, whatever it was that drove him, demand that he stake his claim to her daughter? She'd do anything to avoid that, anything to keep this heartless man from being involved in raising Samantha.

"Dante." Tally hesitated. "I know you're angry but— but you must believe me. I did what I thought was—"

"You told me you were using a diaphragm."

"Yes. I know. But—"

He swung toward her. "But not with him."

Tally blinked. "What?"

"I want to know who he is."

"You want—you want to know—"

"The name of your child's father. The man you took as a lover while you still belonged to me."

She stared at him in disbelief. He wasn't angry because she'd left him without telling him she was carrying his baby. He was angry because he thought she'd cheated on him.

Was that how little he thought of her? That she'd betrayed him while they were lovers? God oh God, she wanted to launch herself at him. Claw his heart out, except he had no heart.

But then, she'd always known that. It was what had made her weep at night toward the end.

She'd never so much as looked at anyone else while they'd been together. She'd never looked at anyone in the years since, either, because she was a fool, a fool, a fool...

"I am assuming," he said, "that you are not going to tell me I sired this child."

*Sired* Sam? He made it sound like a procedure performed in a veterinarian's office...but that was fine. Every word he said assured her she'd been right to leave him when she did.

"Damn you," he snarled, catching her by the shoulders, "answer me!"

She could do that. She could do whatever it took, to get this man out of her life.

"You can relax, Dante. I promise you, I'm not going to tell you that you are Samantha's father. If you want that in writing, I'll be happy to oblige."

A muscle bunched in his jaw. "You still haven't said who he was, this man who took you to his bed while you were still sleeping in mine."

Tally wrenched free. "You have it wrong. It was you who slept in *my* bed, remember?"

"Answer me, damn it. Who is he?"

"That's none of your business."

"I told you, you belonged to me. That makes it my business."

"And *I* told *you,* I am not property!" She looked up at him, hating him for what he was, for what he thought, for what she'd once felt in his arms. "What's the matter? Have I wounded your pride? Will I wound it even more if I tell you I was only with him once? That's all it took for him to give me his child."

He grabbed her, his face so white, eyes so hot, that she thought she'd finally pushed him too far, but that didn't matter. She'd wanted to hurt him enough to draw blood and she had...

With the truth.

She knew exactly when their child—when *her* child—had been conceived. On the night of his birthday. She'd learned the date by accident, when he left his wallet open on the nightstand with his driver's license in view. She'd made dinner, baked a cake, bought him a present because she'd—because she'd wanted to.

After, Dante had made such tender love to her that she'd looked into her own heart and come as close as she'd dared to admitting what she felt for him.

"Stay with me tonight," she'd whispered, as they lay in each other's arms.

He hadn't.

After he was gone, she'd felt more alone than she'd ever thought possible. Not just alone but abandoned. Used, not by his heart but by his body.

She'd cried softly as night faded to morning. Hours later, when she got up to shower, she'd discovered that her diaphragm had a pinpoint hole in it. She'd told herself it was nothing. It was her so-called safe time of the month and besides, what were the odds on becoming pregnant after just one night of unprotected sex?

Six weeks later, a home pregnancy kit proved that the odds were excellent.

Tally had considered the life she'd planned. A career, not for her ego but for security. Money in the bank that would guarantee she'd never have to depend on a man the way her mother had.

She'd visited her doctor. Asked tough questions, made tough decisions. And reversed herself on the subway ride home when she saw a young woman with a baby in her arms, the mother cooing, the baby laughing with unrestricted joy.

Her future had changed in that single instant.

Now, it was changing again. If she'd had any last, lingering doubts about her feelings for the man she'd once come close to thinking she loved, they were gone.

She looked pointedly at Dante's hand, encircling her wrist, then at his face.

"I want you out of here," she said softly. "Right now."

He looked at her for a long moment. Then, slowly and deliberately, he took his hand from her.

"I thought I knew you," he said in a low voice.

She almost laughed at the absurdity of those words. "You never knew me," she said.

"No. I didn't. I see that now." He plucked his leather jacket from where she'd dropped it and slipped it on. "Get yourself an attorney. A good one, because I'm going to start foreclosure proceedings as soon as I return to New York."

Panic took an oily slide in her belly. "I can make the payments on the loan. I *have* made them! All you have to do is check the bank records."

"The amount you've been paying each month is a joke. It has nothing to do with the loan agreement."

"But Walter Dennison said—"

"You're not dealing with Dennison. You're dealing with me."

She watched, transfixed, as he strolled to the door. At the last second, she went after him.

"Wait! Please, you can't... My daughter, Dante. My little girl. Surely you wouldn't punish an innocent child for my mistakes. That's not possible!"

"Anything is possible," he said coldly. "You proved that when you took a lover."

"Dante. Don't make me beg. Don't—"

"Why not?" He turned and clasped her elbows, lifting her to him until his empty eyes were all she could see. "I'd love to hear you beg, *cara*. It would fill my heart with joy."

The bitter tears she'd fought to suppress streamed down her cheeks.

"I hate you, Dante Russo. Hate you. Hate you. Hate—"

He took her mouth in a hard, deep kiss, one that demanded acquiescence. Tally fought it. Fought him as he cupped her face, held her prisoner to his plundering mouth until she knew she would kill him when he turned her free, kill him...

And then, slowly, his kiss changed. His lips softened

on hers. His tongue teased. His hands slid into her hair and she felt it again, after all these years, all this anguish and pain. The slow, dangerous heat low in her belly. The thickening of her blood. The need for him, only him…

Dante pushed her away.

"You belonged to me," he said roughly. "Only to me. I could have you again if I wished." His mouth twisted. "But why would I want another man's leavings?"

Then he put up his collar, opened the door and strode into the teeth of the storm.

# CHAPTER FIVE

HOW MANY TIMES could a man be subjected to the saccharine nonsense of Christmas before he lost what remained of his sanity?

The holiday was still three weeks away and Dante was already tired of the music pouring out of shops and car radios. He'd seen enough artificial evergreens to last a lifetime, and he was damned close to telling the next sidewalk Santa exactly what he could do with his cheery ho-ho-ho.

New York, his city, belonged to tourists from Thanksgiving through the New Year. They descended on the Big Apple like fruit flies, choking the streets with their numbers, unaware or uncaring of one of the basic rules of Manhattan survival.

Pedestrians were not supposed to dawdle. And they were expected to ignore Walk and Don't Walk signs.

New Yorkers moved briskly from point A to point B and when they reached a street corner, they took one quick look and kept going. It was up to the trucks and taxis that hurtled down the streets to avoid them.

Tourists from Nebraska or Indiana and only-God-knew-where stopped and stared at the displays in department store windows in such numbers that they blocked the sidewalk. They formed a snaking queue around Radio City Music Hall, standing in the cold with the patience of dim-witted cattle. They clustered around the railing in Rockefeller Center, sighing over the too big, too gaudy, too everything Christmas tree that was the center's focal point.

As far as Dante was concerned, Scrooge had it right.

Bah, humbug, indeed, he thought as his chauffeur edged the big Mercedes through traffic.

The strange thing was, he'd never really noticed the inconvenience of the holiday until now. Basically, he'd never really noticed the holiday at all.

It was just another day.

As a child, Christmas had meant—if he were lucky—another third-hand winter jacket from the Jesuits that, you hoped, was warmer than the last. By the time he'd talked, connived and generally wheedled his way into a management job at a construction company where he'd spent a couple of years wielding a jackhammer, he was too busy to pay attention to the nonsense of canned carols and phony good cheer. And after he arrived in New York, earning the small fortune he'd needed to start building his own empire had taken all his concentration.

The last dozen years, of course, he'd had to notice Christmas. Not for himself but for others. Those with whom he did business and the ones who worked for him—the doormen, the elevator operators, the porters at the building in which he lived, all expected certain things of the holiday.

So Dante put in the requisite appearance at the annual

office party his P.A. organized. He authorized bonuses for his employees. He wrote checks for the doormen, the elevator operators and the porters. He thanked his P.A. for the bottle of Courvoisier she inevitably gave him and gave her, in return, a gift certificate to Saks.

Somehow, he'd never observed the larger picture.

Had tourists always descended on the city, inconveniencing everything and everyone? They must have.

Then, how could he not have noticed?

He was noticing now, all right. *Dio,* it was infuriating.

The Mercedes crept forward, then stopped. Crept forward, then stopped. Dante checked his watch, muttered a well-chosen bit of gutter Sicilian and decided he was better off walking.

"Carlo? I'm getting out. I'll call when I need you."

He opened the door to a dissonant blast of horns, as if a man leaving an already-stopped automobile might somehow impede the nonexistent flow of traffic. He slipped between a double-parked truck and a van, stepped onto the sidewalk and headed briskly toward the Fifth Avenue hotel where he was lunching with the owner of a private bank Russo International had just absorbed.

He'd be late. He hated that. Lateness was a sign of weakness.

Everything he did lately was a sign of weakness.

He was short-tempered. Impatient. Hell, there were times he was downright rude. And he was never that. Demanding, yes, but he asked as much of himself as he did of those who reported to him, but the past couple of weeks...

No. He'd be damned if he was going to think about that trip to Vermont again.

He thought about it too much already.

And the dreams that awakened him at night... What were they, if not an indication that he was losing his self-control?

Why would he dream about a woman he despised? For the same reason he'd kissed her, damn it. Because the ugly truth was that he still wanted her, despite her lies and her infidelity. Despite the fact that she'd borne another man's child. Nothing kept the dreams at bay. Each night, he imagined her coming to him, imagined stripping her naked, making love to her until she cried out in his arms and said, *Yes, Dante, yes, you make me feel things he never did.*

And awakened hard as stone, angry at himself for an adolescent's longings, for the frustration that he couldn't lose in another woman's bed though, God knew, he'd tried.

What an embarrassment that had been! *I'm sorry,* he'd said, *that's never happened to me before.*

It hadn't, though he doubted if the lady believed him. *He* could hardly believe it!

He was not himself since Vermont, and he didn't like it. One day in a snow-bound village and he'd discovered he was still an old-world *Siciliano* at heart, reacting to things with emotion instead of intellect.

How could a woman he didn't want ruin his sex life from a distance of four hundred miles?

Taylor had—what was the old saying? She'd put horns on his head, sleeping with another man while she was still his. She deserved whatever happened next.

She *had* been his, no matter what she claimed. So what if she hadn't let him pay her bills? If she hadn't lived with him?

She had belonged to him. He'd marked her with his hands. His mouth. His body.

And she'd let another man plant a seed in her womb. She'd given him a child. A child who should rightly have been—should rightly have been—

Dante frowned, gave himself a mental shake and prepared to vent his anger on the half a dozen idiots who'd come to a dead stop in the middle of the sidewalk.

"Excuse me," he said in a voice so frigid it made a mockery of the words.

Then he saw it wasn't only the people ahead of him. Nobody was moving. Well, yes. The crowd was shifting. Sideways, like a brontosaurus spying a fresh stand of leafy trees, heading for a huge, world-famous toy store.

Dante dug in his heels. "Excuse me," he said again. "Pardon me. Coming through."

Useless. Like a paper boat caught in a stream, the crowd herded him toward the doors.

"Wait a minute," he said to a massive woman with her elbow dug into his side. "Madam. I am not—"

But he was. Like it or not, Dante was swept inside.

A giant clock tower boomed out a welcome; a huge stuffed giraffe gave him the once-over. He was pushed past a tiger so big he half expected it to roar.

Somehow, weaving and bobbing, he worked to the edge of the crowd and found refuge behind a family of stuffed bears. He gave his watch one last glance, sighed and took out his cell phone.

"Traffic," he told the man he was to lunch with, in the tones of a put-upon New Yorker. It turned out the other man was still trapped in a taxi. They laughed and made plans for a drink that evening.

Dante put his phone away, folded his arms over his chest and settled in to wait for a break in the flow of parents and children so he could head for the door.

He didn't have to wait long. A trio of pleasantly efficient security guards cleared the way, formed the crowd into an orderly queue outside. Dante started toward the door, then fell back.

What a place this was!

And what would he have given to be turned loose in it when he was a boy. Just to look, to touch, would have been a time spent in paradise.

His toys had been stick swords. Newspaper kites. And, one magical Christmas Eve, an armless tin soldier he found in a dumpster while he scavenged for his supper.

How could he have forgotten that?

Oh, how he'd loved his soldier! He'd kept it safely buried in the pocket of his sagging jeans, bloodied the nose of a bigger boy who'd tried to steal it.

Was that what Taylor's daughter faced? Improvised toys? If she were lucky, a broken, discarded doll to call her own?

Dante scowled.

Talk about giving in to your emotions! The child— Samantha—was not the Poor Little Match Girl. Neither was her mother. Taylor was perfectly capable of earning a living.

Yes, he'd started the legal procedures that would take her house from her, but she'd reneged on the terms of the loan. It was business, plain and simple. She'd understood the risks when she signed those loan papers.

Besides, she wasn't destitute. She had possessions. She could sell them. She had friends in that town, people who'd help her and the child.

Then, why had her coat looked worn? The house, too. Even by candlelight, he could tell it needed work. The walls needed fresh paint. The wood floors needed refinishing. The furnishings were shabby. And where were the shiny, high-tech gadgets women always had in their kitchens?

Had Taylor deliberately simplified her life…or had fate done it for her?

A muscle flexed in his jaw.

Not that he cared. For every action, there was a reaction. That was basic science. She had deceived him, and he had repaid her.

The child was not his problem. Neither was Taylor. He had no regrets or remorse, and if her daughter didn't have a particularly merry Christmas this year…

Something bumped against his leg.

It was a child. A little girl, older than Samantha, clutching a cloth doll almost as big as she was in her arms.

"What did I tell you, Janey?" A harassed-looking woman caught the child's hand. "You can't see around that thing. Tell the man you're sorry."

"That's all right," Dante said quickly. "No harm done."

The child's mother smiled. "I told Janey that Santa's going to bring her some wonderful surprises in just a few weeks but she saw Raggedy Ann and, well, neither she or I could resist. You know?"

He didn't know, that was just the point. He'd never had surprises from Santa, never fallen in love with a goofy bear, like Samantha, or a rag doll like Janey.

Even if he had, who would have understood how important such a simple toy could be?

Dante watched the little girl and her mother fade into the crowd. He stood motionless, long after they'd disappeared from his sight.

Then he made his way out of the store, took out his cell phone to call his chauffeur... And, instead, called his P.A. to tell her he wasn't returning to the office.

He felt—what was the word? Unsettled. Perhaps he was coming down with something. Whatever the reason, walking to his apartment building on such a cold, crisp day might clear his head.

"You're home early, Mr. Russo," said his housekeeper when he stepped from the private elevator into the foyer of his penthouse.

Dante shrugged off his coat and told her he didn't want to be disturbed. Then he went into his study, turned on his computer and did what he could to further prepare for the meeting he'd have over drinks in just a few hours.

For the first time in his life, he couldn't get interested in the complex facts and figures of an imminent deal.

What kind of Christmas morning would Taylor and her child awaken to? There was a time he'd have assumed Taylor viewed the holiday with as much cynicism as he did. After all, he'd spent six months as her lover. He knew her. He knew her likes and dislikes...

Or did he?

She'd shown him a side of her he'd never suspected. Had she really grown up in a small town? If he hadn't seen her in that shabby little house with a child in her arms, even imagining Taylor in that kind of life would have been impossible.

People didn't even call her by that name in Shelby. She was Tally, not Taylor. A softer, more vulnerable name for a softer, more vulnerable woman.

Dante went to the window and looked down at Central Park. Thanks to the influx of out-of-towners, it was alive with people, even on a weekday afternoon. There were probably more people in the park right now than lived in the entire town of Shelby, Vermont.

If Taylor had stayed in New York, if she'd opened her business here, she'd be turning a handsome profit by now. She had contacts in the city, a reputation.

Dante watched the scene below him for long minutes. Children were sledding down a snowy incline; even from up here, he could see the bright flash of their snowsuits.

Would the little girl in the toy store find a sled under the tree Christmas morning?

Would Taylor's daughter?

A muscle knotted in his jaw.

No. The plan running through his head was clearly insane. She'd made a fool of him, wounded him in the worst way a woman can hurt a man.

But the child was innocent.

It was wrong, that children seemed always to pay for the sins of those who'd given them life.

The muscle in his jaw knotted again. Dante went to the breakfront, took out a bottle of brandy and poured an inch into a snifter. He warmed the glass between his palms, stared sightlessly into the rich depths of the swirling liquid.

And put it down, untouched.

Instead, he went to his desk. Picked up the phone. Made calls to his attorney, to his accountant, to the same private investigator who'd found Taylor for him.

If any of them thought his instructions were unusual, they knew better than to say so.

When he'd finished, Dante picked up his snifter of brandy and went up the spiral staircase to his suite.

The view was even better here. Three walls of glass gave him a vantage point a peregrine falcon would have as it swooped over the city.

Lights glimmered, diamonds sparkling against the pall of encroaching darkness, and he recalled the first time he'd stood here, gazing out into the night, the fierce swell of pride he'd felt at knowing all this was his, that his sweat, his struggles, his fight to get to the top had all been worth it.

Taylor had never seen this view. She'd come here for drinks, for dinner, but he'd never carried her up the stairs to this room.

To his bed.

Dante sipped the brandy.

What if he had? If he'd made love to her while the lights of the city challenged the stars in the night sky? If he'd taken her to these windows, naked. Stood with her as she looked out on his world. Stepped behind her. Cupped her breasts. Bent his head and kissed the skin behind her ear.

She'd always trembled when he kissed her there.

Trembled when he entered her.

He closed his eyes. Imagined entering her now, right now, here, as she looked into the night. Imagined holding her hips, pressing against her, the urgency of his erection seeking the heat, the silken dampness that was for him.

Only for him…

His eyes flew open.

*The hell it was.*

She'd been with another man, even while she'd been his because, damn it, she *had* belonged to him no matter what she said.

He turned from the window, turned from the images that assailed him.

What he'd just done had nothing to do with Taylor. It was simply an act of charity. This was the season for charity, after all. What he'd done was for a child. An innocent little girl, trapped in a game played by adults.

That the plan he'd set in motion would also bring Taylor back into his life was secondary. Whatever had happened between him and his once-upon-a-time lover was over.

Dante tossed back the rest of the brandy. The liquid burned its way down his throat and, as it did, burned him, as well, with the ugly truth.

Forget charity. Forget pretending that what had happened was over.

It wouldn't be. Not until he slept with the woman who'd made a fool of him, one last time.

# CHAPTER SIX

WHEN SHE WAS SIX, Tally stopped believing in Santa Claus.

Her grandmother had taken her to the mall the week before. She'd been terrified of the man with the white beard and the booming laugh, but after a lot of coaxing, she'd sat in his lap and whispered that all she wanted for Christmas was a Pretty Patty doll.

Christmas Eve, she crept out of bed and saw her grandmother putting the doll under the tree.

Even then, she'd understood Grandma had to count every penny. That she'd loved Tally enough to buy the doll meant more than if Santa had brought it.

Now, twenty-two years later, she was close to believing in Santa again.

How else to explain the call from a decorator she'd worked with in Manhattan? He'd been in too much of a hurry to offer details but the bottom line was that he knew someone who knew someone who knew someone who was familiar with her work.

That person had recommended her for the commission of a lifetime.

"The guy's richer than Midas," Aston trilled. "Seems

he just bought out some old-line firm and the digs don't suit him, so he's moving the whole kit and caboodle to that new building on 57th and Mad. You know the one? Baby, this is one plum job! A huge budget, free creative rein... Pull this off, your name will blaze in neon!"

A couple of weeks back, Tally would have been flattered but she'd have turned down the offer. She'd have had no choice, not with a shop to open in Vermont. Now it seemed as if Dante's vicious act of revenge might turn out to be a godsend.

"He wants to meet with you first, of course. See if the synergy's right."

For an assignment like this, she'd do whatever it took to make the synergy right.

She splurged on a haircut, had her black suit cleaned and pressed, charged a new coat which she hated to do but appearance was everything in New York. If things went well, she'd be able to pay for it. If not, she was so broke that the credit card company would have to wait the next hundred years for their money.

She even tried to go back to thinking of herself as Taylor Sommers instead of Tally. Her given name had been the one she'd always used in the city. It suited the image she'd needed, that of a cool sophisticate.

The woman Dante had always assumed her to be. The one she knew he'd wanted her to be.

And yet, today, after leaving Samantha with Sheryl, riding the train into Manhattan, now standing across from the glass tower where she was to meet the Mystery Mogul, she felt more like Tally than Taylor.

Taylor wouldn't have butterflies swarming in her stomach.

Tally did.

She was nervous. Hell, she was terrified about meeting the man who held her future in his hands.

He had no name. Not yet.

"You know how these big shots are," Aston said. "Some of them won't make a move unless a camera's pointed at them, but some guard their privacy like lions protecting a kill. This guy's like that. He wants to stay nameless until the deal is struck."

The Mystery Mogul was meeting her in his new offices. Tally looked up, counting the floors even though she'd already done it twice, head tilted back like an out-of-towner.

The butterflies fluttered their wings again.

She wanted this job more than she'd ever wanted anything. Aston's description of it was almost too good to be true.

Her fee would be—well, enormous. More than she'd earn in five years in Shelby. She'd be able to give Sam everything. New toys, clothes, the best possible nanny to care for her while Tally was at work.

Best of all, she could deal with the loan payments she owed the bank—the payments she owed Dante. So much for his plans to destroy her.

She wouldn't even have to tackle the toughest thing about living in New York. The Mystery Mogul, it turned out, owned an apartment building with a two-bedroom, two-bath vacancy.

"Well, of course he does," Aston had said.

The way he said it made her laugh. It was the first time she'd laughed in weeks.

Since Dante's visit.

Since she'd discovered just how ruthless he could be.

Since she'd found out just how much she could hate him.

"The rent's a perk of the job, can you imagine?"

She could. A picture was emerging of a bona fide eccentric with money to burn. The only thing that almost stopped her was that this meant returning to Dante's city. And that was just plain ridiculous. It was her city, too, or had been for five years. Besides, the odds of running into one person in a city of eight million were zero to none.

And even if there was that eight-million-to-one chance, so what? She'd left Dante so he wouldn't know she was having his baby, but it turned out she needn't have worried. She'd told him Sam wasn't his and he'd been only too willing to believe her.

Tally lifted her chin as she strode through the lobby of the glass tower and stepped into a waiting elevator. She should have spat in his face that night in her kitchen. Given the opportunity a second time, she wouldn't pass it by.

"To hell with you, Dante Russo," she said aloud, as the elevator whisked her to the twenty-seventh floor. "You're a cold, contemptible son of a bitch and—"

The doors slid open.

And the cold, contemptible son of a bitch was standing in front of her, arms folded, face expressionless.

"Hello, Taylor," he said, and that was when she knew she'd been had. All this—the wonderful job, the money, the apartment...

It was all a cruel joke.

A joke only one of them could laugh at, she thought,

and then she stopped thinking, called him a word she had never before thought, much less used, and launched herself at the man she would hate for the rest of her life.

DANTE HAD KNOWN this wouldn't be easy.

Taylor despised him. Well, so what? The feeling was mutual.

And she was proud.

He admired that in her; he always had. She'd never shown the weakness so many women—hell, so many men and women—showed, that of needing someone to lean on. Like him, she was independent and strong.

But things had changed.

She did need someone now. Some no-good SOB had gotten her pregnant and walked away, left her with a child to raise, and that made all the difference.

He'd decided to start by telling her that but she didn't give him the chance. The elevator doors opened, she saw who was waiting for her and she came at him like a tiger.

He got his arms up just in time to keep her from clawing his face.

"Taylor," he said, "Taylor, listen—"

"No," she panted, raining blows on his upraised arms, "I'm done listening, you bastard! Wasn't what you did to me enough? Did you need an encore? You no-good, heartless—"

He caught her hands, yanked them behind her back. "Stop it!"

"Let go. You let go of me or—"

She was still fighting him. Dante grunted, tucked his shoulder down and hoisted her over it like a bag of laundry. She shrieked, kicked her feet and yanked at his hair. What in hell would he say if somebody came running to see who was being murdered?

"Put me down!"

"With pleasure," he said grimly.

The former tenants had left behind a couple of chairs, half a dozen file cabinets and a small black leather sofa. Dante strode to it and dumped her on it. Then he stood back, folded his arms again and glared.

What had made him think helping her would be a good idea?

"Don't even think about it," he warned when she scrambled up against the cushions.

"I hate you, Dante. Do you hear me? I hate you!"

"I'd never have known."

She sat up straight, mouth trembling. "How even *you* could do something like this, you—you—"

"Watch what you say, *cara*."

"Do not call me that!"

"Is it your habit to attack your clients?"

"If you think I'm going to be party to this—this schoolboy prank—"

"You're so sure you know everything, Taylor. Is it possible you don't?"

"I know what you are. That's all that's necessary."

She rose to her feet, tugged down her coat, smoothed her hands over her hair. She was still shaking and suddenly he wanted to go to her, take her in his arms and tell her everything was going to be all right. That he would take care of her.

Except, that wasn't why he'd brought her here. It was for the child.

*And for yourself,* a voice in his head said slyly. How

come he'd forgotten his vow to sleep with this woman one last time? That would put her out of his thoughts forever. He didn't need to hear her say she wanted him. Or that she was sorry she'd been unfaithful. He didn't need to hear the words she'd whispered that night three years ago when she'd begged him to stay with her, to stay in her arms, in her bed.

"Get out of my way!"

She was looking up at him as if she wanted to kill him. Fine. The game he'd planned was one that was best played by sworn enemies.

"We'll have our meeting first."

"We've already had it. To think you'd resort to such— to such subterfuge, just so you could make a fool of me!"

"Would you have agreed to this appointment if you'd known I was the man involved?"

"You know I wouldn't." Her eyes filled with angry tears. "Why did you do it? You're taking my house. My livelihood. What more do you want?"

He wasn't going to answer. She could tell by the way he was looking at her but it didn't matter. She already knew the answer. What he'd done to her wasn't sufficient. He wanted to give the knife one more twist.

How? she thought bitterly. How could she have made love with a man like this? How could she have even believed she'd fallen in love with him? Because she had believed it, yes. That was why she'd left him, because she knew he didn't love her, wouldn't love the child they'd created together. She'd left rather than see him look at her as he was looking at her now, as if she had no meaning to him at all.

She took a deep breath, drew what remained of her pride around her like a ragged cloak and started past him.

"Taylor."

She shook her head. She had nothing left to say to him.

His hand closed on her wrist. "You asked me questions. Are you going to leave before you hear the answers?"

She looked pointedly from his hand to hers. "Let go."

"I didn't bring you to New York on false pretenses."

She laughed. "You didn't, huh?"

"Isn't that what I just said?"

"Well, let's see. You got someone to offer me a commission decorating these offices. He mentioned a budget big enough to make my head spin. Oh, and he said there'd be an apartment with the rent a perk of the job." Tally tugged her hand free and put her hands on her hips. "If those aren't false pretenses—"

"The offer is real. All of it. The commission, the budget, the place to live."

Everything from shock to distrust to outright utter disbelief showed in her face. He tucked his hands in his trouser pockets and kept his tone as flat as his eyes.

"It's all yours, if you want it."

She stared at him. "Why?"

"There's an old saying about not looking a gift horse in the mouth."

"I know the saying. Maybe it lost something in the translation. What it means is that an unexpected gift is a gift to beware of."

Dante took a deep breath. "The child," he said.

"What child?" Tally felt her heart beat quicken. Did he know? Had he somehow learned the truth of her pregnancy? "You mean—you mean Sam?"

He nodded. "Yes."

"What about her?"

"I've had time to think." A muscle flexed in his jaw. "And I realized that it's wrong to punish her for your behavior."

He didn't know. Tally almost sagged with relief.

"Your daughter is innocent of all that happened. You deceived me. You left me. But none of that is her doing. The world is filled with children who suffer because of the behavior of adults. I see no reason to add to their number."

She stared at him. Dante Russo, showing compassion to a little girl he thought had been fathered by another man? Why would he show compassion at all? All the months they'd been lovers, she'd waited, she'd yearned to see some show of human emotion in this man.

She never had.

Oh, he supported charities. Smiled at things that were amusing. Frowned at things that were annoying.

But he never lost his composure. Not even in bed.

Not that he wasn't an incredible lover. He was. Alert to her every sigh, her every unspoken desire. He'd given her more pleasure than she'd ever imagined possible.

The way he moved inside her.

The way he brought her to climax.

And yet, he'd always been in control. Always, except that one night when he'd been as tender as he was wild, when she'd asked him to stay with her.

When she'd conceived Samantha.

"Well?"

Tally blinked. Dante was looking at her with barely veiled impatience.

"You asked me why I'd offer this assignment to you and I told you the reason. It's your turn now. Will you accept it? Or will you turn it down because I'm the man making the offer?"

Something was wrong. She felt as if she were looking at a jigsaw puzzle with one piece—the key piece—missing.

"Yes or no?"

She almost laughed. The imperious tone of voice. The straight posture. The cold eyes that said, "I'm in command."

Except, he wasn't.

He couldn't order her around. She wouldn't permit it. She had to think. Nothing was happening the way it was supposed to. She'd worried about being in the same city with this man and now it turned out she'd be working for him.

Impossible.

Better to go home…and do what? Lose the house? Move to a furnished room? Take whatever job she could find? Earn barely enough to live on and, oh yes, impose on Sheryl's kindness by asking her to watch Sam?

"Taylor, I want an answer!"

There was only one answer, but she couldn't bring herself to give it. Not without making him wait.

"I'll call you with my decision."

His eyes narrowed. She tried to move past him as quickly as possible, but his hand clamped down on her shoulder.

"Would you put your pride before the welfare of your daughter?"

"Nice, Dante. Really nice." Tally's eyes blazed with anger. "Don't you try and lay this on me! I never ignored Sam's welfare and I sure as hell never tripped over my own oversize ego! You're the one who came to Shelby, who bought a bank just so you could tear my child's life to pieces."

"That wasn't my intention."

"Maybe not, but it's what you did."

"Yes. And now, I intend to undo it. I will not avenge myself by hurting a child."

"My God, listen to you! So high and mighty. So godlike. Anyone would think you have a conscience. Maybe even a heart."

"Damn you, Taylor!" His fingers dug into her flesh as he pulled her to him. "I want to do the right thing. Why make it so difficult?"

And, in that moment, it came to her. The missing piece of the puzzle. What he'd just called doing the right thing. If that was his intention, there was a much easier way to do it. Why wasn't he taking it?

"If you're serious about not wanting my little girl to pay the price of your revenge—"

"Interesting," he said silkily, "how you manage to misquote me, *cara*. I said I would not avenge myself through her. We both know what that means, that your daughter should not pay the price of your unfaithfulness."

"Put whatever twist you like on it. The point is, if you've suddenly turned into the male counterpart of Mother Teresa, why go through all this? Why not simply stop the foreclosure proceedings?"

There it was, the million-dollar question. The question he'd asked himself a dozen times since coming up with this idea. His attorney and his accountant, each of whom knew only small details of the overall situation, had finally asked it, too, but he hadn't given them any explanations.

A man who answered to no one but himself didn't have to.

That didn't mean it wasn't a damned good question. All he had to do was have the loan payments rescheduled. Or tear up the documents altogether.

End of problem.

Nothing else made sense. Not to his attorney, to his accountant, to him and now to Taylor, who was looking at him with her eyebrows arched.

Dante frowned. She could look at him any way she liked. He didn't owe her an explanation, either.

"It's too complicated to explain."

Her smile was thin. "Try."

"There are banking laws. Rules. And I've already set the foreclosure procedure in motion."

"And I'll unset it by repaying the loan with my earnings from this job." Another thin smile. "Try again."

For a second, he looked blank. "You'd see it as charity. You'd never accept it."

It was a good save. The sudden lift of her eyebrows told him so.

"This way, you'll work for the money," he said, feeling his way carefully through the explanation that had suddenly come to him and knowing it was flawed. Give her too much time, she'd realize that. "I'm simply offering you a practical way out of your dilemma."

Yes, Tally thought. That was how it seemed—but then, the fly that had wandered into the spider's parlor had probably thought she was being asked in for a cup of tea.

And yet, what was the alternative? Could she really say no to his offer and condemn Samantha to financial uncertainty? Besides that, he was right. She'd be working for this money. No favors given, no favors asked.

"Well?"

She looked up. Dante was scowling. Obviously, he had none of her reservations about them being in close contact.

"I can't spend the entire day at this, Taylor. I need an answer. Will you take the job or won't you?"

She took a deep, steadying breath. "I'll take it."

Something flashed in his eyes. Triumph, she thought, but then it was gone, he was smiling politely and holding out his hand. She stared at it. Then, carefully, she extended her hand, too, felt his callused palm against hers as they shook hands.

"I want certain assurances," she said quickly.

"We've already sealed the deal. But go ahead. I'll try and accommodate you. What assurances do you want?"

"Our relationship will be strictly business."

He didn't say anything. His expression didn't change. Was that agreement or was he waiting to hear more?

"Our meetings will occur in public places."

"Such logical choices, *cara*. I'm impressed. Is that all?"

"No. It isn't." She folded her arms. "You're not to call me that."

"What? *Cara?*" He laughed. "You're my employee. I'll call you anything I like."

"I'm not your employee. We'll be working together. Either way, calling me *cara* would be improper."

He smiled, and her heart rose into her throat because everything she'd feared about him, everything she'd adored about him, was in that smile.

"Ah. I understand now." He cupped her elbows.

Slowly, inexorably, he drew her closer. "You're afraid our relationship will become personal."

"It won't," she said stiffly. "How could it, when you're the last man on earth I'd want to become personal with?"

"I used to call you *cara* when you were in my arms. When I was making love to you."

Taylor's breath caught. The sound of his voice at those moments. The feel of his hands on her breasts. The darkness of his eyes as he'd slipped his hands beneath her, as he entered her. Slowly, so slowly, until she cried out with pleasure at the feel of him deep, deep inside her...

"No," she said, "I don't remember. Why would I? It meant nothing. It meant—It meant—"

Dante stopped her lies with a kiss.

*Fight him,* she thought desperately, *don't let him do this to you.*

But the terrible truth was, he was doing what she had dreamed of. What she ached for. She loved the feel of his mouth on hers. The scent of his skin. The way he moved his hands down her spine and lifted her against him so that his erection pressed against her belly.

"Kiss me back," he said, his voice a rough command, and her treacherous body responded, her lips parted and when they did, he thrust his tongue into her mouth and she felt it happening as it always did, her breasts swelling, her bones melting, her body readying for his possession...

Her heart yearning for what he would never give her.

Tally wrenched free of his embrace.

"No." Her voice was hoarse. "I don't want that from you. Not anymore."

He said nothing for a long moment. Then he let go of her.

"As you wish."

"As I insist."

"Please," he said coolly, "no ultimatums. You made your point. And now…"

He glanced at his watch, then plucked his cell phone from his pocket and made a brief call. It was like a slap in the face, a way of telling her that the kiss had meant nothing to him.

"I've arranged for my driver to come for you."

"That's not necessary. My hotel—"

"I've checked you out of your hotel." His hand clasped her elbow; he moved her into the elevator with determined efficiency. "Carlo will take you to your rooms."

"Rooms?" she said, as the elevator plunged toward the lobby. "Aston said an apartment."

"The rooms for you and your daughter are a separate suite within an apartment."

"Whose apartment?" Tally said, heart suddenly racing.

His eyes met hers. "Mine," he answered.

Before she could respond, the doors swept open on the lobby and Dante handed her over to his waiting driver.

# CHAPTER SEVEN

DID HE REALLY THINK she'd live in his apartment?

Not even if the alternative was a tent pitched in the Millers' backyard.

Tally let Dante's driver take her to Central Park West but only because she had to go there if she wanted to reclaim her luggage.

She'd get it, write the imperious Mr. Russo a note telling him, in exquisite detail, what he could do with his contract, phone for a taxi and leave. No. This time, she'd face him. She would not forgo that pleasure.

The driver was new but the doorman was the same as in the past. He greeted her by name, as if three long years had not gone by since her last visit. So did the house-keeper, who added that it was good to see her again.

"This way, miss," she said pleasantly, gesturing not to the library or the dining room or the sitting room, all the places—the only places—Tally had seen when she and Dante had been involved, but to the graceful, winding staircase.

"Thank you," Tally said, "but I'll wait for Mr. Russo in the library. If someone would just bring me my suitcase…?"

"Your things are already upstairs, miss. I'll show you to your rooms."

Arguing seemed pointless. Her quarrel was with Dante, not with his staff. She followed the housekeeper to a door that led into a sitting room as large as her entire house back in Vermont.

"Would you like some tea, miss?"

What she'd have liked was some strychnine for her host, but Tally managed a polite smile.

"Nothing, thank you."

"Ellen's unpacked your things. If you're not pleased with how she's arranged your clothes, just ring."

*But I'm not staying,* Tally started to say, except, by then the housekeeper had disappeared.

Dante wasn't just arrogant, he was presumptuous. She could hardly wait to see him and tell him so, but where was he? And when was the last train to Shelby? Eight? Nine? She intended to be on it. No way could she afford a night in a hotel now that her prospective job had turned out to be a farce.

Tally took out her cell phone and dialed Sheryl to see how Sam was and to tell her that the plans that had seemed so magical had fallen apart, but there was no answer. What a time to be reminded that cell service in Shelby wasn't always what you hoped.

Was nothing going to go right today?

Twenty minutes passed. Thirty. Tally frowned. Paced the sitting room. Checked her watch again. Damn it, she didn't have time for this! She'd wait another half hour, then give up the pleasure of confronting Mr. Russo and his monumental ego.

Getting on that train, getting back to Sam and the real

world, was more important. In fact, why was she wasting time waiting for Dante when she could be packing? She didn't need a maid to toss things into a suitcase.

Chin lifted, Tally marched through the sitting room, though a light-filled bedroom, to a door she assumed led to a closet...

Her breath caught.

The door didn't open on a closet. It opened on a room meant for a very lucky little girl.

For Samantha.

The walls were painted cream and decorated with murals that spoke of fairy tales, princesses and unicorns. The carpet was pale pink. The crib and furniture were cream and gold. A rocker stood near the window, a patchwork afghan draped over it. Tucked away in one corner, a playhouse shaped like a castle rose toward the ceiling, guarded by a family of plush teddy bears.

The room was a little girl's dream.

For a heartbeat, Tally's mood softened. She could imagine her daughter's excitement at such wonders.

Then she came to her senses and saw the room for what it really was.

Did Dante think he could bribe her into staying?

She turned on her heel. There was nothing she'd brought to the city she couldn't do without. To hell with packing. To hell with confronting Dante. All she wanted was to go home.

Quickly she left the suite, went down the stairs and headed straight for the private elevator...

But it was already there.

The doors slid open just as she reached them and she saw Dante standing in the mahogany and silver car.

Dante, with Samantha curled in his arms.

The blood drained from Tally's head.

Of all the things she'd imagined happening this day, she'd never envisioned this. Not this. Not her former lover, with his daughter in his arms.

Sam was so fair. Dante was so dark. And yet—oh, God—and yet they were so right together. The same softly curling hair. The same wide eyes and firm mouths, curving in the same smiles as they looked at each other, Dante with a softness of expression Tally had never seen in his face before, Sam babbling happily about something in a two-year-old's combination of real and made-up words.

Dante and Samantha. A father and his daughter.

The ground tilted under Tally's feet.

Blindly she stuck out a hand in a search for support. She must have made a sound because suddenly Dante looked up and saw her.

His smile faded. *"Cara?"*

I'm fine, she said. Or tried to say. But the words wouldn't come, nothing would come but another soft sound of distress. Dante barked a command. His housekeeper ran into the room, took Sam from him, and then it was Tally who was in Dante's arms, his strong arms, and he was carrying her swiftly through the apartment.

*"Cara,"* he said again, "Tally…"

He had never called her that before. She thought of how soft the name sounded on his lips. Of how the world was spinning, spinning, spinning…

And then everything went black.

WHEN SHE OPENED HER EYES, she was in an enormous, canopied bed in a softly lit room.

Where was she? What had happened? Something

terrible. Something that carried within it the seeds of disaster.

She sat up against a bank of silk-covered pillows— and everything came rushing back. Dante. Samantha. Her baby in her lover's arms. Her baby, here, in this place, where three years' worth of secrets might untangle like a skein of yarn.

Tally started to push the comforter aside. She had to find Sam. Take her home…

"*Cara.* What are you doing?"

Dante's voice was harsh. He stood in the door between the bath and the bedroom, his tall, powerful figure shadowy in the light.

"Where's my baby?"

"Samantha is fine."

He came toward her, a glass of water in one hand, a small tablet in the other. Tally brushed aside his outstretched hand.

"Where is she?"

"She's in the nursery. Asleep."

"I want to see her."

"I told you, she's fine."

Tally swung her feet to the floor. "Don't argue with me, Dante! I want to see her now."

"The tablet first."

She glared up at him. She knew him well; enough to know he wasn't going to let her get past him until she obeyed his command.

"What is that?"

"Just something to calm you."

"I don't need calming, damn it!"

"The doctor disagreed."

"You called a doctor?"

"Of course I did," he said brusquely. "You fainted."

"Only because—because I was stunned to see my daughter. You had no right—"

"Take the tablet." His mouth twitched. "Then you can tell me what a monster I am, for flying Samantha here so she could be with you."

She glared at him one last time. Then she snatched the glass from his hand, dumped the tablet in her mouth and gulped it down with a mouthful of water.

Tell him what a monster he was? No. She wasn't going to waste the time. You couldn't argue with Dante Russo. He was always right, so why bother? She'd take Sam and leave.

But first, she had to get dressed.

The realization that she was *undressed* surged through her. She was wearing a nightgown of pale blue silk, its thin straps scattered with pink silk rosebuds, the kind of gown only a man would buy for a woman.

An ache, sharp as a knife, pierced her heart. Was the woman Dante had bought it for as lovely as the gown? She must have been, for him to have given her something so fragile and exquisitely beautiful. For him to have made love to that woman here, in his home, where he had never made love to her.

Unaccountably, her eyes stung with tears. Angry tears. What else could they be?

Damn Dante Russo to hell! Who had given him permission to have his housekeeper take off her clothes and dress her in this gown that wasn't hers?

"Well?"

She looked up. Dante was watching her, one dark eyebrow raised.

"Aren't you going to tell me I'm a monster?"

"Get away from me," Tally said, her voice trembling.

"After all," he said, a wry smile curving his lips, "you have every reason to despise me. You pass out, I phone for my doctor.... What woman wouldn't hate a man under those circumstances?"

"I want my clothes."

"Why?"

"Dante. You may find this amusing, but I do not. You seem to think you can—you can take control of my life. Well, you can't. I don't want your job. I don't want your guest suite. I don't want you thinking you can decide what's best for my baby, I don't want your housekeeper undressing me, and I certainly do not want your mistress's cast-offs."

"Such a long list of don'ts," he said mildly, tucking his hands into the pockets of what she now realized were soft-looking gray sweatpants. "Unfortunately, not all of them are appropriate."

"Damn you, I'm not playing games!"

"Let's go through them one by one, shall we?"

"Let's not. I told you—"

"I heard you. Now it's your turn to listen. Number one, I'm not trying to control anything. You agreed to the terms of the job."

"If by 'terms,' you mean me living in your home—"

"Two," he said, ignoring her protests, "I cannot imagine that thinking it best for you and Sam to be together as soon as possible was a mistake."

"I was going home to her. Didn't that occur to you?"

"It did, but I have a private plane. Why would you want to spend hours on the train, only to turn around and make the trip here again when I could arrange to bring her to you tonight?"

"Damn it, who gave you the right to think for me? I was not going to turn around, as you put it, and make the trip here again. I told you, I don't want your—"

"And, finally," he said, "finally, *cara,* you're wrong about the nightgown." He took his hands from his pockets, reached out and trailed one finger deliberately across one rose-embroidered strap, hooking the tip under the fabric, lightly tugging at it so that she had no choice but to sit forward. "I bought it for you, along with some other things I thought you might need to help you settle in." His voice turned silken. "And then there's that final accusation. That my housekeeper undressed you. She didn't."

A rush of color shot into Tally's face. Dante saw it and smiled.

"Why would I have her do that," he said softly, "when I've undressed you myself hundreds of times in the past?"

"The past is dead, Dante. You had no right—"

"Damn it," he said sharply, his smile vanishing, "who are you to talk about rights?" His hands cupped her shoulders and he drew her to her feet. "Such self-righteous garbage from a woman who ran like a coward instead of facing a man and telling him she'd cheated on him!"

"I didn't—"

"What? You didn't cheat? What do you call becoming involved with another man, if not cheating? Come on, Tally. I'd love to hear you come up with a better word."

What could she say to that? Nothing, not without admitting the truth. Telling him he'd fathered Sam would
open her to his scorn, his anger and, worst of all, to the
possibility he'd try and take her daughter from her.

"That's a fine speech," she said calmly, even though
her heart was racing. "But you're only making it because I wounded your ego. You were bored. You were
going to leave me. Instead, I made the first move. That's
what really bothers you and you know it."

Was it? She'd just told him exactly what he'd been
telling himself for three years, but now he wasn't sure
it was that simple. Had he planned on breaking things
off because he was bored, or was there some deeper
reason he hadn't wanted to face?

Was that what had driven her into the arms of a
stranger?

Maybe he'd ask himself that question someday, but
not now. Not when all his rage at Tally had turned to fear
an hour ago, when he'd watched her face whiten as she
crumpled to the floor.

Now she stood straight and tall before him, her eyes
fixed on his and glittering with unshed, angry tears. Her
hair was loose; he'd undone the pins himself, let it
tumble to her shoulders in soft, heavy waves. She wore
no makeup; he'd washed it away with a cool cloth and
it occurred to him that he'd never seen her like this
before, that in all the time they'd been lovers, her appearance had always been perfect.

She'd been beautiful then but she was even more
lovely like this, he'd thought, her lips naked of artificial
color, her hair in sweet disarray. She was what they
called her in Vermont.

She was Tally, not Taylor, and something in the softness of the old-fashioned name had made his throat constrict.

Slowly, he'd undressed her, telling himself it was only so he didn't have to ring for Mrs. Tipton or Ellen.

His hands had trembled as he undid the buttons of her suit, as he slid her blouse from her shoulders.

It was so long since he'd seen her breasts. Her belly. The pale curls that hid the sweet folds of flesh where he longed to bury himself. The long legs that had once wrapped around his hips as he lost himself in her welcoming heat.

And yet, despite those images, what he'd felt, undressing Tally, hadn't been sexual desire.

What he'd felt was the desire to protect her. To hold her close. Rock her in his arms. Tell her he was sorry he'd hurt her, sorry he hadn't understood what she'd needed of him, what he'd needed of her all those years ago....

"Even now," Tally said, her voice tinged with bitterness, "even now, you can't tell me the truth."

"You're right," he said quietly. "I was going to leave you." Tally turned away. He cupped her jaw and forced her to meet his eyes. "But I don't know why, *cara*. I thought that I did, but now I'm not so sure." His gaze fell to her lips. "All I'm sure of is this."

"No," she whispered, but even as he lowered his head to hers, Tally didn't pull back. She shut her eyes, felt the whisper of his breath on her mouth, and when he gathered her into his arms and said her name, she moaned and melted against him.

This was the kind of kiss they'd shared on the night that had changed everything. It was a kiss of tenderness and longing so intense she could feel his heart thudding against hers and with a suddenness that stunned her, she knew she wanted more.

"Dante," she said, the word a soft sigh against his lips. "Dante…"

His name, breathed against his mouth. Her breasts, pressed to his chest. Her belly, soft against his. Dante groaned, slid his hands into Tally's spill of cinnamon hair and gathered her closer.

Passion exploded between them.

Tenderness became desire; longing turned to desperate need. Dante's mouth demanded acquiescence and Tally give it, parting her lips so his tongue could seek out her honeyed taste. He groaned, slid down the delicate straps of the nightgown, baring her breasts to his hands and mouth.

"Say it," he demanded, and she did.

Her whispered "Yes, make love to me. Yes, touch me, yes, yes, yes," rose into the silence of the winter night and filled him with ecstasy.

And he knew, in that instant, that taking her to bed once more in a quest for revenge was not what he needed at all.

He needed her wanting him, like this. Crying out as he bent to her and sucked her nipple deep into his mouth. Tossing her head back in frenzied response to the brush of his hand as he dragged up the skirt of her gown, cupped her mons with his palm, felt her hot tears of desire damp on his fingers and sweet heaven, he was going to come, to come, to come…

He scooped Tally into his arms.

"Now," he said fiercely, his mouth at her throat, and she sobbed his name over and over as he carried her through the vast room, heading not to her bed but to his…

A child's voice cried out.

"Sam," Tally whispered.

Dante shut his eyes. Dragged air into his lungs. Turned and carried her to the nursery, where he set her gently on her feet.

He stood back and let her approach the child in the white and gold crib alone.

"Baby," she murmured, "did you have a bad dream?"

"Mama?"

Tally lifted her daughter in her arms. Sam was warm from sleep, sweet from the mingled scents of soap and baby powder. She sighed and laid her head against Tally's shoulder.

"Teddies are sleepin', Mama."

Teddies, indeed. The bedraggled, much-loved bear from home sat in the corner of the crib, side by side with the smallest new teddy from the bear family Dante had bought.

Unaccountably, Tally's heart swelled.

"Yes, baby," she said softly, "I see."

She went to the rocking chair, sat in it and gently rocked Sam back and forth, back and forth.

"'Hush little baby,'" she sang softly, "'don't you cry…'"

Gradually, Samantha's breathing slowed. Tally waited until she was certain she was sound asleep. Then she carried her child to the crib, laid her in it, covered her with a blanket and pressed a kiss to her hair.

When she turned she saw Dante, still in the doorway, watching her, his face unreadable in the soft shadows cast by the nightlight.

*Oh, Dante,* she thought, *Dante…*

Slowly, she went to him and looked into his eyes. A muscle jumped in his cheek. He lifted his hand and reached toward her and she shook her head and pulled back, knowing that if he touched her—if he touched her…

"What we did—what we almost did—was a mistake."

"Making love is never a mistake, *cara.*"

He was wrong. It was a mistake, and Tally knew it. Knew it because she'd finally faced the truth.

She loved Dante Russo with all her heart.

Bad enough she could never tell him she'd borne him a child, but to lie in his arms and pretend it was only sex would be the ultimate travesty.

A heart could only be broken so many times before it shattered into a million pieces.

Tally put her hands lightly on Dante's chest. "Maybe not," she said softly. "But it can't happen anymore."

A smile tilted at the corners of his mouth. "Does this mean I won't have to sue you for breach of contract?"

She smiled, too. "If you mean, will I take the job, the answer is yes. It's a wonderful opportunity, and I thank you for it. And I'll stay here." Her voice grew soft. "This suite is beautiful, and the nursery you created for Sam is a little girl's dream come true." She drew a breath. "But you have to give me your word you won't try to make love to me."

"Is that really what you want?"

No. Oh no, it wasn't. She longed to tell him that, to go into his arms, lift her mouth to his, plead for him to carry her to bed and love her until dawn lit the sky.…

"*Cara?* Is it really what you want?"

She had lied to him already. Now she had no choice but to lie to him again.

"Yes."

Long seconds dragged by. Then Dante took her hand, pressed a kiss to the palm and folded her fingers over it.

It was only hours later, as she lay in bed watching dawn slip over the city, that Tally realized Dante hadn't actually said he'd agree.

# CHAPTER EIGHT

TALLY WAS UP at six the next morning.

Sam was still asleep in the next room, sprawled on her belly in her new crib, flanked by both her teddy bears.

Tally smiled, bent down and pressed a light kiss to her daughter's hair. Then she showered, put on a clean blouse but the same black suit and took a critical look at herself in the mirror.

She needed to buy clothes. If you looked success-ful, people assumed that you were. It wasn't the best way to judge anyone but that was how it went, espe-cially in this town.

Her pay would be based partly on salary and expenses, partly on the cost of the completed project. So far, no one had mentioned when she'd get a check. She hated to ask, especially because it was Dante she'd have to go to, but she'd have to work up to it, and soon.

Tally gave her image another glance, then took a deep breath. Maybe she'd be lucky and Dante would already have left for the day.

No such luck.

He was in the sun-filled breakfast room, seated at

a round glass table with a cup of black coffee in his hand and the business section of the *New York Times* in front of him.

He looked up as Tally entered, and half rose from his chair. She motioned him to stay seated and went to the sideboard to pour herself coffee. It was easier to do that than to think about the fact that this was the very first time they'd had breakfast together.

"Good morning," he said. "Did you sleep well?"

She nodded. "Fine, thank you." A lie, of course. She'd tossed half the night, thinking of him in a room just down the stairs. "Thank you, too, for having that baby intercom installed between my room and Sam's."

"No problem. Actually, I had monitors installed throughout the place. I thought it would make you feel more comfortable, knowing you could hear Samantha no matter where you were."

"That was very thoughtful," she said politely, and sipped at her coffee.

"Sit down and join me."

There was no way to turn down the request, especially since he'd risen to his feet and was pulling out the chair opposite his. She thanked him, slipped into the chair and tried to concentrate on the coffee. It wasn't an easy thing to do.

Dante was a major distraction.

He was—there was no other word for it—he was beautiful. Not in a feminine way but beautiful all the same, wearing what she knew was a custom-made dark-blue suit, a pale-blue shirt from the city's most distinguished shirtmaker, and a maroon silk tie. His dark hair was curling and damp from the shower.

Another first.

They'd never breakfasted together, and she'd never seen him fresh from the shower. They'd had long bouts of incredible sex but afterward, he'd always dressed and gone home to shower. He preferred his own things, he'd told her. His soap, his razor, his toiletries, and she'd understood that what he'd really meant was that sex was one thing but showering was another, that he would only take intimacy just so far....

"Tally?"

She blinked. Dante had pushed a vellum envelope and a leather-bound notebook toward her.

"Sorry." She gave a polite little laugh. "I was—I was just trying to plan my day."

"I've already planned some of it for you. I hope you don't mind, but I want you to get up to speed as quickly as possible."

"Oh. Oh, no. I want that, too."

"There's a check in the envelope. Call it a signing bonus. If it isn't enough—"

"I'm sure it'll be fine. Thank you."

"Don't thank me. You're going to work hard to earn your money. You'll find your appointments for today listed in the notebook. For right now—" Dante glanced at his watch, pushed back his chair and rose to his feet "—I have to get going. Carlo will take you to the office."

"Your driver? Won't you need him?"

"I'm flying to Philadelphia. I'll take a cab to the airport."

Philadelphia. How long would he be gone? Would he be back by evening? It was better if he weren't. Then she wouldn't have to imagine returning here, seeing him, saying something banal as she went to the guest suite and he went out because he would go out, wouldn't he? There had to be a woman in his life. He was too virile a man to be without one.

But if there were, would he have kissed *her?* Would he have said he wanted to make love to her? Would he look at her as he had last night, as if he could almost feel her in his arms, hear her moans, because she would moan if he touched her, and—what was wrong with her today? She couldn't live here and imagine these things.

"Tally?"

"Yes?"

"You seem…distracted."

Heat rushed to her face. "No, not at all." Quickly, to cover her embarrassment, she added, "You said you're flying to Philadelphia?"

"And that my P.A., Joan, will show you around. She took care of furnishing your office. If it doesn't please you, tell her to make whatever changes you wish. Joan's also the one who scheduled your appointments, so if you have any questions—"

"Ask Joan."

Dante nodded and walked around the table to where she sat.

"She's organized meetings for you with half a dozen prospective assistants."

He was leaning over her; his scent drifted to her. Soap, water and pure, sexy essence of Dante. That was how she'd always thought of the smell of his skin. She'd never forgotten it or the memories it evoked.

His taste on her tongue. The feel of him, under her hands.

"I'm right," he said softly.

Tally looked up. His face was close to hers, his eyes a deep, cool gray.

"Something's definitely distracting you, *cara*. What could it be?"

"Nothing. I'm just—I'm concentrating on what you said. My office. Appointments with possible assistants. What else?"

"Did Mrs. Tipton tell you that she and Ellen will be happy to look after Sam, until you've hired a nanny?"

He leaned closer. All she had to do was turn her head an inch and her lips would brush his jaw.

"She told me. That's very—" she cleared her throat "—that's very kind of them. I'll contact an agency first thing and—"

"Joan's already taken care of it. A highly recommended agency is sending over half a dozen women for you to interview. They all have impeccable credentials, but again, if you're not satisfied, all you need do is inform Joan."

His shoulder brushed hers. Was it her imagination, or could she feel the heat of him through all the layers of clothing separating them?

"Tally? Is that acceptable?"

His eyes were on hers. The color had gone from gray to silver. Silver that somehow burned like flame.

"It's—it's fine."

"Because," he said, his voice suddenly low and husky, "because, *cara,* we can always alter the arrangement we made."

He wasn't talking about the office or her appointments, and they both knew it.

"No," she said, "we can't. I want things exactly as we agreed."

"Are you certain?"

The only thing she was certain of was that she had to get herself under control because she couldn't do this. Think about him making love to her, want him making love to her...

She took a deep breath. "Yes."

"In that case, there's nothing left to do this morning." His gaze dropped to her lips. "Except this," he said softly, and brushed his mouth over hers.

"No," she said, hating the soft, breathless quality of her voice.

"You're starting a new career and I'm flying to an important meeting. It's just a kiss for luck. Surely, I'm allowed that?"

"Dante. We can't—"

"We aren't."

He put his hand under her chin, lifted her face and claimed her mouth with his. And she—she let it happen. Let him slide the tip of his tongue between her lips, let him thrust his fingers into her hair, let him deepen the kiss until she was dizzy with wanting him....

Dante let go of her, straightened and took a sleek black leather briefcase from the sideboard.

And then he was gone.

TALLY'S DAY WAS LONG, exhausting—and wonderful.

Her office was a huge, light-filled room, handsomely furnished and perfectly equipped. Selecting an assistant was difficult only because all the candidates Dante's P.A. had chosen were outstanding.

It would have been equally tough to choose one of the nannies but a middle-aged woman with a soft Scottish lilt made things easier when she spotted Sam's photo on Tally's desk and crooned, "Och, the sweet little lamb!"

There was nothing difficult in deciding that Dante's P.A. was the eighth wonder of the world. Joan was fiftyish, elegant, and as warm as she was efficient.

"Just let me know what you need," she said, "and it's as good as yours."

At lunchtime, Tally dashed to Fifth Avenue and did the sort of lightning-fast shopping trip she used to do in the past. Within an hour, she'd bought several trousers, skirts, blazers, cashmere sweaters and a couple of pairs of shoes.

At four, she met with Dante's architect, who showed her the interior changes he was going to make in the new offices. At five, she met with one of her old contacts at the design center. At six, she dismissed Dante's driver and headed for the subway.

Dante would not kiss her anymore, and she would not accept any more favors from him. She was working with him. It was only right that they maintain appropriate behavior.

There was a delay on the subway line. A quarter of an hour passed before the train came and after that, it sat between stations for five endless minutes. When she reached her stop, she went half a block out of her way to buy a chocolate Santa for Sam.

She'd called to talk with her baby half a dozen times and the last time, she'd promised to bring a special treat.

By the time she reached Dante's apartment building,

Tally was feeling wonderful. She was back in the city she loved, involved in a major project, and she'd made peace with the problem of dealing with Dante.

All she had to do was make sure he understood the parameters of their relationship, and—

"Where have you been?"

Dante stood in the entrance to the building, blocking her way. His voice was rough, his face white with unconcealed anger.

"I beg your pardon?"

Mouth set, he clasped her arm and marched her past the doorman to the penthouse elevator.

"I asked you a question. Where the hell were you? You should have been here an hour ago."

She swung toward him, her temper rising to match his as he pushed her, unceremoniously, into the car.

"I should have been here an hour ago?" Tally slapped her hands on her hips. "Are you out of your mind? I don't have to answer to you!"

"You left the office at six. An hour late."

"How nice. You have people spying on me."

"And turned down the use of my car."

"Is your driver a paid informer?"

"And where did you go for lunch? I phoned and you hadn't told Joan or your new assistant where you'd be."

Tally was trembling with anger. "Where I went and why I went there is none of your business. Unless—" The color drained from her face. "Ohmygod, is it Sam? Is my baby ill?"

"No!" Dante stepped in front of her as the car doors opened on his penthouse. "Listen to me. Samantha's fine. This has nothing to do with her."

Sweet relief flooded through her, but it didn't last. She'd accepted a job from this man and moved into his guest suite. If he thought that made her his property, he was wrong.

"Then, get out of my way," she said coldly. "I don't answer to you."

"You damned well will," he said grimly, his hand closing like a steel band around her wrist. "This is New York, not a blip on the map in Vermont. Anything might happen to you on these streets."

"What a short memory you have, Russo!" Tally jerked free of his hand. "I know all about New York. I lived here for five years!"

She had. He knew that. She'd traveled the city's streets, ridden its subways, lived in an apartment alone. Of course he knew that…but things had changed.

He told her so, and she looked at him as if he'd gone crazy.

"Nothing's changed. The city's the same. So am I."

"You're not." His mouth twisted and the ugly suspicions he'd tried to deny while he'd paced the floor and wondered where she was, burst from his lips. "You slept with another man while you belonged to me. How do I know you're not seeing him again?"

Tally's eyes went flat. "You don't," she said coldly, and brushed past him.

Dante let her go. He had to; he was still rational enough to know that if he went after her now, it was a sure bet he'd do something he'd regret.

So he turned his back, strode along the marble floor to the library, flung open the liquor cabinet and poured himself a stiff shot of bourbon. And began pacing again, back and forth on the antique silk carpet before the fire-place, while the hours ticked away.

She'd all but called him crazy.

Hell, maybe she was right.

How come he hadn't thought about this before? All the plans he'd made to bring Tally back to New York and it had never occurred to him that he might be pushing her straight into the arms of her old lover.

The man who'd made her pregnant.

If he wasn't crazy, he was just plain stupid, because the idea hadn't even popped into his head until he'd been at lunch in Philadelphia after a morning of meetings. Somewhere between the salad course and the entrée, he'd suddenly realized he wanted to hear Tally's voice. He'd excused himself, left the table and phoned.

But she wasn't at her office, and Joan had no idea where she'd gone. He'd started to call her on her cell phone, only to realize that he didn't have the number.

He'd gone back to the table. Shoved the grilled shrimps and vegetables back and forth on his plate. Said "yes" and "no" and "how interesting" when it seemed fitting.

And all the while, he'd been thinking, *Where is she? Where did she go?*

That was when he'd first realized that bringing her back to the city might have been a mistake. That even now, while he pretended to pay attention to the details of a billion-dollar deal, Tally might be lying in the arms of the man she'd left him for. She'd slept with the man only once, she'd said, but Tally wasn't like that.

She wouldn't be anybody's one-night stand.

Had she lied about that? Had the bastard been her

lover for weeks? For months? Did she want to go back to him now?

Why would she, when he'd abandoned her when she was pregnant?

He had abandoned her, hadn't he? Because if he hadn't, if something, who the hell knew what, had kept Tally and the SOB apart and that something no longer stood between them—

*You are losing your mind,* Dante had told himself.

The warning hadn't helped.

Everyone ordered coffee. He lifted his cup, frowned, put it down untouched. He was sorry, he said; he had to leave. And he walked away from three men who stared at him as if they agreed with the silent assessment he'd made of his sanity.

He'd flown back to New York, angry at himself, furious at Tally because it was her fault, all of this, his rage, his distrust, his inability to do anything except think about her. If only she'd never run from him…

Her fault. Entirely.

At home, he'd paced the floor, planning how he'd tell her that if she thought she was going to live with him and take someone else for a lover, she was wrong.

He'd kill the other man before he let that happen.

Then he'd told himself that she wasn't living with him, not in any real sense. Besides, maybe she hadn't gone back to the other man. Maybe she'd told him the truth, that she'd only been with that faceless stranger the one time.

One time had been enough.

The son of a bitch had planted a seed in her womb. He'd given her a child he hadn't helped support, a child who was solely Tally's responsibility. A child who by all rights should have belonged to—should have belonged to—

The clock on the mantel had struck the hour. Seven o'clock. Seven at night, and where the hell was she?

Carlo had no idea. Ms. Sommers had sent his car away. Joan, reached at home, didn't know a thing, either.

And Dante, fueled with a rage he didn't understand, had lost control. He'd paced some more, snarled at his housekeeper when she came in to ask what time he wanted dinner served and, when he was alone again, punched his fist into the wall with such force he was surprised he hadn't put a hole in it.

He went down to the lobby, about to head into the street to find Tally—though he had no idea where in hell he'd start—and saw her come sauntering toward the door, with a smile for the doorman and a blank look for him.

He'd wanted to shake her until her teeth rattled.

He'd wanted to haul her into his arms and kiss her.

In the end, because he knew doing either would be a mistake, he'd launched into a tirade that settled nothing except to prove, once again, he was an idiot where she was concerned.

Dante looked at the clock on the mantel. The hours had raced by. It was two in the morning; the city below was as quiet as it would ever be.

Two in the morning, and he was still ticking like a time bomb while Tally undoubtedly slept peacefully two floors above him.

He tilted the glass to his lips and drained it of bourbon.

Did she get a kick out of this? Out of making him

behave this way? Surely, she knew she had this effect on him.

She did it deliberately.

That was why he'd decided to end their affair three years ago. He hadn't been bored. Who could be bored by a woman who could discuss the stock market and football statistics without missing a beat?

A muscle knotted in his jaw.

He could afford a little honesty now, couldn't he? Admit to himself that the reason he'd wanted to end things was because he'd sensed his feelings for her were becoming uncontrollable?

That night she'd asked him to stay, and he almost had. Other nights when she hadn't asked, when he'd had to force himself from her bed because the thought of leaving her had been agony.

Oh, yes.

Tally was manipulating him. Toying with him and the self-discipline on which he prided himself. The self-discipline that had made him a success.

And he didn't like it, not one bit.

Dante's eyes narrowed. But he knew what to do about it. How to regain that control. Of himself. Of the situation. Of Tally.

Back to Plan A. He would take her to bed.

He had perfect control there. Holding back, not just physically but emotionally. Exulting in what happened between them, feeling it as a hot rush of pleasure so intense he'd never known it with another woman and yet, keeping a little piece of himself from her.

Emotions were not things to put on exhibit. Control was a man's sole protection against a hostile world.

Control, goddamn it, Dante thought.

His hands knotted into fists. Anger burned like a fire in his belly. Anger, and something far more primitive.

Tally was asleep, satisfied she'd made a fool of him again, and he was here, wide awake, trapped like an insect in a web of rage.

"Enough," he growled.

Dante flung open the library door and headed for the stairs.

# CHAPTER NINE

MOONLIGHT SPILLED from a sky bright with stars and lay like fine French lace across the floor of Tally's bedroom.

Some other time, she'd have noticed and admired it. Not tonight.

Instead, she sat curled in a window seat, her back to the night, focused only on the turmoil inside her, anger and pain warring for control of her heart.

She hated Dante, hated the things he'd accused her of. How could he think her capable of being a cheat and a liar?

*Maybe because you told him you slept with another man while he was still your lover,* a voice inside her whispered contemptuously.

Yes. All right, but what else could she have done? She'd wanted to protect herself and Sam. Now she knew she'd done the right thing. Dante had shown a side of himself she'd never imagined.

She'd always believed he was a man who suppressed his emotions.

Tonight, he'd been a man out of control, capable of anything.

Tally shivered and drew the silk robe more closely around herself. The night seemed endless, especially without Sam in the next room. The baby had dozed off in her play crib in the little room next to the housekeeper's.

"Let her stay the night, Ms. Sommers," Mrs. Tipton had said. "Why wake her from a sound sleep?"

Now Tally was glad she'd left Sam where she was. Her little girl needed the rest. Tomorrow was going to be a busy day.

She and Sam were going home to Shelby.

She'd scrub floors for a living, move into a furnished flat above a storefront on Main Street if she had to. Better that, better to raise her daughter in poverty, than to raise her here.

Tally rose to her feet and paced the bedroom, the details of her confrontation with Dante as alive as if they'd happened minutes instead of hours ago.

What gave him the right to ask where she'd been? To accuse her of sneaking off to be with Samantha's father? She'd come within a breath of laughing in his face at that, except it really wasn't funny.

Okay. She'd made a mistake, accepting this job. Well, a mistake could be remedied. And maybe some good had come of it. At least now she knew exactly what she felt for Dante Russo.

She despised him.

Tally paused, wrapped her arms around herself and drew a shuddering breath. She had to do something or go crazy. She'd pack. Yes. That was an excellent idea. She'd pack now. That way, come morning, all she'd have to do was take Sam and get the hell out of this snake pit.

Ellen had hung all her clothes in the closet, includ-

ing the things Saks had delivered this afternoon. Tally
dumped her old stuff in her suitcase and ignored the rest.
Let Dante give it away. Let him burn it, for all she gave
a damn.

She didn't want anything his money had bought.

He was a heartless, manipulative, controlling son of
a bitch and it made her sick to think she'd ever imagined
that she loved him. Anybody could be guilty of a bit of
self-deception, but once you knew it you had to do
something about it.

She'd spent years in the city, though maybe she was
still a small-town girl at heart, unable or unwilling to
think she'd slept with a man, borne his child without
loving him.

But no woman could love a man who thought he
owned you. Who believed you capable of lies and deceit
and—

The bedroom door flew open, the sound of it sharp
as a gunshot in the quiet night. Tally whirled around.

Dante stood in the doorway, and her heart leaped
into her throat.

This was a Dante she'd never seen before.

His suit jacket was gone, as was his tie. His shirt was
open at the neck, the sleeves rolled to the elbows,
exposing forearms knotted with muscle.

But it was what she saw in the way he held himself
that terrified her. The tall, powerful body poised like a
big cat's. The dark intensity of his eyes as they fixed on
hers. The cruel little smile that tilted across his mouth.

Tally wanted to run but there was nowhere to go. She
had to face the enemy.

"What are you doing here, Dante?"

He answered by stepping inside the room and shutting the door behind him.

"It's late," she said.

"I agree. It's very late. I'm here to remedy that."

"And—and Samantha is sleeping. I don't want to wake her."

"Samantha is with Mrs. Tipton." He took another step forward. "Taylor."

He was back to using her given name. How could he make it seem menacing?

"Dante." Her voice quavered. "Dante, please. You want to talk. So do I. But it can wait until morning."

"I don't want to talk, Taylor."

A sob burst from Tally's throat. To hell with facing the enemy. She turned and ran. Sam's bedroom was empty. If she could get there before he reached her—

Two quick steps, and his powerful hands closed on her shoulders; he spun her toward him and she looked up into eyes that glittered with the desolate cold of a polar night.

"No! Don't. Dante—"

He captured her mouth with his, forced her lips apart and penetrated her with his tongue. He tasted of anger and of whiskey, and of a primitive domination that terrified her.

"No," she cried, and struggled to free herself from his grasp, but he laughed, pushed her back against the wall and yanked her hands high above her head.

"Fight me," he growled. "Go on. Fight! It'll make taking you even more pleasurable."

"Please," she panted. "Dante, please. Don't do this. I beg you—"

"All those months I made love to you and it wasn't enough. Is that why you went to him? Did he do things I didn't?"

"Dante. I never—"

He ripped the robe apart, tore her nightgown from the vee between her breasts straight down to her belly.

"Tell me what you wanted that I didn't give you."

"You're wrong. Wrong! It wasn't the way you make it sound. I didn't—"

She cried out as he captured one breast in his hand and rubbed his thumb across the nipple, his cold eyes locked to hers.

"Was it the way he touched your breasts?"

Tears were streaming down her face. Good, he thought. Let her weep. It wouldn't stop him. He would do this. Pierce her flesh with his and banish her from his life, forever.

"Was it the way he touched you here?"

He thrust his hand between her thighs, searching, even in his madness, for the welcoming heat, the sweet moisture he had never forgotten...

And found, instead, the cold, dry flesh of a woman who was unready and unwilling. A woman who was sobbing as if her heart were breaking...

As she had broken his.

Dante went still. He looked at Tally's face and felt the coldness inside him melting.

"Tally."

His arms went around her; he gathered her to him, his hands stroking her back, her hair. He kissed her forehead, her wet eyes, and as she wept he whispered to her, soft words in his native language, but she stood rigid within his embrace, still quietly crying as if the world were about to end.

"Tally." Dante framed her face between his hands. "*Inamorata.* Forgive me. Please. Don't cry. I won't hurt you. I could never hurt you." He raised her chin, looked into her eyes and saw a darkness and despair that chilled his soul.

He dragged in a deep breath, hating himself, hating what he had almost done, knowing that what was driving him was not hate or anger but something else. Something foreign to his life and to him.

A fear he'd never known gripped him.

He'd fought toughs on the streets of Palermo. Faced down CEOs in hostile boardrooms. Made believers of financial analysts who'd looked him in the eye and assured him he couldn't do any of the things he'd ended up doing.

He was a warrior. Each battle he survived made him stronger.

But he wasn't a warrior now. He was a man, holding in his arms a woman he'd already lost once before. She had run from him and he knew, in his heart of hearts, that she'd run because he had somehow failed her.

She'd turned to another man for the same reason.

If she ran again, if he lost her again…

"Tally."

He held her closer. Rained kisses over her hair. Said her name over and over, and finally, finally when he'd almost given up hope, she lifted her face to his.

"I wasn't with anyone," she whispered. "I never wanted anyone but you, Dante. Never. Never. Nev—"

He kissed her. With all his heart, his soul, with all he had ever been or ever hoped to be, and Tally wound her arms around his neck and kissed him back. They had kissed a thousand times. A million times…but never like this, as if their lives hung in the balance.

Mouths fused, Dante swept Tally into his arms and carried her to the bed.

At first, it was enough. The taste of her mouth. The warmth of his breath. Her sighs. His whispers. The stroke of her hand on his face, of his hand on her throat…

It was enough.

Inevitably, it changed.

Dante could feel the tension growing inside him. The need to take more. To give more. To suck Tally's nipples, put his mouth between her thighs and inhale her exquisite scent.

It was the same for Tally. She needed Dante's mouth on her flesh. His hands on her breasts. Needed to lift her hips to him, impale herself on his rock-hard erection so that she could fly with him to the stars.

"Dante," she whispered.

Everything a man could dream was in the way she spoke his name.

He eased the robe and tattered nightgown from her shoulders, kissing the hollow in her throat, the delicate skin over her collarbone.

She was lovely. As beautiful as he'd remembered.

There was a new fullness to her breasts now. The child, Dante thought, and felt a swift pain at the realization that someone else had given that child to her, but it left him quickly because there was so much more to the woman in his arms than that one moment of infidelity.

He bent his head, kissed the slope of each breast. Brushed a finger lightly over a pale-pink nipple.

Watched her face as he played the nub of flesh delicately between thumb and forefinger, and felt the fierce tightening low in his belly when she sobbed his name as he drew the nub into his mouth.

She tasted like cream and honey; she tasted like the Tally he'd never forgotten, never wanted to forget, and when she tugged impatiently at his shirt he sat up, tried unbuttoning it, cursed and tore it off. Peeled off the rest of his clothing and took her in his arms again.

The hot feel of her breasts against his chest almost undid him. Dante groaned, clenched his teeth, warned himself to hang onto his control.

But she was moving beneath him, rubbing herself against his engorged flesh. She was slick and hot, and the exciting scent of her arousal was more precious to him than all the perfumes in the world.

"Please," she said, kissing his shoulder. "Please, please, please…"

"Soon," he whispered, but she arched against him and he was lost. Nothing mattered but this. This, he thought, and entered her on one long, hard thrust.

Tally screamed. Her hands dug into his hair; she wrapped her legs around his hips and bit his shoulder and he let go. Of himself, of his past, of the restraints that had always defined his life.

Together, they soared over the edge of the earth, two hearts, two souls, two bodies merged as one.

AFTERWARD, they lay in each other's arms and shared soft kisses. They touched and sighed, and then Tally's breathing slowed.

"Go to sleep, *inamorata,*" Dante whispered.

"What does that mean? *Inamorata?*"

He kissed her. "It means beloved."

Tally smiled and he kissed her again.

"Go to sleep."

"I'm not sleepy," she murmured.

And slept.

Dante gathered her closer against him. How had he endured three long years without this woman in his life?

Except, he had never really let her into his life. They'd been lovers for six months back then but he'd kept his distance. He always did. Dinners out at the city's best restaurants instead of pasta and vino by the fire. Center row seats at the newest Broadway show instead of an evening of old movies on the DVD. Dancing at the latest club instead of swaying in each other's arms to a Billy Joel CD.

How come?

And how come he didn't even know if she liked old movies? If she liked Billy Joel or maybe newer stuff?

Because he'd never let her into his life. That was how come. It was the same reason he'd called her Taylor, when any fool could see that under all the urban glamour, she was really a girl named Tally.

And he—and he felt something special for her.

His arms tightened around her. He wanted to make love to her again but she was sleeping so soundly...

Okay. He'd kiss her closed eyes. Gently. Like that. Kiss her mouth. Tenderly. Yes, that way. Kiss it again and if she sighed, as she was sighing now, if her lips parted so that he could taste her sweetness, yes, like that... If her lashes fluttered and she looked up at him and smiled and linked her hands behind his neck the way she was doing now, would it be wrong to kiss her again? To run his hand gently down her body? To groan as she lifted herself to him, cradled his body between her thighs?

"Make love to me," Tally whispered.

And he would. He would—but first, he lifted her in his arms and rose from the bed.

"Where are we going?"

"To my room," he said huskily. "To my bed. It's where you belong, *inamorata,* where you always should have been." He kissed her. "Where you will be, from this night on."

HIS ROOM WAS SHADOWED, his bed high and wide.

They made love again, slowly, tenderly, until passion swept them up and Dante brought Tally down on him, impaled her on him, and watched her face as she rode him to fulfillment. They slept in each other's arms and awakened again at dawn, Tally wordlessly drawing Dante to her, sighing his name against his throat as he rocked into her and took her with him to the stars.

When she awoke next, it was to the kiss of the morning sun. Dante lay next to her, head propped on his fist, watching her with a soft smile on his lips.

Tally smiled, too. "Hello," she whispered.

He leaned over and kissed her mouth. "Hello, *bellissima.*"

She stretched with lazy abandon. The sheet dropped to her waist. Dante seized the moment and kissed her breasts.

"Sweet," he murmured.

She smiled again. She might never stop smiling, she thought, clasping his face between her hands and pressing a light kiss to his lips.

"I love it when you kiss me," he said softly.

She loved it, too. She could spend the morning like this, just kissing, touching, locked away from reality....

Oh, God. Locked away from Samantha.

"Tally. What's wrong?"

Everything, Tally thought, and it was all her fault. She moved out of Dante's arms and sat up, suddenly conscious of her nudity.

Dante sat up, too, and caught her in his arms. "Talk to me. What's the matter?"

"Sam's an early riser."

"Is that what's worrying you?" Smiling, he drew her to him. "So is Mrs. Tipton."

"Sam is my daughter. My responsibility. Not your housekeeper's."

"Damn it, Tally, don't look away from me." He clasped her face, forced her eyes to meet his. "Moments ago you were in my arms. Now you're looking at me as if we're strangers. Talk to me. Tell me what you're thinking."

Tell him what? That the long, wonderful night had been a mistake? Because it had been. Yes, he'd brought her to his bed, but nothing had changed. She loved him. Why lie to herself? She loved him, she always would...

And all he felt for her was desire.

It hadn't been enough three years ago. It was why she'd decided to leave him, even before she'd known she was carrying his baby. She'd loved him so much that hearing him say he'd tired of her would have killed her.

Now she'd put herself in the same position. He wanted her because she'd defied him, but the novelty would wear thin. He'd tire of her as he had in the past and they'd be right back where they started, with one enormous difference.

This time, she wouldn't be the only one who'd pay the price for her foolishness.

Samantha would pay, as well.

Her daughter. Dante's daughter. God, oh God, oh God...

"Tally?"

She pulled free of his embrace, plucked his robe from the chair beside the bed and slipped it on.

"Dante." Tally got to her feet. "This was—it was a mistake."

He sat up, the comforter dropping to his waist. "What are you talking about?" he said, his voice sharp.

"I shouldn't have slept with you." She tried not to look at him as he rose from the bed, naked and beautifully masculine. "I—I enjoyed last night." The look on his face made her take a quick step back. "But it shouldn't have happened. I have a daughter. That makes everything different. I can't just live for the moment anymore, I have to think of her. Of how much what I do affects her."

"You're a fine mother, *bellissima.* Anyone can see that."

"I try to be. And that means I can't—I can't sleep with you and then go about my life as if nothing's happened. I can't—" Tally caught her breath as he reached for her. "You're not listening."

"I am," he said softly. Gently, he brushed his lips over hers. "You don't want your little girl to see her mother take a lover."

"That's part of it."

"To live a life with her, and a separate one with him."

Tally nodded. He was more perceptive than she'd given him credit for. "She won't understand. And I can't do something that will confuse her. Do you see?"

"Better than you think, *cara*." He hesitated. "I only wish my own mother had thought the same way."

The words were simple but they caught her by surprise. He had never mentioned anything about his past before.

"She took lover after lover," he said, his mouth twisting, "if that's what you want to call them. Sometimes she brought them home. 'This is Guiseppe,' she'd say. Or Angelo or Giovanni or whoever he was, the man of the hour. Then she'd tell me to be a good boy and go out and play."

"Oh, Dante. That must have been—"

"When I was six, seven—I'm not certain. All I know is that one day, she took me to my *nonna's*—my grandmother's. 'Be a good boy, Dante,' she said. And—"

"And?" Tally said softly.

He shrugged. "And I never saw her again."

Tally wanted to take him in her arms and hold him close, but she didn't. She sensed that the moment was fragile, that it would take little to tear it apart.

"I'm sorry," she said quietly. "That must have been— it must have been hard."

Another shrug, as if it didn't matter, but when he spoke, the tension in his voice told her that it did.

"I survived."

"And grew into a strong, wonderful man."

Dante looked at her. "Not so wonderful," he said, "or you wouldn't have left me three years ago."

This time, she did reach out, even if it was only to touch her hand to his cheek.

"I grew up living with my grandmother, too," she said quietly.

"In that little house in Vermont?"

She nodded. "My mother was—Grandma called her flighty." She managed a quick smile. "What it really means is that she took off when I was little and never came back. My father had already done the same thing, even before I was born."

Dante gathered her into his arms.

"What a pair we make," he said gently.

Tally nodded again. "All the more reason that I can't—why we can't—"

"Yes. I agree," he murmured, tucking a strand of hair behind her ear, "and I have the perfect solution."

"There is no solution. I have to protect Sam." *Sam and me.*

"Of course there is." Dante tilted her face to his. "You'll move out of the guest suite."

One night? Was that all he'd wanted? Tally forced herself to nod in agreement.

"Of course. I'll find an apartment and—"

"And," he said softly, "you'll move in with me. We'll let Sam see that we are—that we are together. That we are part of each other's lives, and that she is, too."

Tally stared at him, her face a mask of confusion. Was she trying to find a way to tell him she wouldn't go along with his plan? It had come to him during the night; he'd been pleased with it until this moment, when he realized that Tally might not want to be with him this way.

"Tally." His hands slid to her shoulders. "Please." His fingers bit into her flesh. "Tell me want to be with me. I don't want to lose you again. Say yes."

Her head whispered of reservations, of questions, of why the arrangement would never work…

But Tally listened to her heart and said, "Yes."

# CHAPTER TEN

THROUGHOUT THE AGES, wise men caution that a man
who makes decisions in the heat of the moment might
very well live to regret them.

Dante had always agreed.

He was not impulsive. He made choices only after
he had examined all the facts. If a man did anything less,
he might, indeed, live to regret his decisions.

And yet, he'd acted on impulse when he'd asked
Tally to live with him.

It should have been a mistake. The worst mistake of
his life, considering that he'd never asked a woman to
do that before. Living together, spending your days and
nights with one woman, was the kind of involvement
he'd always avoided. He liked to come and go as he
pleased, to spend time in a woman's company only
when he was in the mood.

Add a small child to the mix and a man would
surely go crazy.

At least, that was what he'd have said of this new arrangement a week ago. A disaster in the making, he'd
have called it…

Dante smiled as he stood at his office window and watched the lights wink on over Manhattan.

He'd have been wrong.

Asking Tally to live with him had turned out to be the best decision he'd ever made. Being with her, with Samantha, had already changed his life.

He'd lived in New York for more than a dozen years and most of that time he'd lived very comfortably. As his fortune grew, he'd become accustomed to a certain start and finish to his day.

In the morning, his housekeeper would ask if he'd be home for dinner; in the evening, she'd inquire pleasantly as to how his day had gone. If the doorman made a comment beyond "Good morning" or "Good evening" it was about the weather. His driver might exchange a few polite words with him about European soccer or American football.

Dante's smile became a grin. How that had changed!

Mrs. Tipton regaled him with stories about Sam. Carlo, whose grandson turned out to be Sam's age, was a font of helpful advice. Even the doorman got into the act with details of Sam's latest adventure among the big potted plants in the lobby.

Sam herself, a bundle of energy with big green eyes and a toothy grin, started and ended his days with sloppy kisses.

Amazing, all of it.

But most amazing was his Tally, who fell asleep in his arms each night and awoke in them each morning. She was the most incredible woman he'd ever known, and he wasn't the only one who thought so.

His architect told him she had the best eye for detail

he'd ever seen. His contractor said she made suggestions that were as innovative as they were practical. Even his P.A., a woman who had seen everything and was surprised by nothing, called her remarkable.

His household staff flat-out adored her.

But not as much as he did.

Dante tucked his hands in his trouser pockets and rocked back on his heels. He'd never believed in luck. What you got out of life was in direct proportion to what you put into it, and yet he knew it was luck, good fortune, whatever you wanted to call it, that had given him this second chance with Tally.

He'd lost her through his own callous behavior. He understood that now. He'd treated her like a possession, taking her from the shelf when he wanted to show her off, returning her when he'd finished. It was how he'd always treated his lovers. Kept them at a distance, bought them elaborate gifts, and politely eliminated them from his life when he got bored.

Dante's jaw clenched.

But Tally had never behaved like his other lovers. She'd kept herself at a distance. That was why she'd refused his elaborate gifts and left behind the ones he'd insisted she accept. And she had never bored him. Never. Not for a moment, in bed or out.

At some point, he'd realized it. And it had shaken him to the core. He'd reacted by pushing her away because he hadn't been ready to admit what she had come to mean to him. As recently as a few weeks ago, he'd still been lying to himself about his feelings for her.

That whole thing about wanting to sleep with her to get revenge, get her out of his system...

Sheer, unadulterated idiocy.

It had always been easier to pretend she was just another woman passing through his life than admit his Tally was special. That what he felt for her was special. That what he felt for her was—that it was—

"Dante?"

He swung around, saw her in the doorway and felt his heart swell. And when she smiled, he thought it might burst.

"I knocked," she said, with a little smile, "but you didn't—"

Dante held out his arms. She went into them and he held her close.

"You look beautiful," he said softly.

She leaned back in his embrace. "Not too dressed up?"

He shook his head. "Perfect."

That was the only word to describe her in a softly clinging silk dress and matching jacket in a color he'd have called green but he suspected women gave a more complex name. Her shoes were wispy things, all straps and slender heels, the kind that made a man imagine his woman wearing them with whatever was under the dress and nothing else.

Dante had a pretty good idea of what was under that dress. He'd bought Tally a drawer full of wispy lingerie from The Silk Butterfly, a shop he'd passed on Fifth Avenue.

"Hand-sewn lace," she'd said, her cheeks taking on a light blush. "I'll feel naked under my clothes." And he'd taken her in his arms and shown her just how exciting that would be for them both.

"I know tonight's important to you."

"You're what's important to me."

"Yes, but tonight—the Children's Fund dinner…"

"Tally. We don't have to go. I told you that. We can have a quiet dinner at that little place on the corner and—"

"No. No, I don't want you to change anything because of me. Everyone you know will be there."

"Everyone *we* know. And they'll see how happy we are to be together again."

She nodded, but her eyes were clouded. "There'll be questions."

Dante raised one eyebrow. "No one will dare to ask questions of me." That made her laugh, just as he'd hoped it would. He took her hand, brought it to his mouth and kissed it. "I missed you."

"You saw me an hour ago," she said with another little laugh.

"And that's far too long to be without you." He drew her closer. "It's going to cost you a kiss."

"Dante. Someone will see."

"I don't care."

"But—"

"If I don't get a kiss from you this very minute," he said dramatically, "my death will be on your hands."

She laughed again. He loved the sound of her laugh, the way her lips curved into an eminently kissable bow. He loved everything about her.

The truth was, he loved—he loved—

Dante bent his head and kissed her.

THEY ARRIVED a few minutes late and found five of their dinner companions already at the table. A well-known real estate agent and his third trophy wife. Dennis and Eve. A used-car salesman turned self-help guru, whose latest feel-good book had just gone into its fifth printing.

Tally remembered them all.

And, clearly, they remembered her. She could almost hear their jaws hit the table when they saw her.

Dante had his arm firmly around her waist.

"Good evening," he said pleasantly. "Tally, I think you know everyone here, don't you?"

"Yes," she said brightly, "of course. How are you, Lila? Donald? Eve and Dennis, how good to see you again. And Mark. Your newest book just came out, didn't it? I hope it's doing well?"

Dante pulled out her chair, whispered, "Good girl," as she slipped into it. He sat down beside her, took her hand and held it in his, right on the tabletop where everyone could see. Five pairs of eyes took in the sight. Then someone said, "Well, I see we're going to have chicken for the main course. Surprise, surprise."

Everyone laughed, and that broke the ice.

People began chatting. Wasn't the weather particularly cold for December? Was snow in the forecast again? Wasn't the ballroom handsomely decorated?

*I might just get through this,* Tally thought...

"DanteDarling," a woman screeched.

And Tally looked up, inhaled a cloud of obscenely expensive perfume, saw Charlotte LeBlanc swoop down to plant a kiss on Dante's mouth even as he jerked back in his chair, saw the woman's hate-filled gaze fix on her before she switched it to a big, artificial smile...

And knew, instinctively, that Charlotte LeBlanc had, probably until very recently, been Dante's mistress.

"Taylor," Charlotte said. "What a surprise!"

"Yes," Tally said, "yes, I—I suppose it is."

"A wonderful surprise," Dante said, squeezing Tally's hand, but he was looking at Charlotte, his eyes cold with warning, and any doubts Tally might have had about her lover's relationship with the LeBlanc woman vanished.

Conversation swirled around her, the polite stuff people discussed when they were casual acquaintances. Eve talked about her new hair stylist. Dennis said he was buying a new yacht. The self-help guru was also buying one. The real estate agent was too busy eating his shrimp cocktail to say anything. His trophy wife was silent, too, perhaps because her face was frozen in Botoxed bliss.

And suddenly, in a lull in the chatter, Charlotte leaned over, her breasts almost spilling from her neckline, and laid a taloned hand on Tally's arm.

"Taylor," she cooed, "you must tell us all where you've been the last few years."

"She's been in New England," Dante said smoothly. "Building a successful business."

"New England. How quaint." Her smile glittered with malice. "And are you here on business?"

"Taylor's working on a project of mine."

"How nice." Her head swiveled toward Dante. "And you, DanteDarling. Are you and I still on for Christmas in Aspen?"

Dante's eyes went black. "No," he said coldly, "we are not. I told you that weeks ago,"

"Oh, but everyone knows how you tend to change your mind, DanteDarling. How fickle you are, well, not about business but about, you know, other things."

There was no mistaking what "things" she meant. Heads swiveled from Charlotte to Tally to Dante, who snarled a word no one had to speak Sicilian to comprehend.

Charlotte turned red. Everyone else gasped. And Tally pushed her chair back from the table.

"Tally! Damn it, Tally…"

Luck was with her. The band was playing and the dance floor was crowded with couples. Tally wove through the mob, pulled open the door to the ladies' room and slammed it behind her. A sob burst from her throat.

How could she have been so stupid? He'd been with that woman. With Charlotte. He'd been with God only knew how many women these last three years. She'd dreamed of him, yearned for him, wanted only him despite all the lies she'd told herself, but Dante…

"Tally!"

His fist slammed against the door.

"Tally! Open this door or I'm coming in."

One of the stall doors swung open. A woman stepped out and stared at her.

"Tally, do you hear me? Open this goddamned door!"

Tally went to the sink, splashed cold water on her face. She would have ignored the hammering on the door but the woman who'd come out of the stall was looking at her as if she'd somehow wandered into the sort of situation that ended in bloodshed.

There was nothing for it but to square her shoulders and walk out of the ladies' room, straight into a muscled wall of male fury.

"Dante," she said quietly, "please, step aside."

He answered by clasping her shoulders and hauling her to her toes.

"If I'd known that bitch would be at our table," he demanded, "do you really think I'd have brought you here tonight?"

"It doesn't matter. Step aside, please."

"Of course it matters! Damn it, she means nothing to me!"

"Dante. Get out of my—"

"Are you deaf?" His hands bit hard into her flesh as he lowered his face to hers. "She doesn't matter."

"She matters enough so you were going to take her to Aspen."

"She suggested it. I said no. In fact, I never saw her after that evening. We were finished and she knew it."

Tally looked into his eyes. They were the color of smoke, and without warning, the pain inside her burst free.

"You slept with her," she whispered.

His mouth twisted. "Tally. *Bellissima...*"

"You should have told me. So I—I could have been prepared to see the way she looked at you. To know you'd been with her, made love to her—"

"It was sex," he said roughly. "Only sex. Never anything more."

She stared into his eyes again. *And what is it with me?* she longed to say, but her heart knew better than to ask.

"How many were there?" Her voice trembled and she hated herself for it. She'd known a man virile as Dante wouldn't live like a monk but to see the proof for herself... "How many women after me?"

His grasp on her tightened. "What does it matter? All

the years we were apart, I never stopped thinking of you. I hated you for leaving me, Tally—and hated myself for not being able to get over you."

Tally looked away from him, certain that her heart was going to break. If he couldn't get over her, how could he have betrayed her with other women? In the endless years since leaving him, she had never even thought of anyone else. She had never betrayed him...

But she had.

Running away had been a kind of betrayal. Even the cold, cleverly worded note she'd left had been a betrayal.

And then there was the cruelest betrayal of all. She'd told him she'd cheated on him with another man, that she'd given birth to that man's child.

"Tally." His voice was thick with anguish. "There's never been anyone but you. You must believe me!"

Slowly she lifted her eyes to his. "What I believe," she whispered, "is that we've both been fools."

He nodded. She could see color returning to his face.

"Yes. We have been, but we won't be any longer." He framed her face with his hands and raised it to his. "I'm not going to lose you again, *inamorata*. I won't let it happen."

Tears gathered on Tally's lashes. Gently Dante kissed them away. Then he wrapped his arm around her shoulders.

"Let's go home."

She smiled. "Yes. Let's go home."

He led her past the curious little group that had been watching them, out of the hotel and into his waiting limousine. Part of him wanted to go back to the ballroom, put his hands around Charlotte's throat and make her pay for what she'd done.

But he was every bit as guilty.

Not for having slept with Charlotte. Tally had been out of his life then. Not even for having not told her about Charlotte. He was a man, not a saint. What man would deliberately tell the woman he cared for that he'd slept with someone else, even if he'd been absolutely free to do so at the time?

He pressed a kiss to Tally's hair as she sat curled against him, her head on his shoulder.

His guilt was over what he'd done three years ago.

He'd let Tally slip away. And he should have gone after her. Should have faced what she meant to him because the truth was he didn't just care for her, he—he—

"Dante?"

Dante cleared his throat. "Yes, *cara?*"

"I'm sorry."

"No! It wasn't your fault."

"Not about tonight. I'm… I'm sorry for…for—" She took a deep breath and sat up straight, her eyes locked to his. "We need to talk. But not here. Someplace… someplace where we can be alone."

Suddenly he knew that was what he wanted, too. A quiet place where they could be alone. Where they could talk—and he could finally confront what was in his heart.

"I have an idea," he said slowly. "Christmas is next week. What if we spend it alone? Just the three of us. You and me and Samantha. We'll go somewhere warm, where we can lie in the sun in each other's arms, where Sam can run around to her heart's content. Would you like that?"

"A place where we can talk," Tally said softly.

Talk about what had really made her run away, she thought as Dante drew her against him, because tonight, she'd finally faced the truth.

No matter what happened, she had to tell Dante that she loved him.

That there'd never been another man.

That he was Sam's father.

# CHAPTER ELEVEN

WHAT COULD BE more wonderful than lying in the curve of your lover's arm on a white sand beach under the hot Caribbean sun?

Tally turned her head and put her mouth lightly against Dante's bronzed skin, savoring the exciting taste of salt and man.

How she adored him!

Her Dante was everything a man should be. Strong. Tender. Giving. Demanding. Fiercely passionate, incredibly gentle. She loved him, loved him, loved him…

And it killed her that she'd lied to him.

That she was still lying to him, because she'd yet to tell him the truth about Sam.

Soon, she thought, as she closed her eyes and burrowed closer to his warm, hard body. She'd confess everything to him this evening, after dinner, when they were both tucking Sam in for the night. Or tomorrow morning, at breakfast. And if the time didn't seem right then, she'd wait just another few hours. Another few days…

Tally swallowed hard. *Liar,* she thought, *liar, liar, liar!*

She wouldn't tell him tonight, or tomorrow. Or ever,

at the rate she was going. She wanted to. Wanted to say, *Dante, I've done an awful thing. I lied to you about Sam. About being with someone else. Sam is your child. Ever since we met, there's only been you.*

The problem was, she could see beyond that.

She had let him think she'd been unfaithful.

She had denied him knowledge of his own child.

Who could predict how he'd react?

Some days, she was sure he would understand. Others, she was afraid he wouldn't. She'd thought it would be so easy to admit everything once they were here, on this beautiful island in the midst of a sea as clear as fine green glass, tucked away from the world in a magnificent house on its own long, pristine, private beach. Just the three of them: she and Dante and Samantha. No housekeeper. No maid. No nanny or chauffeur. Just she and the man she loved and her little girl.

Their little girl.

Except, Dante didn't know that yet because she was a coward, because she was terrified of what he'd say, what he'd do when he knew she'd deceived him in the worst way possible—

"*Bellissima,* what's wrong?" Tally's eyes flew open as Dante brushed his lips over hers. "You were whimpering in your sleep, *cara.* Were you having a bad dream?"

"I… I… Yes. Something like that."

Smiling, he kissed her again. "You've been in the sun too long. That's the problem."

*Now. Tell him now!*

"Dante."

"Hmm?" He bent to her and kissed her again, parting

her lips and slowly slipping the tip of his tongue into her mouth. "You taste delicious."

*So did he. Oh, so did—*

"Dante." Her breath caught. His mouth was at her throat, her breast, nipping lightly at the rapidly beading tip through the thin cotton of her bikini top. "Dante…"

"I'll bet you taste even more delicious here," he whispered as he slid his hands behind her, undid the top, his eyes shining brightest silver as he exposed her breasts. "Let me see if I'm right."

Tally cried out, arching against him as he drew her nipple into the wet heat of his mouth; even as he began easing her bikini bottom down her thighs, she felt it starting to happen, the shimmering heat building inside her, the hot rush of desire as he stroked her dampening curls, put his mouth to her until she was begging him, pleading with him, to take her.

Slowly, so slowly that she thought it might never end, prayed it might never end, he entered her. Filled her, stretched her, moved deep inside her while he whispered to her in Sicilian, words she didn't know but somehow understood, and she thought, *I love you, Dante. I've always loved you. Only you.*

And shattered like crystal in his arms.

AFTER, HE CARRIED HER into the house, past the room where Samantha lay sleeping, to their bedroom and their canopied bed overlooking the sea.

Gently, he lay her in the center of the white sheets, came down beside her and drew her into his arms. Tally put her face in his neck and sighed.

"I love it here," she said softly.

"I'm glad."

"The house is so beautiful. And the sea... I've never seen a sea this clear."

Dante smiled as he stroked his hand gently up and down her spine. "There's a beach on the Mediterranean where you can stand knee-deep in the water and watch tiny fish swim by like flashes of blue and green light."

Tally tilted her head back so she could see his face. "Is that where you lived with your *nonna?* In a town by the sea?"

"Nothing so postcard-perfect, *cara*. I grew up in Palermo, on a street that was already old when Rome ruled the world."

"It sounds wonderful. All that history—"

"Trust me, Tally. There was nothing wonderful about it. Everyone was dirt-poor, except for us." He gave a self-deprecating laugh. "We were poorer than that."

"Then, everything you have today—you built it all, from scratch?" She smiled. "The amazing Mr. Russo."

He grinned, lifted her so that she lay stretched out along his length.

Well," he said, "if you want to call me that—"

Tally rolled her eyes, brought her mouth to his and kissed him. "Don't let it go to your head," she said softly, "but you really are. Amazing."

Dante framed her face with his hands. "What's amazing," he whispered, "is you."

That brought her back to reality. "Dante," she said carefully, "Dante, do you remember what I said the other night? That we have to talk."

"I agree. We do." His eyes grew hooded. "But not right now."

"Dante. Please—"

"Please what?" He cupped her hips, eased her to her knees above him. "Please, this?" he whispered, and she felt the tip of his erection kiss her labia. "Tell me and I'll do it. I'll do whatever you want, *inamorata*. Anything. Everything…"

Then he was inside her, and words had no meaning. All that mattered was this. This…

This.

AN HOUR LATER, Dante eased his arm from beneath Tally's shoulders, touched his mouth lightly to hers, slipped on a pair of denim shorts and went to check on Sam.

The baby woke just as he peeked into her room. When she saw him, she grinned, said "Da-Tay" and held out her chubby arms. Dante grinned back, picked her up and gave her a kiss.

"Hello, *bambina*. Did you have a good nap?"

"Goo'nap," she said happily.

"I'll bet you need a diaper change."

"Di-chain," Sam gurgled, and Dante laughed.

"You're a regular little echo chamber, aren't you?"

"Eck-chame," Sam said.

Dante laughed again, put her on the changing table and replaced her wet diaper with a fresh one. Then he carried her through the house, into the kitchen, put her in the booster chair at the table while he filled a sippy-cup with milk. She liked it warm so he heated it in the microwave oven, tested a drop on his wrist, screwed the top on, plucked her from the booster, went out on the porch and sat down with her in his arms.

She could handle the sippy-cup herself and he knew

it, but he liked holding her, liked the warm weight of the baby, her sweet smell, the little noises of delight she made as she fed.

He liked caring for Samantha in general. Well, maybe not the poopy-diapers part, which he'd done when he heard her babbling softly to herself early this morning. Why wake Tally when he could change the diaper himself, even if it had been a rather interesting learning experience?

The truth was, he'd never imagined himself with a baby in his arms. Oh, he'd figured on having children someday. A man wanted children to carry on his genes, his life's work, but his thoughts had been of faceless miniature adults and a faceless perfect wife. Now, of course, he knew better.

He wanted a little girl exactly like Sam.

A wife exactly like Tally.

Dante caught his breath.

And, just that easily, came face-to-face with the truth.

He loved Tally. He loved her daughter. He had his family already, right here, the baby in his arms, the woman he adored in his bed.

He rose to his feet, ready to rush to the bedroom, wake Tally with a kiss, tell her what was in his heart—

No. He wanted this to be just right. All the romantic touches he'd always scoffed at. Candlelight. Flowers. Champagne.

The travel agent had given him the name of a respected island family that lived nearby. He waited until Sam finished her milk. Then he kept her safely in the curve of his arm while he made some phone calls. When he was done, he'd arranged for a babysitter, reserved a secluded table at a five-star restaurant on the beach, and ordered a ten-carat canary-yellow diamond in a platinum setting from the delighted owner of the island's most exclusive jewelry shop, with instructions to have a messenger bring the ring to the restaurant promptly at nine that night.

He was about to order flowers when Sam giggled and said, "Mama!"

Dante looked up and saw Tally.

"Hey," she said, smiling.

"Hey," he said softly, smiling back at her.

"You should have woken me."

"Your hear that, kid? Your mother doesn't think we can handle the tough stuff on our own." He paused. "Tally?"

"Hmm?"

*I love you. I adore you. I want to marry you and adopt Sam, raise her as our very own daughter…*

"What on earth are you thinking" she said, with a little laugh. "You have the strangest look on your face!"

"Do I?" He cleared his throat. "Maybe it's because—because what I was thinking was that I want to celebrate Christmas this evening."

Tally laughed. "Christmas is two days away!"

"You don't think I'm going to permit a little detail like that to stop me, do you?" Smiling, he came toward her. Sam held out her arms and he handed her to her mother. "In fact, I've already made plans for us tonight."

"What plans?" Tally said, hugging her daughter, putting her face up for Dante's kiss, thinking how right all this was, being here together, the man she loved, the child they'd created together. "What plans?" she said again and knew that tonight, no matter what happened, she would tell him everything.

His smile tilted. "It's a surprise. A good one," he added softly, "one I hope will make you happy." He put his arms around them both, the woman he loved and the child he would make his.

The child that should have been his, if he hadn't been so stupid and self-involved.

He felt the dull pain of regret settle over him.

If only Sam really were his. He loved her but sometimes—sometimes it hurt to know that Tally had lain with another man. That someone else had joined with her to create this beautiful little life.

"Dante," Tally said softly, "what's wrong?"

"Nothing." He cleared his throat. "I was just thinking about tonight."

"You looked—you looked sad."

"Sad?" He smiled, forced the dark thoughts away. "Nonsense," he said briskly. "I'm just making sure I've thought of everything. Sam's babysitter. Our dinner reservations."

"Are we having dinner out?"

"We are. At that place on the beach."

Tally gave him the look women have always given men who are too dense to understand life's basic rules of survival.

"That place? But I don't have anything to wear! You said we'd only need swimsuits. Shorts. Jeans. I can't go there in jeans, Dante!"

He thought she could go there in what she wore now and still be more beautiful than any woman in the place, but this played right into his hands. He still had things to arrange. The flowers for their meal and for the house when they returned to it later. Candles for the bedroom.

More champagne, to drink on the beach once she had his ring on her finger.

"I agree," he said solemnly. "That's why you're going to take my credit card, taxi into town and buy whatever you need for tonight."

"But—"

He silenced the protest with a kiss.

"Find something long and elegant. Something so sexy it will make every man who sees you want me dead so he can claim you for his own." He kissed her again and she leaned into him, the baby gurgling happily between them, and half an hour later, holding Sam in his arms, both of them waving as the taxi and Tally pulled away, Dante knew he was, without question, the luckiest man alive.

HE MADE THE BALANCE of the phone calls, arranged for the delivery of white orchids, white candles and bottles of Cristal. The last call went to his attorney in New York, where he left a message asking him to research the state's adoption laws and to determine the quickest way to effect an adoption.

"I think that about does it, Sammy," he said, grinning at the way Samantha looked when he called her that. It wasn't elegant, but he liked it.

Then he turned all his attention on the child who would soon be his.

He took her into the pool, rode her on his shoulders in the warm water as she laughed and clutched at his hair with her fists.

He held her hand as they walked along the beach, helping her pick up shells, making a show of putting them into his pocket for later while surreptitiously letting ones that were too small for her safety fall to the sand.

He made himself a cup of coffee, handed Sam a sippy-cup of juice and shared an Oreo cookie with her, chuckling as he imagined what all those who trembled at his presence in a boardroom would think if they could see him eating the chunks she handed him, baby drool and all.

Late afternoon, with the sun high overhead, he sat on the palm-shaded patio, Sam playing at his feet. She gave a huge yawn.

"Nap time," he said.

Sam, who was, of course, brilliant for her age, puckered up her baby face and yowled.

"Okay, okay, forget I mentioned it."

The baby smiled, yawned again, put her head down and her rump up, and promptly fell asleep on the blanket at his feet. Dante yawned, too, picked up the magazine he'd been leafing through, wondered if Tally—his Tally—would be as happy as he wanted her to be when he proposed tonight.

She would—wouldn't she?

She loved him—didn't she?

He hadn't really thought about it until now. Yes. Of course she loved him. The way she sighed in his arms. Smiled into his eyes. The way he caught her watching him sometimes, that little smile curving her lips—

What was that? A dark shape, near his foot.

"Dio mio!"

Sam woke up screaming as a thing with eight legs raced across her outflung hand. Dante scooped the child into his arms, stomped on the ugly black thing and saw the bite marks of its fangs on Sam's tender wrist.

"Sam," he said, "Sam, *mia figlia*—"

Her shriek of pain rose into the air. Even as he scooped her into his arms, Dante saw the flesh around the bite start to swell. He paused only long enough to tie a scarf around her arm above the bite and to pick up the dead spider, place it in his handkerchief and tuck it into his pocket.

Heart racing, he ran for his car.

HE PHONED THE HOSPITAL when he was two blocks away. Two physicians and a nurse were waiting outside the emergency room. The nurse tried to take Sam from his arms but he refused to give her up.

"I'm staying with her," he said, and neither the doctors nor the nurse doubted his determination.

They led him into an examining room. Sam clung to his neck, sobbing. He soothed her with words he barely knew, things he'd heard people say to weeping children, things he'd once wished his *nonna* had said to him when he was small and he'd skinned his knee or bloodied his nose, except this wasn't a bloody knee or nose, he thought, as he dug in his pocket and produced the ugly corpse.

The nurse grimaced; one of the physicians barked out a command, and Dante's heart turned over when the nurse appeared with a tiny needle and reached for Sam's hand.

"Shh, *bambina*," he whispered, "everything will be all right."

But Sam was past listening. Her little body arched; Dante cursed as a convulsion tore through her.

"Do something," he snarled.

"Wait outside," the doctor snapped.

Dante flashed him a look the man would never forget. "I will not leave my baby," he said.

He didn't. Not until Sam finally opened her eyes and looked at him.

"Da-Tay," she whispered, and for the first time since his mother had left him, Dante wept.

IT TOOK TWO HOURS and a dozen calls to the house by the sea before Tally answered the phone.

She was, as Dante had anticipated, frantic.

"Dante! Dear God, where are you? Where is Samantha? I came home and the place was empty and—"

He interrupted. Told her everything was fine, that they were at the hospital, in the emergency room. Lied and said he'd let his worry over a little bug bite get out of hand. He didn't want her to know the truth until he could take her in his arms and hold her and she could see for herself that the crisis was over.

He was waiting at the big double doors of the emergency room when she came flying through them.

"Where's my baby?"

Dante caught her in his arms. "She's fine, *cara*."

"Tell me the truth. My baby—"

"Tally." He held her by the shoulders, brought his eyes level with hers. "I would never lie to you. Never."

She nodded, though he could feel her tremble in his embrace. Slowly, carefully, he explained what had happened. When she swayed, he gathered her against him, rocked her gently until she pushed her hands against his chest and looked into his eyes.

"Where is she?"

He kept his arm around her, let his strength seep into her as he led her to Sam's room. The room was private; so was the nurse who sat beside the baby in the white crib, peacefully sleeping. The danger was past but the IV was still in her arm.

Tally bent over the crib and put her hand on her daughter's back. Tears fell from her eyes.

"My baby," she whispered, "oh, my sweet little girl! I could have lost you."

"Your husband did all the right things, Mrs. Russo," the nurse said softly. "Without his quick thinking, things would have been much worse."

Tally looked at the woman. "But he isn't—"

Dante slid his arm around her shoulders. "Let's let Sam sleep, *cara*. Come into the hall and we can talk."

Bewildered, Tally followed him from the room. "She thinks you and I are married?"

"I don't know the laws here, *cara*. But I remember reading about a child somewhere who died because a hospital wouldn't provide emergency treatment without the permission of a parent." He clasped her shoulders. "I wasn't going to run that risk. Not with our little girl."

Tally swallowed hard. *Our little girl. Our little girl.*

"Don't look at me that way, *cara*. I had no choice. Our Samantha—"

It was her fault, all of it. She had denied Dante knowledge of his child, denied Sam her father. And now, dear God, and now Sam might have died if Dante hadn't thought quickly—

"Tally."

She looked up at him. His face was drawn. He had gone through so much today for a child he didn't know was his, a child he loved.

"Tally." Dante paused. "I know my timing is bad but—*cara*, I want to marry you. And I want to adopt Sam. I want to be her father."

Tears swam in Tally's eyes. "Oh, Dante…"

"I love you. And I love her, as much as if she were my daughter."

Tally began to weep. There was no hiding her secret, not anymore.

"Dante," she said brokenly, "Sam *is* your daughter!"

There was a long silence, broken only by the sound of Dante's breathing and Tally's sobs. When he finally spoke, his voice was without inflection.

"What do you mean, Sam is my daughter?"

"I should have told you. I wanted to tell you—"

She gasped as his hands bit into her shoulders. "Tell me what?"

"There was no other man. I made it up. Samantha is—she's your child."

Moments, an eternity, slipped by. Tally waited, trying to read Dante's face, to see something of what would come next.

"Let me make sure I understand this. You didn't sleep with someone else."

"No."

"You didn't get pregnant by another man."

"I know I should have told you, but—"

"You knew you were pregnant, and you left me anyway?"

"Dante. Please. Listen to what I'm saying. I knew

you'd grown tired of me. How could I have told you I was having a baby?"

"My baby." His voice was like a whip; he caught her wrists and pushed her back against the wall. "*My* baby!"

"It isn't that simple!"

"On the contrary, Taylor. It's brutally simple. You became pregnant with my child and didn't tell me. You were going to raise her to think she had no father."

Tally wrenched her hands free and slapped them over her ears. "Stop it!"

"You were going to raise Samantha—my daughter— as I was raised. Fatherless. Impoverished."

"It wasn't like that, damn it! I did what I thought was right."

"For who? Surely not for Samantha. And not for me."

"Remember when I said I wanted to talk to you? It was about this. About you and Sam. But I had to wait for the right time."

He gave a hollow laugh. "Another lie. How many more will you tell before I know the entire truth?"

Tally stared up into her lover's enraged eyes. He was right. It was time for the truth. All of it.

"No more lies," she said, her voice trembling. "Here's the truth. Sam is yours. There was never anyone else. And I left you—I left you because I knew I'd fallen in love with you."

"Such a pretty story."

"I swear it's true! I still love you. I always will."

"As soon as my daughter is fully recovered," he said, as if she hadn't spoken, "we'll fly back to New York."

"Damn you, Dante! Listen to me!"

"You will move back into the guest suite. I'll permit

that because I don't want my child to be traumatized by too many changes all at once."

A cold knot of fear gripped Tally's stomach. "What does that mean?"

Dante smiled thinly.

"It means," he said silkily, "that Samantha is mine. That you stole her from me. That you are an unfit mother." He paused. "And that I intend to gain custody—sole custody—of her."

"No!" Tally's voice rose in horror. "You can't take her from me. No court will permit it!"

Dante ignored her, walked to the room where Sam lay sleeping and sat down in a chair beside the crib. So much for love. For putting your heart in someone's hands. For being foolish enough to think life was ever anything but a cruel joke.

He took his cell phone from his pocket, called his attorney, cut through the man's perfunctory greeting and told him he'd just learned he was the father of a two-year-old child.

The lawyer, who dealt with several wealthy clients, cut to the chase.

"How much does the woman want?"

"You misunderstand me," Dante said. "I don't want to deny my paternity of the child, I want to claim her. I want full custody. Will that be a problem?"

He listened, answered a couple of questions, then smiled.

There were times having money, power and the right connections paid off.

# CHAPTER TWELVE

MOMENTS LATER, TALLY entered the room.

Dante, still seated beside the crib and the sleeping baby, looked at the nurse.

"Please take your dinner break now."

He spoke politely, but that didn't lessen his tone of command. The woman left without a backward glance. Tally looked at him, but he didn't acknowledge her presence.

Anyone looking at him would assume he was angry.

She knew better. He was furious. And it frightened her. Dante was a powerful adversary in any situation. Now he would be formidable.

But he wouldn't win. She would do whatever it took to keep her child and defeat him, and that meant facing up to him, starting now.

She moved the nurse's abandoned chair to the other side of the crib and sat down. Her face softened as she looked at her little girl, so peacefully asleep.

Samantha was hers.

No court in the land would separate a mother from her child, not even to satisfy Dante Russo. None, she thought…and maybe because she wished she really believed it, she spoke the words aloud.

"You won't win," she said.

He looked at her, his eyes empty. "Of course I will."

Her face paled. Good. He was happy to see it. She deserved what would come next. She had brought it on herself with her lies.

His attorney was already earning his million-dollar-a-year retainer, drawing up motions and citing precedents even though the hour was late and Christmas was only a couple of days away.

Dante had no doubt as to which of them would gain custody. Tally had apple pie and motherhood on her side, but he had the things that really mattered.

What a fool he'd been, imagining himself in love. He almost laughed. He, of all people, knew that the word had no meaning. His mother had claimed to love him, right up to the day she kissed him, told him to be a good boy, and vanished. His *nonna* had claimed to love him, too, and proved it by beating the crap out of him at every opportunity until he finally ran away.

Emotion was weakness. Self-discipline was strength. This woman had made him forget that, but he would not make the same mistake again.

The one thing he couldn't understand was why she had kept her pregnancy from him. He was rich. She could have milked him for a lot of money. He knew men who'd had that happen to them. A woman got pregnant, deliberately pregnant, and dipped her manicured hands into a man's bank account.

Anyone could see that Tally could have used the cash. The old house in Vermont, the business she'd attempted... An infusion of dollars would have changed her life.

All right. She had not been after his money. He had to admit that. And he had to admit that she seemed to be a good mother.

Why, then, had she lied? Why had she left him?

Because she loved him. That was what she'd said.

What a joke!

A woman who loved a man didn't run from him. She didn't give birth to his child and tell him the child was someone else's. *Dio,* the anger and pain that had caused him. The nights he'd lain awake, held Tally in his arms, tried not to wonder if she were dreaming of him or of her other lover.

His mouth thinned.

It was some consolation, at least, knowing she had not belonged to anyone else. That she had been his. Only his. That no one else had made love to her, held her close, felt the whisper of her breath against his throat while she slept in his arms.

He'd blanked his mind to the rest. To what she'd looked like when she was pregnant. Now, knowing Sam was his, that was impossible to do.

Her breasts would have been full, the skin translucent over the delicate tracery of her veins. Her belly would have been round, lush with the life they'd created. She had denied him the wonder of those months. The feel of his child, kicking in her mother's womb. The moment of his child's entry into the world.

All those signs, the proof of their love...

Except, it had never been love.

Never. Love was just a polite four-letter word men

and women used in mixed company. Taylor's lies were the issue here, not love.

He'd had the right to know the truth. She should have told him.

He looked up. Tally sat with her head bowed. "You should have told me," he said coldly.

She raised her eyes to his.

"You're right. I should have."

"But you didn't."

"No. I didn't. I've tried to explain, to say I'm sorry—"

"I'm not interested in apologies or explanations."

She gave a sad little laugh. "No. You're only interested in you. That's one of the reasons I didn't tell you I was pregnant. I was afraid you'd react exactly this way, as if our baby's existence concerned only you."

"You're good at making excuses."

"Not as good as you are at feeling nothing for anyone but yourself." Her voice trembled. "I think you do care for Samantha, though. And that surprises me."

"A compliment, *cara*. I can hardly bear it."

"Dante. Don't take her from me. I know you want to hurt me, but you'll hurt her, too."

"Hurt her?" His lips drew back from his teeth. "You have nothing. I have everything. I'll give my daughter a life you can only imagine."

"She's my daughter, too. And what she needs is love. It's what everyone needs. How can you not understand that?"

"*Love*," he said, his mouth twisting, "is a word without meaning. *Honesty. Responsibility.* Those are words that matter. How can you not understand that?"

Then he folded his arms, fixed his eyes on the sleeping baby and ignored Tally completely.

DAWN HAD JUST TOUCHED the sky with a delicate pink blush when Samantha stirred.

"Mama?"

Tally, who'd fallen into a fitful sleep, sprang to her feet, but she was too late. Dante had already leaned into the crib and lifted the baby into his arms.

*"Bella figlia,"* he said huskily, *"buon giorno."*

Sam grinned. "Da-Tay," she babbled, and wrapped her arms around his neck.

Tally felt her throat tighten. All the time she'd been pregnant, the months and years after, she'd never pictured this. Dante and Samantha as father and daughter. She'd never dreamed of this softness, this sweetness in her lover.

The door opened. The physician who'd treated Sam stepped into the room.

"Well, look at this! It doesn't take a trained eye to see that our patient's made a full recovery."

"Thank you, Doctor. For everything."

"My pleasure, Mr. Russo. Just let me give your little girl the once-over and you can take her home."

"To New York?"

"I'd wait a couple of days, just to be on the safe side." He grinned. "Quite a hardship, having to spend Christmas in the Caribbean, huh, folks?"

Tally made a choked sound. Dante forced a smile.

"We'll manage," he said.

Tally hoped he was right.

COEXISTING in a three-level penthouse, as they'd initially done, was simple.

Coexisting in a one-level house built to take full advantage of the sun was not.

Rooms opened into rooms; doors were almost non-existent. Tally moved her things into the third bedroom, but it was impossible to walk to the kitchen or Sam's room without running into Dante.

"Excuse me," she said, at the beginning.

After a while, she stopped saying it. What was there to apologize for? He was as much in her way as she was in his.

And how did he manage to get to Sam's side so quickly? All the baby had to do was whimper and Dante, damn him, was there.

Tally told herself she'd at least have the pleasure of watching him suffer through the horrors of a full diaper but apparently he'd mastered Diaper 101 on his own. All right, she thought with petty satisfaction, at least he wouldn't know how to mash a banana just the way Sam liked it—and she was right. He didn't.

It didn't matter.

Her sweet little traitor liked Dante's method just fine. She liked everything he did, including taking her for hand-in-hand walks along the beach, the warm water lapping at her ankles.

When Tally attempted the same thing, Sam shrieked with horror.

Dante could charm any woman he set his eyes on, including two-year-old females.

But he couldn't charm Tally. Not that he tried. He looked right through her. That was fine. She'd gone back to hating him. She'd never let her little girl be raised by such a cold-hearted tyrant, never mind the performance he was putting on with Sam, never mind the way his face lit each time the baby toddled toward him...

Never mind the numbing sense of sorrow in her own heart at glimpses of what might have been.

As midnight approached, with Sam sound asleep and the house silent, Tally was close to tears, but it wasn't over Dante.

Never over him.

"Never," Tally whispered, and wept as if her heart might break in half.

TALLY'S SOFT SOBS carried through the walls.

Lying on his bed, arms folded beneath his head, Dante stared up at the dark ceiling. Let her cry, he thought coldly. For all he gave a damn, she could cry enough salt tears to fill the sea.

After a long time, the sound of her weeping grew softer, then stopped. A muscle in his jaw flexed. Good. Now, at least, he might get some sleep.

Half an hour later, he sat up.

To hell with sleep. He was going crazy, trapped in a house that was rapidly becoming a prison. He pulled on a pair of shorts, opened the patio doors and strode over the beach until he reached the surf.

The moon, full and round, was bright enough to carve shadows into the sand. Dante's mouth thinned. It was the kind of night you saw on picture postcards. The endless stretch of sand. The white ruffle of the surf. The dark sea stretching to the horizon under the elegantly cool eye of the moon.

Once, he'd considered buying a house in these islands. He'd even mentioned it to Taylor. The idea had come from out of nowhere…or maybe not. Maybe he'd thought of the beauty of this place because Taylor was so beautiful. Because, fool that he was, he'd imagined he was feeling something for her he'd never felt for another woman.

He'd stepped back from that precipice.

And here he was, three years later, with her in the very setting he'd imagined, except all he wanted was to get away from her and return to New York.

*Dio,* the irony of it!

Dante kicked at the sand as he walked slowly along the beach.

A beautiful island. A beautiful woman, but what good was her beauty if she had no heart? Not when it came to him.

And why should that mean a damn anyway, when he'd never thought the human heart was responsible for anything more than pumping blood through the body?

Wrong, he thought, tilting back his head and staring blindly at the moon. Dead wrong, and it had taken a two-year-old imp to teach him the lesson.

A painful lesson.

For the first time in his life, he'd begun to think about a different existence from any he'd ever known. A house in the country. A dog, a couple of cats, a station wagon. A little girl to run to the door when she heard his key in the lock and maybe a little boy, too...

And a wife, to step into his embrace.

Not just a wife. Tally. His Tally. Because that was how he thought of her, how he'd always thought of her, even three years ago...

*What was that?*

Dante cocked his head. Music? Chimes. No. Not chimes. Bells. Church bells. Of course. It must be midnight, and this was Christmas Eve.

He swallowed hard. So what? Christmas was for fools. A holiday that celebrated a miracle, except miracles were in painfully short supply in today's world.

When was the last time he'd seen anything remotely like a miracle?

*When was the last time he'd held Tally in his arms?*

The sound of the bells came to him again, filled with poignancy and hope that floated on the soft sea breeze. Dante swallowed again but he couldn't ease the constriction in his throat.

"Tally," he whispered, and the name was sweeter than the music of the bells.

Tally was his miracle. She always had been.

And he'd turned his back on that miracle, ruined his one chance at love, at happiness, out of pride, arrogance, all the things she'd accused him of, rather than admit the truth.

He loved Tally. Now, three years ago, forever. He adored her.

And he knew exactly why she'd left him.

He *had* been about to end their affair, just as she'd said, and it hadn't had a damned thing to do with boredom. The truth was the great Dante Russo had been terrified of putting his heart in a woman's hands, of saying, *Here I am, cara. A man, nothing more. A man who loves you and can only hope you love him in return because without you, I am nothing. My life is nothing....*

Dante took a shuddering breath.

"Tally," he whispered, and turned toward the house.

TALLY LAY HUDDLED in her bed, eyes hot and gritty with tears.

Ridiculous, wasn't it? To weep over Dante? He wasn't worth it. Not anymore.

He had shown his true colors today. He was the cold, brutal, arrogant tyrant she'd always called him...

Tally rolled onto her back and stared up at the dark ceiling. No. That wasn't true. Dante had been wonderful today, quick and courageous and tender with Sam, and with her...

Until she'd told him what she should have told him a very long time ago.

She could be honest about this, at least. Dante wasn't a tyrant, he was a man in pain. She had told him a lie that had cut to the bone. Now he was hurting. And a man like Dante Russo knew only one way to deal with pain.

He struck at its cause.

And she—she was the cause.

A sob caught in Tally's throat and she rolled over and buried her face in the already-damp pillow.

If only she'd told him the truth that day in Vermont, when he'd first seen Sam. If only she'd said, "Dante, this is your child. I kept her from you and I kept myself from you, too, because—because I loved you. Because I knew I'd die if you turned away from me."

Would he have laughed? Or would he have opened his arms to her? She'd never know. It was too late. She'd finally told him the truth, that Sam was his and that she loved him, but it didn't matter.

He wanted Sam, not her. And she couldn't blame him for that. Her lies had destroyed everything.

Too late, the beat of her heart said, too late, too late, too—

*What was that?*

Tally sat up, head cocked. Bells? Yes. Bells, chiming sweetly through the night. Why would bells be...

Of course.

It was Christmas. Christmas! The bells were heralding the start of the holiday, singing of joy, of wonder...

Of miracles.

Tears streamed down Tally's face. She'd had her own miracle. A man. Proud. Strong. Protective and, yes, loving. And she'd let that miracle slip through her fingers out of cowardice. She'd been afraid to tell him about Sam.

And terrified to tell him about herself, that she loved him, that she'd always love him, until it was too late.

Almost too late, she thought, and drew a ragged breath.

Tally threw back the covers and rose from the bed. Her footsteps were hesitant at first but they quickened as she ran from room to room.

"Dante," she said brokenly, "my beloved, where are you?"

The bells rang out again, just as she hurried into the sitting room. A beam of ivory moonlight illuminated the French doors that led to the beach. Tally flung them open—

And saw Dante, just as he turned toward the house.

"Dante," she said, and she began to run across the sand, "Dante..."

Moonlight touched his face. She saw love, understanding, the same hope that burned in her heart, and she flew into his embrace and clung to him.

"I heard the bells," she said, crying and laughing at the same time, kissing his mouth as she rose to him, luxuriating in the racing beat of his heart. "I heard them calling and I thought, I can't lose him again, I can't, I can't, I can't—"

"I love you," Dante said fiercely, cupping her face in

his hands. "I've always loved you, *inamorata,* but I was too proud—and too afraid of needing you—to admit it."

"And I love you," Tally said, "I always have. It's why I left you three years ago. The thought of having you end things between us was more than I could bear."

"I was a fool, *cara,*" he said, tightening his arms around her. "How could a man end what is destined to last through eternity?"

Tally laughed through her tears. "Is that all?"

He smiled, too. And then his mouth was on hers, the taste of her tears was on his lips, and as he lifted her into his arms and carried her to the house, the bells rang out, telling the world that miracles are always possible.

All you have to do is believe.

SOMETIMES, HAVING WEALTH and power and all the right connections really did pay off.

They flew back to New York early in the morning the next day, Tally wearing the diamond solitaire Dante had bought for her in the Caribbean.

"It's beautiful," she whispered, when he slipped the ring on her finger.

"Not as beautiful as you," he said, and kissed her.

All the municipal offices were closed, but such details weren't enough to put a crimp in the plans of Dante Russo.

"I know someone who knows someone who knows someone," he said, laughing when Tally rolled her eyes.

"Such arrogance," she said, but her smile, her voice, her eyes shone with love.

By noon, they had a wedding license and a judge who said he'd be happy to marry them in Dante's penthouse.

By one, the penthouse was filled with Christmas

garlands. Mistletoe hung from every doorway. Dante loved catching Tally under the mistletoe, whirling her in a circle and kissing her.

The enormous sitting room was filled with baskets of crimson and white poinsettias. Holly leaves, bright with berries, lay draped over the top of the fireplace mantel. But the room's centerpiece was a blue spruce so tall its branches reached the ceiling.

The tree was beautiful.

It filled the air with its fragrance; it glowed with what Tally was sure were a thousand white fairy lights. The flames on the hearth in the wall-long fireplace danced on the gleaming surfaces of the gold and silver balls that hung from the tree. Gaily wrapped packages spilled from under the branches, though Sam, squealing with delight, had already opened most of hers.

Champagne was chilling in silver buckets; caviar sat in a silver dish. Everything was perfect...and a little before two, the doorman brought up an enormous white box. Inside was a magnificent gown of lace and seed pearls, straight from the atelier of a world-famous designer.

It was the sort of gown princesses wear in the fairy tales little girls read.

Except, Tally thought when she finally stood beside her gorgeous groom and looked up into his eyes, except, this was no fairy tale.

This was real. It was true love, and it would last forever.

"Do you take this woman," the judge intoned, and Dante short-circuited things by saying "Yes."

The perfect P.A., who was one of the guests, laughed. So did Mrs. Tipton and so did Samantha, who she held against her bosom.

Dante brought his bride's hand to his lips. They smiled into each other's eyes. Then they gave the judge all their attention. Slowly, and with deep meaning, they took the vows that would forever unite them.

Moments later, they were husband and wife. Dante gathered his bride to him and kissed her again.

"I will love you forever, *inamorata*," he said softly.

Tally smiled through tears of happiness. "As I will love you," she whispered.

"Me, too," Sam said.

Everyone laughed as the baby made her pronouncement.

"Down," she told Mrs. Tipton, with all the imperiousness of a two-year-old. She toddled to her parents and held up her arms. "Up," she commanded.

Dante, a man who never took orders from anyone, happily took this one and settled his daughter into the curve of his arm.

"Mama," Sam said, touching a chubby hand to Tally's cheek.

She looked at Dante, who smiled and waited for her to call him Da-Tay.

But she didn't.

Instead, she put a little hand on each side of his face and said, "Dada."

Dante's eyes filled. He looked at his wife, and Tally smiled.

"Merry Christmas, beloved," she whispered.

*"Buon natale, inamorata,"* he said softly.

Their daughter laughed, and flung her arms around them both.

# LAYING DOWN
# THE LAW

AND SUSAN STEPHENS

**Susan Stephens** was a professional singer before meeting her husband on the tiny Mediterranean island of Malta. In true Modern™ Romance style they met on Monday, became engaged on Friday and were married three months after that. Almost thirty years and three children later, they are still in love. (Susan does not advise her children to return home one day with a similar story, as she may not take the news with the same fortitude as her own mother!)

Susan had written several non-fiction books when fate took a hand. At a charity costume ball there was an after-dinner auction. One of the lots, 'Spend a Day with an Author', had been donated by Mills & Boon® author Penny Jordan. Susan's husband bought this lot and Penny was to become not just a great friend but a wonderful mentor, who encouraged Susan to write romance.

Susan loves her family, her pets, her friends and her writing. She enjoys entertaining, travel and going to the theatre. She reads, cooks and plays the piano to relax, and can occasionally be found throwing herself off mountains on a pair of skis or galloping through the countryside. Visit Susan's website: www.susanstephens.net—she loves to hear from her readers all around the world!

Dear Reader,

Christmas is such an emotionally warm time of year for me as I contact much-loved friends and family across the globe, and I want to share that sense of warmth and love and friendship with you.

I want you to know that every day, when I sit down at my desk to write, I'm thinking about you, the reader, and how best to share my thoughts and dreams with you. I feel as if I'm reaching out with this Christmas book just as I do with all those other messages at this time of year and I hope that, as you read, you will smile and escape into another world for an hour or so.

This book is based on some quite hair-raising and amusing stories brought home by my elder daughter when she first became a barrister, so it's good to know the legal profession isn't quite as stuffy as we sometimes think—though I hasten to add that your friend the author has taken considerable liberties with the truth!

With my warmest good wishes to you at this special time of year,

*Susan*

Www.susanstephens.com

# For Wiggy

# PROLOGUE

PARTIES BORED HIM. Office parties bored him most of all. But he'd been too busy to meet anyone in the hectic city chambers since he'd arrived in the country to head up an exchange programme between promising young lawyers in the UK and the US, and this was an opportunity to show his face, as well as to weigh up the raw material.

He paused in the entrance to the room. The reception was being held in honour of the latest judge on the local circuit to be elevated to the House of Lords. An uneasy silence had fallen and he knew immediately that something was wrong. The room was packed with the local legal aristocracy, together with a swarm of pupil barristers all hoping to be noticed. His gaze was drawn to the podium where a red-faced girl was struggling to make an introduction, while next to her stood the guest of honour, Judge Deadfast of Dearing. His Lordship appeared less than amused by the fact the girl appeared to have forgotten his name.

He held his breath as she tried again. *Judge Dredd?* It was time for him to step in….

The elderly man at Carly's side shifted impatiently as she tried again. 'And it is my great pleasure this evening to introduce

Judge…' Why had her mind chosen now to blank? Was it because the most incredible looking man she had ever seen in her life had just entered the room? Tall and fierce, with dark flashing eyes, he took in everything at a glance, including her red face, no doubt. With his tan, athletic build and thick, chocolate-brown hair, he was the quintessential Latin lover made flesh. While she was the quintessential fat girl battling to introduce a geriatric judge with eyebrows that badly needed shearing.

No wonder she'd lost her audience! Who wouldn't prefer to look at that gorgeous man?

Would she be defeated? Sucking in a deep breath, she tried again. 'Ladies and gentlemen—'

Response: nil. Humiliation: a bottomless pit.

She was a back-room girl, not an MC. But if she hoped to pursue her career at the bar and become an effective advocate she had to get over her stage fright fast. But now it was too late! The cavalry had arrived in the form of the man with more testosterone flying off him than sparks off a Catherine wheel.

A path formed in front of him as he strode across the room. 'Ladies and gentlemen,' he said, smiling confidently at his audience as he rescued the microphone. 'My apologies for being late…' He wasn't late of course, but no one knew that, did they?

He turned his charm on the judge next, keeping the microphone close to his lips. He could feel the rustle of interest in the room, the shower of pheromones in the air. He could also feel the abject misery of the girl who had failed, but he'd see to her later.

'Your Lordship, what an honour…' He continued in this vein until the apoplectic look on His Lordship's face had paled into his usual sepulchral pallor.

He stood back well pleased with his performance as the

grimly smiling judge left the podium to be toadied by his colleagues. Courting judges was his area of expertise; courting
women, his passion. His spirited Italian mother had taught
him that keeping women happy was fundamental to life. He
had since learned that it was fundamental to his sanity. The
red-faced girl was next in line for some TLC, but not before
he'd won back her audience.

'My Lords, ladies and gentlemen… Some appreciation, if
you please, for my learned colleague.' As he spoke he laid a
protective arm over the culprit's shoulders and drew her
forward. 'Who amongst us would have made the connection
between our honoured guest Judge Deadfast of Dearing and
that legendary comic-strip character Judge Joe Dredd, law en-
forcement *par excellence?*' He paused to allow the mood
against the young woman under his protection to change. He
had His Lordship's interest now. 'And let us not forget,' he
added, raising his hands to silence the oohs and aahs of understanding rippling through his audience, 'that Judge Joe
Dredd has the power to arrest, sentence, and even execute
criminals on the spot. So I advise prudence tonight…' As His
Lordship led the laughter, he relaxed, job done. 'Enjoy the rest
of your evening, everyone!'

He turned to rescue his charge and found her gone. His
mouth firmed when he spotted her at the bar.

She knocked back a second glass of wine, but nothing helped.
She was over; finished. She wasn't a natural party animal, or
speech-giver. Perhaps that was why her fellow pupil barristers had set her up by making her the compere…

As she picked up the wine bottle to pour herself some more,
he made his move. Realising he was coming over she fired
red and turned away, but not before he'd had a chance to

assess the voluptuous figure. It appealed to his Latin soul, like the tilt of her chin and the abundance of Titian hair. Those were the points in her favour. On the reverse side of the coin she had the fashion sense of a—

Of an Englishwoman, he reminded himself as she glanced around to see how close he was.

She gasped to find him right behind her. 'I'm really, *really* grateful,' she blurted, drawing his attention to her wine-dampened lips. 'I don't know what came over me…'

She gulped as he took the wineglass out of her hand. 'Thanks for rescuing the situation. Can't imagine why you did it,' she finished awkwardly.

Chivalry would sound outdated to her, and he'd moved on in any case to urges and fantasies that had yet to be explored. His body, like his mind, was meant to be used. Years of study hadn't robbed him of the need to express himself physically, hence the workouts, tarmac, the gym, the sparring he indulged in twice a week. 'Think nothing of it,' he said, pouring her a glass of water. 'Here, drink this—you'll feel better in a minute.'

'Thank you,' she said, sipping demurely.

*Dio!* She was a contradiction. In unguarded moments her green eyes flashed fire, which gave him a hint of the busy thoughts beneath her frumpy exterior, and now he was close enough he could see her skin had the translucency of delicate porcelain. She might be considered gauche and awkward compared to the polish of the other girls in the room, but she had his attention. Taking the wine bottle she thought she had so cleverly hidden behind the punch bowl, he replaced it in the ice bucket where it belonged. 'I think you've had enough. It doesn't do to blunt the senses…'

His gravelly voice made her toes curl. He was so gorgeous. She had no coping strategies for a man with the body of a kick boxer dressed by Savile Row. Which hardly mattered. With his stubble-darkened face and commanding manner he could have any woman in the room. He would pour himself a drink, give her one of those dangerous half smiles, and walk away.

How did she know this? Because she had dressed carefully so as not to draw attention to herself, just as every other woman present had dressed to impress, and now she should get out of his way and spare herself the indignity of being asked to move. Unfortunately her feet refused to agree with this proposition and remained where they were. Glaring at them, she noticed his feet: shoe size large. She blanked out the obvious correlation to other parts of his anatomy.

As he flipped back his jacket to slip a hand in his pocket, he raised the line of one trouser leg enough to display the most extraordinary socks. A man in a traditional three-piece suit wearing crazy-coloured socks? Which said what about the workings in his head?

'Feeling better now?' Dark eyes probed deep, and the voice that went with them was intriguingly foreign: mid-Atlantic with a dash of chilli. He was waiting for her to say something, but her quickness of mind—the only worthwhile attribute she possessed—deserted her. All she could think was, You don't normally look at teeth and think, Bite me. But this man's teeth were very white, and very strong, and something in his mocking expression promised a very pleasurable nip indeed. He had the sexiest lips on earth, and his eyes…were expressive pools of wicked thoughts and sardonic humour; perfect.

But who was he? She was a pupil barrister in this busy city chambers, a freckle-faced country bumpkin with a lively interior mind, but the man towering over her was film-star perfect. 'Are you Italian?' It was the best she could come up with going on nothing more than his looks.

'Italian American,' he said, staring at her empty wineglass. 'I don't think you like parties any more than I do. Am I right?' He didn't wait for her answer. Taking hold of her arm, he drew her across the room, guiding her in and out of the alcohol-fuelled mayhem with an arm outstretched in front of her face.

To protect her?

No one had ever done that before. Everyone assumed she could look after herself. As they should; she was big and capable, but this was nice for a change.

As they walked she worked out that, as a stranger in town, he must want her to point him in the direction of the nearest taxi rank. But then he tested this assumption, taking her past the elevators and heading for the offices. She ran out of feasible alternatives as to what would happen next. And okay, maybe she would regret this in the morning, but tomorrow was another day...

'This office is being used as a cloakroom, I believe.' Trying the door, he held it open for her.

She stared at him blankly.

'You do have a coat, don't you? It's cold outside...'

All he wanted to do was help her on with her coat? That lively interior mind had let her down badly this time! 'You're assuming I'm ready to go—'

'Aren't you?'

Of course she was, but was that an invitation to leave with him? Her heart started thundering even though she doubted it.

'Shall I call a taxi for you?'

Not an invitation! 'It's only walking distance to my flat.'

'Are you sure?' He dipped his head to give her the type of stare a ringside doctor might give a boxer he suspected of being punch drunk.

'Absolutely sure...' The punch had been good, come to think of it. She'd made it herself to an old family recipe, and in hindsight perhaps the glasses of white wine on top of it had been a mistake. She tapped her foot, starting to feel uncomfortable beneath the scrutiny of a man who had taken grooming to new heights—six feet two or thereabouts, she guessed. 'Something wrong?' She grabbed her coat.

'Not at all. I just think you've had rather a lot to drink.'

'Are you judging me?'

The raised brow and almost-smile were the signal for her heartbeat to go crazy. 'Well, if you don't mind…' She stared pointedly at the door. He was way out of her league, so there was no point in prolonging the agony.

'Of course…' With a mocking bow, he stood aside.

Who was that man? she wondered again. Crunching frost beneath her boots, Carly realised his socks were the only clue she'd come away with. They'd been extraordinary: bright green with a motif of red boxing gloves, garnished with the badge of some club he must belong to… Which made sense when you considered the evidence—there was nothing soft about him—so maybe he was just that: a particularly desirable kick boxer with a keen sense of style. Whatever the case, she was too busy developing her career to think about men.

Her body disagreed. Her body wanted things her mind would never allow. Fortunately, reason prevailed. If his intentions had been dishonourable when he had led her by the hand towards that darkened office she would have pulled back. She would never have given way to lust.

Never.

*Never!*

Oh, all right then, she might have done.

Fortunately the opportunity to test her resolve would never arise. She might not be Brain of Britain, but she was bright enough to know the ugly duckling never got the prince.

# CHAPTER ONE

YOU COULD HEAR a pin drop in the lecture theatre. A fly on the wall might say the man teaching law could only be Italian. One thing was certain. With his striking Latin looks, impeccable tailoring and autocratic stare, Lorenzo Domenico could hold an audience spellbound. Women had stampeded the law school to secure a place in his class and on this first morning they outnumbered the men ten to one. Lorenzo Domenico might be new in town, but he was already a legend.

Lorenzo paced as he spoke, pausing occasionally to shoot an impatient glance at his adoring audience. He wanted to check if they were listening. He intended his standards to be the highest on the faculty. He'd worked hard, and now he expected that same application from his students. He tested them constantly, often in the most unexpected ways. In Lorenzo's opinion anyone who possessed a photographic memory could pass an exam, but could they fathom the intricacies of law and come to the best result for their client? He called it lateral thinking. Some of his students called it unreasonable; they were the ones who didn't make it through the course.

Along with heading up the scholarship programme he had agreed to mentor a pupil barrister at the top flight chambers in the city where he had tenancy. Multitasking was his speciality, intolerance of those who couldn't keep up his only failing—though his adoring Italian mother would have disagreed, and persuaded him he had no failings. Lorenzo smiled. Mama was always right.

Pausing mid-stride, he checked his register. There was someone missing. Instinct made him glance out of the window. He tensed. 'Will you excuse me? That wasn't a question,' he added as a groan of disappointment rose in the lecture theatre. He was already halfway through the door. The student who was late had just slammed her rusty old bike into his pristine Alfa Romeo.

'You cannot wipe it off,' he roared, exiting the outer doors like an avenging angel. He had arrived just in time to see the young woman's pink tongue flick out to wet her finger.

'It's a very small scratch,' she explained, her green eyes rounding with sincerity. 'Oh…' The blood drained from her face. 'Hello…'

He stood motionless, taking in the facts. Whichever way he looked at it, this was bad.

Carly paled as her mind absorbed the information: Carly Tate crashes into the car of her senior tutor Lorenzo Domenico on her first morning in his class. Not only that, she'd just received a letter to say he'd been appointed her pupil master in chambers, plus he chaired the committee for the Unicorn scholarship; the scholarship she had promised her parents. How much better could it get?

No prizes for guessing his thoughts: Oh, no, not her again! Shortly followed by, Do I associate with failure? She could hardly pretend the fiasco last night had escaped his notice. And now this! To distract them both she pointed to the damage on his car. 'You can see how small it is…' But now she looked again the gouge seemed to have grown.

'Small?' he said with a curl of his lip.

No wonder she hadn't recognised him last night. Since arriving in the UK Lorenzo Domenico had barely settled long enough to register a shadow. Winning a no-hoper case in his first month in town had raised his profile to the extent that the clerks who managed his diary were looking at a twelve-month waiting list. Lorenzo wouldn't be returning home any time soon—or ever, if the rumours were to be believed—so it was time to build bridges. Fast. 'I'm really sorry about your car—'

'You will be.' He cut her off crisply.

He hadn't been dubbed the scourge of the courts for nothing. What a perfect start to her scholarship hopes! Her fellow pupils had all landed some elderly old duffer who schooled them in an atmosphere of calm and dusty academe, while she had scored Torquemada, Chief Inquisitor.

She had been so sure she could deal with a man like Lorenzo Domenico when she had first read the letter, in fact she'd been rather thrilled, but there was a huge gulf between the written word and the man standing in front of her now. And ominously his socks were tartan, suggesting he was poised to dance a jig on the grave of her ambition. But she wasn't going down without a fight. 'I think you'll find that the scratch will polish out—'

'Do not presume to practise your advocacy skills on me, Ms Tate.' His eyes turned cold. 'Take a look at my car.'

'Very nice—'

'I mean the damage to my car, Ms Tate. Look at that. If you examine it closely you will see that the scratch will not polish out.'

She shook her head like a wayward pony, sending shimmering auburn curls flying round her shoulders. He admired the hair, but it distracted him. She was a student and his sole purpose in life was to whip her into shape.

'I can hardly see it,' she protested.

Her determination to fight pleased him. He liked a fight. 'And a *very small* scratch on a hired car will affect my deposit how, *Ms* Tate?' He would drive her hard like all his students. Time was short, and they had to learn more than the letter of the law, they had to absorb an immeasurable lexicon of nuance and interpretation. If they weren't up to it, it was better to find out now. 'Come on, come on,' he goaded her. 'Aren't you supposed to be a lawyer?'

'I am a lawyer,' she retorted, holding his gaze.

Another rush of pleasure hit him. He didn't want his students to fail; he wanted them all to excel—even this sorry excuse of an MC. 'You may be a lawyer one day,' he said, 'but not yet. And if you're late for my class again, you never will be. You will fail the course and lose your chance to be considered for the scholarship.'

'I'm really sorry—'

'Sorry doesn't cut it with me, Ms Tate.'

'*Very* sorry…'

She raised her head to confront him in a way that almost made up for her blunders, because now he caught a glimpse of a strong inner core. She would need that when she stood up in court. Her face was easy on the eye too. Though not glamorous or attractive to him, she had a fresh-faced look he found appealing. After all the painted sophisticates he'd been introduced to on the so-called social scene she was a refreshing change.

And then there were his students. His impression of them to date was that the females were slightly less good-looking than the men, which, as a serial heterosexual, was a serious concern to him.

He'd read the report on Carly Tate, as he had read the reports on all his students. She was the brightest of the bright, but was she right for law? That was what he meant to find out. But if she was going to work with him she'd have to clean up her act. For instance, what was she wearing? A jacket with bald cuffs, which she had teamed with ripped and faded jeans, and on her feet something that looked as if she had made them herself out of a couple of hides and a yard of ribbon.

She hadn't made the slightest effort to impress, which insulted him. She looked as if she'd just climbed out of bed, which enraged him. Women should be chaste and available and waiting for him to notice them. His eyes darkened as he pictured his ideal woman waking slowly and languorously with the memories of the previous night still heavy in her eyes, and on her plump, perfectly formed lips...

Why was he staring at her lips? Did she have a milk moustache?

Clearing her throat, Carly made that her excuse for swiping a hand across her mouth.

Charming! Such grace and style, these Englishwomen. 'So,' he rapped, staring at her, before turning to look at the one thing that could distract an Italian man from thoughts of family, football, fashion or fornication: his car. 'What do you intend to do about the damage and my claim for reparation?'

She recited the relevant passages of law to him flawlessly, but then, remembering the preliminary notes he'd circulated prior to the course, he realised what a good teacher he was. 'I see you've read my notes.'

'Of *course* I have,' she said, pinking up again.

'I'll leave you to report the damage, in that case,' he said coldly. 'Arrange for repairs and keep me informed...'

He was pleased to see how well she responded to instruction. But as he turned to go he could have sworn she clicked her heels. He almost swung round to challenge her, but then contented himself with the thought that dealing with trouble-makers was something he excelled at. He loved trouble; his career had been built on it.

Reaching the entrance to the building, he stopped and turned abruptly. Her cheeks flamed red as he fixed a stony stare upon her face. Pleased with the effect, he moved in for the kill. 'As you've already missed the main thrust of my lecture I'd like you to return home and dress for court.'

Her face brightened. 'Court?'

There wasn't a student barrister alive who didn't ache to ease the tedium of study with some real-life drama in the courtroom. 'Yes, court,' he said evenly. 'I left my wig and gown there. You can collect them for me.'

It amused him to see her eyes fire bullets at him while her face remained carefully blank. He revised his opinion of her again—upwards. She'd make a great lawyer if she possessed the will to do so. But he hadn't finished with her yet. 'You can't go to court as my representative dressed like that.'

'Oh, don't worry about me,' she said, starting to gather her spilled belongings. 'This suit will brush down fine.' Retrieving some rag from the gutter, she shook it out.

'In case it's escaped your notice, Ms Tate, that suit is covered in mud, and you work under me now.' An unfortunate turn of phrase, perhaps, but too late to call it back. He added some iron to the mix. 'I forbid you to go to court dressed like that. What will people think?'

'That I can't afford cleaning bills…?'

There was such an expression of innocence on her face he considered his grounds for launching a rebuke uncertain. Everyone knew that pupil barristers existed largely on fresh air and the charity of their parents, plus her face was already flaming with mortification, and his intention had never been to crush her. While he contemplated this she rallied. Angling her chin, she waited, as if expecting him to pat her on the head for arriving at the right answer. He knew her type immediately. She was the child who had always known the right answer in class, and who had shot up her hand before anyone else had a chance to, oblivious to how unpopular that made her. He could only contrast that with his own childhood when he'd only had to burp for everyone to applaud him in breathless admiration. Nonetheless, he had to set her right. 'No, Ms Tate. They will not think that. They will think you so rushed this morning you didn't have a chance to look in the mirror. Do you want to leave an impression of incompetence behind you? No, I didn't think so.'

Inconvenient images invaded Carly's mind as Lorenzo delivered his ultimatum, of flinging the wretched suit at his feet and jumping on it. Did he think bespoke suits like his grew on trees? Did he think parking across the cycle path was a good idea? But these images were swiftly followed by her parents' anxious faces. She couldn't let them down, and while there was life left in her scholarship hopes she had not the slightest intention of doing so.

# CHAPTER TWO

'AND YOUR SECOND TASK for today, Ms Tate…'

They were in Lorenzo's office. He was seated; she was standing in front of him like a recalcitrant child. She kept her expression carefully neutral. It wasn't that she had suddenly become immune to the power storm swirling round Lorenzo, but the fact that her feet were killing her. She had made a real effort to conform to the image she imagined he would have in mind for a successful female applicant for the Unicorn scholarship, and if that involved wearing the type of heels that were almost impossible to come by for farmyard feet, then that was what she would do.

'You're a front runner for the scholarship,' he said. 'You do know that, don't you?'

Say yes, and be damned for complacency, or say no and appear a wuss. She decided not to comment and straightened her back, assuming what she hoped he would take for a determined stance. And while she did that she gave full rein to her lust. Playing poker face was an area in which she excelled.

'You do realise what's hanging on your performance over the next few weeks?'

She might have known Lorenzo wouldn't give up until he had forced an answer out of her. Thinking about her parents made a clean sweep of her mind and the lust. Her parents had talked of nothing but the scholarship for months now, and both the bridge club and golf club were waiting agog for news of her latest triumph, apparently.

'Ms Tate.' Lorenzo snapped her out of the reverie.

'Yes?' She held back on the temptation to salute.

'Do I have your total commitment to this project?'

'One hundred per cent.'

'Good.' He relaxed a little, which was enough to give her a grandstand view of his socks…as well as just a hint of the tanned and deliciously muscular hairy legs above them. Her cheeks fired up like warning beacons when he caught her staring.

'Something wrong?' he said.

'No…of course not—'

'That outfit won't do,' he said, turning his attention to her clothes. He wrinkled his nose as he scrutinised the same suit he'd seen lying in the gutter. She had sponged it down since then with a pungent though effective mix of hot water and vinegar. She had wanted to look her best for this momentous first one-on-one meeting with her pupil master, except, of course, this wasn't their first one-on-one encounter. 'I'm sorry about your car—'

'Never mind that now,' he said impatiently. 'I expect you to deal with that in your own time. This is my time, and while you're under my tutelage I expect you to prove you're a lawyer worth sorting out.'

'Oh, I am,' she said eagerly. Her cheeks fired as her body entertained some frenzied notions involving Lorenzo sorting her out. 'What I mean is, I won't disappoint you—' The fire in her cheeks went up a notch when she noticed his interested gaze lingering on her breasts. Her suit jacket wouldn't close over them and was hanging open, revealing a paper-thin shirt that had seen much better days. 'I'm ready to be sorted out,'

she blurted recklessly. 'And I promise to try and find something more suitable to wear.' As she spoke she clutched the
edges of her jacket in a last-ditch attempt to make it close.

'Be sure that you do.'

Carly couldn't tell if Lorenzo was amused or angry as he
turned his attention to the documents on his desk, but now it
was her turn to study him. The fine wool of his dark, bespoke
suit clung attractively to his powerful frame, and she guessed
he would have to have suits made for him as the spread of his
shoulders was so wide—

Looking up, he snapped, 'I thought I told you to go home
and change?'

Change into what? Ally McBeal? She was wearing a thrift-
shop find, and going home to change her clothes would
involve donning another thrift-shop find. She had to come
clean and explain. 'I would, but—'

'But?' Lorenzo let the word hang like a dead rat. 'No
excuses, Ms Tate. If you intend to succeed you must do what
I say, when I say it.'

Had she signed up to join the army? And what would it
take to soften that firm mouth?

'If you have difficulty following a simple instruction perhaps
we'd better sort that out before we go any further,' Lorenzo
rapped, jolting her back to full attention. Holding up a list with
the logo of the Unicorn scholarship printed prominently on the
top of the sheet of paper, he said, 'If you're not willing to go
the extra mile in every area of your professional life I think it
better for both of us if I cross your name off this list now.'

'Are you threatening me?' She couldn't believe she'd said
it, but something made her blunder on. 'Did you spare a
thought for the consequences of parking your flashy new car
across the cycle path? Or was it more important to leave a
gleaming Alpha Romeo where you could admire it from the

window? That way, I suppose, when the cogs of your students' minds failed to turn swiftly enough you'd got at least one piece of outstanding machinery to admire.'

'Finished?' Lorenzo demanded coolly. He shifted in his chair. 'Passion, Ms Tate. I like that in an advocate. But I'd also like you to consider the perils of over-larding your assertions when you're standing up in court.'

His eyes were like black diamonds, and the ice in his voice was a salutary reminder that Lorenzo Domenico had not risen to the top of the legal levee on a tide of emotion.

'Yes or no, Ms Tate?' he demanded, pen poised.

Her heart was racing. Her lips were parted…

She was aroused!

And not just aroused, she was thoroughly stirred up, which was unusual—no, make that unique! This unexpected confrontation with Lorenzo was rousing parts of her that had remained dormant for years. And at this, one of the most crucial moments in her life!

She had to get over it, and let her mind rule; her parents needed this. 'You can put your pen down,' she said with matching calm. 'I'm up to the challenge.'

If only Lorenzo didn't have quite such a direct and perceptive stare, but she had to be up to the challenge. She hadn't moved from a sleepy village—where her parents were pillars of the local community—to the city, only to fail them. Her goal was to make her parents proud, and if that meant jousting with Lorenzo like this then she would. She wanted the Unicorn scholarship more than anything. *Other than a hug sometimes…* 'You mentioned a second task?' she prompted, rattling her brain cells into order.

'I'd like you to organise the Christmas party.'

The poisoned chalice! Her stomach clenched.

'The holidays come around each year, Ms Tate,' he said

briskly. 'There's no need to look so startled. I have been informed that we host a spectacular Christmas party each year, and I'm offering you the chance to make this year's the best. I would have thought you would be grateful for an opportunity to shine.' He said this wearily. 'You have four days,' he added in a harder tone.

*Four days?* He made it sound as if four days was a generous amount of time in which to achieve the impossible. Lorenzo had unerringly settled on the one task for which her finely-tuned brain was most ill equipped. She was a swot, not a party planner. She collected scholarships like other people collected golf trophies. But Lorenzo was right in saying this was a chance to impress, if not the chance she had been hoping for. She didn't have sufficient polish to lay on something grand for a group of sophisticated lawyers.

But polish could be acquired, Carly reminded herself, whereas ambition had been stamped on her forehead at birth. She was going to nail this.

'If you don't feel up to the task I can always ask someone else.'

'That won't be necessary,' she assured him. 'I can handle it.' If he'd asked her to walk up and down Oxford Street with a sandwich-board on her back advertising ambulance-chasing services, she'd do that too. All it took to cement her determination in place was the thought of her mother's face if she failed, or her father's friends shaking their heads behind his back, if she returned home empty-handed. She had to win Lorenzo's respect somehow if she was going to land the wretched scholarship. She was going to grasp this nettle and shake it in his face. She was going to put on the best Christmas party there'd ever been.

Somehow.

'Are you sure?' he pressed, staring at her intently. 'You can't afford to get this wrong, Ms Tate.'

Thanks for the confidence boost! 'I'm positive. You've got nothing to worry about.' She tipped her chin and found a confident, businesslike smile to match the brave words. She had already fathomed how she was going to turn what her mother was sure to see as a menial task into a positive: Lorenzo had *entrusted* her with the task of organising the most important chambers event of the year. The fact that you didn't need an honours degree from Cambridge to do that would never occur to her mother.

She hoped.

'Very well, then…' Lorenzo's dark eyes glinted as the challenge began. 'Well? What are you waiting for? You'd better make a start.'

It was the ultimate test for Carly. He doubted she had ever attended the type of party where networking and point-scoring were a given, champagne and caviare just a starting point. He wanted to push her; he wanted to find out about those hidden depths. Would she ring a party planner and take the easy way out? He'd known that to happen in the past. It usually ended in disaster with the student forced to ring Mummy and Daddy to provide extra funds when they realised how little they would be receiving from him.

Yes, this was one of his favourite tests.

Back in the cubby-hole that passed for her office, Carly reviewed her position. Planning a sophisticated party took her so far out of her comfort zone her first inclination was to laugh hysterically. Carly Tate, the girl least likely to party, was now expected to arrange one!

Her mother expressed serious doubts when she rang up for advice. 'If only your sister were there to help you…' But Livvie wouldn't be there to help…

She felt a pang as she thought about her sister. Livvie had a talent for bringing people together and making them smile and could sprinkle fairy dust over any gathering. But, clueless or not, this was her party. It was just one more mountain to climb. And climb it she would.

Dusting off the crampons of her ambition, she got to work. The phrase 'party planner' sang in her mind as she spotted the telephone directory, but then remembering the tone of Lorenzo's instructions, she changed her mind. He had asked her to organise the party; he hadn't asked her to delegate. This was just another of his little tests, Carly concluded, determined to play Lorenzo at his own game.

Playing Lorenzo at his own game involved seeing him again during his working day, and he didn't welcome her interruption. But he could turn on the hard stare all he liked, she wasn't going anywhere until she had the information she needed. 'I must know more before I can start to plan.' She used a firm voice to distract him from the papers he was studying.

'For instance?' His gazed pierced her.

'Budget?' She held her ground even though Lorenzo was so tensely poised behind his desk he looked like a cougar about to pounce. 'I must know the budget I'll be working to…' It was hard to block out images of chocolate fountains and multiple crates of champagne. Having perused the guest list, she knew a number of eminent QCs and judges from other chambers would be attending, and they'd expect the best. Her confidence was growing by the minute. Party planning wasn't so bad. It was just a question of making lists and sourcing suppliers—

'Budget?' Lorenzo barked, cutting her off mid self-congratulation. 'Slim, Ms Tate!'

Was that an instruction? She sucked in her stomach, just in case.

Lorenzo fixed her with a basilisk stare. 'Bring every quotation to me. Don't agree to anything without my direct permission. Do I make myself clear, Ms Tate?' His voice had dropped to a penetrating whisper.

Crystal. She would use lawyer's discretion, which meant that anything she could get away with, she would. Unfortunately she didn't have such an immediate answer to the irresponsible behaviour of her body, which was responding frantically to the stern note in Lorenzo's voice. She liked that. She liked it a lot. Probably because she could see all sorts of erotic possibilities in her mind's eye. She gave a brisk nod to cover for her abstraction as her fantasies played out.

Lorenzo scribbled something on a pad, which he handed over to her. 'Here's your guideline spending limit…'

Taking the paper from him, Carly read it and tried not to gulp. Her scholarship was definitely teetering in the balance, not on a champagne fountain, as she had hoped, but on a beer mug and a plate of curling sandwiches. She could forget the graceful twelve-foot tree, tastefully decorated with colour-coordinated baubles and flashing lights—clear, of course, she knew that much. With the budget Lorenzo had just handed her she'd be lucky if she could afford a pot-plant and a torch.

'If the task's too much for you—' he began wearily.

'Not at all,' she interrupted him.

'Then, if you don't mind…' He stared pointedly at the pile of papers on his desk.

'Of course,' she said coolly. 'I'll start working on it right away.'

When the door had shut behind her he sat back. Would she crumble? He hoped not. Closing his eyes briefly, he thought he could detect the faint aroma of wildflowers in the air. Ms

Tate was proving a lot harder to blank from his mind than he had anticipated. And his body would have some striking images to dip into as well if she didn't find a suit jacket that fitted. The end result was he found it impossible to concentrate.

Springing up, he paced the room. So what if the task he had handed her was impossible? A working lawyer rarely encountered anything ordinary or expected in court. He wanted to see how she reacted, how she thought on her feet when she was up against a wall…

He had to shake his head to drive away that disturbing image before he could progress his thoughts. Her development as a lawyer was under his command. On paper she was the front runner for the scholarship, but was it enough? She was a hopeless public speaker, which put her future as an effective advocate in jeopardy. And maybe she did have the best possible paper qualifications, but was her memory suspect? Was it possible she had forgotten what was happening tonight? She certainly hadn't mentioned it. Yet she faced a crucial test. Had it slipped her mind? And if it had, what could possibly have distracted her to that extent?

Lorenzo. Lorenzo. Lorenzo. Why couldn't she get him out of her head? He seemed to have taken up permanent residence in there, Carly thought, raking her hair in frustration. And it was imperative she concentrate on the task at hand. Four days was hardly enough time to organise a cup of tea in this place, let alone a full-blown Christmas party!

Chewing the top of her pencil, she wracked her brain for that one brilliant idea that would astound everyone.

And failed.

The only clearly focused thought in her head was the knowledge that Lorenzo would never look at her in the way her body thought he should. Why would he, when he was older and worldly-wise, wildly successful and far better looking? Face it, he wouldn't, and that was that.

Lorenzo rasped his beard with one firm thumb pad. He was still pondering Carly's inexplicable lapse of memory. Tonight was the Grand Court, a legal ceremonial notorious as the killing ground of pupils. He would have thought she'd be prepared for it. The Grand Court was geared to weed out the weaker members of the bar before they had chance to gain a foothold in the profession. It went without saying that any pupil of his would succeed and pass the test with flying colours—and without any prompting from the sidelines. But on this occasion he wondered if there might be too large a gulf between his expectation and Carly's performance. He refused to believe she could simply forget, just as he refused to give her an unfair advantage over the other pupils. He felt a little reassured when her determined face flashed into his mind. Of course she had everything in hand. If she hadn't she'd be squashed like a bug.

Back in her cubby-hole Carly sat with her head in her hands. There wasn't a chance she could organise the type of party Lorenzo was expecting on the measly budget he had allowed. Hard work wasn't enough in this instance. She needed a miracle.

Her head bounced as her eyes fired with inspiration. *Of course!* Why hadn't she thought of it sooner? She didn't have to compete with some glitz and glamour event. All she had to do was land on something bold and different, something novel and unexpected—

And hope she didn't fall flat on her face.

# CHAPTER THREE

SLURPING COFFEE without tasting it, Carly continued scribbling notes. The ideas were coming thick and fast now, and driving her hard towards party nirvana was the knowledge that she had less than a week to put everything in place…food, drink, music, decorations, dress—

*Dress!*

Pushing back from the desk, she yelped in alarm. How could she have forgotten tonight? How could she have forgotten a night as crucial to her career as the Grand Court?

Lorenzo. She blamed him entirely.

He had shot everything from her brain in less time than it took to…

Clear your mind, Carly.

Pressing her fingertips against her temples, she battled hard to erase images of her stern pupil master performing all sorts of pre-sentence examinations on her all too eager and totally irresponsible body.

And failed.

She was doing quite a lot of that recently.

But the Lorenzo effect was a concern for another day. The Grand Court was so important to her future she couldn't believe it had slipped her mind. *Nothing* slipped her mind *ever.*

Before Lorenzo.

The Grand Court was a rite of passage for every pupil barrister, and as such should have taken precedence over everything. And she didn't have a thing to wear. If there'd been room in her cramped cubby-hole she would have paced up and down. It was too dreadful to contemplate. All the senior lawyers, including Lorenzo, would be attending; there was no getting out of it. And she hadn't given it a thought.

He'd known that and let her stew?

His sardonic face flashed into her mind. Of course he had.

So she would fight fire with fire. The Christmas party would just have to take a back seat until tomorrow. If she failed the Grand Court she wouldn't make the Christmas party anyway, Carly thought, grimacing. Plus the golf and bridge clubs would be forced to fly their flags at half-mast, which was out of the question.

Settling back down, she tried to remain calm. The Grand Court was no picnic—unless you took into account the bread rolls flying your way if you messed up. The ceremony was held annually in the vaulted dining hall of one of the ancient Inns of Court. If you failed the test you were a laughing stock, and if you succeeded you could expect no praise. Following centuries of tradition the senior lawyers were expected to heckle the pupils as they stood to make their formal application to join the circuit. There were no rules, no quarter given, and only last year a judge's daughter had been sick in her own handbag. She told herself to concentrate on the positives.

All one of them.

Her middle name was Viola, like Shakespeare's heroine in *Twelfth Night*. The play had first been performed in 1602 in the very same hall where the Grand Court was held. What more mojo did she need? Everything would be fine.

Hopefully.

All she had to do was stand up and state her name, along with the date of her call, and the ancient Inn that had called her to the bar. After that, she just had to declare her wish to join the circus—

Circuit, Carly corrected herself grimly.

A slip like that could cost her her career. If she stumbled over the words, tradition demanded she start her little speech all over again, which was when the seniors' fun began. It was their task to shout her down, drown her out, and ultimately destroy her.

Calm, Carly commanded herself a second time, sucking in a deep, steadying breath. Everything would go to plan, but she must leave no stone unturned, which brought her thoughts full circle to the question of her outfit for the occasion. Fortunately, she had a secret weapon…

Madeline Du Pre, the most senior pupil in chambers, was Carly's elder by three years. Madeline was the recognised expert in fashion by virtue of a stint at a Swiss finishing school. Rumour had it that Madeline had been forced to repeat her first six months of training several times due to… Well, no one really knew, and Madeline wasn't telling, but the pupil master in charge of broadening her experience, one Judge Roger Warrington, never visited Madeline's office unaccompanied these days.

Madeline the modiste if not the modest, Carly thought as she rapped smartly on Madeline's door.

Carly didn't have long to wait for Madeline's verdict.

'Black? Are you mad?'

'Black's safe,' Carly protested. 'Legal-black is practically a definition,' she pointed out. 'In fact it should be a colour in the paint box. I can see it now—black, with a silvering of dust, and a touch of green mould… Don't look at me like that, Madeline. You know as well as I do that wearing black will take you through anything.'

'Except a wedding.' Madeline sniffed. 'For you…' cocking her head to one side, she gave Carly a long, considering look '…it has to be orange.'

'Orange?' Carly's eyes widened as she pictured her flame-coloured hair framed in orange. 'Are you sure?'

'Quite sure… Orange will be perfect with your colouring.'

It was important to get this right, and Madeline's scarlet talons were already drumming the desk.

'If you really think so…' Carly's voice trailed away as a horror snap in some down-market journal flew into her mind. There would be a banner heading with her looking fat, proclaiming, ORANGE JUISTICE!

But Madeline was already leading her by the arm towards the door…

'Stop worrying. Orange is absolutely your colour,' Madeline soothed. 'You mustn't even think of wearing black. You can only wear black when you've been accepted by the Grand Court. You'll cause an uproar if you go against tradition, Carly. Now, fortunately I can help you out. There's a fabulous second-hand designer clothes place, just about half a mile from here. I saw a dress in their window this morning that would be perfect for you. I even have their card…'

She handed it over and Carly read, 'One Starry Night: Model gowns by Madame Xandra… Available to hire, or to buy…'

'Thank you,' Carly said, frowning uncertainly.

It wasn't that Carly was fat, Madame Xandra explained helpfully, it was just that ball gowns were meant to fit snugly.

Which was all right for Madame Xandra, Carly thought mutinously, since she was thread-thin. Viewing her red face in the mirror, she knew she couldn't possibly hold her breath like this all evening, but on the other hand she couldn't bear the humiliation of trying to squeeze her plumpness into any more undersized Barbie-frocks. 'Yes, this one is absolutely perfect,' she said in answer to Madame Xandra's pained look.

The day could only get better, Carly told herself firmly, taking a final look at herself before setting out. Somehow she had managed to shoehorn her way into The Dress unaided, but she wasn't keen on looking too closely at the bulges of flesh fighting with an abundance of closely draped tangerine satin. The only good thing about it was that the gown seemed to answer the 'formal' dress stipulation on the gilt-edged invitation.

Edgily humming a song, she attempted last-minute to twirl her abundant red hair into some sort of sensible and therefore noticeably more compact style. She tried telling herself that everything was going to be all right, but that didn't work. How could it when she felt like a galleon under sail, roped, braced and mortally constricted? It was hardly the mood of choice for a night out in the spotlight!

Did the first person she had to see the moment she stepped down gingerly from the taxi have to be Lorenzo? And looking more like a film star than ever in his dark Alpaca coat, under which Carly knew he would be wearing a similarly impeccable tailored evening suit.

She stood for a moment to watch him greeting the other guests. He was so regal, and so confident of approval. And no wonder when he drew people to him like a magnet. Everyone wanted to bask in Lorenzo Domenico's darkly glittering glamour, no doubt hoping some of it would rub off on them…

The white silk scarf around his neck fascinated her. It was lifting in the breeze—not flying off as it would have done had she been wearing it, causing all sorts of hullabaloo, nor landing in his face and sticking on his lips, just…lifting.

Carly shut her mouth, conscious she was gawping. Her pupil master looked simply gorgeous with the wind ruffling his thick, dark hair. Where style was concerned Italians always got it right, she mused, unlike dumpy Englishwomen named Carly Tate, with her big feet and truly enormous breasts.

Lorenzo remained standing, a solitary figure, as the crowds peeled away. Staring up, he seemed transfixed by something. Following his gaze, she saw he was admiring the ancient buildings. She had forgotten how beautiful the Inns of Court were, but seeing them through Lorenzo's eyes was like seeing them anew. They were such totems to power, and such incredible monuments to the men who had designed and built them. Verging on Gothic with a special serenity all their own, they were truly awe-inspiring…

Carly shifted guiltily when, turning, Lorenzo noticed her. 'Carly,' he said, coming over. 'You're looking very—' The all-too-familiar ironic expression was firmly in place.

'Colourful?' she supplied, wanting the painful moment over with. She hadn't failed to notice as the crowds streamed past that everyone else was dressed in black, plus she was the only woman sporting a ball gown and showing her breasts. She had been set up, and it was too late to do anything about it. She just had to smile and get on with it.

'Are you ready for your ordeal?' Lorenzo murmured, trying very hard not to smile.

'You mean it hasn't started yet?'

Her dry comment unleashed something in him and he laughed. Unfortunately for her that sexy rumble had the same effect as a low-voltage charge to her most sensitive regions, which was the last thing required if she was to keep her wits about her tonight.

'Shall we go inside?' he suggested, offering his arm.

Lorenzo was offering to escort her inside? Did the most lusted-after, successful lawyer in London really want to be seen with a country bumpkin dressed in an orange meringue, or was Lorenzo merely using her as a foil to make himself look better?

He hardly needed to do that, Carly concluded.

'Well?' he pressed, a suspicious tug appearing at one corner of his mouth. 'Are you coming inside?'

Her exhalation of breath was noisily ragged as she considered this suggestion.

'Carly?' He dipped his head to look her in the eyes. She didn't dare to breathe on him. But he wouldn't wait for ever. Her options were obvious—she could turn tail and run, or she could brave it out.

Walking in on Lorenzo's arm felt good. People stared. At him, of course, she knew that, but still it proved, if proof were needed, that the only accessory a girl really needed was a bed-worthy man.

Standing beneath the brilliantly lit chandeliers, Carly felt her new-found confidence draining away. Everyone else looked so elegant, while she felt like an orange marker buoy set adrift in a sea of penguins.

'Shall I take your shawl?' Lorenzo suggested. 'It will be quite safe with my coat in the cloakroom,' he reassured when she hesitated.

But would she be safe? Carly wondered as he twitched the yards of fabric away. She needed something substantial to cover the acres of chest on show.

As Lorenzo strode away Carly noticed how the crowd parted for him. She would never be able to make the same sort of impact. In fact she noticed now that the space around her suggested people feared bad taste might be catching. She was so wrapped up in humiliation she gasped out loud when Lorenzo returned.

'I didn't mean to startle you.'

But his eyes were sparkling. No doubt he was already anticipating the fun he was about to have at her expense.

'Which table are you sitting at? Haven't you checked?' he added with a frown when she didn't answer.

Actually, no, she hadn't checked. She had been frozen to the spot, too embarrassed to move and show herself and her terrible dress off in the sombre gathering. 'No, I haven't checked.'

'There's no need to raise your voice,' Lorenzo pointed out smoothly. 'Why don't I take you now to find out where you're sitting?'

'Because I don't need you to?' It was just a shame for the sake of her defiance that her voice was trembling.

'Clearly you do, *Ms* Tate,' Lorenzo contradicted her with a raised brow.

Staying hidden in the shadows held far more appeal than making herself the subject of gossip on Lorenzo's arm as she walked across the crowded ballroom, but what option did she have when he had taken a firm hold of her?

Just as Carly had anticipated, everyone turned to stare, but at her, this time—or, at least, at the orange meringue. 'This is so kind of you, Lorenzo,' she ground out through gritted teeth.

'Don't mention it,' he murmured in a sardonic tone, bringing his head close to hers. 'If I'd left you to your own devices I imagine they would have been passing the port by the time you found your table, and I don't want you to miss your slot tonight. I'm *so* looking forward to it…'

Shaking her arm free, she walked ahead. Lorenzo could suck all the rational thought out of your brain with a single look, and she had no intention of being distracted by him tonight, or mocked. But, having escaped his protection, Carly became aware that she was getting even more amused looks. And no wonder when she was the only woman showing her breasts, and they were big, bouncing breasts that refused to be hidden. Right now they felt like barrage balloons beneath her rigidly corseted top. And it didn't help her confidence any to see Madeline du Pre sailing past in a sharp Armani suit!

Reaching the table plan, she stared up. Grinding her teeth so hard they almost chipped, she forced herself to concentrate as a sound of disappointment rang out somewhere close to her left ear.

'You're not sitting with me.'

Lorenzo's comment sent a buzz of awareness spinning down her spine. 'Are you disappointed?'

'Disappointed?' he said. 'Without eye protection I'll feel much safer observing you from a distance.'

She should have known taking on Lorenzo would end in tears. But perhaps tears wouldn't be stinging the backs of her eyes if she hadn't felt so ridiculous. 'You could have warned me about the black dress code.'

'And show favouritism to my own pupil?'

She held his gaze and hardened her heart. Would any of the seniors have finer feelings? No, they were here to have fun at their pupils' expense. Tipping her chin, she went for a forceful gesture that was meant to demonstrate her nonchalant acceptance of her fate, but which unfortunately lifted her breasts clear of the constraining bodice. It was harder to appear defiant now while she was hastily stuffing them back in, and, to make matters worse, Lorenzo showed no intention of turning away as any gentleman should.

'I'm impressed,' he murmured, taking a leisurely ocular stroll down the Grand Canyon of cleavages.

'By what?' Carly challenged, frowning.

'By your sang-froid,' Lorenzo said easily with a smile. 'Why, Carly, you're shivering,' he said as she shuddered with awareness. 'Are you cold?'

All the tiny hairs on the back of her neck were standing to attention, and her nipples were about to explode, but cold? No, she wasn't cold.

'It's time you made your way to your table. I trust you won't let me down?'

'I won't let myself down,' she assured him pleasantly. 'What are you doing?' she said with suspicion as he uncapped his pen.

'Not taking any chances,' he murmured.

'Meaning?'

'I'm changing our names around on the seating plan so I can watch your back…'

She was tempted to relent and think that, for once, Lorenzo was trying to be nice, when just at that moment Madeline Du Pre wafted past with a coterie of admirers. The sight of her main rival for the scholarship flagging up her good sense in front of Lorenzo was all it took for Carly to decide to stay and fight in her orange armour. Removing the pen from Lorenzo's fingers, she changed their names back again, scratching his alterations out with such force she bent his nib.

There had been catcalls and wolf-whistles all night as pupils rose one by one to make their application to join the circuit. Silence fell when Carly stood. Maybe everyone was bored of the sport; her name was pretty close to the end of the alphabet. Or perhaps the seniors had simply exhausted their catalogue of jibes. Or, and this seemed the most likely explanation, the orange gown had come into its own and stunned everyone into silence.

'My name is Carly Viola Tate, and I was called to the bar by the honourable society of...'

It took the space of a heartbeat for her mind to blank. Her lips tried to form the words she needed to speak while her mind was in freefall. *Which of the ancient Inns of Court had she been called to the bar by?* Her darting gaze met Lorenzo's. She only had to take one look at that lazy, mocking stare to know she had no intention of allowing him to see her fail. He must have been through a similar ordeal at some stage of his career...

*As had all the seniors here before her!*

Tipping her chin, she started over.

The seniors would have to look elsewhere for their sport. Lorenzo didn't know when he had felt so relieved...or more aroused. And that did stop him in his tracks. But as he basked in the compliments of his peers over the outstanding performance of his pupil he could only agree with them that Carly was indeed exceptional—and in so many ways. She had obliterated his addiction to all that was perfect, replacing it with new standards of her own. She was quirky and different and fresh. Or, to put it another way, her breasts were extraordinarily large and she was divinely plump in all the right places...though he had to admit that her fashion sense still left everything to be desired.

But, of course, he had to forget this moment of weakness and remember their relative positions in life. He was dominant, while she was...

No.

*No!*

She was not spread-eagled on his bed!

She was his *young* student, and the development of her career devolved on him. She was inexperienced and innocent, and it was up to him to defend her. And didn't he excel in defending the innocent?

He curbed his smile, confining himself to a grave nod of approval as she glanced at him in triumph before sitting down to a chorus of cheers and wolf-whistles. She had been so charming, so endearing when she stumbled over her little speech, everyone had loved her for it. Even the seniors had forgotten to heckle, and the dreadful gown had been over-looked. As her pupil master, restraint was the only sensible option to him, but unfortunately that had no effect on his libido. Lucky for him he was about to be removed from temptation. The courts were about to close for the Christmas recess and when they did he would work off his excess energy on the ski slopes.

With his conscience set at ease, Lorenzo turned his attention to the man seated next to him, and was soon involved in the sort of work-based discussion lawyers thrived on. But try as he might he couldn't keep his thoughts from wandering back to Carly. He wanted her so badly his balls ached.

# CHAPTER FOUR

SHE HAD RETURNED HOME in triumph to this? Cramming a
pillow over her head, Carly tried not to hear the noises coming
from the next room. Her flatmate appeared to be indulging
in some sort of technically advanced sex moves, which
required the bed to bang against the wall in one rhythm while
Louisa cried out in another. The result was a complex synco-
pation of which Stravinsky would have been proud.

Didn't anyone sleep these days?

Was everyone in London, except for her, having sex?

Swinging out of bed, Carly squinted at the clock and saw
that it was one o'clock in the morning. Great. Shuffling out
of the room in her dinosaur-claw slippers, she fumbled for the
light switch and turned it on.

'Hello, Carly…'

'Lorenzo! What on earth are you doing here?'

'Nice to see you too…' Sliding the silk scarf off his neck,
he looked her up and down, bestowing sensation upon each
one of her erogenous zones in turn.

Her cheeks fired automatically. Knuckling her eyes she tried
to convince herself that this could only be a very bad dream.

'Well?' he said when she stood in his way. 'Aren't you
going to invite me in?'

'You *are* in,' she pointed out.

Shrugging off his coat, Lorenzo handed it to her with the scarf. She was wearing a paper-thin nightshirt that covered nothing. Tugging hard on the hem in an attempt to cover her bottom, she exposed a breast.

Lorenzo watched without comment, and then his gaze tracked down to study her dinosaur-claw slippers.

Turning on her heel, she hung up his coat. What was she doing *waiting on him?* She could only excuse herself by pleading the lateness of the hour and her exhaustion after the ordeal of the Grand Court.

He had telephoned every hotel in London when his new flat flooded. Not a chance of a bed in town with Christmas looming, he'd been told. He had tried absolutely every option until bunking down in the spare room of a flat owned by an old school chum became the only option. The repairs to his own apartment would be completed within the next couple of days, but until then, this was it…

As Carly stared at him in disbelief, he asked himself if a park bench have been a better option? Did he want to take up residence with his pupil? Did he want to have temptation thrust in his face? Did he want to smell her warm, fresh, sleepy smell and see her hair in wild disarray? Her face was attractively sleep crumpled and she was half-naked…

'What are you doing here, Lorenzo?' she challenged him.

He was guilty of musing while Carly's mental faculties had stormed back onto full alert. 'I might ask you the same question,' he returned smoothly.

'Louisa is my friend, and this is her apartment,' she told him, coughing noisily to cover the sounds of passion erupting from a bedroom down the hall.

'And Louisa's brother is my friend,' he explained. 'They

share joint tenancy on the flat. So while some emergency repairs are being carried out on my new apartment I'll be using the spare room here—'

'You can't,' she exploded. 'I live here.'

'And for the time being, I do too,' he informed her. 'Is the coffee on?' He strolled down the hall following the odour of old pizza and tea bags.

What did Lorenzo imagine this was? Carly raged silently. *A service flat?* Counting to ten, she took the opportunity to rattle her brain cells into some sort of order.

'Do you have anything better than instant coffee?' he called from the kitchen.

She found him rooting around and peering into cupboards. 'There might be some beans in there, somewhere…' There might be lions too, for all she knew.

'Along with the spaghetti hoops, Pop Tarts and… What are these?' He held up a tub and pulled a face. 'Pot Noodles?' He narrowed his eyes in disapproval as he looked down at her.

She responded in the usual way to Lorenzo in stern mood, and, after enjoying it for a moment or two, told him, 'I haven't had time to go shopping recently. I've been very busy at work.'

'Really?' he said, as if this came as a complete surprise to him. 'Well, you still have to eat.' He looked her up and down. 'We wouldn't want you shrinking away…'

We wouldn't? Clearing her throat to muffle another of Louisa's moans, she became obsessed by turning all the labels on the tins to the front.

'You must keep up your strength,' Lorenzo advised, reaching past her into the darkest part of the cupboard.

For the battles to come, she could only presume. 'You mean I should arm myself for disappointment?'

When Lorenzo turned to look at her his arm was still outstretched and very close to her face…so close it made her cheeks tingle.

'Disappointment?' he queried.

She watched his lips work in fascination.

'Why do you say that? You did well tonight. I'm proud of you…'

Lorenzo was proud of her? For a moment she just stared and inhaled his cologne—sandalwood and amber, with a hint of wild fig and cassis. And still her analytical mind refused to shut down. What was Lorenzo really up to? Why was he here? Was he serious when he said they were going to be living together? Even in the short-term that would be more fuel for her fantasies than she could safely handle.

*Living together?*

It was time for a dash of cold reality in the face. This was not a dream come true; this was her worst nightmare. Where would she take refuge from Lorenzo's scorn now? She would be on duty every minute of the day and night. 'How long did you say you would be staying?'

'I didn't.' He turned back to his search.

'Weeks?'

'*Dio!* No!'

He sounded about as excited by that prospect as she felt. 'Oh, well, that's a relief.'

'Because my being here is your worst nightmare, I presume?' He turned slowly to look at her, erasing all sensible thought from her mind. 'Don't look so worried,' he murmured, turning back to his search. ' I'll only be staying here until they repair the pipes and restore all the damage done to my apartment.'

His apartment… Images of leopard skin rugs dressed with naked women sprang unbidden into Carly's mind. All the women would be slim and beautiful, of course. How long would that take to organise?

Unfortunately, she didn't get a chance to progress this thought as a series of shrieks erupted from Louisa's bedroom.

'Where is Louisa, by the way?' Lorenzo said, frowning as the shrieks continued unabated.

'Asleep in bed,' Carly said hurriedly. 'She must be having a nightmare.'

'It sounds like a good one to me,' Lorenzo murmured. Taking a step towards the kitchen door, he turned. 'Do you think she's all right, or should I intervene?'

'I'm sure she's fine.' Carly wasn't sure whether to be more horrified by the screams or by her restraining hand on Lorenzo's arm. She removed it smartly before telling him, 'I think we'd better leave her to sleep now, don't you?'

'All right,' he agreed, clearly enjoying every moment of her discomfort.

'Why don't you and I have a drink?' she suggested, keen to keep Lorenzo occupied in the kitchen until things calmed down a bit along the hall. 'Coffee, water, or something stronger…?'

'In the absence of decent coffee, water, please,' he said.

She added ice to the glass of water before handing it to him.

Lounging back against the counter-top, he tipped his glass towards her in an ironic salute. 'Goodnight, Carly…'

Yes, why exactly was she hanging around?

'I wouldn't advise you to be late for my class twice in one week…'

He let out a breath of relief as the kitchen door shut behind her. Five minutes in Carly's company had left him in torment, real physical pain. This was the craziest situation, and he only had himself to blame. Had he really thought it would be easy to be under the same roof as Carly just because his palate was so jaded?

Jaded?

Not tonight!

She was different and he wanted her. It was that simple and that complicated. This was torture. He'd be close to her night and day and couldn't touch. He'd award himself a medal when this was over.

Tossing and turning on her bed, Carly tried telling herself what a relief it was Lorenzo didn't want her 'that way'. But as Louisa's sexual marathon continued she knew she didn't want to be a dumpling with freckles; she wanted to be a fully formed sex kitten with the power to bring Lorenzo to his knees. But Lorenzo was glamorous and rich, while she was not. He was at the top of the greasy career pole, while she was at the bottom—and would never climb any higher if she went on like this.

Stifling the alarm clock with a well-aimed pillow, Carly concluded that the only way to impress Lorenzo was in the professional arena. She would win the scholarship, and she would arrange the best Christmas party in the history of Christmas parties. How, she hadn't a clue, but that was a minor detail right now. Stumbling out of bed, she blundered blindly into the hallway where fortunately Lorenzo was there to catch her when she fell over a shoe.

'Don't be late,' he said, steadying her back on her feet.

Was she imagining it, or had he snatched his hands off her body as he might from a live electric cable? She'd got quite a charge herself, but in her case she wouldn't have minded waiting around until her hair sizzled.

For the sake of her career she decided prudence must be her watchword. 'Good morning, Lorenzo. I trust you slept well?'

He made a humming sound as he looked her up and down, reminding her to hide her fat rolls beneath a robe in future. As the door slammed behind him she found herself waiting for a thunderclap, but of course there was only silence and a great big empty hole. Lorenzo didn't so much as glance behind him; any erotic thoughts floating about were confined to her own head.

Deflated, Carly trundled towards the kitchen, where a double-sized bowl of honey-sweet-quadruple-the-calories pops awaited her.

Flat share with Lorenzo was shaping up to be about as appealing as eating her way through a case of stewed prunes. Shelving the scholarship plan suddenly seemed like a very good idea, but nothing would disappoint her parents more. They had sacrificed everything for her, and she owed them this last and most prestigious scholarship, which in turn meant she couldn't afford to fall foul of Lorenzo because her pupilage hung by a thread he could cut.

Pupilage, the system whereby a practising barrister monitored the training of a graduate law student, was like gold dust. If you lost your pupilage for any reason your career at the bar was as good as over. Failure wasn't an option, especially not to a Tate. The law had bypassed a generation in the family, and Carly had always known her destiny as the plain sister. She had to uphold the family tradition. Some grizzled ancestor had probably dipped a nib in their own blood to sign the Magna Carta.

At least she wasn't late for her appointment with Lorenzo. Knocking on his door and entering the room, she found him lounging back in his chair.

'Progress report, Christmas party,' he instructed with a wave of his hand like some maestro bringing in the soloist.

Carly's mind blanked as she looked at his socks. They were pink today. And not just pink—fuchsia-pink!

Did it matter if his socks were pink? This was a man who

could wear a dress and look virile, which he almost did in
court, come to think of it, in his wig and gown—

'Ms Tate, are you still with me?'

The voice was impatient.

'The list?'

The hand signal unmistakable.

'Of course.' Tilting her chin at a businesslike angle, she
offered him the sheet of paper listing everything she had
prepared. 'It doesn't include all the details yet.'

'I don't like guessing games.'

'And this won't be one.' She sincerely hoped.

Scanning the page, he made no comment. He was beginning to make her feel nervous. Why was life so unjust? Why
did Lorenzo look as if he was ready for a photo shoot for the
world's most desirable man, while she felt as usual like the
dumpling on parade? She forced herself to meet the icy gaze
unflinching as he glanced up.

'Not bad, but it would be better if you work to a theme.'

Praise indeed! What a shame she wasn't ready to reveal
that in fact she *was* working to a theme, if not the sort of theme
she guessed Lorenzo would be expecting.

'What I need now,' he said, 'are specifics. Detail, Ms Tate.'

Resisting the urge to salute, she stared past him out through
the panoramic windows overlooking the city. Somewhere out
there were all the answers to her problems. At least, those connected to the party. 'I need a little more time. You'll just have
to trust me.'

'Trust you?' One ebony brow shot up, showing Lorenzo's
opinion of that suggestion. 'I thought I'd explained to you that
the only thing I'm interested in is fact?'

But this wasn't a court case, and she wasn't on trial. She
held her ground, staring straight into his incredible eyes. 'I
don't want to spoil the surprise.' This was a phrase she had

often heard trip off her mother's tongue. It was only as she grew to be older that she realised her mother employed it to cover a bottomless pit of panic.

Lorenzo wasn't even slightly fooled. 'Arranging the Christmas party isn't a leisure activity, Ms Tate; it's part of your brief as my junior. It's also an opportunity to show everyone what you're capable of.'

Exactly, Carly thought uncomfortably.

'I want a detailed summary of everything you've arranged up to now. Come,' he said, offering her a pen, 'write them down for me now.' Ripping a clean sheet of paper from his pad, he handed it to her and sat back.

It was a very large sheet of paper for what was destined to be a very short list. 'Why don't I take it with me so I don't disturb you?'

'Sit down,' he rapped.

They stared at each other unblinking for a moment, but then an image of her parents' anxious faces swam into Carly's mind and she folded. 'Okay…'

'And while you're writing your list I'd like you to start thinking about guidelines for some of the younger members of chambers. There will be a number of senior judges attending this year, some of whom wear ermine and sit in the House of Lords. I don't expect anyone here to let the side down.'

He watched her face carefully. Sometimes he surprised himself with the ingenuity of his tests. This one was particularly harsh, because it put her in the firing line in front of her colleagues. Could she rise above that and act professionally? Could she swallow her misgivings? Or was this the moment when she told him to go to hell and walked out? He decided to find out.

'You will need two lists,' he told her as if she were in infant class. 'One will have the heading "Christmas Party", and the second will have the heading "Christmas Party Guidelines for Junior Members of Chambers".'

That should win her a few friends! Was there a way out? If there was she couldn't think of one. For now she would have to be satisfied with some fiendish revenge sequences reeling through her mind involving Lorenzo naked and a pair of stiletto heels. But later, when she got back to her cubbyhole, she would have to work something out that didn't risk the scholarship, or her easy working relationship with her younger colleagues...

'What?' Lorenzo said, glancing up.

Had he felt the sparks flying his way? Carly wondered, composing her face into its customary bland mask. Composing a cautionary note for her fellow pupils as Lorenzo had instructed was nothing short of an insult to them, and to her...

'What is it, Ms Tate?'

'Nothing,' she said innocently, but an idea was forming; an idea that involved two lists for Lorenzo as he had requested, and a third, somewhat less reverential, list for her friends.

'Well, if that's all?' Lorenzo said, turning back to his notes. 'Get on with it.'

He was right. There was no point in prolonging this. She was a realist, if nothing else, and as Lorenzo was all male, while she was undeniably female, there was no common ground.

'Write,' he insisted, staring hard at her sheet of paper.

She tried. She sucked the tip of her pen and tried really hard. She had the ideas—too many of them! The problem was assembling them in front of him. Lorenzo made it so hard to concentrate. She was drowning in waves of testosterone, and then there was his distinctive scent, warm, clean, male and spicy. She could close her eyes and inhale that all day quite happily… Except at the same time she would have to wriggle now and then to give the type of sensations he provoked chance to express themselves. Come to think of it, she hadn't been so obsessed by sex for years—not since she had lost her virginity to a spotty youth on the back seat of his car; a skirmish that had hardly prepared her for encountering Lorenzo. She'd had no idea she had been so repressed—

'Okay, leave now and take your work with you,' he snapped impatiently. 'I can see you're not concentrating, and you're distracting me.'

He watched her leap away as if she were attached to a spring. Was he such an ogre? Or had that wriggle signalled more than a desire to get away? 'Before you go…'

'Yes?'

Her face had reddened guiltily. What had she been dreaming about—his demise, perhaps?

Okay, so maybe he was being hard on her, but he expected the best of his students, and Carly was the best of the best. Organising the Christmas party was a thankless task; the list of guidelines he had proposed she draw up a mockery. He could imagine the reaction of her colleagues to any suggestions she might make! But lawyers had to keep a cool head under fire. Would she? He decided to push a little harder and find out. 'I'm meeting a friend tonight.'

A muscle jumped in her jaw though her face remained carefully expressionless. This ability to hide her thoughts was yet one more reason she currently headed up the list of potential Unicorn scholarship candidates. 'I'm going to bring my guest back to the flat, and I thought you might like to make yourself useful…'

If her face grew any tighter she would implode. He pressed on. 'Make sure the wine is chilled, prepare a few canapés, that sort of thing?'

He could see her feminist principles raging against her lust to win the scholarship. He could also see her wanting to take him by the throat and choke him. And throughout all this they continued to stare at each other impassively.

Easing her neck, Carly fought to stay calm. 'Canapés?' She could only comfort herself with the thought that the reports of her numerous culinary disasters hadn't reached Lorenzo's ears yet.

*The successful candidate for the Unicorn scholarship will be both resourceful and creative...*

'Of course, no problem,' she replied.

'That's good,' he said, relaxing. 'You might want to sit in when my guest arrives as we'll be discussing the possibility of extending the reach of the scholarship. It's such a great opportunity.'

To make canapés? Carly thought, staring back without expression.

'As I'm sure you'll agree?' Lorenzo challenged, searching her gaze for the slightest hint of insubordination. 'Canapés at eight, then?'

Why not? She had no intention of being tripped up by a cocktail sausage now.

# CHAPTER FIVE

CARLY GAZED AT the work she had completed with satisfaction. It felt good to be properly organised, almost like the old times before Lorenzo had exploded onto the scene. She had compiled three lists, two of which, being dry and sensible, were the ones for Lorenzo.

The Christmas Party list would show him how bookings for various services were working out as well as the ordering system she was using—everything except food was either on a short-term hire agreement, or a sale and return basis, so he could find no room for concern there. The Christmas Party Guidelines for her colleagues would appear equally sensible—because, of course, Lorenzo wouldn't be seeing the copy she'd actually send to her colleagues, or, indeed, her own copy, upon which she had added some rather graphic doodles.

In addition to this she had stuck a Post-It note to the desk on which she had scrawled, 'Canapés at eight!' To date she had made no entries to suggest what form these canapés might take. But there was plenty of time to worry about that. Canapés were tiny, which suggested they were easy to prepare. It was more important to concentrate on her doodles, which in Carly's modest opinion were starting to rival the illustrations in the Kama Sutra. Well, a girl could dream, couldn't she? And with Lorenzo tied up in court she had hours in which to indulge every flight of erotic fancy she'd ever had…

By noon Carly's Christmas Party list had a pleasing line of ticks down the side of the page. Father Christmas had been booked, along with a couple of elves, and even on such a slim budget she had managed to organise good, wholesome food, that could best be described as interesting. Or, at least, she hoped it would prove so to the sophisticated palate of those attending. Anyway, she liked it, and it was in line with the theme she had chosen, so Lorenzo could hardly complain.

When it came to the advisory notes for her colleagues she had thought long and hard before deciding on something they could stomach. She knew Lorenzo had set her up for a fall and she had every intention of staying upright.

With this intention in mind she kept the tone light, listing the warnings beneath a picture of Lorenzo looking suitably stern and yet rather stunning in his wig and gown. Her fellow pupils would get the joke. Especially after she'd added some doodles to their list—the one Lorenzo wouldn't be seeing—the list she would compile after this one to illustrate the form any rebellion might take. But meanwhile Lorenzo's list was complete:

*GUIDELINES CHRISTMAS PARTY*
REMEMBER…
MERRY NIGHTS MAKE SAD MORNINGS!
And here are a few handy tips to help *you* avoid the pitfalls…
1. Arrive early and make a point of speaking to your immediate superior!
2. Above all, please remember that first impressions count!

3. You must remain visible at all times and maintain a pleasant and interested smile on your face.
4. You must try to engage every judge in light-hearted chit-chat, and maintain an air of quiet confidence as you do so.
5. Absolutely NO dancing drunkenly on tables!
6. In the unlikely event that you begin to feel the effects of too much alcohol you must take yourself outside the building IMMEDIATELY!
7. The importance of thanking your host at the end of the night cannot be overstated.

Lorenzo should be pleased with that. Folding the sheet of paper neatly, she placed it safely inside an envelope.

And now for the list her colleagues would receive, which would be basically the same, but with certain additions. Her intention was to make it recognisably the same, so they wouldn't be caught out if questioned, and yet, so very, *very* different…

Beneath the legend *'GUIDELINES CHRISTMAS PARTY'* the banner heading still read 'MERRY NIGHTS MAKE SAD MORNINGS!' But now there was a smaller sub-heading, which advised,

Expert Schmoozing, Without Resorting To Being A Creep, Helps You Move *UP* The Ladder!

Below this she had written another list of bullet points.

*Arrive early and make a point of speaking to your immediate superior!*

Carly frowned, reading the point through again. The chance of engaging Lorenzo in a conversation that didn't involve her saluting and him instructing seemed remote. And weren't parties supposed to be fun? She added fangs and horns to his picture before printing out a dozen for distribution.

*The importance of thanking the host cannot be overstated.*

She frowned again. Well, that was all very well, but Lorenzo hadn't made it clear who would be hosting the party. She added a handwritten note to suggest her colleagues assume the customary grovelling position with every senior who attended.

*You must remain visible at all times and maintain a pleasant and interested smile on your face.*

No problem! Smiling while inwardly yawning was a skill every pupil perfected within their first six months. But she added a further helpful point anyway:

*You must try to engage even the most curmudgeonly judge in light-hearted chit-chat, and maintain an air of quiet confidence as you do so...*

Even if they fell asleep on the bench last time you were in front of them, presumably.

*Absolutely NO dancing drunkenly on tables!*

After a moment's contemplation she moved this item to the top of the list and reprinted everything, shredding the first draft and anything else that might prove incriminating. Then she popped the lists into envelopes ready for distribution. It

was crucial to ensure they didn't get into the wrong hands—
i.e. Lorenzo's hands. To make certain of it she would deliver
them to the various offices herself.

Sitting back, Carly congratulated herself on a job well
done, and then, remembering that there was still time to per-
sonalise her own set of guidelines, she got started…

First off she jotted a note next to Lorenzo's photograph:
'Carly's Christmas Present to Herself', while down the side
of the page she sketched some imaginative and energetic
matchstick people—one of whom wore Technicolor socks,
while the other boasted enormous breasts…

He had just walked back into chambers when Carly rushed
past him with a distracted look on her face. She was mutter-
ing something. He thought she said, 'Canapés…'

As she ran out of the door a note fluttered out of her pocket.
Strictly speaking he shouldn't read someone else's mail, but
lawyers did it all the time…

Returning to his office, he drew out the note and scanned
it. It was a list Carly had headed, '*GUIDELINES CHRIST-
MAS PARTY*'. So far so good, but then he realised that this
list bore scant resemblance to the one she had put in his
pigeon-hole. His gaze returned to study the various doodles
she had drawn down the side of it. Her inventions were impressive. He read on: 'Inappropriate behaviour at the
Christmas party can SERIOUSLY limit your career…'

How fortunate for him that rules were made to be broken, and
when you reached the inner circle you broke them all the time.

Canapés!

Carly woke up with a start. For a moment she couldn't
remember where she was. Where she had been was far prefer-
able…in Lorenzo's arms, and he had been just about to kiss

her. She rubbed the back of her hand across her mouth just
to check she hadn't been playing Sleeping Beauty and missed
something wonderful.

Not a chance! It was so hot in her little cubby-hole she had
fallen asleep, that was all. And no wonder she was exhausted
after her shopping expedition. Propelled into panic by the
sight of Lorenzo in Reception, she had rushed to the supermarket, but halfway there she had spotted a sign advertising
a sale of designer shoes…

Glancing at her wrist-watch, she let out a shriek.

All thoughts of Lorenzo and stiletto heels flew from her
mind. Flailing about, she battled to organise her wayward
thoughts and only succeeded in knocking everything off her
desk, then banging her head against it when she dived to
retrieve it. Nursing the bump she ordered her inner self to
calm down. Canapés were no problem. They'd been in her
head all the time she'd been asleep, so the planning was
already done. All she had to do now was buy the ingredients
and assemble them. The menu she had decided upon was
divine… Shrimp in a light batter with sweet chilli sauce;
slivers of tomato on tiny rye crackers with an anchovy curled
artistically on top and—the pièce de résistance—miniature
parcels of smoked salmon and cream cheese decorated with
chopped chives.

Inwardly, she dribbled.

'You're in a hurry today…'

Lorenzo's lazy drawl caught her between the shoulder
blades and brought her screaming to a halt. She turned to look
at him and felt her senses flare like the bright socks he was
wearing—purple with orange flags today. She made a silent
vow to carry out intensive research on international marine
signals the moment she got the chance.

'Canapés all in hand?' he said, giving her a dark stare.

Her throat dried. 'In component form…'

'Excellent…'

There was something different about Lorenzo; she couldn't quite pin it down. Maybe it was the way he was looking at her. Normally he made inscrutable seem an understatement; he wasn't a top lawyer for nothing. But today there was a definite smoulder in his gaze as he leaned back against the wall.

So, who was he thinking about?

The sting of jealousy that brought on took Carly by surprise. She ran a mental check-list of all her female colleagues, wondering which one of them had served Lorenzo's best interest that lunchtime, and knew she didn't stand a chance of making that list. Lorenzo probably thought plain girls didn't need sex like pretty women, but that didn't stop her wanting him. Especially now when he looked so gorgeous…absolutely gorgeous—

'No time to hang around,' he cautioned, stamping on her fantasy.

It was a waste of time dreaming, Carly thought, heading for the door. Lorenzo was on another planet, one where men ruled and women served—mostly in the bedroom when they weren't trying to fold towels a certain way, or create the world's most impressive canapé…

She took one last look at him before the door swung shut and decided he looked pretty pleased with himself. No wonder! The clerks probably kept his little black book alongside Lorenzo's court appointment diary to enable him to take full advantage of each adjournment. Plus he'd just gained a slave of cuisine. Who wouldn't be feeling smug?

So, how did she explain why the heart of this independent-minded woman was racing with delight at the thought of serving him?

Because like a cup of hot chocolate thick enough to stand a spoon in, Lorenzo Domenico was wicked, but irresistible.

Carly's hope of presenting the perfect canapé faltered at the entrance of the twenty-four-hour supermarket. She stood outside staring through the plate-glass window at people fighting over Christmas food and just knew she couldn't face it. Turning on her heel, she hurried across the street towards Greasy Jo's. The local pizza parlour had never let her down…

By half past seven she was back at the flat carving up pizza in the kitchen. She heard the front door open and Lorenzo and his friend come in.

Lorenzo and male friend…

Thank goodness! She wasn't sure that even for the sake of the scholarship she could have waited on some It girl with the hots for Lorenzo!

Giving her hands a final lick, she wiped them down the front of her jeans, and then, picking up the platter of oozing pizza, she backed her way into the sitting room and turned around with a flourish. 'Gentlemen…'

Two pieces of pizza flew off the plate.

She ignored the startled glances and carried on. Dipping low, she offered, 'Gorgonzola and gherkin, pickled onion and pastrami, or…' and she was rather proud of this one '…squid ink and pineapple…'

Beneath his tan Lorenzo paled. 'Thank you, Carly. Perhaps you'd like to put them down over there?' He indicated the furthest corner of the room. 'And then perhaps you'd like to pour the chilled white wine?' He said this in a slightly harder voice.

The *chilled* white wine?

'Of course…' She gave a little laugh, scooping up the pizza on the floor as she made her escape.

* * *

Exchanging an amused shrug with his friend as he went to retrieve the plate, Lorenzo said, 'Excuse my pupil. She's embarked on a rather steep learning curve—'

'Drawn up by you?' Ronan's lips pressed down. 'Pass the pizza, will you? I'm starving.'

'Me too,' Lorenzo confessed. He and Ronan had been students together; they'd eat anything. Not that Carly needed to know that! 'So, what d'you think of her?'

'You're a lucky man. She's gorgeous.'

'Do you think so?' He played it cool.

Ronan gave him a look. 'How long do you intend to keep up the tough-tutor act?'

'For as long as it takes.'

Ronan raised his yet-to-be-filled glass in a toast to him, while he called unrepentantly, 'Carly—wine.'

'Lorenzo…' Ronan remonstrated, shaking his head in disapproval.

But he knew he'd be lucky if he didn't get that wine poured over his head, Lorenzo thought, already smiling as he anticipated the banter that would ensue between him and Carly once Ronan left.


Carly ignored Lorenzo's summons. Leaning against the kitchen door, she thought back to when she had been such a together sort of person—that was before Lorenzo came along, of course. Now she barely knew her own name, let alone remembered to chill the wine. There was only one thing for it…

Rinsing off some ice cubes from the back of the box, she dropped them into the wineglasses, filled them to the brim with warm white wine and stirred vigorously.

Lorenzo's stare found her face like a heat-seeking missile

the moment she came back into the room. Lifting the wine-glass, he held it up to the light without comment.

'So you liked the pizza?' she said with relief, glad something had gone well. She handed Ronan a glass of wine.

'We had to throw it down,' Lorenzo said solemnly, staring out of the window.

'Into the dumper?' Carly exclaimed, glancing in the same direction and then at the empty plate. But even as she gasped she was sure she saw Lorenzo exchange one of his wicked grins with Ronan. As she stood there the two men clinked their glasses, and with gusto the ice cubes collided.

'Ice?' Lorenzo's stare didn't so much burn into her as presage Armageddon.

Ronan tried to soften the situation, suggesting pleasantly, 'Aren't you going to join us, Carly?'

He turned to look at his friend as a stab of something unaccustomed took him by surprise. It wasn't jealousy, of course, more head-of-the-herd instinct. Well, Ronan was no angel, and it was up to him to defend his pupil. 'My apologies, Carly,' he said sternly. 'Allow me to present Ronan O'Connor, a friend of mine and a trader in futures. Ronan, this is my pupil, Carly Tate…'

Ronan gave Carly a sympathetic look as he stood to shake her hand.

'We're discussing the possibility of extending the Unicorn scholarship to the City,' Lorenzo explained to Carly. 'Would you care to join us?'

Sit between them while they drank Lorenzo's expensive wine, which she had watered down with ice cubes? No, thank you! It was time to head for the badlands away from Lorenzo's accusing stare!

She didn't want to brood in her bedroom either, Carly

realised, not with Lorenzo in her head darkly mocking. She was going to dress up, go out, and show him!

After making a somewhat feeble excuse about leaving the men to it, she went to her room to get ready. Faded jeans wouldn't cut it, and so she ditched them in favour of a black spangled top from a charity shop, along with a short denim skirt from the same place. And then, because she'd always known they'd come in useful, she unpacked the killer heels she'd bought at the sale.

Lorenzo would never guess it was all a sham. The tip tap of heels on a laminate floor would tell him everything she wanted him to know. She was a sophisticated city girl in full control of her life.

# CHAPTER SIX

THE BAR CARLY was heading for was popular with young city types, and tonight it seemed busier than ever. Odd for mid-week, but perhaps not when you considered that this was the lead up to Christmas...

Peering in through the tinted windows, she felt daunted. She had only been for a drink in a crowd before. She tried to identify a free table before taking the plunge, but then a few spots of rain hit her in the face, forcing her to act.

Noise and warmth hit her as she walked inside. An earnest young man in designer jeans and a smart black top came towards her right away. 'Ah, good,' he said, as if he had been expecting her. 'You're just in time.' Without any explanation he grabbed her elbow and started steering her through the throng. She was about to protest he'd got the wrong person, but then she noticed he was leading her towards an empty table. At least she'd get the chance to sit down and read her book. Buzzy? The place was heaving.

At least this wasn't Lorenzo's type of place, Carly consoled herself, pulling out her novel. But as she tried to read Lorenzo's face replaced the cover, the first page, the second, and the— Slamming the book shut, she tried to attract a waiter. This was an emergency! What she needed was coffee: hot, sweet and strong.

* * *

Lorenzo made coffee and then settled down with Ronan to chat about old times, but he kept thinking about Carly and an image of her alone and unprotected in the city sharpened in his mind.

He'd caught sight of her as she click-clacked past the door, and she'd been dressed up by Carly's standards. Surely he'd have heard on the chambers grapevine if there'd been a party, which left a meeting in a bar or in a restaurant. It had to be close by because she hadn't called a taxi, and the nearest tube or bus stop was over a mile away. She had definitely planned to walk, but not far in those heels…

It was pitch-black outside and the rain was turning to sleet. He couldn't kid himself any longer; he'd been hard on her and that was why she'd gone out. What was more important to him? Carly's safety and happiness, or an evening chatting with his pal?

'Oh, no, thank you, I brought a book with me…'

'But not this book,' the young woman said confidently, plonking one from the pile in her arms down in front of Carly before disappearing back into the crowd.

She tried to attract the attention of an attendant to hand the glossy booklet back. She was here to relax, not to be drawn into something that put such a flush on people's faces.

Having failed, she found as she had suspected that it wasn't so much a book as a marketing tool, entitled, *Raise Your Market Value,* but it was the subheading that caught her attention: 'Make contact, make chat, make love…' She jerked around to take a closer look at everyone else in the bar.

'Is this chair free?'

She panicked and stood up.

'Please don't go,' the man said plaintively. 'I'm desperate to make contact with something other than a cyber chip—'

Knocked back into her seat by a fresh rush of people she

made a silent pledge to give it five minutes and then she was out of here.

'Is this your first time?' the man asked her.

And the last, Carly decided, noticing he seemed fixated by her breasts.

'We've made a good start, haven't we?' he said.

Had they? Had they made a good start? If so she was giving out the wrong signals! Glancing round, she dreaded Lorenzo walking in, and yet wished he would.

Then just as a bell sounded a man stepped out of the rain. The collar of his rugged jacket was pulled up tight, revealing a hint of the casual chequered shirt underneath. Snug-fitting blue jeans teamed with workman-like boots added to the piratical image created by the rough, dark stubble on his face. His unruly black hair curled damply round his chiselled cheekbones, and his eyes were narrowed as he searched the room.

Lorenzo!

Waitresses swarmed round him, and then looked her way.

*Escape!* was the only thought in her head, but the bell had been a signal for everyone to move, or so it seemed. She was jostled and staggered as she tottered determinedly towards the nearest door. The handle seemed so temptingly close, yet as she launched herself forward to grab it the man who had been at her table got in the way.

'No,' he said, shaking his arm free as she clutched hold of him to steady herself. 'Only we men move around. You women have to stay at your table.'

'I'm sorry?'

'You've had your five minutes with me,' he explained self-importantly. 'If I tick your box at the end of the evening you might get five minutes more.'

*Tick her box?* Urgh! That sounded horrible! But the

thought of Lorenzo delivering one of his fire-and-thunder sermons was even worse—

Deciding the man was the best shield she'd got, Carly hid behind him, but he made some rude comment, which prompted everyone to turn to look at them. And now Lorenzo was staring too!

'Ah, there you are,' Lorenzo said with satisfaction. 'What's this about?' His dark gaze switched to the face of the other man, forcing a nervous laugh from him.

'Perhaps you should ask your young lady—'

'Perhaps I will,' Lorenzo said icily. 'Intending to take advantage of her, were you?' he suggested.

'Not at all! She came on to me—'

'To you?' Lorenzo's raised brow was enough for some of his audience to start laughing.

'Yes. I think she was trying to kiss me!' *Shock! Horror!* 'She doesn't seem to appreciate the finer points of speed dating. The regulations demand—'

*Speed dating?* What a clutz! Carly felt as if someone had sewn a running thread through her stomach and pulled it tight.

'To which regulations are you referring?' Lorenzo demanded in his deceptively mild court tone, commanding everyone's attention.

'We get given five minutes with each woman, and then I tick her box if I'm interested. I haven't made up my mind yet,' the man declared with affront.

'I think you have,' Lorenzo told him. 'Did you come on to this man?' he demanded, switching his attention to Carly. 'Did you want him to kiss you?'

'Of course not!' she protested hotly in possibly the most humiliating moment of her whole life.

'Then why did you come here?' the man cut in.

'If you want a kiss so badly, I'll kiss you,' Lorenzo offered.

Was there anyone else in the world who could *accidentally* speed date? He thought not. And it only made Carly all the more adorable in his eyes. How alone she must have felt to come here in the first place. And whose fault was that? Time to make amends.

Carly gulped as Lorenzo dragged her into his arms. What happened next was less a kiss, and more a lifetime achievement award in seduction, and it went on and on until people started applauding. First he laced his fingers through her hair, while with his other hand he caressed her cheeks. He made her feel as if she were the most beautiful woman in the world, stroking her jaw with his thumb as he kissed her, and kissing her so tenderly she could hardly believe this was what people did. And then the kiss morphed into something so stirring and passionate, she had to wonder if he'd forgotten himself as he plunged and withdrew in what was surely a dress rehearsal for a performance she had no part in.

Drawing back at last, he stared deep into her eyes, and then, taking her by surprise, he came back for more. This couldn't be a mistake, could it? She hoped not. Lorenzo's face was still cold from the night air, and his stubble felt rough against her cheek, but his lips were hot with a persuasive heat that ran riot through her body and as he continued to kiss her their audience egged them on.

'I think I'd better get you out of here,' he said, pulling away at last.

He was still holding on to her. 'I think you better had,' Carly agreed, her eyes sparkling like diamonds.

# CHAPTER SEVEN

HE WAS TAKING CARLY out of the bar when a girl approached him with a clipboard, to ask if, under the happy circumstance, he would be prepared to give her company an endorsement. She might have spared a thought for Carly's opinion on that, he thought, but the young woman's gaze was fixed on him.

'I don't sign my name to anything unless I've read the small print,' he told her, concentrating on ushering Carly safely towards the door. He took the pamphlet anyway and stuffed it in his pocket. 'I'll study this later, and find out what exactly your company is asking people to sign up to.'

The girl looked as if she wanted it back. He didn't blame her.

Carly noted the incident, but was still reeling from what had happened. With Lorenzo's arm around her shoulders it was hard to think straight, and with Lorenzo's astonishing kiss branded on her swollen lips for all time, it was impossible. Maybe she would never think straight again. But then she wouldn't win the scholarship, Carly realised, quickly shaking herself out of it.

'All right?' Lorenzo said, looking down at her.

'Absolutely fine. Thank you for rescuing me.' She eased herself free, knowing he was only being kind.

As they reached the door two representatives from the

speed-dating company almost collided in their haste to open it for them. Lorenzo glanced at them, and then, leaning across her, held the door open for her himself. There was something about him, even without his wig and gown, that inspired fear in the heart of every wrongdoer, including her! 'If this means I'm finished I'd rather you told me straight,' she said, trying to keep up with him as he started back towards the flat.

'We'll talk about it later. Right now it's more important to get you out of this weather.' Lacing his arm through hers, he slowed, matching his pace to her shorter stride, seemingly oblivious to the sleet hitting them in the face.

'Lorenzo, I'm really sorry to bring you out on a night like this. I was just—'

'Trying to pick up a man in a bar?'

'It wasn't like that.'

'What was it like, Carly?'

'I wouldn't do anything I thought might bring chambers into disrepute.'

'Work? Is that all you think about? What about your own reputation?'

The lamplight was reflected in his eyes, making them appear to burn fiercely. The look reached inside her and twisted something. 'Lorenzo, I—'

'Lorenzo?' he interrupted. 'Do you think I have all the answers? Or maybe you think the scholarship will fill that empty space inside you? Do you even have a clue what you want out of life, Carly?'

As she stared at him in shock his jaw firmed. 'No, I didn't think so.'

As he swung an arm around her shoulder and urged her on she shrank into him, relieved that, though clearly exasperated, Lorenzo wasn't prepared to abandon her to her fate. Keeping her scholarship hopes alive was important, but meanwhile it felt good snuggling up to him, and she was going to enjoy it as long as she could. Even in the freezing cold her lips still burned from his kiss, and everywhere his hands had touched, held or stroked bore little imprints of strength and warmth and protection. Dreaming again, maybe, but it was a dream that didn't cost a broken heart to indulge in.

When they arrived back Lorenzo let them in and left her under strict instructions to strip off her clothes in the hallway. And pose nude? Catching sight of herself in the mirror, Carly quickly doused that thought. She could hear Lorenzo running a bath and, clutching her damp clothes in front of her, she draped her jacket over her shoulders for good measure.

'I thought I told you to get undressed?' he said, barely sparing her a glance.

'I am undressed…underneath…'

Zero reaction. The promise of that kiss in the bar had cooled, leaving stern Lorenzo a little sterner, but no more interested in taking her to bed than he'd ever been. This wasn't lust that ached inside her; it was something more, she realised in panic. The thought that she might have fallen in love with Lorenzo put her at more risk than a broken heart, because it made it impossible to work with him. And what about her scholarship hopes then?

'Are you coming to have your bath?' he said, distracting her. 'I'll get some towels.'

As he walked away her dreams seemed ridiculous, like the fantasies of a schoolgirl with a crush.

'Don't wait for me,' he called back.

What point would there be?

Closing her eyes, she inhaled deeply. Lorenzo was way out of her reach. Even the oil he had added to the bath water was expensive and exclusive; a man like that would never settle for anything ordinary.

This time he only put his arm round the door, brandishing thick-piled, toffee-coloured towels, each one of them big enough to swaddle her from head to foot. 'They're still warm,' he said. 'If you hang them over the radiator they'll stay that way…'

She thanked him and then settled back in the warm water so she could listen to him moving about in the kitchen. Tea and sympathy? Or maybe he was preparing a stiff drink for her to ease the news that her scholarship hopes were dashed.

'Ten minutes and then we talk,' he called to her from the hallway.

At least she didn't have long to wait to hear her fate! Relaxing back, she closed her eyes. There was little she could say in her defence. She'd been feeling low and had sought refuge in a bar, which hardly sounded like the reasoned actions of a Unicorn scholarship candidate.

Lorenzo's knock on the bathroom door made her spill bath water on the floor.

'Are you decent?'

'Yes…' Well, she was cloaked in a glittering foam blanket.

'I'm coming in.'

She sank beneath the foam.

'Drink this.'

She cautiously pushed herself back up a bit. Lorenzo was offering her a mug of warm milk. 'I hate warm milk.'

He ignored her complaint. 'Drink it while it's hot. I added honey and a sprinkling of cinnamon.'

Great. Nursery food.

'Good girl…'

She curbed the urge to spit out a milk fountain in favour of sipping slowly to see if he would stay.

'Don't move.'

It worked.

'I'm going for some more towels…'

She'd made an impression!

He returned with an armful of towels, but now it came to it he was rather more man than she could handle. Her body might be telling her to prepare for contact with some hard, tanned flesh, but she was losing her nerve.

He hunkered down.

'What are you doing?'

'Drying your hair. Maybe that way you won't catch a chill and take time off work.'

Some impression!

When Lorenzo had finished drying her hair he held out a bath sheet, allowing her to climb out of the bath with her modesty sadly intact. As if that weren't humiliating enough he told her to clean her teeth and stood aside.

Fantasies would be the death of her.

They went into her bedroom.

'Night clothes?' Lorenzo prompted.

She reached inside the bedside drawer where she stored her sexy sale bargains.

'What's that?' Lorenzo demanded as she held up a wisp of lace. 'Haven't you got anything sensible?'

Like grandma's bloomers?

'How about these?' Fishing deeper than she had, he emerged triumphantly with a pair of pink flannelette pyjamas. 'These will keep you nice and warm.'

So could he…

'Climb into bed,' he ordered, returning to the door.

This was not going to plan. This was not going anywhere. For all she knew Lorenzo might have sisters, but she didn't want to be one of them.

'Don't worry about over-sleeping. I'll wake you in the morning.'

'What about our talk?'

'We'll have it tomorrow…'

'Carly…'

'Mmm…'

'It's time to get up.'

No. He couldn't wake her now. 'Leave me,' she said grumpily. 'I'm asleep…' She had no intention of getting out of bed so soon after Lorenzo had taken so much trouble to make sure she stayed there. 'Did you have to do that?' With a groan of disapproval she tried to shield her eyes. From arrows of sunlight?

'Did I have to pull the curtains at ten o'clock in the morning? Yes, I most certainly did, young lady.'

'Ten o'clock in the morning?' Carly shot up and rubbed her eyes. The evidence was undeniable. Lorenzo was wearing his three-piece suit, and he'd shaved. He was ready for work, and the thin winter sunshine was streaming into the room.

'You've slept long enough.' His eyes narrowed. 'You wouldn't want to be late for work.'

There was an edge to his voice that suggested she had better not be.

'I won't be late.'

'Half an hour in my office.'

*Half an hour?* 'I'll be there.'

Last night had been his biggest test yet, and the night of the Grand Court had been the turning point in his mind between Carly Tate, promising law student, and Carly Tate, promising innumerable erotic delights. But this was question time and office time, Lorenzo reminded himself. He wanted to know more about her before writing his report for the scholarship committee. 'So, your parents are supportive?'

'Absolutely…they couldn't be more so.'

He rearranged himself in the chair. 'Do you have brothers and sisters?'

'One sister, Olivia…'

Her gaze flickered.

'Do you get on well?'

'Oh, very well. She's the pretty one.'

She gave a nervous laugh, and he wanted to tell her that he wasn't interested in pretty sisters, only Carly Tate. He had to dig deep if he was going to find out if she was committed to the programme. 'So what drew you to law?'

'It missed a generation.'

'And you felt you should fill the breach?'

'I wanted to,' she argued passionately.

'There are other worthwhile careers you could have pursued. Didn't you consider any of them?' He waited for her reply, already knowing the answer—there had only ever been one path open to her. 'How about your hobbies, Carly?'

'Hobbies?' Her eyes went blank.

'Yes, hobbies—sport, dancing, theatre—'

'Oh, I read a lot,' she interrupted.

'Law books?'

She clammed up and blushed red. She didn't want him grilling her on the latest hot reads. 'Anything else?' he pressed.

She bit her lip, drawing his attention to the other redness where his stubble had abraded her tender skin. He remembered his hackles shooting up when he'd thought the man in the bar was trying to humiliate her. He'd acted purely on instinct, but he could still remember how she'd felt beneath his hands, his mouth, and the way she'd tasted against his tongue. He wanted her now. He wanted to take her to bed right now—

'Anything else you'd like to tell me?' he said, needing the

distraction badly. But he couldn't look at her without recall-
ing how fragile she'd been in his arms. And the thought of
sinking deep into that warm, soft body—

'Do I have anything else to say?' she said, interrupting his
stream of thought. She looked thoughtful. 'I want the scholarship.' Lowering her chin, she delivered him a level gaze. 'It
means everything to me…'

'And to your parents too, I have no doubt…' He glanced at
the door, a signal that their interview was over. He needed space.

The rest of the day flew past, not that there was much left of
it. She was free to concentrate on firming up the arrangements
for the Christmas party. That and ensuring Lorenzo's car was
returned to him on time.

'Everything going to plan?' he said, making her heart stop
when he poked his head around the door of her cubby-hole.

'Really well. Your car should be returned to you this evening.'

'And the party?'

'All going to plan.' At least something was, she thought wryly.

'Just don't be too proud to ask for my help if you need it. Will
you, Carly?' Lorenzo pressed in a way that required an answer.

'Don't worry—everything's under control.'

As he pulled away from the door she spun a smile and sent
it flying in his direction. She waited motionless until his footsteps had died away. It was stupid to go on feeling like this.
She had to stop pining for something that was never going to
happen. What she should be doing was making the hard call
home—the one that told her mother she wouldn't be back for
the annual gathering of the clan, because this year she had to
stay in London and organise the Christmas party. 'Which, yes,
Mother, includes cleaning up after it. That's right, Mother,
menial tasks.' She was already rehearsing the conversation in
her head. 'Someone has to do them.'

The phone call began better than Carly could have expected. Her mother was in high spirits and even swallowed her version of the party being an honour she had been entrusted with, right up to the point where she mentioned tidying up afterwards.

'Stay and clear up?' her mother exclaimed in disapproval. 'Have we paid for all that education in order for you to carry out menial tasks?'

Someone has to do them, Carly mouthed silently, and then as her mother exploded into shrill indignation she held the phone away from her ear. Her mother couldn't be expected to know what a scholarship race entailed. How you had to grovel and study until your eyes turned bright red and popped out of your head. It was better if she never knew. How could you explain that pride had no place when you were clinging on to an opportunity by your fingertips? 'Really, it's considered an honour,' Carly said during of one of her mother's rare pauses for breath.

'*An honour?* I can't see your sister agreeing to emptying slops—'

'Mum, please, it's not like that—' But her mother was in no mood for listening.

'You say yes too easily, Carly. You might be thought the clever one, but you're not shrewd or worldly-wise like Olivia. Just be sure you're not being taken for a mug. Here,' she finished impatiently. 'Speak to your father. I can't talk any sense into you. But for his sake, if nothing else, I'm asking you to rethink.'

Her father was gentler, but she could hear the disappointment in his voice. 'Dad, they're hardly likely to invite me to host the chambers party when I've so recently been granted a pupilage. Organising the Christmas party is not so bad. It's a chance to prove myself—'

'As a cleaner?' her mother prompted from the wings.

'Anyway, I'll let you know how it goes, shall I, Dad?'

Carly waited as the silence lengthened. She was longing for a word of encouragement. She heard her mother say something in the background. 'What did Mum say? I couldn't hear her.'

'She says don't eat too much at the party,' her dad reported. 'You can't afford to put on any more weight…'

# CHAPTER EIGHT

'THANKS, DAD…' Carly stared at the dead receiver in her hand. Her father had been bustled off the phone because her mother wanted to make a call. She remained very still for a moment, and then emotion welled inside her. She needed air…now.

'Hey…'

Lorenzo had to move fast to avoid a collision. In her flight across Reception she'd been blind to everything, including him.

'Didn't you see me?' His lips curved up in the half smile that could turn her legs to jelly, but on this occasion seemed like one more mocking jibe.

'I saw you,' Carly lied, standing tall. She made a point of strolling to the door as if she had all the time in the world, but inside she felt like a washing machine on its final spin, whirling mindlessly, endlessly. She was frantic for space, air, rain, anything other than the claustrophobic atmosphere inside her tiny cubby-hole because that was drenched in reproach and disappointment. All she wanted was to make her parents proud, and she could never seem to do so.

Lorenzo reached across and opened the outer doors for her. 'I'm leaving too,' he said. 'Why don't we walk back together?'

She could think of a thousand reasons why she shouldn't

do that, and did her best to put him off. 'Oh, that's okay,' she said. 'I might do some shopping first.'

But he slipped into stride beside her. 'I'll worry if I leave you wandering the streets alone looking for men to kiss.'

'Last night was a one-off.'

'Okay, so if you don't want me to join you—'

'What, on my hunt for kissable men?'

Lorenzo refused to take offence. 'Kissing men has never been my style,' he said dryly.

She felt so miserable she snapped back, 'Well, I don't make a habit of it either.'

'In that case I'm glad you made an exception last night.'

Right. Lorenzo had only been trying to save her from embarrassment. He would have done the same for any of his female students. Lorenzo gave kisses easily, because kisses came easily to him; they had rarity value where she was concerned.

'Stop frowning,' he instructed, slanting a glance her way. 'Your face might stick that way. We're off duty, and even lawyers can't take themselves seriously all the time.'

Says the inquisitor-in-chief! 'So where are you heading?'

'Back to the flat. I'm going to make some supper. You can have some too. You have to eat, don't you?' he said, responding to her surprised look.

'I didn't think you could cook.'

'How many Italians do you know who don't cook?'

'I don't know many Italians.'

'Then you don't know what you're missing.'

Her cheeks blazed red on cue.


When they arrived, he suggested she take off her suit and relax. It was exactly what he planned to do. It was just unfortunate as he said it that the bits of lace she kept stored in her bedroom flew into his mind. He quickly prescribed an outfit: 'Jeans and a top—something you don't mind spilling food down.' He wanted to take her to bed and it should have been straightforward, but, as he'd told his inner self before, nothing was straightforward with Carly Tate. 'My food is messy,' he said when she looked at him.

Someone had hurt her; he could see it in her eyes. So much for seduction! How could he when that same someone was putting roadblocks in his way? But the anger that surged inside him came from longing to bring her detractor to account.

'I won't be long,' she said, walking off.

Who the hell had done that to her? His work made him acutely aware of body language and she couldn't hide the strain on her face.

He went to his bedroom and took his clothes off. Hanging up his suit, he made for the bathroom. He needed a shower to clean away everything he'd seen and heard that day. Working as a criminal lawyer was all he'd ever wanted to do, but the cases he handled were real-life dramas and he could never relax until he'd washed the day away.

He felt refreshed by the time he reached the kitchen. Women loved it when he cooked. It always threw them—usually in the direction of his bed. He was a perfectionist in cooking, advocacy and sex, and knew better than most that practice made perfect. But this wasn't a cynical exercise. He was right to have doubts about Carly's future. Confidence was a prerequisite for a successful career at the bar, and it took more than a sharp brain and dedication for a student to achieve their potential. Carly carried a load of expectation on her shoulders, but what did *she* want?

'Hungry?' he said, forced to break off his cogitations when she walked into the kitchen.

'Starving,' she admitted, but then her cheeks flamed red as if she'd said something wrong.

'I promise not to poison you.'

'No need to go to any trouble—I'm not that hungry.'

'You said you were starving.'

'Are you cross-examining me, my learned friend?' She was only half joking.

'If I make it, you eat it, is that understood?' This time he was only half joking.

She blushed and looked away. To spare her the spotlight he started making a home-made salad dressing. 'To go with the pasta,' he explained, feeling pleased when she came a little closer to see what he was doing. 'Food allergies?' he queried without looking up as he added seasoning.

'None.'

'And you're not on a diet?'

Her cheeks pinked up. 'What makes you say that? Do you think I should be?'

The tone of her voice shocked him. 'No, I don't. You work long hours and you need your strength.'

Like a sumo warrior? Carly thought, watching Lorenzo wield his wooden spoon. Truthfully, she was ravenous, and this already smelled good.

'I'm going to put the dressing in the fridge,' he said, moving past her, 'and start on the tomato sauce for the pasta.'

She pressed back against the work surface. It was torture being this close to him. The jeans he'd changed into hugged his hips, and the heavy-duty belt he'd threaded through the denim loops drew her attention to things she shouldn't be sneaking looks at. Then there was the top clinging tenaciously to his hard-muscled arms.

'Taste?' he said, having beaten his sauce into submission.

She did an instant calorie calculation and agreed: tomato,

chilli and onion were safe. 'And is this your idea of a simple pasta?' It was simply delicious, that was for sure.

The look he gave her confirmed nothing was simple where Lorenzo was concerned. And then, looking for an indication of his mood, she glanced at his feet and saw they were bare. For some reason that gave her a sexual charge, which took her by surprise. Was she so desperate she was finding feet sexy now? But Lorenzo's feet *were* sexy. Tanned, with a fabulous pedicure, her eyes reported. And his hair was still damp from the shower, which she found incredibly arousing too. In fact—

'Try this now I've seasoned it again,' he said, breaking into her thoughts.

She opened her mouth as he touched the spoon to her lips. 'Better?' he said.

She licked her kiss-bruised lips, and hummed approval.

'Take a bigger mouthful. Unless you're afraid of food, of course.' He'd meant it as a joke. 'You're not, are you? Why, that's ridiculous. While I live here you're going to eat properly.'

Her stomach growled on cue, making them both laugh and relaxing the tension.

They sat down to eat. Lorenzo's ragu was rich and perfectly seasoned, and as she slowly dropped her inhibitions Carly found her tension unravelling as fast as a piece of loosely-knit cotton. 'Ice cream?' she asked, after Lorenzo had cleared their plates away and returned with dessert. She felt a moment of guilt, but only a moment. 'Oh, no, you're spoiling me.'

'It's a special Zabaglione…my own recipe. Open wide…'

It was the most indescribably delicious spoonful of food she had eaten in her life.

'The alcohol content makes the mixture soft, and so—'

She didn't listen to the rest, because Lorenzo's sleepy gaze was soothing, and the brush of his minty breath on her face was making her tender lips tingle.

'And like many things it must be eaten without delay,' he went on. 'Carly? Are you still with me?'

Barely, and yet never more so, she thought as Lorenzo dipped his head to stare her in the eyes.

'Has someone said something to upset you?'

The telephone conversation with her parents was still fresh in her mind, and the concern in Lorenzo's voice was the last straw for her tear ducts. 'No, of course not.'

'Then why are there tears in your eyes?'

'Don't be silly, there aren't any,' she said, sniffing violently. She wasn't about to reveal her weaknesses to him.

He let it go and made coffee. He put his questions down to professional interest, but it was more than that. It was new to him, this impulse to nurture. It certainly got in the way of sex for recreation. The trouble with Carly was she made him want things he couldn't have, things he didn't have time for. 'Tell me more about yourself…' He wanted to hear her speak; her voice soothed him, and right now he badly needed soothing.

'What can I tell you? I'm boring,' she said.

'Why don't you let me be the judge of that?'

'Another test? I thought we were off duty?'

'These are scholarship questions,' he lied.

'How am I doing?' Her eyes fired.

He didn't want to answer that. He wasn't prepared to commit himself either way. Carly was a strong candidate. On paper, at least. Or was that being unfair to her, because he wanted her in his bed?

It was more than that, Lorenzo reflected. He doubted Carly's commitment to the scholarship programme. She had allowed herself to believe she wanted nothing more on earth than the Unicorn scholarship, but in his view her motives were wrong. The scholarship was a prize she'd take home for her parents like an eager puppy might take a ball. He doubted she'd thought further than the winner's name being announced. Where the Unicorn would take her was immaterial, it was where it would take her parents that obsessed Carly. 'So, what's the boyfriend situation?' he said to distract them both. And, yes, because he wanted to know. He had an obsession too—the thought of sex with Carly, and right now it was driving him hard.

'There isn't one,' she said, turning on a frank stare. 'I don't have time.'

Should that answer please him quite so much? 'So you won't be leaving anyone behind if you're awarded the scholarship?'

*Only you...* With a head and heart full of Lorenzo it wasn't easy to stare straight at him and convince them both there was no one she cared about. 'No one,' she repeated, avoiding his gaze.

'Surely your parents have someone lined up for you?'

'Maybe, but I didn't approve of their selection.'

'You make them sound like a box of chocolates.'

'That's just what they were,' she agreed. 'But they were all strawberry creams, when I was looking for—'

'Bitter chocolate and a hard nut?' he suggested dryly.

'Exactly...' She looked at him, wishing the comparison between men with grey socks and darkly, dangerous Lorenzo could have been a little less extreme. 'Anyway—'

'Anyway?'

'Like I said before, I don't have time for men.' It was a useful lie. 'The speed-dating fiasco was a mistake. I found myself in the right place at the wrong time, and then I just got swept away by the prospect of—'

'Sharing a man's bed with countless others?'

'No!'

He hummed sceptically as he might have done in court. 'Are you sure your parents don't know what's best for you?'

He poured coffee, but she wondered at the tense line of his jaw. 'I'm positive.' She passed the cream. 'So-called society can be incredibly dull.'

He sat back. 'Tell me about it.'

'Bores who think their stories are irresistible, and when you try to get to know them, you wonder why you—'

He cut in. 'I didn't mean tell me literally, I was agreeing with you.'

'You were?'

'Yes, I was, Carly.'

Well, that had to be a first! The way Lorenzo was looking at her now was unfathomable. The only thing she could say for sure was that it made her heart melt.

She would get over him and get on with her life, Carly told herself firmly. This little chat was nothing more than a fishing expedition on Lorenzo's part so he could write a proper report. 'Thanks for taking the time to talk to me.' She was just congratulating herself on a great exit line when she missed her footing and landed in his arms.

'Bed?' he suggested.

She stared into his eyes, hardly daring to breathe.

'I need you back working full tilt tomorrow.'

Ah.

He steadied her back on her feet and said goodnight. She'd almost made it out of the room when he added, 'Your parents must be very proud of you.'

'Yes, of course they are.' She stiffened.

'And this scholarship would mean a lot to them?'

'Of course…'

'And to you?'

When she didn't reply immediately, he added, 'I should

think they're already proud of you. You don't need the Unicorn scholarship on top of everything else.'

Her stomach clenched. Was Lorenzo trying to tell her something? If he was she'd rather he just came out and say it. 'Lorenzo, please don't mess me about—I'd rather know.'

'And you know I can't tell you my decision.'

She gripped the door handle for a moment and then left the room. He fought the urge to go after her. He had been trying to let her down lightly and he'd messed up. He waited until she shut her bedroom door and then only managed to stop himself punching the wall because it wasn't his wall to punch.

He was suspended between business and pleasure with a bridge of lust in between. If he had been searching for a recipe for disaster, he couldn't have found a better one.

# CHAPTER NINE

ONLY ONE MORE NIGHT until Carly's Christmas party. That was her second thought as she woke up. The first—since it contained Lorenzo—was censored.

There was a street lamp outside the window shedding a grudging light inside the room. She lay in bed staring at the ceiling, telling herself she was stealing the last few moments in a warm bed before getting up, when really she was listening for Lorenzo. And fretting. He had dug and dug last night until she'd given up who knew what innermost secrets. One thing was for sure: he'd read more into what she'd said than anyone who wasn't a top-flight barrister might. She wasn't fooled for a minute by his cosy chit-chat; he'd been using his tried-and-tested courtroom technique to find out everything he could about her. So had she blown her scholarship chances out of the water? Only Lorenzo knew that, and he wasn't telling.

It shouldn't be hard to avoid him today she'd be so busy, but it was when they were both home like this and the apartment hummed with his energy she found it so difficult to relax. How long would it take to fix a leak at his flat? When would she be rid of him?

Who was she trying to kid? She was aching for sex; aching for Lorenzo.

Burying her head under the pillows, she tried to shut out the sound of his shower running. The thought of him naked beneath the spray was nothing short of torment, but, short of a miracle, aching for sex was how she was going to stay. Lorenzo Domenico might be the hottest thing on two hard-muscled legs, but he wasn't interested in her.

The bathroom grew silent again. Sitting up in bed, she hugged her knees, resting her chin. The best thing to do was work twice as hard to prove to Lorenzo that her parents' expectations weren't the only thing driving her.

Lifting the envelope containing Carly's lists, he picked up the phone and summoned her. Minutes later she was in his office.

He eased back in his chair, acting as if the sight of her had no effect on his libido. 'Let's go over these lists,' he said, handing her the copies.

Lists plural? He had *both* her lists?

'Lists?' she squeaked, delving frantically through her memory bank. She distinctly remembered stuffing Lorenzo's list inside an envelope and popping it inside his pigeon-hole. She knew it was his envelope because she had marked it For Your Eyes Only. For one look into Lorenzo's eyes she would do a lot of things…but not, *surely,* mix up her lists?

'You put an envelope into my pigeon-hole, didn't you?' he said, confirming it was all right to relax. But then a suspicious curve tugged at his lips. 'And I picked this list up when you dropped it…'

He'd got the wrong envelope! It wasn't just a list she'd dropped, it was the bottom out of her world!

'Is it getting too hot for you?' Lorenzo murmured as she eased the neck of her shirt. 'I can easily turn the central heating down.'

He could turn the air-conditioning up and it wouldn't

impact on her discomfort. Toughing it out was the only way left to her. She played it cool. 'Oh, *that* list. I still have one or two additions to make, so if you wouldn't mind…' She held out her hand in a way that would make any normal person act immediately.

'Additions?' Lorenzo said dryly. 'Can it be possible you've left something out?'

Her cheeks fired as she thought about it. Her cravings, her fantasies of everything she'd like Lorenzo to do to her—all of them written down in note form, some with explicit doodles…

'No, I didn't think so,' he said. 'I think you'd better explain yourself, Carly.'

Inwardly, she shrank. Explain what? That she wanted to go to bed with Lorenzo—and not once, but many times, and each of those times was going to be more inventive than the last—

'I hope you haven't circulated this list to your colleagues,' he said, showing a distinct absence of humour.

'No, of course not!' That was the one thing she could be sure about. The list Lorenzo had just placed on the desk in front of him was one of a kind.

'Good,' he said evenly. 'It could corrupt in the wrong hands…'

Forget toughing it out! 'Sorry.' Snatching the list off his desk, she ran out. If she was going down she was going down with all guns blazing!

Back home that night, wanting to take her mind off Lorenzo, and inspired by his prowess in the kitchen, Carly baked a cake. And not just any cake. A cake decorated with emerald-green icing. The bottle of colouring had been tiny, the bowl large—who knew you were supposed to put in a drop of green colouring and not the whole bottle?

In spite of this small setback she decided stubbornly

that it would make an excellent centrepiece for the buffet table at the Christmas party.

'Emerald-green icing?' Madeline stared.

'It's festive,' Carly pointed out. She had drawn quite a crowd on her arrival in chambers, and was prepared to defend the first cake she had ever baked to hell and back again.

'It will brighten up the buffet table no end,' one of the clerks agreed. 'You could use it for a centrepiece.'

'That's the plan…' She was smiling again by the time she replaced the lid on the tin.

'You have got everything ready for tonight, haven't you, Carly?' Madeline asked anxiously as everyone peeled away. 'Only Lorenzo went off to court like a bear with a sore head—'

'Did he…?' she asked, trying to sound indifferent while she inwardly groaned. This was it. She was finished. After the encounter in his office and the wretched list she should have expected it. 'Of course I'm ready.' She changed track quickly, seeing Madeline's suspicious nose was already twitching at the thought of something juicy to spread around.

'What will you wear?' Madeline gave her the quick up and down.

She wasn't falling for that one again. 'I haven't decided yet,' Carly replied vaguely, her mind on other things—like the tirade of anger due from Lorenzo.

'Don't you think you should?' Madeline demanded with a frown, taking a large bite out of a succulent Krispie Kreme. 'Want one?' she offered, holding out the box. She didn't just offer, she held the box stuffed with freshly-baked doughnuts right under Carly's nose. 'I didn't have time to stop for breakfast,' Madeline explained as the mouth-wateringly sugary smell invaded Carly's quivering nostrils.

Carly's stomach growled in disappointment as she refused the offer. But what could she do? She had nine hours to drop a dress size, and no intention of squandering a single minute. 'I had breakfast before I left the flat, thank you,' she lied glibly. 'And now, if you will excuse me, Madeline, I really should be getting on...'

'Of course...' Madeline looked curiously at the hefty brief beneath Carly's arm, tied ostentatiously as all briefs were supposed to be with bright pink ribbon. The sight of it didn't have quite the same effect on Madeline as the box of Krispy Kremes had had on Carly, but at least it made Madeline's predatory gaze narrow, which was something.

'Lorenzo entrusts you with his briefs?'

'I'm looking this one over for him, actually,' Carly said, excusing her fib on the grounds of extreme provocation. The truth was Lorenzo had left the papers behind in the flat, and she thought he might need them. And returning them was as good an excuse to see him again and beg for his mercy.

'What about your dress for tonight, Carly?' Madeline pressed.

'Who said anything about a dress?'

'You surely can't be thinking of turning up in trousers?' Madeline looked fit to faint.

'Now, Madeline, you know that everything about the Christmas party is supposed to be a surprise.'

'A surprise, not a shock,' Madeline pointed out, taking another monster bite from her doughnut. 'But if you should need any help...'

And see you coming? I'll run a mile, Carly thought, smiling sweetly as she pressed the elevator call button. She had enough trouble on her hands as it was.

'Only I saw this dress, and it's just you—'

Carly breathed a sigh of relief as the elevator doors closed right on cue.

Carly smiled with satisfaction. She was ready. She had arranged for everything to be delivered at least two hours before it would be needed for the party, and so far her plan was running like clockwork. Everyone else had gone home at lunchtime to prepare. She hadn't managed to see Lorenzo, which she told herself was a good thing as she plonked the brief down on his desk. Actually, it was; she was anxious enough. She had warned the security guard at Reception that no one, apart from her suppliers, was to come anywhere near the main hall. If she was going down, she was going down with the most spectacular bang.

How could you go without food for a whole day and still not lose weight? Having raced back to the flat, Carly was now struggling with the skirt she had planned to wear for the party—black lace over a flesh-coloured skirt. If you didn't look too closely, it gave the illusion of lace over naked skin—though whatever had possessed her to imagine anyone would want to see her naked flesh escaped her now. Tugging it off, she discarded it on top of the ever-growing clothes mountain at the foot of her bed.

She was getting desperate, but then she noticed the snow drifting past the window. Snow was good news, because snow made it possible to pile on layers which, hopefully, would conceal everything underneath. Plus, if she transformed herself into something shapeless and sexless, no one would care how much she ate. Brilliant. When she wasn't handing out food she could be eating it.

There was a far bigger turnout than Carly had expected, and everyone was in party mood, including Madeline.

'Carly, you're a star!' Madeline enthused, managing at the same time to frown with incredulity that Carly could have achieved something so enjoyable. 'Everyone's saying that no one but you would have had the nerve to put on a Northern night.'

'Really?' Was that good, or bad? Carly wondered. And where was Lorenzo? She gazed around nervously. The sooner they could have their confrontation and get it over with, the better. She knew she was finished. She just didn't know the mode of execution Lorenzo would choose to despatch her with yet.

'I can see now why you didn't need my fashion advice,' Madeline commented with a critical gaze. 'How clever of you to get that grunge outfit exactly right.'

'Thank you,' Carly said, trying not to chip her teeth in the process of grinding her jaw into the approximation of a smile.

'I'm having such fun,' Madeline confided. 'Beer and skittles! Who'd have thought you could come up with such an original idea?'

'Have you seen Lorenzo?'

'Oh…' Madeline's face took on a concerned look. 'Did I forget to say? He asked to see you in his office the moment you showed your face…'

The *moment* she showed her face? This was bad. 'So he's here?' It was too late to hide her feelings from Madeline. Her guard was down, and everything she felt about him, all the longing and apprehension, was on her face for everyone to see.

'He's been here for some time…monitoring the situation,' Madeline said ominously. 'There's nothing for you to worry about. You just have to accept that a man like Lorenzo isn't used to this kind of entertainment. I'm sure he'll get over it.'

'Is he very angry?'

'Who knows? Lorenzo never shows his feelings. Surely you've learned that by now?'

If nothing else? Carly wondered, maintaining a neutral expression as she crunched on Madeline's barb.

Madeline shrugged. 'But never mind. At least I'm enjoying your party…' She gave Carly a consoling hug, dropping a greasy sausage-and-onion kiss on the cheek for good measure. 'Can't stop!' she exclaimed happily, having wrought the appropriate level of havoc on Carly's nerves. 'Must go and sign up for the snooker tournament.'

Carly's insides were lashing about like crazy, but there was no escape. Whatever anyone thought there was only one person who mattered, and he was waiting to see her in his office.

She should have known Lorenzo would be here from the start. She should have known he wouldn't like this sort of casual, rowdy party. And on top of everything else that had happened it was the final straw; the straw that proved she had made a complete hash of things.

Carly elbowed her way across a crowded dance floor as she attempted to reach the corridor where the seniors' offices were located. She gleaned some comfort from the fact that the dance floor was crowded with judges and QCs, all jiggling about. At least they were having fun. She hadn't been able to afford a DJ and so she had hired a beat-up jukebox from a friend of Madame Xandra's. The skittles had been thrown in along with a dartboard and a snooker table, as well as several boxes of dominoes and Shove Halfpenny boards, which were being fought over this very minute. When she had queried the minuscule cost of so much entertainment, Madame Xandra had explained that retro was finished. Maybe it was, but the legal world was centuries behind, meaning that for most of her guests retro had barely arrived.

As she walked briskly down the corridor towards her fate she tried to picture Lorenzo in his sober three-piece suit throwing darts… It wasn't easy; in fact, she failed.

*What had she been thinking?*

\* \* \*

She hesitated briefly, and then rapped firmly on Lorenzo's door.

'Come in.'

Seated behind his desk he looked suitably stern.

'Before you say anything—'

'I'd like to congratulate you,' he said, ignoring her. 'Your party's a huge success.'

There was a 'but' in there somewhere; there had to be. His face gave nothing away. 'Did I do something wrong?'

'I'd be happier if it weren't for this.' He held out the list.

'I can only apologise…' Not prepared to give up yet, she sidled up to his desk and tried to take it.

He lifted it out of her reach. 'Shut the door, please,' he said briskly.

A sense of failure swept over her as she closed the door. A black cloud sat on her head as she thought about her parents and the disappointment that was about to envelop them.

Lorenzo remained seated, remained stern. She bit her lip and then bit back tears. However hard she tried, she always let people down. 'I'm sorry,' she started, but then, just as she began to speak she had a vision of Madeline Du Pre gloating. It was time to stop feeling sorry for herself and defend her corner. 'I did my best,' she said robustly, 'and if you don't like it—'

'I can what?' Lorenzo challenged in a lazy voice, unfolding from his chair.

She swayed back. How could she have forgotten how big he was? Was every bit of him in proportion? She reddened as her thoughts ran riot. He towered over her. Ominously.

'What are you wearing?' He came a step closer.

Did it matter? Did he care? Would anyone notice what she was wearing when she left the building? And at least she was warm, which was something! 'It was snowing outside when I left the flat—'

'But that's hardly a party outfit,' Lorenzo commented, viewing it disparagingly. 'You're hot,' he said.

Obviously! But then she noticed the look in his eyes and blushed. Did he mean what she thought he meant? 'Really?' she said in a different voice.

'Absolutely. Now, I think we should make a start by removing some of these layers... This shawl, for instance,' he said, unwinding it, 'is quite unnecessary in a centrally heated building.'

'I didn't have time to take it off,' she stuttered as he tossed it aside. 'Look, I know I'm not hot on fashion, but—'

'But what?' he said. 'You've cornered the market in cardigans?'

Okay, maybe she had added one too many. She gasped as first one cardigan and then another hit the floor.

'Or caftans, perhaps?' he said, fingering the heavy cloth of the garment she was wearing underneath.

'This isn't a caftan,' she said with affront. 'This is a genuine beaded *abaya* from the souk. I only bought it last year—'

'Well, it looks like a Bedouin tent to me. Are you sure you bought it from a clothes stall?'

'Quite sure...' She gasped as he lifted it over her head.

'This won't do, Ms Tate. Apart from your rotten taste in clothes, you've broken the first rule on your list. Or was it the second?' Rasping the stubble on his chin, he thought about it. 'You do remember the rule to which I'm referring?'

'Of course I do.' She drew with relief upon her flawless memory bank, which unlike her social skills and doodling, never let her down. '"Arrive early,"' she quoted, '"and make a point of speaking to your immediate superior—"'

'But you didn't make a point of speaking to your immediate superior. I was waiting here to see you.'

Her breath rushed out in shock as Lorenzo started undoing

the laces at the neck of the traditional shirt she was wearing underneath her abaya.

'Now this is an ugly thing,' he said, 'so we'll discard it.'

'I'm really, *really* sorry.' She glanced anxiously at the growing mound of clothes. 'I'll get some help—a personal shopper…a full make-over—'

'Let's forget your fashion crisis for now,' Lorenzo soothed, 'and concentrate on your rules.' He referred to the list again, while she could think of nothing other than the lurid activities her matchstick people had indulged in.

'I like this rule,' he said, looking up. Lorenzo's eyes were so dark they were almost black. 'You must remain visible and maintain a pleasant and interested smile on your face at all times… Well?' he prompted softly. 'What do you have to say about that, Ms Tate?'

She gasped again as the first of her vests hit the floor.

# CHAPTER TEN

'I WROTE THOSE GUIDELINES at your instruction,' Carly reminded Lorenzo in a voice that refused to stop trembling. 'Just like you said, they're meant to help the less experienced members of chambers in stressful party conditions—'

'And are they helping you?' he said in a murmur as he peeled off another vest.

'Lorenzo…what are you doing?' She eased her neck, subconsciously presenting it for his attention…

'You don't know?'

Lorenzo's face was very close to her ear. His warm breath was making it tingle, and she gave a little groan.

'Are you cooler yet?'

Was he joking?

He was so close now the harsh cut of his beard grazed her skin, and before she had chance to recover from that he licked her ear.

'Shall I stop?' he said when she trembled.

Only if you want to, she wanted to say, but her lips moved and no sound came out—other than a ragged sigh that was half a moan. 'Don't you dare,' she managed to force out.

He backed her up against the door, taking it slowly,

crossing the room step by inevitable step, until she could feel the cool wood against her back and he could reach the lock.

'Exactly how many garments are you wearing?' he murmured, perusing them.

'Quite a few yet…' Suddenly all those layers seemed more of a blessing than a curse; the unwrapping process made her wish she'd put on more.

'You must be steaming,' Lorenzo growled against her ear.

He had no idea!

'The best thing we can do,' he said, 'is remove everything…'

'What about the party?'

'The best parties run themselves…and you have put on an excellent party.'

'What a relief…'

'Indeed. Now…is this a thermal vest?'

'One of two,' she admitted.

'Will you take it off, or shall I?'

Reaching up, she hesitated a second, and then instead of taking her vest off she loosened his tie.

Lorenzo cocked his head to one side with a slow smile burning. 'Why, Ms Tate, that's very forward of you…'

'I think I'm beginning to get the hang of this.'

'I always knew you were a good student.' He whipped off her vest as she pushed his jacket from his shoulders.

'Now, this is very nice,' Lorenzo approved, discovering another of her lucky sale finds in silk, lace and satin.

Teasing him, she crossed her arms over her *décolletage*. The aquamarine camisole, which was her very last top, thank goodness, was so fine it hid nothing.

'How interesting,' Lorenzo observed softly, 'that in spite of wearing everything else you possess you have forgotten to put on a bra.'

'They're so confining.'

'At last, we agree—' his lips tugged at one corner and his eyes lit with humour as he gazed down at her '—but I should warn you that inappropriate behaviour at the Christmas party can seriously limit your career.'

'While expert schmoozing without resorting to being a creep helps you to move up the ladder,' Carly retorted with a look that was almost as wicked as Lorenzo's.

Taking hold of her arms, he removed them gently but firmly from her chest and placed them at her side, drawing a soft moan from her lips as he ran the tips of his nails very lightly down them. 'That list was an excellent piece of work,' he commended huskily. 'It gave me all sorts of pointers as to what you might like—'

'Did you need them?'

Lorenzo was concentrating on stroking her breasts beneath the filmy fabric and didn't welcome her interruption. 'Not really,' he murmured, without looking up. She groaned as he moved on to tease the tip of her nipples with his thumbnails.

'Watch out for horns,' he reminded her when she reached up to lace her fingers through his hair.

'You read the wrong list,' she complained.

'I read every list,' Lorenzo husked against her lips. 'Surely you know by now how very thorough I am?'

'I'm counting on it…'

He backed her up towards an intricately inlaid Linley table, positioned at a convenient height against the wall. He lifted her onto it. 'My only complaint—'

'Yes?' she said anxiously.

'Is that I can think of a much better use for a table than dancing on top of it.'

'Merry nights make sad mornings…' Carly warned.

'Not necessarily,' Lorenzo countered, his hands running down her torso to her thighs.

Her fingers flew down his shirt studs and sent them flying, and while he was otherwise occupied she ripped his shirt off too. He teased her with almost kisses, making suggestions based on her doodles in between, while she pulled down his zip. His low, husky voice had made her wild for him, as did the expression in his eyes. And his chest…she explored it greedily. It was like polished bronze, like a statue by Michelangelo, and his body was made for sin…

As her camisole floated to the floor they fell on each other like starving men at a banquet. Lorenzo tasted great, and she did too, judging by the way his kisses were migrating down her neck. The kiss in the bar had been nothing compared to this; she'd been constrained by convention when they were in public, but now, when she was alone with him—

Carly gasped with disappointment when Lorenzo stopped touching her abruptly to rip open a foil packet.

'So you're…'

'Not a virgin,' she confirmed happily, shrieking with excitement when his warm hands cupped her buttocks. 'But you were a Boy Scout,' she asserted as he settled her in position.

'A Boy Scout?'

'Be prepared?' she reminded him.

'I would certainly recommend it,' he advised, nudging his way between her thighs.

Lovely desk, wonderful desk, perfect desk, it was just the right height. She was completely at his mercy now, naked, available, and panting for release. 'Oh…!' she breathed in a long-drawn-out ecstatic sigh.

'Delicious,' Lorenzo murmured, testing her.

'Delicious?' she breathed against his hard, warm, naked chest.

'You're plump in all the right places, and juicy like a fig—'

'I swear if you stop now… If you start to tease me, or make me wait—'

'You'll what?'

'Oh, Lorenzo!' The breath shot out of her as he plunged deep.

'You approve?'

'You know I do,' Carly gasped, grinding her fingers into Lorenzo's buttocks to urge him on. 'I've waited long enough—' Her voice broke off and then came back again, but this time without words and in a series of fractured shrieks. He was moving faster now, thrusting into her efficiently while holding her in place.

She should have known when she first saw his feet, Carly reasoned wildly. If feet were any indicator Lorenzo should have been huge, but he was even bigger than that, and most importantly he knew what to do with it. 'Oh, you're good…' Groaning with pleasure, she let her head fall back. She had started out quite prepared to take an active part, but with a man like this the wisest thing was to relax into it, and allow him to amaze her.

Which he did.

She had no idea any man could stretch her like this and massage every part of her at once. Lorenzo was hot, hard, huge and incredible. 'You're incredible!' she moaned, to which he replied by grinding his hips round and round. 'That's amazing!' Another shriek.

'I'm only taking your advice that first impressions count.' He rotated his hips again and again.

'Oh, they do, they do,' she yelped again, writhing greedily against him. 'Just…don't…be tempted to leave the building,' she managed to gasp out.

'When I leave, I leave with you,' he said, holding her safe as she grew frantic with excitement.

'I can't hold back.'

'You're not supposed to.'

She worked her hips to match each of his powerful thrusts, digging her fingers into him and sinking her teeth into his shoulder like a wildcat. 'Faster! Faster!' she ordered him, until the climax hit her and she was powerless to resist. It was bigger than anything she'd ever known, all-consuming, and massive, extraordinary, wonderful.

It took for ever for the pleasure waves to subside, and when they did she slumped against him.

'Better now?' he asked her.

'Getting there,' she admitted cautiously in case there was any more.

Tilting her chin so he could look into her eyes, Lorenzo brushed her mouth with his lips and kissed her deeply again.

'Did you mean it?' she said when he pulled back.

'Did I mean what?'

'What you said about us leaving together?'

'I've never been more serious in my life,' Lorenzo whispered, and, cupping her face in both his hands, he kissed her again.

He made her feel special. But she shouldn't get used to it. This was Lorenzo and Carly Tate. 'I mustn't keep you from the party—'

Lorenzo shushed her by placing a finger over her swollen lips, and then he replaced his finger with his mouth and kissed her into oblivion again. She was lost in an erotic haze but even something this good had to end.

'I'd better get out there,' he said.

'Must you?'

Lorenzo laughed.

He wanted nothing more than to yield to temptation. It was the best sex he'd ever had. Ever. Carly Tate was everything he'd imagined and more. *Caro Dio!* She was a real woman with real breasts and real hips; she had everything, including an appetite that matched his own. She was perfect, better than perfect, and this wasn't the end, it was just the beginning. After a feast like that he couldn't wait to get her into bed and for the banquet to begin.

But unfortunately they had to get back to the party. 'Why don't you take a shower in my bathroom,' he suggested, punctuating the words with kisses, 'while I use the staff facilities?' He smiled down at her, loving everything about her—the look in her eyes, the touch of her soft skin against his, her warmth, especially her warmth. 'And then we'll go back to the party together, and celebrate your triumph…'

She was in such a state of bliss it took her a moment when she shut the bathroom door to notice what was hanging on the back of it. As she took it in her heart stopped beating, and all the strength drained from her body. How could anyone be so cruel? 'Lorenzo…' Her angry voice shook.

'Yes?' he called back, sounding completely unconcerned.

'What is this?' Carly demanded, flinging the door open. She couldn't bring herself to look at him. She refused to believe he could be such a monster.

'What on earth's the matter with you, Carly?'

She was determined not to cry or lose her cool, and so instead she tilted her head towards the fabulous Chloe dress hanging on the back of the door, still in its clear Cellophane wrapper. To add insult to injury, it was the most beautiful dress she had ever seen. Low-necked in a clear blue silk, it had a defined waist and spaghetti straps, and a skirt that was softly flaring and would fall just below the knee. It was a dream of a dress, a dress that only a beautiful and slender woman would wear.

Lorenzo frowned at her. 'Don't you like it?'

Her response sounded like an animal in pain.

'It's not that bad, is it?' he said incredulously, coming closer to look. 'I spent a long time choosing it, but if you don't think it's right—'

'Right for what, Lorenzo?' she managed to choke out.

'Right for you,' he said, as if that were obvious. 'Look, it's no big deal. If you don't like it I won't be offended. Wear it tonight, and then throw it away.'

'No, just a minute…say that again.'

'Say what again?'

She wanted to wind back time over and over, and hear him say it a thousand times. 'The dress is for me?'

'Well, there's no one else here,' he said, 'and I'm certainly not going to wear it.'

But what if it didn't fit? He'd bought her a dress; he'd gone to all that trouble just for her? And it wasn't just any dress, but the most beautiful dress in the world… Of course it wouldn't fit. She went hot and cold at the prospect of trying it on. Clothes like this were made for thin, elegant women… She threw an anxious glance at it and then looked away. She couldn't bear to see it. She dreaded the look of disappointment on Lorenzo's face when he realised that the dress wouldn't even make it over her breasts, let alone her hips.

'Take your shower,' he said, 'and then call me in if you have any trouble putting the dress on.'

She'd rather die and was already looking for a window wide enough to climb through.

'There are some shoes over in the corner to go with it.'

Her cheeks blazed as she stared at them… They were gorgeous too. 'You guessed the size of my feet?' She blushed scarlet; size yeti.

'No…' He came back and caressed her face, making her look at him. 'I went into your bedroom and checked.'

Of course!

'What's the problem?' he said. 'You're going to look beautiful. Or is that a problem? Do you still want to hide yourself away beneath bundles of old clothes? I think it's time to show off that fabulous figure and walk tall at my side in five-inch heels.'

'I'm already tall,' she pointed out. And her mother had advised that flat shoes were the best option, because no man wanted a woman to tower over him.

'I'll still be taller than you,' Lorenzo told her. Taking hold of her shoulders, he drew her in front of him. 'Carly,' he murmured, staring into her eyes. 'You're beautiful. Why can't you believe that?' He tipped up her chin, making her look at him. 'You are not going to tie your gorgeous hair into a knot, and you *are* going to wear the dress and shoes I have chosen for you. And if I tell you you're beautiful, then that's what you are. All you have to do is believe…'

He kissed her brow, her eyes, her lips… 'You're beautiful,' he said again. '*Siete una donna giovane bella…* Now go and take that shower or people will wonder where we've got to.' As usual he made no attempt to hide his wicked smile. 'Go,' he said, urging her into his private bathroom. 'I'll take the staff bathroom, and I'll be back in a few minutes to help you dress…'

After she had showered, Carly stared at the fabulous dress beneath its polythene cover. She'd left her hair down as Lorenzo had requested, so that it floated round her naked shoulders. The bronze and copper curls seemed to have taken on a life of their own, and it was a life that defied her attempts to scrape it back and flatten it down. She had even put the shoes on…and was sure she was now about ten feet tall. She felt as if it was her first day in court, or the day she sat her first exam, or—

'Oh, to hell with it!' Carly exclaimed, ripping the dress

from its hanger. If she was going to be humiliated she might as well get it over with.

The designer gown fluttered over Carly's naked skin like a caress. The fabric settled on her curves as if it had been fitted properly in a couturier's atelier. The colour couldn't have provided a better foil for her auburn hair, and the length was perfect. She stared at her reflection in astonishment. She was transformed. She had never worn a party dress in her life before. She had never shopped for one. Why would she? She had never worn anything that embraced her figure rather than concealing it.

'Can I come in yet?' Lorenzo called.

Opening the door a crack, she put her face close to it. 'I can't manage the zip—' The moment she spoke she wished she hadn't. Would it even do up?

Lorenzo opened the door fully and stood, staring at her.

'Will I do?' she asked nervously.

*'Buon cielo!'* he exclaimed. 'Did I say you were beautiful? I lied. You are exquisite. You are the most beautiful woman I have ever seen. Where have you been hiding yourself, Carly Tate?'

'I'm not sure if the zip will fasten up.'

Placing his hands on her shoulders, Lorenzo dropped a reverent kiss on the nape of her neck as he reached behind her. 'It fastens easily,' he said. 'The dress fits you perfectly, as I knew it would. And now I'm going to be the proudest man at the party, and everyone will envy me...'

'You're the kindest man I know.'

'Kind?' he said wryly. 'Someone should tell you there's a degree of self-interest when a man buys a beautiful woman a gift.' His smile eased into a grin. 'Well, what are you waiting for?'

As he offered her his arm she caught a flash of the kingfisher silk lining beneath his sober three-piece suit. His socks would be equally exotic. What was a man like this doing with her? He was so different from every other man. He was so dazzling, he blinded her. Lorenzo dared to be different. He dared. And that was what she loved about him...

She loved him, Carly realised with a jolt. It wasn't just in her imagination as she had thought. She loved Lorenzo. She had fallen in love with Lorenzo Domenico.

# CHAPTER ELEVEN

'OH, NO, LOOK at my cake.' Carly stared in dismay at the buffet table.

'It looks fine to me.' Lorenzo ran a hand through his shower-damp hair.

'You look fine to me, but the cake doesn't,' Carly argued, darting a glance around to make sure they weren't being overheard.

Lorenzo's eyes warmed with a new familiarity. 'Carly?' he said, removing a strand of hair from her love-stained lips. 'Try and concentrate, will you?'

'That's exactly what I am doing,' she insisted, holding his gaze.

'On the party,' he reminded her. 'I want you to see how well it's going. Look,' he said, turning her to see as another colleague squeezed past them with a loaded plate of food. 'It's a huge success.'

'Unlike my cake,' she said, grimacing. 'No one's brave enough to try a slice of green cake.'

'I am.'

'But it's oozing unattractively beneath the lights.'

'All the more reason to eat it quickly,' Lorenzo pointed out, squeezing her arm. 'I'm sure it will taste fantastic. Why don't you cut me a slice, and let me start a trend?'

The cake almost made it as far as the plate, but then she dropped it. As she was crouching down to clear up the mess Lorenzo joined her. 'I'm sorry,' she said.

'For what?'

For being clumsy, for not sticking to her diet, for not remembering to cover her freckles with fake tan before she set out for the party this evening...

The list went on and on. But most of all she was sorry she was determined to believe everything Lorenzo said when it could only end in tears. 'For not being a better baker,' she fudged, realising he was still waiting for her answer.

'There are classes for things like that,' he said dismissively. Springing up he cut a slice of cake, and then proceeded to feed her.

'No more, please,' she begged, fearing for her disappearing waistline.

'I don't want to risk you shrinking away.'

'No danger of that,' she said self-consciously.

'Haven't you noticed the way people are staring at you?'

'They're wondering why I've changed my clothes, that's all,' she said, turning to glance around.

'I don't think so,' Lorenzo disagreed. 'They think, as I do, that it's great to see you happy and great to see you looking so lovely and so loved...'

'Loved?' She laughed and made a joke of it. 'I'd hardly win a popularity poll here.'

'Oh, I don't know,' Lorenzo argued.

She looked round in embarrassment, hoping no one had heard him. 'If you carry on like this I won't be able to get my head out of the door.'

'I think we've got a long way to go before we reach that stage,' he said. 'But in the meantime, Carly, why don't you enjoy your triumph?'

\* \* \*

At the end of the evening the party was declared a success, just as Lorenzo had predicted. Everyone said that in future all social events must be left for Carly to arrange.

As for Carly, she had just one regret and that was if she won the Unicorn scholarship she wouldn't be around to organise anything. It had surprised her to discover how much she had enjoyed the challenge of arranging the Christmas party, and in no way did she see it beneath her, or a menial task. How could she, when it had brought pleasure to so many people? Plus it was a way to get to know them better, which she'd never had the confidence to do before.

'You worked a miracle tonight,' Lorenzo told her as they walked home together. 'You took my measly budget and turned it into something everyone will talk about for years to come.'

'I'm not sure I can top my Northern night.'

'You don't have to. You'll think of something else for the next time, and whatever you do will be well received. Tonight's triumph will become your badge of honour, your success story by which you will be known from now on.'

'You talk as if there's going to be no more law.'

'You can do whatever you want to do,' he told her in a voice that had suddenly turned serious.

Alarm bells sounded, but she didn't want to break the easy mood between them by raising the spectre of the Unicorn scholarship. 'You make it all sound easy, so romantic.'

'You know me better than that, Carly. An event planner couldn't have done better than you did tonight. I'm just pointing out that the world's your oyster. Now stop fumbling with the lock and give me that key.'

'You're impatient.'

'There are some things that can't wait, and you're one of them—'

But the first thing Carly saw when Lorenzo opened the front door was a letter from her mother sitting on the mat.

'Leave that now,' he said, dragging her close so he could bury his face in her hair.

At first she couldn't stop thinking about it. She was far too tense as she held the letter in her hand, but Lorenzo took matters, or, rather, Carly, into his own hands, and made her forget.

Tugging off their clothes as they ran, they laughed and stumbled their way down the hallway. Carly was heading for her bedroom, but Lorenzo cut her off at the pass. 'My room,' he insisted, swinging her into his arms. 'The bed's bigger, and we're going to need every inch of it.'

A bed! A real bed! Oh, bliss. She threw herself down on top of it, making Lorenzo laugh. She didn't care what he thought, she only knew she wanted him. Reaching up, she demanded he kiss her without further delay. The blue dress had clearly worked some magic, because he took her in his arms and told her she was beautiful again.

'Okay, okay,' he murmured as she laced her fingers through his hair and tugged. He dropped a kiss on her swollen mouth. 'I get the message…'

'But not quickly enough,' she complained.

The gorgeous silky dress floated to the floor with her lacy thong, and then the bed dipped as Lorenzo came to lie down beside her.

'I can't,' she said in a moment of panic as he loomed over her. 'Just wait a minute…I'm not ready… Oh…'

'Really?'

'Oh,' she said again, this time more quietly and with wonder. How could she have forgotten how big he was in so short a time?

'There,' Lorenzo teased softly against her lips as he pressed her knees back. 'There, you see, you can… What a good, brave girl you are.'

'Yes, aren't I?' Carly agreed, groaning with satisfaction as he remained quite still, giving her every opportunity to savour the moment.

She grew bolder, and wrapped her ankles around his neck. He supported her, holding her bottom and kneading it gently as he sank slowly inside her. 'How does that feel?' he murmured, as if he didn't know.

It felt delicious. With Lorenzo nudging and rubbing places that only seemed more receptive to his touch now they had known it she could barely manage to voice a ragged sigh. He knew everything she liked as if by instinct. He took his time, moving slowly, and even withdrawing completely, so that she knew the pleasure of having him re-enter her again and again and again, and he was right about them needing every inch of the bed. He was intent on working his way steadily through all the positions suggested by her ambitious doodles until he found the ones that pleased her most.

'You greedy girl,' he murmured softly, placing one finger over her swollen mouth.

'You make that sound like a compliment,' she whispered.

'That's because it was…'

Words dissolved into sensation as Lorenzo made lazy passes with his tongue against her lips. Then he plunged deep, matching that action with another, and repeating it until her hips moved convulsively beneath him. 'I want it… I want it again,' she panted in desperation.

'And you shall have it,' Lorenzo assured her. 'When I tell you to, you'll let go with me, and it will be bigger and fiercer and stronger and scarier than anything you've ever known.'

'I believe you,' she cried, beside herself with excitement.

She opened herself as wide as she could for him, holding herself in place, offering herself; wanting it, wanting him—

'Now!' he rasped fiercely in her ear, taking her with him.

But this time he didn't stop when she quietened, but kept right on moving, slowly to begin with and then building the pace until they were working fiercely together. When the moment came it was like an explosion of pleasure, and when she cried out in amazement approaching fear he looked at her and knew he couldn't enjoy sex more than this. He needed this...

He needed her.

He shook himself round in time. What he needed was sex, pure and simple.

He needed Carly...

The words kept on like a siren call in his head. He drove it out and moved to take her again.

'Don't you ever need to rest?' she asked him.

'If you've had enough—'

'I didn't say that,' she assured him breathlessly, writhing sinuously on the bed. Putting her arms above her head, she allowed them to rest on the pillows in an attitude of wanton seduction. 'I just thought you might need to recharge your batteries.'

'I don't know which brand you use,' he said, progressing the metaphor, 'but I suggest you find yourself a more reliable supplier.'

'I think I just did.'

'Good...then why don't you shut up, relax, and let me do the work?'

That was the sort of instruction she was more than willing to take.

It was much, much later when Lorenzo suggested they take a shower together. 'And after that I suggest we indulge ourselves in a feast of chocolate and champagne.'

'I love your suggestions.'

He carried her into the bathroom and turned on the shower.

He didn't warn her about the icy water, and she shrieked as it cascaded over them.

'Not too cold for you, I hope?' Lorenzo queried dryly, and when she complained that it was he suggested a cure.

'You're insatiable,' she accused him.

'Aren't you glad?'

'I'm not complaining,' Carly assured him, 'merely offering an observation…' And now it was impossible to speak. Lorenzo had one arm braced against the wall, while the other held her bottom in place. The contrast between icy water and the heat inside her was incredible. 'You're amazing,' she groaned as he thrust into her.

'I can't fault your judgement,' he agreed.


'Shall we have macaroons in bed, as well as the champagne?' Lorenzo suggested when they were dry.

'When we've just had a shower?'

'Half the fun is getting dirty.'

'And the other half is getting clean?'

'You guessed it,' he said dryly with a grin.

He padded naked to the door, and as he turned back to her she thought again how beautiful he was.

'Or shall I just bring you chocolate and champagne?' he asked.

'You really do know the way to a woman's heart, Lorenzo.'

'As long as I can find my way to yours…'

Did he mean it? Carly turned her face into the pillow when Lorenzo left the room. Of course not! Words, like kisses, came so easily to him.

When he returned with a loaded tray she switched on her bright face. The truth was all that activity had given her quite an appetite. Lorenzo had brought champagne and chocolate, as well as a plateful of dainty multicoloured macaroons.

'From Ladurée, the best tea shop in Paris,' he told her. 'I had them flown in especially for you.'

'Of course you did.'

'No, I really did,' he insisted, 'as a reward for arranging the party—and that was before I knew how good it was going to be. Now as this is something of an experiment for me I shall expect your full concentration...'

Carly tried to hide her smile as they gazed at each other, and failed. 'You've got it,' she said. Lorenzo could do that to you—however many times she warned herself to hold back on the emotion he could obliterate common sense with a look.

Carly soon discovered that one tiny chocolate macaroon could go a long way when it was crumbled. 'Oh, that's bad,' she gasped in the throes of recovery as Lorenzo finally came up for air. 'I'm going to make sure you go down for a very long time indeed.'

'I sincerely hope you do,' he said, smiling wickedly as he reached for another macaroon.

His good intentions were shot to hell, Lorenzo accepted as Carly lay sleeping in his arms. This was supposed to be emotion-free sex, no ties, no long-term repercussions for either of them. His judgement had always been flawless in the past, and now this! He wasn't sure he would ever be able to think straight again. The only thing he was sure about was no more female pupils *ever!* The best thing he could do was find an order of monks and hope they needed legal representation—

'Lorenzo...'

She'd sensed his restlessness and woken up. He sensed her need for reassurance. Kissing her, he brought her back into his arms. 'What is it, *cara mia?*' As he stared down into her trusting face he wanted to tell her everything he had decided, but how could he do that when it would shake the foundations of her life?

'What is it?' she said, sensing the shadow passing over him.

'Not now, baby…' Drawing her close, he kissed her again. Having seen her confidence blossom while they'd been together, he couldn't bring himself to destroy it now.

# CHAPTER TWELVE

CARLY WENT INTO chambers early one morning the following week to clear up some papers before facing her final interview for the Unicorn scholarship that same afternoon. It was due to take place in front of a panel of senior lawyers chaired by Lorenzo. She hadn't really seen him since the night of the party but she felt confident, if anxious. She was going incommunicado until it was over, she decided, switching off her phone.

Now she wanted to be anywhere but here. She had never felt this apprehensive about an interview before, maybe because this time there had been vibes coming off Lorenzo, telling her however well prepared she was it wouldn't be straightforward.

She bodged the interview. And not just bodged it; by the time she left the room she was suffused in waves of uncertainty as to whether law was even the direction in which she wanted to go. Scrunching her mother's letter into a tiny ball, she braced herself to make the call.

What made it all the harder was that Lorenzo had let her down. He hadn't appeared on the panel. He hadn't even bothered to turn up and wish her luck. And okay, her phone was off, so he couldn't reach her that way, but surely he could have sent her a message somehow? She'd known all along her love affair with Lorenzo was one-sided: she was in love with Lorenzo; he was in love with sex. She'd had her eyes wide open from the start, but surely common human decency demanded some explanation for his absence?

Her mother picked up the phone, stemming her train of thought. She couldn't get a word in as her mother explained excitedly that everyone was waiting at the house for her news…

'I didn't get it—'

'Your father's poised to open the champagne—'

'Mum, please listen to me. Can't you tell him to hold the champagne?' Too late! She heard the cork pop. She waited for the cheers and the laughter to die down. 'Mum, I didn't get it…'

'What did you say?' Her mother's strangled whisper silenced the excited chatter in the background.

'I didn't get it,' Carly repeated dully, knowing how badly she'd let everyone down.

Her mother turned shrill as all the wasted dreams spilled out of her. 'How could it go so wrong?' she finished.

'It was my fault,' Carly confessed. 'I made a mess of the interview.'

'Is that all you have to say?' Her mother's voice had dropped to a driven whisper. 'Don't you care what this means to us?'

'I'm sorry… I don't know what else to say.'

'There must be a mistake,' her mother insisted, rallying. 'You'd never make a mess of the interview. You're overreacting, Carly. Why are you doing this to me?'

'I'm really sorry—can I speak to Dad?'

'You know what this is going to do to him, don't you? You read my letter, I hope! I told you about his stress levels—what do you think this is going to do to him?'

'Would it be better if I came home to break it to him myself?'

'No,' her mother shot back. 'I think you'd better stay away and lay low for a while until everything's died down.'

'Okay…' Carly bit down on her lip as the line went dead. Covering her head with her arms she let out a shuddering sigh. It was no use thinking the bottom had just fallen out of her world, even though it had; she had to pick herself up and carry on however much it hurt. And this time it really hurt. The panel had told her that her pupil master had absented himself from the panel.

Deserted a sinking ship, more like!

Lorenzo walked briskly round the luxury store with a personal shopper in tow. He knew how much winning the scholarship had meant to Carly and he was determined to soften the blow for her. He had resigned from the panel with immediate effect. He couldn't bring himself to endorse something that could never make her happy. At the end of the day he hadn't needed to say as much to the panel; they had come to the same conclusion he had—that her heart wasn't in it. She had talked a lot about her parents during her interview, apparently, but very little about herself. They assured him that although she was an outstanding candidate it wasn't what she really wanted in life, but she just hadn't seen that yet.

He'd seen her type before, Lorenzo reflected as he paid the bill and thanked the personal shopper—ambitious young lawyers on the threshold of life, following a route map laid out for them by their parents. Carly was so much more than that, she deserved so much more than that. He'd tried to ring her, but he could understand she must want some time alone.

The flat was empty when she got back. Louisa had already left for the Home Counties, and Lorenzo was…

Practically moved out!

Carly's stomach contracted painfully as she scanned his room again just to make sure. She knew his apartment was ready for him to move back into, but she hadn't realized he'd leave so abruptly—and so soon. She sat down on his bed to get over the shock of his desertion, but then she sprang up right away. She didn't want to touch, see or think about Lorenzo's bed. She didn't want to remember anything that had happened there.

The sound as she slammed the door echoed round the empty apartment, mocking her. Leaning back against a wall, she wrapped her arms around her waist and expelled a shuddering sigh. What a bright spark she'd turned out to be! She had slept with a man who held her fate in his hands, a man who didn't care, and now she'd lost the scholarship.

The scholarship… Closing her eyes as she thought about it, she relived the moment in the interview room when she had realised she didn't want it. What she had wanted was to please her parents. The scholarship meant nothing to her. What she wanted was Lorenzo and a working life where she could feel a real sense of achievement as she had after the Christmas party. Closing her eyes, she wished violently that Lorenzo were out of her head and she could identify the route she really wanted to take in life.

The clerks, the backroom boys at chambers who managed the barristers' diaries, had been kind to her when she had told them she'd flunked the interview. 'Why don't you plan some more parties?' they'd chorused. 'You're good at that.'

She had laughed with them, and then realised they were serious.

An event planner?

She shook her head, dismissing the idea at once. Her Northern night had been a one-off. Like Lorenzo.

And, like Lorenzo, never to be repeated, Carly told herself, switching on her phone.

She waited for it to initialise, and then saw that there were seven missed calls from Lorenzo. Frowning, she tried returning them, but he didn't pick up. Leave a message? She couldn't think of one—not one polite enough to write down, that was.

Determined to have it out with him face to face, she went to his new apartment where the smell of fresh paint caught her throat the moment the elevator doors opened. He hadn't been kidding about the flood; everything had been recently decorated. It must have been bad.

The elevator she'd travelled up in was private and reserved for the exclusive use of the owner of the penthouse in a prestigious block, one Lorenzo Domenico. It was all very impressive, even by Lorenzo's exacting standards. The concierge had greeted her in the lobby and had checked her credentials carefully before allowing her upstairs. Mr Domenico was out, he'd told her, but there was a mailbox outside his apartment in which she could leave her package of important documents.

Important documents? She had collected together as many A4 sheets of paper as she could find and had tied them ostentatiously with bright pink barristers' tape. The bundle was her passport up to Lorenzo's apartment, and nothing more. The hallway was impressive enough; Lorenzo's apartment, which took up most of the top floor overlooking London, must be sumptuous, Carly concluded, ringing the bell.

He wasn't in. She'd known that right away; his energy was missing.

She looked around as she waited, uncertain as to what to do next. For all its luxury the entrance to Lorenzo's palace lacked the patina of a home. It was just a new apartment in a new apartment block. There were no cooking aromas seeping under the door to suggest the gorgeous Italian-American who loved to cook, no scratches or stains, no finger smudges on the walls, everything was pristine, and completely soulless. Quite suddenly she missed the trappings of a home, somewhere filled with love and warmth. Love and warmth, she mused, those were the elusive magic ingredients, like the seasoning in Lorenzo's sauce. But perhaps this was enough for him, this gilded cage. Men measured success in terms of money and possessions, while women lusted after nests to feather, homes to clutter with memories…

Hefting the papers she'd brought with her into the waste shoot, she returned to Lorenzo's mailbox and posted the small gift-wrapped parcel she had bought for him before everything went wrong. She didn't want it hanging around and she couldn't bring herself to throw it away. It wasn't much in the monetary sense, even though she thought it special, and she would have bought her pupil master something for Christmas anyway, she had managed to persuade herself.

Lifting her chin, she started back to her flat. Bypassing the elevator she chose the stairs. Why hurry when she had almost two weeks to kill before the courts reconvened?

Lorenzo hit the button to the top floor. He considered an elevator essential. Shopping had to reach the penthouse somehow, and experience had taught him that if he didn't have a fast, reliable means of reaching the top floor, any grocery service he selected would complain.

The smell of newness hit him the moment he opened the front door. Tossing his jacket aside, he opened all the windows. He had thought about ordering flowers, and then realised it would have to wait until after Christmas. The best he could do for now was brew coffee and start cooking.

There was only one thing, one person, missing: his sparring partner, Carly Tate. He missed their verbal jousts as well as their tangles in the bedroom. But he wouldn't chase. He knew she'd probably be angry and she needed time to consider the suggestions he'd made in his letter. She might not take them well at first; she might not take them well ever, but he'd had to say what was on his mind.

She turned back when she was halfway home. She wasn't going to take this on the chin. She was fed up with doing that. Lorenzo couldn't just walk out on her. If she put this down to experience she would never forgive herself. She would sit on his doorstep if she had to and wait until he got back. A lack of self-confidence didn't mean you were a coward; it just meant you had to work harder at persuading yourself that a man hadn't bought you a fabulous dress as incentive to have sex with him.

And who needed an incentive to sleep with Lorenzo?

So had it been pay-off time?

No. Lorenzo had far more style than that.

Another woman, then? Madeline flashed into her mind.

The little green devils were always the hardest to deal with, but in all honesty she couldn't remember Lorenzo looking at Madeline that way. Maybe that was because she couldn't bear to think about him and Madeline after…

After what? Carly asked herself impatiently. Had there ever been anything between them except sex?

'Carly…' Madeline stood back in Lorenzo's hallway. 'This is a surprise!'

Not half as much for Madeline as it was for her, Carly thought angrily. Well, if she was about to make a bigger fool of herself than ever she might as well get on with it. 'Is he in?'

Waving a champagne flute, Madeline backed deeper into

Lorenzo's apartment. 'He's cooking in the kitchen. Shall I call him?'

Madeline was definitely weaving, Carly decided, narrowing her eyes. So they'd been drinking together. Everything inside her shrivelled into dust and then it exploded into cold, hard fury. Cooking was Lorenzo's preferred path to seduction; he'd made no secret of it. She should have known he wouldn't be without a bed-mate for long. And Madeline was the perfect choice—another lawyer, glamorous, clever, witty, and even now, slightly drunk, she looked amazing.

Absolutely amazing.

While she looked a fright, Carly realised, feeling her spirit drain away as she caught sight of herself in a mirror. She had really outdone herself today. She was wearing the usual thrift-shop suit, and now she saw she'd spilled something down it. And she'd gone into the interview looking like that? She grimaced. It was so humiliating. Nothing, *nothing* could be worse than this—

'I got the scholarship,' Madeline announced. 'Did you hear?'

'You…' Pressing her lips together, Carly made her head move up and down. 'That's such great news. I'm really pleased for you.' And she was, strangely, but her nose was stinging, really hurting, in the way noses did when tears were threatening.

She took the opportunity to escape when Madeline turned around to call Lorenzo from the kitchen. She didn't need anyone to explain to her what was happening here, though as she fled she heard Lorenzo say something she didn't catch. She did hear Madeline's reply.

'Oh, it was nothing important, and they've gone now…'

Make that no one important, and Madeline had got it right, Carly thought, clutching the cold stone handrail on the bridge.

The river Thames was moving slowly to the sea, a dull, grey dish-rag of a river, reflecting a sullen sky. It perfectly mirrored her mood. She was transfixed by the rolling water, and by the tears dripping off the end of her nose into it. She could see now that she had been too complacent about everything; too naïve, too fat—

'Carly?'

'Lorenzo!' She bridled and backed away. 'What are you doing here?'

'Is this your private bridge?'

She glared at him.

'What are you doing here, Carly? Not planning a swim, I hope?'

Emotions churned inside her as she looked at him. She wanted to kill him. She wanted to launch herself into his arms... And kill him.

'I saw you from the window. I couldn't believe it was you. Where on earth have you been?'

'Where have *I* been?' Anger ripped through her, made all the more intense by the realisation that she had gone to pieces right under his balcony—she couldn't even get that right.

'You're coming with me,' he said. 'You look frozen.'

He was right about one thing: she was ice inside, and not about to thaw any time soon. 'I'm not coming back with you.' Not while Madeline was there!

'Did I say you had a choice?'

And have Madeline stare at her pityingly the whole time? It just wasn't going to happen. 'Lorenzo! Let go of me.'

'I have a sauce on the go, and woe betide you if it burns.'

She struggled furiously, and then stopped. If she went with him she could have her say, and, Madeline or no Madeline, she was going to let him have it with both barrels.

# CHAPTER THIRTEEN

STANDING WITH HIS pleasure-giving hands planted on his ecstasy-dealing hips, Lorenzo glanced round his new apartment with pride. 'Well,' he said to Carly. 'What do you think?'

What did she think? She could smell Madeline's perfume! Still tender from his incredible love-making, she was still stinging from his vanishing act, and on the edge of rage. What threw her a little was the warmth and enthusiasm in Lorenzo's eyes where she failed to detect the slightest hint of guilt. She glanced round suspiciously. The apartment was even more magnificent than she had imagined, with stripped pine floors, cream walls, and splashes of colour provided by well-chosen modern art. There was a state-of-the-art sound system in one corner, and all the other technical gizmos she might have expected a man like Lorenzo to own. All in all it was fabulous: light, airy, and mostly open plan—so little chance for anyone to hide.

'What?' Lorenzo said, watching her.

'Where's your friend?' Carly tipped her chin at an aggressive angle.

'My friend?' Lorenzo paused for a moment and then enlightenment struck him. 'You mean Madeline?'

'This isn't funny, Lorenzo,' Carly snapped, seeing the suspicion of a smile hovering round his mouth. 'Where is she? In your bed?'

This was answered with a quizzical look. Refusing to be deterred, she set off on her hunt. Flinging open the first door, she peered inside. The bedroom was immaculate, and looked as if it had been put together by an interior designer. She couldn't imagine Lorenzo arranging the fabulous buttermilk suede cushions with such precision. Behind the next door she found a broom cupboard. Slamming it, she wheeled around.

'Why do I get the feeling you're not happy with me?' Lorenzo said.

He looked so gorgeous standing there she almost relented. Almost. 'Why do *I* get the feeling your sauce is burning?'

'What?' He whirled around and rushed to pull the pan off the cooker, shaking his hand and cursing after he did so.

'Too hot for you, Lorenzo?' Carly demanded pointedly.

Turning to face her, he granted her an ironic look.

Behind the next door she found the most sumptuous bathroom she had ever seen...all marble and glass with steel fittings and a bath big enough for two...

'I'd happily show you round,' Lorenzo offered.

She paused with her hand on the next door handle.

'Just a thought,' he murmured. 'Oh, and by the way, are you staying for supper?'

'You've got a nerve,' Carly said, turning. Her throat dried. If only she'd had some mental armour to deal with the way her body responded to Lorenzo. He was standing in the open-plan kitchen with his hands on his hips, looking magnificent. His jeans moulded every inch of his impressive lower body, and with such brazen accuracy her cheeks burned. His sleeves were rolled up, revealing the muscles on his arms. He was seriously good-looking, as well as a serious distraction.

Carly dragged her thoughts back to the reason for her

visit. 'Where were you today?' Disappointment and distress rang in her voice, but it was too late to stop now. 'Were you too busy coaching Madeline on scholarship technique to have time for me? I bet you found time to attend her interview—'

'Are you jealous of Madeline?'

'Don't be so ridiculous! And don't you dare try to turn this round on me. You should have been there. You're the chairman of the scholarship committee, and my pupil master—'

'Which is a good enough reason for me to step out, don't you think?' Lorenzo cut in calmly.

'No, I don't!' But even as she raged at him her sensible self insisted he was right. She shook her head and when she spoke again her voice was husky. 'If you felt that our relationship affected things why didn't you warn me sooner?'

'Because you were incommunicado,' Lorenzo reminded her. 'Because no one knew where you were.'

'But didn't you think I'd want to see you before I went in?' As her voice broke she turned away.

'I've had enough of this,' Lorenzo said. Crossing the room, he seized hold of her. 'Look at me, Carly...'

He had never wanted to kiss a woman so much in his life. When Carly was aroused she was magnificent. Her cheeks were flushed, her lips were crimson, and the tip of her nose with its sprinkling of freckles had turned white in her fury. Her wild Celtic hair rose above her shoulders like an inferno painted in red and gold, and yet coppery baby fronds were pressed to her brow. It was more than humankind, or at least he, could withstand—

'Get off me, Lorenzo, I'm warning you!'

Her slap began at her knees, and travelled like a comet to his chin, by which time her tiny hand had turned into a fist. He blessed his lightning reflexes. Catching hold of her wrist just as her hand connected with his face, he snatched her other wrist too, just to be on the safe side. But then he found it impossible to stop laughing, which on reflection was a mistake. She had taken some of his fashion advice on board, including how good she looked in stiletto heels. He cursed violently when she stamped down hard on his toe. 'God save me from women and from redheads in particular! You don't need a mentor, you need a keeper with a whip—'

But their struggles were too enjoyable to come even close to anger, and as she writhed against him, making the little sounds of frustration he knew so well, he could only thank God she'd found emotion, and wasn't afraid of showing it. He guessed she had spent her whole life listening to other people emote while she got on quietly with her work. Maybe his family went too far the other way, but at least they had never been afraid of expressing their feelings. When he let her go she said, 'I'm sorry... I don't know what came over me—'

'Passion,' he suggested. 'Maybe that came over you. Anyway, forget it.'

Forget it while Lorenzo stood nursing his chin? She was mortified and ashamed of herself. She had never resorted to violence, and never would again. But he was right; there was a lot bottled up inside her, and she hadn't even realised how much up to now. That was one thing Lorenzo understood about her; he knew how to free the stopper that kept all the feelings in.

She looked at him. They had invoked a world of passion; an electric storm of passion. She had always believed herself to be one of the dullest people alive, but that was before she started seeing herself through Lorenzo's eyes. Maybe there was hope for her after all...

'Madeline's not here,' Lorenzo confirmed. 'She came

round to share her news, and I opened a bottle of champagne. It seemed the decent thing to do. Then she left. She was already pretty merry by the time she arrived.'

It made sense, Carly admitted to herself. Her gaze strayed, as it always did, to Lorenzo's socks: the barometer of his mood. They were green, with angry red polka dots, which couldn't have been more appropriate for the way she was feeling, for a change.

'You haven't read my letter, have you?' he said.

'Your letter?' She looked up.

'You didn't go back and check your cubby-hole after the interview?'

She gave a shrug. 'I didn't exactly feel like hanging around.'

'But you collected up your stuff.' He glanced at the heap of things she'd brought with her from chambers.

'Of course I did. It's the Christmas recess. But I didn't look at it. The clerks packed it all up for me—'

'So you don't know that I've resigned from the scholar-ship committee?'

'What?' she said softly. 'Why would you do that?'

'Don't you know?'

Everything went very still. 'No…'

'Because you're more important to me than any seat on a board. Don't ask me why,' he added dryly before she could go starry-eyed.

'What exactly are you saying, Lorenzo?'

'I got out before the scandal broke.'

'What scandal?'

'This one.' He dragged her close. 'I'm not so sure there would have been a scandal,' he said, looking down at her, 'but I wasn't taking any chances, and it's you I care about. You and your future, Carly Tate. I want what's right for you—'

'And you think you're going to determine my future now?'

With an angry cry she pushed him away. She'd had enough of people deciding what she should do. But when Lorenzo looked at her as if to say it was her decision—her life, her career, something only she must decide—her pummelling fists softened to searching hands, and a jolt of pure longing drew a sound from her throat.

He brought her back into his arms then and held her firmly the way she liked. His lips were cunning as they prepared the way for his tongue, and the intrusion, the sudden penetration, the taste, the strength and the scent of him all combined as they always did to steal her strength away. Lucky for her he was so strong. He took her weight easily with the smallest adjustment of his powerful frame, and all the while he kept on kissing her deeply and intimately, until her nipples grew painfully tender again, and she was drowning in waves of needing him.

'*Santo Dio!* I've missed you,' he murmured.

Should she swim against the tide of arousal, or should she sink beneath it and drown? 'Just don't treat me like a child, Lorenzo. You can't pick me up and put me down again when it suits you.'

'Who said anything about putting you down?'

'I needed you, Lorenzo. I needed your support—'

'I was moving into my new apartment. I left you a letter to explain…' He sighed. 'And I was shopping.'

'Shopping?' Now she was incensed.

'Christmas?' he reminded her. 'I thought you would have read about my decision regarding the committee. I thought you needed time. I guessed you would be going home to your family for Christmas.'

That clearly wasn't on the cards, he guessed, judging by the look on her face, but as he reached out to her she thrust him away again. 'What am I going to do with you?' he demanded with frustration. They were facing each other like warring tigers. He hadn't felt this way since…ever, he guessed.

'Next time you kiss a woman, kiss her because you mean it, Lorenzo! Because you want to! Because you can't stop yourself.'

The irony wasn't lost on him. He had never wanted to kiss a woman more, but he blamed himself for upsetting her even though he suspected he wasn't aware of the cause of half of it. There was so much going on inside her head he didn't know about. 'Why don't you tell me what's really upset you?'

'You…and other things.' She gave him a cold stare that warned of her feelings switching off.

With a sound of frustration he jutted out his chin. 'Okay, if it makes you feel better, punch me. Go on,' he urged, angling his head to make it easy for her. 'Why hold back now?'

She stared at him tensely for a moment, and then she made a little noise—not quite a laugh, but getting there.

'You're impossible!' she flung at him, shaking her head.

'And you're perfectly reasonable,' he said back. 'Now let's get real. I've got a bottle of Krug open waiting for someone to take a slug out of it. Interested?'

She hesitated and then followed him as he turned to the kitchen.

Climbing up on one of the bar stools, she waited in silence while he found some glasses and poured the champagne. 'Cheers!' he said softly, clinking glasses with her.

'Happy Christmas, Lorenzo…' She wouldn't look at him.

'So, what plans have you made?' he prompted.

Thanks to the revolving chairs and the way she'd angled herself he couldn't see her face, but then he saw her shoulders shaking and swung her round. He stopped her sobbing the only way he knew, with a kiss, and with his arms binding her close so she would know how it felt to be safe. 'You taste salty,' he said, pulling back so he could smile against her mouth.

'So do you,' she said with a little laugh that made his heart swell.

'Well, are you going to tell me what's wrong, or not?' He tipped her chin, giving her nowhere to look but in his eyes.

'My mother doesn't want me home.' She tossed the words off as if they were of no importance to her; she even managed the approximation of a smile.

'She doesn't want you home?' he repeated incredulously.

'That's right. She said it would be better if I left things to calm down a bit after the scholarship fiasco.'

He was raging inside. What sort of family made a child feel that it couldn't come home unless it brought a prize? It put a price on love, and it seemed to him Carly could never meet that price however hard she worked.

'I didn't think it would hurt so much,' she admitted with a frankness that brought them closer.

Lifting her face, she stared him right in the eyes as if to say she was all right now. He didn't believe her for a minute. 'So, what shall we do about it?' he said.

'We?'

'Well, *I* don't want to be on my own for Christmas.' He had meant to make it easier for her, but the last thing he wanted happened—more tears, and this time they were tears of humiliation.

'You don't have to be kind to me, Lorenzo.'

'Kind?' He gave her one of his looks. 'Me?'

'Stop it. You know what I mean. I'll be fine—'

'I don't *have* to do anything, but if I want to…'

Lorenzo would do exactly as he pleased, Carly thought, silently finishing the sentence for him. But she didn't want to be anyone's charity case, and she wasn't sure how long she could keep this up, this casual pretence that sex was fun, kissing was fun, eating together was fun, when there was so much love inside her scorching a trail for him through her heart.

# CHAPTER FOURTEEN

'I'VE COME TO a decision,' Carly told Lorenzo. 'I'd like to be alone for a few days. I need to sort out my head. I need to learn how to stand on my own two feet.'

'You've been doing that all your life, as far as I can tell. You're strong, Carly. Why can't you see that?'

'I'll admit to being determined and driven, but I've always walked in the direction someone else has pointed me. What I want now is time to work out where I want to go.'

'You'd consider quitting law?' His eyes narrowed. He wasn't going to tell her what to do, though it was so obvious, at least to him. The last thing she needed was someone else pulling her strings.

'I haven't made any decisions yet. I thought the scholarship was what I wanted, and that it would be an end in itself, but I was wrong, and now I need a new goal.'

'How about personal happiness?' he suggested. He was growing impatient with her inability to see how easy it was to throw a life away on someone else's aspirations. 'Your parents will get over this—'

'You don't know them.'

And, increasingly, he didn't want to. 'You'll do lots of things to make them proud.'

'I understand why they're disappointed,' she said. 'They gave up so much for me. They're entitled—'

'Parents aren't entitled to live their children's lives for them,' he cut across her. 'They can only love them, and equip them for the world as best they can—'

'That's your way of thinking, Lorenzo, not mine—'

'But it's your life—'

'And I'm not sure what my life is right now, so please—'

'I won't stop you going,' he said as she glanced towards the door. He eased away from the cabinets to let her get by him. 'If you need me you know where I am.'

An expression crossed her face that told him she was surprised and hurt he could just back off like that. His intention had been to give her space, but maybe space wasn't what she needed.

'Enjoy your supper,' she said.

It was a crossroads, a turning point in his life. She let herself out of the front door while the energy they had created was still springing round him. He wasn't about to wait around for it to fade. Snatching up his jacket, he went after her.

The moment she opened the front door of her flat he knew she'd been crying. 'Go wash your face. I'm taking you out,' he said.

She stared at him blankly, and then to his absolute relief she opened the door fully, murmuring, 'Come in…'

He wanted to take her in his arms straight away. She was so vulnerable, he would do anything to heal the hurt inside her, but he held back, respecting her desire to find the path she wanted by herself.

Thankfully, she rallied quickly, the way he'd hoped she would. 'Where are you taking me?' she said after a protracted tidying-up session in her bedroom.

'That's my surprise.'

'But it's Christmas Eve,' she reminded him. 'Won't everywhere be too busy for us to find a table?'

'It will be fine,' he reassured her. 'Trust me.'

She gave him an ironic look. 'You'd better tell me if I'm dressed appropriately?'

If she'd been wearing a dustbin liner tied with string she'd have looked just as beautiful to him.

'No comment?' She gave a twirl.

The ice-blue sweater against her ivory skin made her look ethereal, beautiful. He had only one suggestion. 'Let your hair down…'

Reaching up, she removed the tortoiseshell pin holding it, and the whole glittering cascade fell and bounced around her shoulders.

'Perfect. Do you have a warm jacket?'

'How warm do I need to be?'

'No clues,' he said. 'You're too good a lawyer. If I'm not careful you'll have the whole story out of me before I'm ready for you to know.'

The smile on her face was the only reward he wanted.


Her face turned ashen when she realised where they were going.

'You said nothing when I asked if you trusted me,' he reminded her.

'Yes, I know, but I *hate* flying.'

'I'll ask you again—do you trust me?'

She gulped and stared up the steps of the small aeroplane. 'Are you the pilot?'

He laughed. 'Unless you'd like to take a turn?'

'No! I just—'

'What you'll just do,' he said, 'is sit in a very comfortable seat, reading a selection of magazines, while sipping champagne and nibbling some delicious snacks.'

'I will?' she said uncertainly.

'You will.'

'Will it be a long fright…flight?'

'Quite a short one, actually,' he soothed, escorting her up the steps. 'And now, if you will excuse me, I have a plane to fly…'

Lorenzo must be taking her to Italy, Carly guessed as they took off. She knew he had family there. Or perhaps a Christmas ski trip. But if that were true, why hadn't he suggested she pack even warmer clothes?

It was no use worrying about it now she was buckled into her seat. She just had to accept they were heading somewhere—

And landing already?

Not Italy, then.

So where?

Peering out of the window told her nothing. One runway looked much like another in the dark.

'Did you enjoy the flight?' Lorenzo said, ducking his head as he came back into the cabin to collect her. 'I told you it wouldn't be long.'

'So where are we?'

'That's my surprise.'

As they stepped outside the aircraft and the sleet hit her in the face she read the sign.

'I told you it would be a surprise, didn't I?'

But not a good one, Carly thought in silence.

Linking arms with her, Lorenzo hurried her across the tarmac towards a waiting limousine. 'I'm taking you home,' he said as if that should please her. 'Families should be together at Christmas. It's a time for reconciliation, and for love…'

It wasn't much of a village, though she was right; it was in the middle of nowhere. He wasn't sure what he'd been expecting, but this wasn't it. Carly's talk of an English village had conjured up an impression in his head of a picture-perfect place like something you might find on the front of a greeting card. This was more like a village some local planning team had come up with fast on a Friday afternoon. It had been built without thought for the eventual inhabitants' convenience, either side of a busy main road. He could see why Carly would want to escape; it was harder to understand why anyone would want to settle there in the first place.

He turned to smile reassurance at her, having noticed how quiet she had become. He had hoped this trip back home would give him the answers she wouldn't, but now he was beginning to wish he'd had more patience and had waited until she was ready to tell him.

When the limousine had halted he helped her out. He was using a driver because he had wanted to sit with her, but she'd put acres between them on the back seat. She was going home, he thought, frowning inwardly. Shouldn't that have been a cause for celebration? Maybe those answers he was looking for were right here.

He stood close to her as she rang the front door bell. She had nodded when he had asked her if she was okay, but the set of her shoulders told him something different. He wanted to tell her it would be fine, and that he was there for her, but suddenly even he wasn't so sure he could make it right. For a start, it was up to Carly to decide how much or how little she wanted to tell her parents about them...

The door was opened by a thin, pinched-face woman who looked as if she sucked lemons for a treat.

'Mum!'

The excitement in Carly's voice contrasted starkly with the way the older woman flinched.

'Mrs Tate,' he said, extending his hand formally. His hope

had been to distract Carly so she wouldn't notice her mother's reaction to her. The calculation in Mrs Tate's eyes as she turned her attention to him was a real eye-opener.

'This is Lorenzo, Mother,' Carly said, blissfully un-aware, he sincerely hoped, of the undercurrents running from the house to the step. 'Lorenzo Domenico…my pupil master in chambers?'

Mrs Tate stood back to take a proper look at him. 'To what do we owe this honour?' she said.

'Can we come in?' Carly prompted with an edge of anxiety in her voice.

'Of course you can,' her mother said, standing back. 'What are you waiting for?'

A welcome, maybe, he thought.

Once inside they walked down a narrow hallway and into an impressively neat sitting room. An older man was sitting in an easy chair watching football on the television. He looked weary, and barely glanced up, though judging by his slippers he had little enough cause for exhaustion.

'Mr Tate?' It was a relief when the man turned to look at him, and even more of a relief to see his gaze brighten.

'Yes, that's me,' he said, a little awkwardly, as if he were unused to being in the spotlight. Then his face transformed, and he sprang up. 'Carly!' he said, going to her.

'Dad!'

It was touching to see them embrace; it brought some warmth into the chilly atmosphere.

'You've put on weight, Carly.' Her mother's voice shattered the touching tableau. 'You need to watch that,' she said.

Carly's cheeks reddened, and her father returned mildly to his seat.

'My other daughter will be back soon.'

He realised Mrs Tate was addressing him, and speaking as if she expected him to be riveted by this piece of information.

'Olivia,' she prompted, as if news of her younger daughter had travelled far and wide. 'The beautiful sister,' she added, in case he was in any doubt.

'Oh?' He smiled pleasantly, after shooting a glance at Carly. He had to remember they were discussing her sister, but in his opinion there was no one more beautiful than Carly.

Olivia chose that very moment to breeze in, in a flurry of cold air and childish perfume.

'Carly!' she exclaimed as if all her Christmases had come at once. Ignoring everyone else in the room, Olivia threw her arms around her sister and danced about with her. She was deaf to her mother's pleading that if she didn't stop she might break something.

From what he could see there was already a litter of broken hearts in the room.

'Carly, come with me.'

His jaw worked with annoyance as her mother uttered this instruction. She had broken father and daughter apart, and now she was doing the same to her two daughters. What was wrong with the woman? He held back from comment; his up-bringing wouldn't allow him to countermand an instruction from Carly's mother in her own home. He would just have to fix the damage later.

'Are you pregnant?'

Carly's eyes widened. Her mother had barricaded them in the tiny kitchen, and now she stood barring the only escape route with her back firmly planted against the door.

'Why do you ask?' If she was pregnant, she would need her mother's support, surely?

'Because I can't think of a single reason why a man like

that pupil master of yours would fly you up here in a private jet just to see us.' Her mother's thin lips pursed as she waited for a response.

'He said it was Christmas, a time for families to be together.'

'That's never bothered you in the past.'

'I only ever missed one Christmas at home, and that was when I was on a gap year from university—'

'But you didn't fly back then, did you?'

'You know I didn't. I was in India. I'm sorry. I didn't realise…I should have been here—'

'Yes, you should,' her mother said impatiently, frowning. 'So *are* you pregnant?'

She had been brought up to tell the truth, and everyone knew condoms failed, and people got pregnant all the time. 'I don't know…' Carly met her mother's cold gaze steadily. They could both hear Lorenzo, his deep voice providing a melodious counterpoint to Olivia's delighted laughter.

'Well,' her mother said with a knowing air. 'You needn't think a man like that's going to marry you…' Glancing towards the door, she made it clear whom she considered the more suitable candidate to be. 'If he has got you pregnant the best you can hope for is a pay-off. Any mistress to a man like that would have to be—'

'Beautiful, Mother?' Carly cut in. 'Stylish? Content to live in the lap of luxury provided by Lorenzo? We both know I don't fit any of those categories, don't we?'

'Don't turn your bitterness and disappointment on me,' her mother shot back. 'If you're pregnant, have an abortion.'

The moment's silence rang on and on.

'Don't look so scandalised,' Carly's mother insisted. 'You've always been the practical member of the family. If there's a problem there's a solution—wasn't that what you always used to say to me?'

Carly flinched. She hadn't realised that so much bitterness had built up over the years. It might be too late, but she had to try one last time. 'You gave up so much for me.'

'Yes, I did,' her mother said. 'But that's behind us now.'

Was it? Would it ever be behind them? No, Carly thought, it was here with them now in the tiny kitchen like a malign force—every penny spent, every missed hair appointment that had gone to provide for some expensive textbook. And she hadn't seen it. Had she been too self-absorbed to see it? She had—and this was the price she had to pay. 'If I am pregnant you wouldn't really want me to abort your grand-child, would you?' Her throat constricted as she waited for her mother to answer.

'Make up your own mind,' her mother said dismissively. 'You never listen to me anyway. I just hope you're not on your way to making a bigger fool of yourself than usual.'

As Lorenzo's laughter sounded from the other room Mrs Tate moved away from the door. 'You'd better go back in if you're to have the slightest hope of hanging on to him.'

Blinded by tears, Carly blundered through the door.

'Carly…'

Lorenzo got to his feet the moment she entered the room. He was smiling, and there was such a change in the atmos-phere after the frost in the kitchen it took her a moment to adapt. The small sitting room was unusually full of life. Her father had even switched off the television. But as Lorenzo stepped forward to take hold of her hands she got the horrible feeling he was about to make an announcement. She was so disorientated and distressed after the talk with her mother she managed to persuade herself that Lorenzo wanted to comfort her when he explained that he was going to marry her sister. It was the only thing that made sense; they were both so beautiful. She could even hear him saying it: 'Mr and Mrs

Tate, I have been struck by a thunderbolt and have no alternative other than to ask for the hand of your daughter Olivia—'

'Carly?' Lorenzo said, dipping his head to stare her in the eyes. 'Where are you now?'

In the middle of a nightmare. Blinking, she refocused. Her mother and father had returned to their usual places either side of the fire. Her mother sat on the edge of her easy chair, while her father sat well back, as if bracing himself for confrontation. Olivia sat in silence on the sofa staring up at her.

For the first time in her life she couldn't bring herself to meet her sister's gaze. This time it wasn't a question of yielding a favourite toy, or the last chocolate in the box, it was the threat of losing the man she loved.

The man at the centre of the drama stood in front of her, making the tiny sitting room seem claustrophobic. Whatever had happened, whatever misunderstandings there had been between them, Lorenzo was the only person who made sense of her life. He was the direction she wanted to take; she just hadn't realised it before. And now it was too late.

# CHAPTER FIFTEEN

'CARLY'S OVERWHELMED at returning home,' Lorenzo said to explain her silence. 'I'm glad you two had time together,' he told her mother, but something in his eyes left Mrs Tate in no doubt that he knew what she had done.

The tension that followed was suddenly too much for Carly, and she bolted for the stairs. She was halfway up them before she remembered she didn't have a room in the house any longer. Fortunately, Olivia was right behind her.

'My room,' Livvie said. 'Left at the top of the stairs.'

'My old room...' Carly smiled as she looked around. Plain fabrics had been replaced by chintz, and there was lace at the window.

'It's a bit frilly for you,' Livvie said, reading her sister's thoughts. 'I hope you don't object to my taking it over, only it was bigger than mine. You don't mind, do you, Carly?'

'No, of course I don't mind. You get the rooftops...' Carly turned to stare out of the window at a view she knew so well. She used to imagine all the hidden miles rolling back behind the chimney pots...

'I thought I'd better take the bigger room since it looks like I'm stuck here for life.'

Carly turned to look at her sister. Olivia had flopped down

on the bed. 'You're not stuck here any more than I was. Not unless you want to be, Livvie.'

'I've missed you…' Livvie patted the bed by her side.

'And I've missed you…' They hugged.

'So, is this Lorenzo special?'

There could be no secrets between sisters as close as they were, Carly realised. 'Lorenzo?' She gave a dry laugh. 'Anyone can see Lorenzo's special—far too special for me.'

'No one's too special for you,' Livvie argued hotly. 'And why would he bring you all this way if he didn't care for you?'

'His good deed for the year, maybe.'

'Carly, what's happened to you? You never used to be so cynical.'

'I never used to be much of anything, unless being a bookworm counts—'

'That's not true!' Livvie exclaimed with exasperation. 'You've always been the most wonderful sister to me. You're kind and loyal and brave. And you had the courage to escape.'

'You have that same courage. We're sisters. We're out of the same egg.'

'The same bitter old husk, don't you mean?'

'Livvie… Don't say that about Mother. She's done her best. But it's never enough, can't you see? She never quite managed to catch up with those wealthy friends of hers.'

'Then she should get herself some real friends,' Olivia argued fiercely.

By the time the two girls returned to the sitting room Lorenzo seemed to have worked magic. He had certainly put their parents at ease.

The atmosphere could hardly remain tense while Lorenzo was around, Carly reflected, but she wasn't ready for her mother's next remark.

'Why don't you stay over?' her mother invited. 'We've got two spare rooms now Carly's gone. Of course,' she hurried to explain, 'Christmas Day is a simple affair in the Tate household, and not up to your usual standards—just lunch at the golf club, followed by a few drinks. If I make a call now I'm sure they'll put on a couple of extra places.' Her eyes were already gleaming at the thought of introducing Lorenzo round.

'How kind of you, Mrs Tate,' Lorenzo said politely. 'I'd love nothing more, but I must admit I've made other plans for your daughter.'

As her mother tensed Carly felt sure the whole world was holding a collective breath.

'Are you ready, Carly?' he said, turning to her.

Why had she ever doubted him? Why had she ever doubted Livvie? Throwing her arms around Livvie's neck, she hugged her tight, begging her softly, 'Come and see me soon.'

'I will,' Livvie assured her in the same passionate undertone.

Lorenzo was quiet on the drive back to the airport and Carly's cheeks were burning as she imagined what he must be thinking. Her family home was shabby and parochial in comparison to his elegant city centre penthouse. She'd never seen her childhood home through a visitor's eyes before, never felt the tensions that existed between her mother and father to this extent.

The saddest thing was that she could remember a time when love was king, and possessions, like people's position in life, took second place. But that had been a long time ago, and seemed now almost like a dream that had never existed outside her imagination.

He was quiet because he was thinking about the suburban house they'd just left. In so many respects it was superior to the chaotic family home where he'd been brought up, but in the ways that mattered Carly's family home was impoverished. There were many more ways that cruelty could be dealt than in a blow, and Carly had done well to get away and forge a life for herself. He was so proud of her; her strength of character shone through everything he'd seen today.

'Lorenzo, I'm so sorry—'

'Sorry? For what?'

'I would have thought that was obvious.' She met his gaze fearlessly as she always did.

'Not to me.' He squeezed her hand.

'You don't have to be kind,' she insisted, pulling away. 'I know what you were trying to do back there.'

'Do you?' He smiled as he saw her cheeks pink up. 'You have no idea,' he assured her. Dragging her close, he brushed the tears from her cheeks with his thumb pads and then he kissed her and kept on kissing her until she believed him.

It was too late and too stormy to fly back to London, and so Lorenzo asked the chauffeur to take them to the nearest luxury hotel that had a room to spare.

'On Christmas Eve in Manchester?' Carly said, turning to look at him in surprise.

Her eyes were tear-stained and he knew she was still hurting. The damage her mother had done wasn't something that could be eradicated in a few hours; it would take a lot more time than that. Frustration was gnawing away inside him because he'd failed to shield her from the hurt. He wanted to reach inside her and wrench it out. He wanted to take her in his arms and reassure her and kiss that look off her face. He wanted to hold her hand and take her into a park where they could fool around and feed the ducks, and she would laugh. She didn't laugh much, and now he knew why.

'So what did you think of my family?' she asked him.

'I liked your sister.' He smiled as he spoke. What was not to like? Livvie was childlike and eager to please, and almost as wounded as Carly in her way.

'She's very pretty, isn't she?'

His brows drew together as he thought about it. Olivia was certainly a pleasure to look at in the same way he might enjoy looking at an interesting work of art, but did she move him? Did she make him feel like Carly made him feel? Not in a million years. He felt warm towards Olivia because of the way Olivia felt about her sister, and that was it. 'She's not as beautiful as you,' he said, holding Carly's gaze. And then he kissed her. She made him feel so good. She was beautiful inside and out. Maybe Olivia was too, but he had no interest in finding out. He'd found the woman he wanted.

'And my father?'

'Henpecked,' he said bluntly, pulling back to answer her as she deserved. 'Though an interesting man with an interesting story to tell about his life and his hobbies.'

'Do you really think so?' She looked astounded.

'Yes, I do. Did you know, for instance, that he builds model airplanes in his shed?'

'No,' Carly said with amazement. 'I only hope mother doesn't put a stop to it. I can't imagine she'd like all that dust and glue flying about—'

'Talking of flying,' he interrupted, 'I've promised to take your father up with me one day.' As he spoke his jaw firmed in a way that told her he would do that regardless of what anyone else thought about the idea.

'And my mother?' she asked him softly, staring down at her hands.

'Your mother is tense and anxious like a lot of people are

when they encounter something new, or something beyond their control.'

She seemed relieved he hadn't gone on the attack. 'Taking my father flying is certainly that!'

'She loves him in her way, and I think she'll worry about him in the same way she worries about you.'

She made a dismissive sound at that. 'Don't get carried away, Lorenzo. I know you're good with words, but we're not in court now. I don't mind. You can tell me exactly what you think.'

But she would mind. Whatever Mrs Tate was like she was Carly's mother. 'Your mother might relax more if she trusted her children to get on with their lives,' he said carefully. 'She doesn't need to find a husband for Olivia or a career for you. You're both capable of doing that for yourselves.'

'Do you think Olivia should have a husband?'

There was an edge in her voice.

'It's up to Olivia. I think she should start by finding some work outside the home she cares about, and then she would feel liberated.'

'And me?'

'A home life outside your work?' he suggested dryly.

'How profound you've become, Signor Domenico,' she mocked him.

'Carly, I haven't changed.' He touched her hand. 'And now...I think we've arrived.' He gazed out of the tinted window as the limousine slowed to a halt.

As Lorenzo came round to her side of the car Carly couldn't help wondering how far he would go to give all those things he'd talked about for Olivia and for her a helping hand. She pushed her concerns to one side as he gave the driver a generous tip and then asked the man to pick them up early the next morning.

'Early?' The word slipped out before she could stop herself.

'Was that a complaint?' Lorenzo challenged softly, taking hold of her hand.

'Lorenzo, this is fabulous…'

He had brought her to an exquisitely restored Georgian manor house deep in the Cheshire countryside. It was an award-winning hotel, Carly learned from reading one of their embossed cards while Lorenzo checked them in. The village was chocolate-box picture-perfect, the house lovely, and their welcome warm and unpretentious. It was very Lorenzo, she concluded.

'Only the best is good enough for you, *bella signorina*,' he said, gesturing towards the staircase.

The best turned out to be a sumptuous suite with a vast four-poster bed in the centre of the bedroom. The bed was dressed with ivory silk, and there was every conceivable aid to comfort in the room. There was also a space-age bathroom down the tiny hallway full of luxury products that could easily tempt you to stay for ever, and a small sitting room with an elegant dining room off. 'You really didn't have to go to all this expense,' Carly exclaimed as she gazed around. 'But I'm glad you did,' she added mischievously.

He started to laugh. Nothing made him happier than seeing Carly smile. As he watched she tried out the mattress, bouncing on it. He'd restrained himself long enough. Dropping down beside her, he brought her into his arms. She tasted wonderful; her skin was soft and fragrant like a peach, and he was ravenous for fruit…

'We're wearing far too many clothes,' she pointed out sensibly.

'I couldn't agree more.' His face was close to hers and he smiled against the plump, yielding cushion of her lips. 'But there's one thing I want you to do first…'

She yelped in disappointment as he moved away. 'What?'

she said, running her hand down his back in a way that was guaranteed to change his mind if he didn't move fast. 'My letter,' he reminded her. 'Did you bring it with you?'

The erotic mist slowly lifted from her eyes. She'd searched for the letter after he'd told her about it, but she hadn't quite been able to bring herself to read it. 'Yes, of course I did... It's in my handbag—'

'Good. I want you to read it...'

Fear took the place of desire on her face. 'Now?' she said, frowning anxiously. At his nod she slipped off the bed without another word.

She handled the heavy vellum fearfully, tracing her finger over Lorenzo's bold black writing. How was it that every time things were going well reality stuck its oar in and spoiled everything? She stood with her back to him so she could hide her feelings, but then, as if some internal starter gun had gone off inside her head, she ripped furiously at the envelope, pulling out the single sheet.

Her gaze, so well trained, so accustomed to studying each word in sequence to be sure she didn't miss anything important, hopped straight to the bottom of the page where Lorenzo had written the three most important words in the English language: I love you.

She stared at them unblinking for a while, standing motionless until it finally sank in, and then, returning to the beginning of the letter, she read it through. When she'd finished she held the sheet to her chest, and then pulled it away again to read it through once more. She was terrified as she began reading that the words might have changed, or disappeared; that they might be nothing more than a figment of her imagination. But they were still there: I love you; signed, Lorenzo.

He loved her? Lorenzo loved her?

'I'm so sorry,' she whispered, turning to face him. 'If I'd

had any idea… If I hadn't been such an idiot after the interview, I'd have read this and saved us both a lot of trouble…' Lorenzo had resigned from the scholarship project, but had decided to continue his career at the bar in London. He was asking her to stay with him whatever she decided to do in life, but he asked her to think about the future very carefully and not to hurry into anything.

'So many thoughts in your eyes,' Lorenzo observed quietly. 'Are you going to share any of them with me?'

'I love you too…more than anything in the world.'

'And you're not hurting too badly because of the scholarship?'

'The scholarship? No.' She had almost forgotten it. It was behind her now, and only the shadow of her parents' disappointment remained.

'And the future?' Lorenzo prompted her.

She did have an idea what she would like to do, but every time she thought about it her mother's face flashed into her mind.

'You must have thought about it.'

'I have…' And him. And his reaction when she told him. She wasn't sure she was ready to face that now. 'I think…'

'Yes?' he prompted.

'I think I don't want to think…' Her expression took on meaning.

'Well, I want you to think,' he said, still not coming any closer. 'And I want you to share those thoughts with me. All I want is for you to be happy, and I know you well enough to know that drifting aimlessly through life isn't your style. To be happy you have to have a goal, Carly. You know that. You've always grasped the nettle in the past and made something good out of it. What's holding you back now?'

She knew what she wanted to do, but also knew it would

sound ridiculous when she told him. 'I love you, and that's enough.'

'Really?' His expression changed from sultry to sober in a heartbeat. 'Love takes more than words, Carly. It takes commitment and hard work. And you won't have the energy for that if you become bored, which, knowing you, I know you will. Look at your sister, Olivia—don't you think she longs to find something to do?'

'If law isn't for me I'm not sure I have the confidence after all these years of training to try anything else. It's a lot to give up—'

'Rubbish. I never heard such nonsense. If the past is holding you back it's time you moved on. Learn from it and then break free.' He paused for a moment and then said, 'Are you ready to share a glass of champagne?'

That was a loaded question, and everything hung on her reply.

# CHAPTER SIXTEEN

CARLY CHOSE MARINATED goat's cheese with mandarin and honey-peppercorn dressing, followed by grilled swordfish with red pepper and fresh tomato coulis, while Lorenzo selected Thai-style rosti fish cakes, followed by Cajun-spiced tuna with cucumber crème fraîche, but then he ordered chocolate fondue for two with fresh dipping fruit…

'And champagne,' Carly reminded him.

'Are you sure?' His eyes were serious.

'Never more so…'

He placed the room-service order briskly and then dragged her into his arms. 'This is all I want, all I care about; you—' His voice was laced with passion, and as he kissed her champagne quickly became an afterthought, though he had ordered a second bottle to be kept on ice for them, just in case. 'We might need a few crates more,' he pointed out when she exclaimed at his extravagance. 'If you decide to take a bath in it…'

'Shall we leave that for the tabloids?' Carly suggested, wondering if she might burst with happiness.

'As long as we don't part with the hot chocolate sauce,' Lorenzo said wickedly.

'You read my mind again,' Carly said happily.

Lorenzo insisted on feeding her the best bits from his plate, and the chocolate fondue was no exception, though he seemed to be keeping most of it for himself. Not that she objected to being a fruit plate. The peach was cool, the segments of orange cooler still, and with a dribble of icy cold cream, augmented by hot chocolate sauce and a sprinkling of nuts she was nothing if not deliciously aroused.

There wasn't a part of her to be left neglected, Lorenzo declared, and he was as thorough as he had promised to be, right down to the swathes of towels he made her lie on while he ministered to her needs on the bed. Her clothes were scattered round the floor, as were his. Her body was in raging torment for him, but he refused to hurry. She must learn to be patient, he insisted, slipping one of her legs over his shoulders. He was going to finish every scrap of the chocolate sauce, he assured her, dribbling it in a warm stream onto her most sensitive, her most secret place.

Not a secret any more, at least, not to Lorenzo. She had never felt a sensation like it. The insistent pressure of the stream of chocolate, the rasp of Lorenzo's tongue and the heat of his breath, the rhythmic sucking motion of his lips; sensation didn't come any better than this, and yet every time she drew close he drew back.

'Are you determined to send me mad?'

'Haven't I taught you anything about the benefits of delay?" he countered, licking chocolate off his lips as he stared down at her.

'You have a very healthy appetite,' Carly observed, moving restlessly as Lorenzo examined the fruit bowl to see what was left.

'And I love apple, in particular. It's so firm and juicy,' he said, doing incredible things with it.

She bucked towards him as he continued his experiments with the fruit salad. 'You can't leave me like this,' she complained when every piece of fruit had been eaten, and Lorenzo paused to wipe his hands on a hot towel. 'I might die of frustration.'

'Somehow I doubt that,' he said with a confidence that raised her to new levels of arousal. 'So you want me?' he said.

'Don't tease me, Lorenzo, you know I do.'

His wicked gaze challenged her. 'Show me…'

Drawing her knees back, she offered herself to him.

'Tell me…'

She begged him to take her in words she hardly recognised, begged him to ease the ache inside her where she needed him to be, so firm and hard and strong. He came to her then, and she writhed beneath him, inviting him on. He took control, his strong hands positioning her; one cradled her buttocks, while the other cupped her face, holding for his first impassioned, love-hungry kiss. The time for subtlety had long passed and now desire overtook them.

Lorenzo's first thrust sank deep. It was a raw display of sexual power and sexual need that filled and stretched her, and sent them both to the very edge right away, but as he knew this he withdrew slowly…withdrew completely. She whimpered her complaint, and so, with his lazy, confident smile tugging at the corners of his mouth he took her very slowly again. He went as deep as he could, taking his time to allow her to relish every moment, until every muscle and nerve ending she possessed was mad for more. 'Faster,' she begged him hoarsely. 'Faster now…'

Lorenzo's answer was to repeat the sensation-packed stealth invasion again and again until she couldn't remain still beneath him a second longer. Lifting her hips towards him, she claimed him greedily, drawing him deep into the heart of her womb where she held him with powerful muscles until he obeyed her wishes. Pulling out, he thrust firmly, once, twice, and then in a gloriously rhythmical pattern at a much brisker pace.

'More…more,' she begged, working her body in the same rhythm as his. She craved fulfilment, but wanted it to last for ever. Lorenzo ground his hips against her to heighten her pleasure, while she clung to him in desperation until ecstasy claimed her. She was only dimly aware as she called out wildly that her abandoned cries had mingled with those of Lorenzo.

Each time they made love it was a revelation, Carly reflected drowsily as she lay safe in Lorenzo's arms. They had showered, made love again and now they were sleeping together. She loved him, she loved everything about him. She loved his body and loved his mind. The feel of his naked flesh beneath her hands was addictive; the slide of muscle, the shift of limbs, the sheer weight of him and the power he exuded. Not to mention his finesse, Carly thought with pleasure, listening to her body's quiet satisfaction. Lorenzo was magnificent, and he had put himself and all his skills at her disposal. What more could she ask? Gazing at him as he sprawled in contentment at her side, she had to confess he was even more beautiful than she had imagined when they first met. Perfectly proportioned, he was steel to her cushioned softness; they fitted perfectly together, and for the first time in her life her generous curves made sense. When she pressed her lips against his chest she could feel his heart beating steadily and strong; he was her anchor, her port in a storm…

Carly wasn't sure how long she slept, but she woke to find Lorenzo on one elbow at her side, looking down at her. He brushed the tangles of hair from her face.

'I enjoy watching you sleep.'

She made a sound of contentment. 'I don't know how you're still awake when every inch of me is exhausted. Where do you find the strength?'

'You're my inspiration?' he said dryly.

But there was a look in his eyes she hadn't seen before. 'What are you thinking about, Lorenzo?'

'I heard you talking to your mother in the kitchen. I have good hearing and plenty of practice at speaking while I listen. I heard her ask you if you might be pregnant.'

'Well, I'm not.'

'Can you be sure?'

They'd just made love unprotected, so, no, she couldn't be sure.

'Would you be disappointed if you found that you were not pregnant?' Lorenzo asked her.

She didn't want children...of course, she didn't. The only thing she had ever wanted before Lorenzo came along was a career... All her mother had ever wanted for her was a career, Carly amended silently. She had a major rethink on her hands.

Lorenzo pressed her for an answer.

'I'd be disappointed,' she admitted softly.

'You can have it all,' he said. 'You do know that, don't you? Career, family—'

She gave herself a warning, knowing she couldn't even begin to face the pain if she talked herself into believing Lorenzo wanted a family with her.

'Yes, but as I'm not pregnant—'

'We can soon put that right—'

'Lorenzo—'

'Are you complaining?'

'No,' she gasped.

'Happy Christmas, baby...'

It took everything she'd got to open one eye, and then Carly saw that Lorenzo was not only up and about, he was shaved, dressed, and ready to hit the road.

'Half an hour and the driver will be here,' he reminded her. 'You'd better get up.'

'Must I?' She brushed the hair out of her eyes to look at him. 'Unfortunately, yes.'

She swung her reluctant limbs over the side of the bed. 'Merry Christmas, Lorenzo…' She had barely enough strength left to form the words. 'I think you drained every ounce of energy out of me last night.'

'I'm sure there's plenty more where that came from. I only wish we could stay longer and find out,' he said, folding her in his arms, 'but we have a take-off slot to fill.'

'Okay,' Carly murmured reluctantly, snuggling close. Winding her arms around his neck, she turned her face up for a kiss, and then complained when Lorenzo lifted her out of bed and steered her towards the bathroom.

'It's lucky that one of us has some self-control,' he said.

'Yours wasn't so hot last night.'

'That was a one-off,' he assured her. 'Go on,' he urged, 'I won't relent.'

Good, Carly thought with satisfaction, leaning back against the closed door. And wasn't that what she loved about him, the challenge, the wall to kick against? But what if her mother was proved right? What if Lorenzo was just using her for sex? No. He loved her. She firmed her jaw. Lorenzo loved her.

'Don't take too long,' he called through the door. 'We can't miss that slot.'

'Move in here,' Lorenzo suggested when they got back to his apartment.

'Are you serious?' Carly stared at him.

'Why not? What's the point in keeping a room at Louisa's when you're going to be here with me? I'm going to have to put a lot of time and effort into satisfying your demands, and I'll need you on site for that.'

The way Lorenzo was talking made living together sound like a building project. But maybe it was a project to him, something to carry out with his usual efficiency before finishing it and walking away... Giving him chance to start again on a fresh *project*. Carly's heart squeezed tight as she thought about it. 'You mean like a temporary arrangement?'

'Carly...' Lorenzo's lips tugged up at one corner as he shook his head. His thumbs were lodged in his belt loops with his fingers pointing the way to an impressive bulge, which took her mind off...everything.

As they ripped clothes off she couldn't help noticing his socks were covered in rabbits. 'Are these prophetic?' she said, laughing as she tugged them off.

'What do you think?' Lorenzo demanded, throwing her down onto the bed.

'I think you'd better show me.'

'My pleasure,' he said.

'Mine,' Carly argued with a gasp.

'You have a real talent for making me forget everything,' she said much later, turning her head on the pillows to look at Lorenzo.

'I've had years of practice in court—but I haven't succeeded in making you forget everything, have I, Carly?'

She sighed as he stroked her breasts.

'There's still all this hurt inside you...'

'Hurt?' Capturing his hand, she held it in place. 'If you mean that visit home, I'm over it. I'm made of stronger stuff than you seem to think.' His face assumed the masklike quality she recognised from court. 'I can't thank you enough for flying me up there.'

'You don't need to thank me.'

'And I'm not hurting,' she assured him.

He had only done what anyone with the means would do for someone they loved. Had no one ever made a gesture to Carly before that wasn't connected to the advancement of her career? Perhaps her father and sister were frightened to. The treats and surprises his parents had heaped on him made him realise how lucky he'd been and he wanted that for Carly. 'Let's get up and take a shower,' he suggested, 'and then we'll open our Christmas presents.'

'Presents plural?' she said, already sounding worried. 'But I only got you one—' Her cheeks reddened.

'You're my present; the only present I want.' He would drum that guilt out of her however long it took. He raced her to the shower, giving her a head start, and she shrieked with excitement as he closed in. Her eyes were already darkening in anticipation as he shut the doors. She was in his arms with her legs locked around his waist before the water had turned warm, and this time her shrieks came fast and furious and had nothing to do with the temperature of the water.

'And you call me insatiable,' he said.

'The more I get, the more I want,' she admitted.

'Love can do that to you,' he said.

'Love…'

'Don't tell me you're just using me for sex,' he teased her.

Her anxiety dissolved into a cheeky smile. 'Now there's an idea…'

It was some time before they emerged from the bathroom swaddled in warmed towelling robes. He had to carry Carly, because his spare robe was far too big for her. He had to carry her anyway, because he wanted to. 'We'll get dressed, and then have presents,' he said, ignoring her complaint. If they didn't get dressed soon, Christmas would never happen. 'And if we don't hurry up we'll miss supper—'

'Supper out on Christmas Day?'

'A friend of mine has opened a restaurant. It's open, and he's saving us a table.'

'You were pretty confident I'd come back here with you.'

'You should know from court I always plan ahead.' He dipped his head to look her in the eyes. 'And I never doubted it…'

Carly gulped when she saw how many carrier bags Lorenzo had hidden behind the sofa. 'These can't all be for me!'

'I wasn't hanging around to edit the contents. Half an hour in that place was enough for me.'

Lorenzo shopping? Now she understood. 'So where do I start?'

'With the underwear—that's usual, isn't it?'

The ribbon-trimmed box from her favourite store was unmistakable, the contents racier and more expensive than she would ever have dared choose. Plus Lorenzo seemed to have taken one of everything—in pink, in aquamarine, and in…gulp!

'For when you're feeling frisky. Shall we move on to the outer casing?'

Which just happened to be the softest cashmere dress in pale caramel, which he'd teamed with knee-high suede boots in a slightly darker shade. The heels could most safely be described in polite society as wicked in the extreme. 'Oh, Lorenzo, they're fabulous,' Carly exclaimed, trying them on.

'And there's a jacket.' He angled his chin towards the remaining carrier bag.

'You shouldn't have bought me all this. It must have cost you a fortune.'

'Won't you try it on?'

Carly was speechless. She had never bought clothes of this quality for herself.

'If you don't like anything you can change it. I won't be offended,' Lorenzo assured her.

'I don't want to change a thing,' she said, finding her voice. Everything was just perfect, and in the classic styles with a quirky edge she looked almost fashionable.

'You'd look beautiful in a sack,' Lorenzo argued.

'If you don't mind I'll pass on the sack and stick with the clothes you bought me.' She leaned back against him and sighed. 'Honestly, Lorenzo, I don't know what to say... I'm overwhelmed.'

'Say you're happy; say you believe me when I tell you you're beautiful...' Clasping her shoulders in his warm hands, he nuzzled her hair out of the way and planted a kiss on her neck.

'But—'

'No buts...' Turning her to face him, he silenced any remaining doubts she might have had with a kiss.

Lorenzo was wonderful, and she loved him with all her heart, but what would he say when she told him her dreams for the future?

'You're doing it again,' he said.

'What am I doing?'

'Thinking too much...' He looked at her seriously for a moment and then his lips tugged up. 'Do I get my present now?'

He'd taken the parcel out of his mailbox and it was sitting on the coffee-table. 'It's nothing compared to all this,' she said, gesturing around.

'If you chose it I'll love it, just as I love you...' He kissed her hand as he spoke, and then, turning it, kissed her palm too.

He loved her. She would never get used to it. Did he love her? In her head her mother huffed.

Lorenzo ripped the paper off her gift and then sat staring at the book she'd bought him.

'How did you know?' he said at last. 'How did you know that Frank Frazetta is one of my all-time favourite artists?'

'Call it an educated guess.' But it was more than that. Frank Frazetta was a famous American artist who drew fantasy heroes and larger-than-life battle scenes. He idealised the fight for right, and celebrated heroes and heroic principles, and in her opinion every one of Lorenzo's dragon-slaying qualities existed between the pages of that book.

She looked over Lorenzo's shoulder as he turned the pages depicting another man's incredible flights of imagination. Some people might think the images off the wall, but Frazetta had been a student of anatomy, and was an impressive artist in every way. His work seemed a perfect match for Lorenzo. Wasn't he off the wall with his austere front, his sensual nature, and his crazy-coloured socks?

'It's a perfect gift,' he said in a way that made her heart clench.

But it was more than that for him, Lorenzo realised as he stared into Carly's eyes. She had reached into his soul and plucked something out of there. In a way he wasn't even surprised she'd bought him the book of illustrations; they were like two sides of the same coin. Frank Frazetta had been his late father's favourite artist too. 'While there are men like this around,' he used to say, stabbing a work-worn finger at one of the illustrations, 'everything will be okay. You gotta be like them, Lorenzo. In here...' He'd thump his chest at that point. It was a regular Sunday night routine to prepare them both for the rigours of the week ahead—his at the private school, and his father at the meat factory where he worked to pay the fees.

'Do you really like it?' she said.

He realised Carly must think him distant, when nothing could be further from the truth. 'You have no idea what this little book means to me,' he assured her.

# CHAPTER SEVENTEEN

'I LOVE IT.' Lorenzo put the book in pride of place on the coffee-table. 'You couldn't have bought me anything I'd like more.'

When he'd stopped kissing her Carly asked what time they had to be at the restaurant. 'Soon, but first I want to know what you've decided about the future.'

'You'll think me silly…'

'Try me…'

She gazed at his socks, sombre blue, decorated with the scales of justice. Somehow that made it harder to tell him, but she couldn't put it off for ever. 'Not law,' she said.

She waited, but Lorenzo didn't cut in as she had expected him to. 'I've had a wonderful training and a wonderful time at chambers. And it's all been worthwhile, because I wouldn't have met you if I'd chosen another path. So I have a lot to thank my mother for…'

He let that one pass. 'Well?' he said. 'What's it to be?'

'I'm going to be an event planner…'

Not, I want to be; I'm going to be. For once in his life he couldn't keep his mask in position. He knew she would eventually realize what he'd wanted her to. 'Carly, I'm delighted!' He swept her into his arms.

'You are?'

She looked amazed, but whatever the rest of the world thought of him he was a simple man with simple goals. He wanted to make a difference and raise a family, and to do that Carly had to be happy. What she'd just told him would finally bring her the sense of personal achievement that had proved so elusive in the past. 'I know you'll be fantastic. And if you get cards printed and circulate them amongst all the people who attended your Christmas party I'm sure you'll be snowed under with enquiries.'

'You really mean that, don't you?'

'I never say anything I don't mean. Now, come on, or we'll be late for Father Christmas—'

She shook her head. 'Don't tell me you're a believer?'

'Of course I am.'

As she laughed he made a silent pledge to fight each one of her demons in turn until there were no shadows left.


The restaurant Lorenzo took her to was a surprise. It was situated in something that looked more like an aircraft hangar than a glamorous eatery, and it was only when they walked inside and Carly smelled the food she realised why the huge space was packed out.

The smiling host had been waiting for them at the door, a man of similar age to Lorenzo, but with more dream than scheme in his dark blue eyes. He led the way for them through the tables.

'Don't be misled,' Lorenzo whispered discreetly in Carly's ear as they headed towards a generous-sized table overlooking the river. 'Tre's dreamy expression comes from his eternal quest for that coveted third Michelin star.'

'Can you read all my thoughts?' Carly challenged him softly.

'Most of them,' he admitted. 'That's why I know we'll make such a good team.'

She had to try very hard not to read anything into that. 'This is really lovely,' she said as Lorenzo attracted the attention of the wine waiter.

'I thought it would make a nice change from Greasy Jo's,' he teased her.

'Don't remind me,' she protested, laughing. 'I'm never going to live that one down, am I?'

'Never,' Lorenzo assured her.

They both laughed.

He ordered champagne. 'You'll need a glass to toast Father Christmas,' he explained. 'And look… Here he is, right on cue…'

The celebrations allowed everyone to shed their inhibitions, Carly thought as Father Christmas wove his way through the tables; even she was excited.

The wine waiter filled her champagne flute to the brim, and reaching across the table, Lorenzo found her hand and linked their fingers together. 'I just hope you like your gift.'

'I'm sure I will.' She had seen some of the other women opening packages that contained a beautiful orchid in a tiny glass vase. The men's gifts appeared to be miniature tins of coffee beans, which she knew Lorenzo would love. 'But mine's different to everyone else's gift.' It was a lot smaller, and Lorenzo had a different gift too.

'I get a personal gift from Tre because we've known each other so many years,' he explained. 'He can never resist his annual dig at my fashion sense.'

'So you get socks?' Carly guessed.

'That's right,' Lorenzo confirmed. 'And what do you make of this one?' he said as Father Christmas left the smaller gift in front of Carly.

'Why would Tre buy me something when we don't even know each other?'

'Who said Tre bought it for you?'

'You said— No, you didn't,' Carly amended.

'For a moment there I really thought all those years of legal training had been wasted,' Lorenzo said dryly.

'Can I open it?'

'After me.' He was already ripping the Christmas paper off his socks.

'Reindeer socks with bells on?' Carly laughed. 'At least I'll hear you coming.'

'Why don't you open yours now?'

There was a tiny jewellery box beneath the Christmas paper. Possibilities raced through Carly's mind—collar studs? This was embarrassing. She had only just told Lorenzo about her intention to leave law and now it looked as if he had bought her something she would use in court: collar studs, or cufflinks engraved with the crest of her inn of court, perhaps—they were very popular. 'You shouldn't have,' she said awkwardly.

'How do you know what it is until you open it?' he pointed out.

Maybe it was a joke present. She went hot and cold at the thought that she might have made a fool of herself confessing her love for Lorenzo, just as her mother had predicted. But he'd said he loved her. He did love her. She firmed her resolve, and, pressing the catch, released the lid.

'Well?' Lorenzo said as she sat in silence. 'What do you think?'

She wasn't capable of thinking, or speaking, or anything else at the moment. She was too busy staring in disbelief at the biggest solitaire diamond she'd ever seen. 'Is this thing real?'

'No, it's glass. I got it out of a cracker,' Lorenzo observed dryly. 'Now would you like to try it on?'

'But what's it for?' All her brain cells had collided in a heap and the ring was firing all the colours of the rainbow at her, confusing the issue.

'What's it for?' Lorenzo repeated. 'Now, let me think... Maybe it's a bonus for good behaviour? No—' he shook his head '—you don't deserve that. You've been extremely naughty over these past few days. For good work, then?' His lips pressed down. 'Well, that can't be right, because you haven't started your new job yet—'

'Lorenzo!'

'Carly.' Angling his head, he stared at her with exasperation. 'For someone with so much brain power you have precious little common sense. Why can't you just accept that I love you, and that I want to be with you for ever? I want to marry you. I *want* to buy you a diamond ring.'

'And what Lorenzo wants Lorenzo gets?' Carly's face started to relax into a smile.

'Something like that,' he admitted.

'Are you sure it's for me?'

'Unless you have an invisible friend?' He stared over her shoulder.

'Lorenzo...'

'Give the ring to me,' he instructed.

She gave him the box with the ring still intact. She couldn't believe such a fabulous piece of jewellery was destined to find its home on her finger. She was already braced for the punchline and the laughter. If Lorenzo mentioned crackers one more time she would—

'I'm surprised you can't recognise a Tiffany box—'

'A Tiffany box?' she said. 'Let me see that again...'

She held out her hand, but he just laughed. 'I can see I have a lot of educating to do. Now hold out your hand, Ms Tate...'

The ring fitted perfectly.

'Do you like it?'

Carly studied the fabulous diamond on her wedding finger. 'I don't know what to say.'

'Say you love me—say you'll marry me…'

'You do mean it, don't you?'

Lorenzo took hold of her hand. 'Don't you know how much I love you yet? Don't you know how much I want to marry you?' His lips tugged up in a wicked grin. 'Don't you know how much I want to make babies with you? I thought I'd made at least that much clear. Seems I'll have to put in a lot more time convincing you…'

'I will marry you, Lorenzo—' She broke off.

'Are you all right?' He was instantly concerned as she swayed a little in her seat.

'It's just the shock,' Carly explained. 'I felt a little faint…'

'Can you describe your feelings exactly?' Lorenzo said, staring at her intently.

'Lorenzo,' she reminded him, 'we're not in court now.'

'My mother felt strange every time, and she had seven of us.'

'Your mother? Lorenzo, please, whatever's wrong with me, it has nothing to do with whatever your mother suffered seven times.'

'How can you be so sure?'

She looked at him and then at the ring. 'Because anyone would faint with shock when they saw the size of this diamond.'

'Oh, come now, Carly,' Lorenzo argued dryly. 'There isn't a woman alive who would faint at the size of a diamond— unless it was tiny, of course.'

# CHAPTER EIGHTEEN

IT WAS SOME WEEKS before Lorenzo had the opportunity to tell Carly, 'I told you so,' and nine months before he held their beautiful daughter, Adriana, in his arms. He brought his two girls home from hospital to the country house he and Carly had chosen together in the latter stages of Carly's pregnancy. The Georgian manor house was reminiscent of the boutique hotel in Cheshire where their baby had almost certainly been conceived. The property was an easy drive from the city, and provided them both with a much-needed break from the hustle and bustle of city life. An Internet connection had been set up to ensure that the newest party planner in town could continue to grow her business while heavily pregnant, or nursing a baby, and Carly's inbox was already bulging with an impressive number of potential clients.

She was integral to his life in every way, and his only concern was her happiness. He had settled effortlessly into the role of devoted husband, and now devoted father, and, following in the footsteps of his parents, he was determined to share that happiness around.

'My mother won't come,' Carly stated confidently six weeks after the birth of Adriana, by which time he judged her ready to face the storm. 'She'll never forgive me for leaving law.'

'We'll see, shall we?' When had he ever allowed a small thing like a mother-in-law to put him off his stride?

'Who said your mother wouldn't come?'

Carly couldn't believe her eyes as her father's car pulled into the yard. Livvie piled out first, and then her father hurried round to open the passenger side door.

'Mother?' she breathed incredulously.

'And bearing gifts, by the look of it,' Lorenzo observed, watching as Mrs Tate marshalled her handbag, her carrier bags and her troops.

'She looks lost,' Carly said, staring transfixed through the window. Her father and Livvie were hurrying excitedly up the path, while her mother remained in the same spot, gazing up at the façade of Carly and Lorenzo's beautifully restored home.

'She *is* lost,' Lorenzo pointed out. 'She's not in her kingdom now, she's in yours.'

'I've got to go to her…'

Lorenzo's voice stopped Carly halfway across the hall. 'Take it easy,' he said. 'Don't intimidate her—'

'Intimidate my mother?'

'Just remember the tables have been turned, Mrs Domenico. Be gentle with her…that's all I'm saying.'

Carly's face softened as she looked at Lorenzo holding their baby. He was such an amazing man. 'You know I will…'

'Yes, I do. That's why I love you.'

'I love you too…'

As Carly opened the door Livvie fell into her arms, hugging her as if she would never let her go. 'Can I hold the baby?' she asked the moment they released each other.

Lorenzo made the careful transfer, and then went to greet Mr Tate. Giving the older man a firm handshake, he drew him into the house as if they were old friends. 'Your father and I have things to discuss,' he said to Carly as father and daughter hugged, 'so you can't keep him long.'

'My flying lesson,' Carly's father confided. 'Good man. He remembered.' Holding Carly's face between his hands, he searched her eyes. 'That's better,' he said quietly, releasing her.

As Lorenzo led him away towards the kitchen, and Livvie followed with baby Adriana, Carly waited with apprehension to greet her mother. She felt anxious, but she told herself she couldn't possibly feel half as awkward as her mother.

'Carly...'

The voice hadn't changed, and they didn't attempt to embrace each other.

'Come in...' Carly stood back, remembering Lorenzo's counsel. 'Welcome...'

'Very nice,' her mother observed, walking past her. 'You've done very well for yourself, Carly.'

Lorenzo always made her feel that he had done very well for himself too, but the moment her mother spoke the doubts set in again. As she turned and raked her face with the narrowed gaze, searching for signs of insecurity, it took all she'd got to respond openly with a smile. 'Won't you come into the kitchen? Everyone's there.'

'Don't rush me, Carly. I bought you something.' She pushed a carrier bag into Carly's hands. 'I expect you've got something better. It's only a quilt cover for the baby's cot.'

'But it's beautiful,' Carly exclaimed softly as she looked inside the bag. 'I love it. Thank you.'

'Your father chose it,' her mother said awkwardly. 'And we bought a little gift for Lorenzo too, which I chose.'

Carly hid her astonishment. 'That's very generous of you, and there was absolutely no need.'

'There was every need,' her mother argued. 'This is Lorenzo's house, and we're enjoying his hospitality.'

Carly nodded. The barb might sting, but she refused to let it show.

'Well, go on...look at them,' her mother urged impatiently, handing over a small stiff bag. 'You'd better make sure I got it right.'

'I'm sure you did,' Carly reassured. When she looked inside the bag she had to try very hard indeed not to laugh. Her mother's gift to Lorenzo was socks. Grey socks. It would take more than that to turn Lorenzo into a strawberry cream, Carly reflected, pressing her lips down hard to keep from smiling. 'They're lovely,' she said. 'And it was very kind of you to think of it.' Her mother didn't seem such a dragon any more, and impulsively she leaned forward and kissed her on the cheek.

Her mother jerked back as if she'd been hit. 'I'm not interested in whether you like them or not. What I want to know is will Lorenzo like them? We'd better keep on his right side. You'll need someone to support you now you've thrown away your career.'

'And got another one,' Carly reminded her mother, who responded with a cynical hum. 'I'm sure he'll love the socks,' she lied, for the sake of her mother's feelings.

'This way, is it?' her mother said briskly, turning away.

'That's right.' And don't stop walking until you find the tall, dark handsome man wearing jeans, a rugby shirt and ruby-red, heart-festooned socks, Carly thought happily. For the first time in her life her mother couldn't hurt her; in fact she felt sorry for her and for everything they'd missed over the years. Lorenzo was right; her mother was far more vulnerable in this situation than she was.

Carly followed her mother into the kitchen where she found her hovering just inside the door. It was as if she couldn't bring herself to walk into the room, which was strange, Carly thought, because she found the scene idyllic. There was home-cooked food on the table, and the people she loved were standing around it. Her very own newborn baby was lying contented and asleep in her sister's arms...

Lorenzo found her gaze and smiled reassurance at her. His look told her how much he loved her, and how he was always there for her, whatever might happen.

'Won't you come and join us, Mother?' Carly said, returning to the door where her mother was still standing. Taking her mother's arm, she drew her gently inside the room.

Lorenzo came forward and put his arm round her shoulders. As he did so Carly noticed her mother's gaze flinch away and land on Olivia...with disapproval. She'd never seen that before. Her mother started to say something and then stopped herself. As she looked at Carly's father for support her mouth hardened when she realised he was too engrossed in his grandchild to notice her.

'Support the baby's head, Olivia,' she said, her voice sounding cracked and strained. 'Olivia, are you paying attention?'

'Of course I am, Mother,' Livvie crooned, gazing adoringly at her niece. 'Don't you think she's lovely?'

'What do I think? Does anyone care what I think?' When this received no answer, Mrs Tate went on. 'I think it's hard to credit Carly got married before you and had a baby.' The harsh words were out, but somehow they'd lost their sting; everyone was too happy to take it in. 'You'd better hurry up and find a man, Olivia,' she pressed on, 'or all the best ones will be gone.' She flashed a meaningful glance at Lorenzo.

'Olivia is taking her time to pick out the best of the best. Isn't that right, Livvie?' Lorenzo said kindly, and perhaps only Carly detected the thread of disapproval in his gaze as he looked at her mother, but then she knew his court mask.

'Well, she'd better hurry up, that's all I've got to say—'

'Mother—' Carly began, noticing that Livvie was now paying attention and was on the verge of tears.

'Your mother always did have to have the last word,' her father cut in to everyone's surprise. 'Me? I've always known what a lucky man I am to have two exceptional daughters.'

'Well said, Mr Tate,' Lorenzo agreed.

'Call me Arthur. And now you and I had better discuss that flying lesson—'

*'What?'* Exploding out of her brooding silence, Mrs Tate clutched her chest.

'Don't worry, Enid, I won't be taking you with me,' Carly's father said dryly.

There was another moment of silence, and then Carly noticed her mother was blinking back tears. She was about to go to her when her mother looked at her beseechingly. 'Can *I* hold her?'

There was such hope and fear in her voice it was as if the world as Carly knew it had come to an end, and something far better had taken its place. 'Of course you can,' she said warmly.

Olivia carried her baby niece across the room and placed her carefully in her grandmother's arms. 'Adriana, meet Granny,' Carly said softly, smiling at Livvie and Lorenzo before backing away.

'Thank you.' Her mother's gaze flickered up, and then quickly flashed back to her grandchild.

As she was the child of two such strong-minded parents it came as no surprise to anyone that Adriana had her own thoughts on reconciliation. Curling her tiny fist around her grandmother's forefinger, she held on tight.

'This is a new beginning,' Carly's mother murmured, entranced.

'Yes, well, let's hope so,' Carly's father commented. 'Are you coming, Lorenzo? Your study, didn't you say? I think we can safely leave the ladies in peace now.'

Lorenzo shot a look at Carly as if to say this division of the sexes wasn't their way, but for a day, if it made her parents happy, it would be worth it.

Carly put her arm around Livvie's shoulders as they watched their mother with Adriana. 'Your turn next,' she whispered. 'That's if you want a baby.'

'Perhaps I'd better find a man first?' Livvie suggested.

'Good idea,' Carly agreed, sharing a smile with her sister.

Later that night Lorenzo suggested they leave everyone to it. Adriana had so many nursemaids her parents were superfluous for once. He didn't wait for an answer before drawing his beloved wife out of the room.

'You worked a miracle today,' he told Carly, 'and I'm proud of you.'

'You worked the miracle,' she argued.

'Can we agree just this once to reach a compromise?' Lorenzo suggested, starting to unbutton her blouse. 'I think the miracle is Adriana...'

'Well, I'm not going to argue with you about that...'

Easing her head back to give Lorenzo better access to her neck, Carly knew that arguing was the last thing on her mind now, though there was definitely a storm brewing—of the most tempestuous and physical kind.

'Your breasts are enormous,' Lorenzo approved as if he'd never seen them before. 'I adore them...' Casting her bra aside, he swung her into his arms. 'Shall we?' he invited, moving towards the bed.

'Only if you take your socks off.'

'I'm not sure I can wait that long.'

But they did take his socks off—they took every single piece of clothing off.

'We don't always make it this far,' Carly said, laughing as

Lorenzo lowered her down onto the bed. 'Do you think the fire is dying down?'

Taking hold of her hand, he placed it over the throbbing proof of his continued interest. 'I'm not sure,' he said. 'What do you think?'

'I think I need regular reminders,' she told him wickedly.

He raked his stubble against her neck in the way he knew she liked, but when she reached for him he told her, 'Be patient... Haven't I taught you anything?'

'So much, I hardly know where to start.'

'Fortunately, I do,' he said, muffling her cries with kisses until she grew frantic underneath him. Carly's appetite was a source of constant pleasure to him, and he never tired of giving her the satisfaction she craved. Watching pleasure unfold on her face was one of his greatest joys in life. She was fierce in bed, demanding and passionate, and she was the mother of his child, sweet, kind and loving. She was the lynchpin of his family around which everything else revolved. 'I love you, Carly Tate.'

'Carly Domenico,' she corrected him in the scant few seconds he allowed her before finding another way to silence her.

Later, when she had quietened, he told her about the plans he'd made. 'I've taken an island for a month—'

'Of course you have,' she said, stroking his face.

'No, really, I have...'

'Are you serious?'

'Never more so. I'm going to fly the wife I adore and our baby, along with Adriana's nurse, to a tiny Caribbean island where my beautiful wife can lie in the sun all day and dream about...me.'

Carly laughed. 'You're impossible.'

'We've already established that,' Lorenzo said, kissing her into submission. 'And, of course, for this trip my wife will need some new clothes...' He reached beneath the bed for the parcel he'd put there earlier. 'For instance, she will need some new bikinis...' Reaching into the parcel, he showered some vivid scraps of fabric down on her. 'And, of course, she will require this season's must-have, ridiculously impractical underwear—'

'But, Lorenzo, I'm fat—'

'Carly, you have never been more beautiful in your life.' Bringing her hand to his lips, he planted a lingering kiss on her palm, staring into her eyes until she believed him.

'You are the most wonderful man in the world,' she whispered, 'and so generous. But, Lorenzo, I must buy something for you. What would you like?'

Her earnest expression made his lips curve in a smile. 'Isn't it obvious?'

'No...'

'How about socks?' he said wryly.

# Special Offers

Every month we put together collections and longer reads written by your favourite authors.

Here are some of next month's highlights— and don't miss our fabulous discount online!

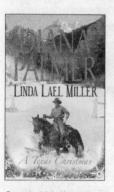

On sale 16th November　　On sale 16th November　　On sale 7th December

Find out more at
**www.millsandboon.co.uk/specialreleases**

Visit us
Online

1212/ST/MB392

# *Sparkling Christmas kisses!*

Bryony's daughter, Lizzie, wants was a *dad* for Christmas and Bryony's determined to fulfil this Christmas wish. But when every date ends in disaster, Bryony fears she'll need a miracle. But she only needs a man for Christmas, not for love…right?

Unlike Bryony, the last thing Helen needs is a man! In her eyes, all men are *Trouble*! Of course, it doesn't help that as soon as she arrives in the snow-covered mountains, she meets Mr Tall, Dark and Handsome *Trouble*!

**www.millsandboon.co.uk**

# Come home to the magic of Nora Roberts

Identical twin boys Zeke and Zach wished for only one gift from Santa this year: a new mum! But convincing their love-wary dad that their music teacher, Miss Davis, is his destiny and part of Santa's plan isn't as easy as they'd hoped…